SOMEONE IN THE WOODS

"Hold on to me," Jake said softly into her ear.

Roberta put her hands on his chest and felt curly, fine hair beneath her palms; heat pulsated into her fingertips. He smelled of the sun and the forest.

She leaned into him as he used his body to press her against the broad tree at her back. His lips, when they met hers, were warm and supple. The kiss was deep, sweet, and searching. Her mind reeled with the sensations of the moment. His smell, his taste, his warm skin beneath her hands.

She wanted him. Here, now, on a bed of pine needles and maidenhair ferns, the warm night air permeated with the earthy aroma of all organic life around them.

Somewhere behind them a dry branch snapped.

"MIND-BOGGLING . . . THE SUSPENSE IS UNBEARABLE . . .
DORIS MILES DISNEY WILL KEEP YOU
ON THE EDGE OF YOUR SEAT . . ."

THE MYSTERIES OF DORIS MILES DISNEY

THE DAY MISS BESSIE LEWIS DISAPPEARED	(2080-5, $2.95/$4.50)
THE HOSPITALITY OF THE HOUSE	(2738-9, $3.50/$4.50)
THE LAST STRAW	(2286-7, $2.95/$3.95)
THE MAGIC GRANDFATHER	(2584-X, $2.95/$3.95)
MRS. MEEKER'S MONEY	(2212-3, $2.95/$3.95)
NO NEXT OF KIN	(2969-1, $3.50/$4.50)
ONLY COUPLES NEED APPLY	(2438-X, $2.95/$3.95)
SHADOW OF A MAN	(3077-0, $3.50/$4.50)
THAT WHICH IS CROOKED	(2848-2, $3.50/$4.50)
THREE'S A CROWD	(2079-1, $2.95/$3.95)
WHO RIDES A TIGER	(2799-0, $3.50/$4.50)

Available wherever paperbacks are sold, or order direct from the Publisher. Send cover price plus 50¢ per copy for mailing and handling to: Zebra Books, Dept.3661, 475 Park Avenue South, New York, NY 10016. Residents of New York and Tennessee must include sales tax. DO NOT SEND CASH. For a free Zebra/Pinnacle Catalog with more than 1,500 books listed, please write to the above address.

NIGHT PREY

CAROL DAVIS LUCE

ZEBRA BOOKS
KENSINGTON PUBLISHING CORP.

With love and kisses
to Alex, Cody, and Cory . . .
little bits of heaven on earth

ZEBRA BOOKS

are published by

Kensington Publishing Corp.
475 Park Avenue South
New York, NY 10016

First printing: February, 1992

Printed in the United States of America

Prologue

Gigantic pines, white fir, and quaking aspen passed along each side of him, casting deeper shadows across his boots and the deer trail he followed. The creature sounds in this shadowy stretch of the woods seemed more guttural. Unreal. Menacing. Birds shrieked. Predators growled low in their throats. Prey screamed in the throes of death.

The large man moved stealthily through the thickets of chokeberry and manzanita. He bent his head to avoid the low-hanging boughs, hunched his shoulders, his arms swaying apelike as he lumbered down the worn path.

In the heat of the afternoon, when the air smelled of roasted pine nuts, baked earth, and granite, he would find her in the cool waters of the pond. His pond.

He slowed. He was close. Once he spied the pond he would have to move more cautiously. This was the hardest part. For at this point he always wanted to rush ahead and join her in the sweet, cool water. But he must not reveal himself. Not yet.

At the edge of the darkness, through a tunnel of brush, he saw sunlight glitter off the water's surface.

From tree to tree he advanced furtively to the fringe of the woods. Still deep in the concealing shadows he became a watcher. The dim forest devoured him.

Her horse was tethered to a clump of dry brush. Her clothes lay scattered over a large flat rock. He scanned the pond for her, seeing only distorted reflections of the tall trees lining the western shoreline.

He waited. Watched.

The girl shot out of the water in an explosion of droplets, shimmering like precious metal, in the afternoon sun. He heard the sharp intake of her breath. He felt her energy.

Like a water nymph she stood waist-deep in the shallows, her skin golden in the sunlight. Her breasts were at last beginning to swell with weight and size.

He felt the silence of the forest, the denseness of the air, the cool shadows. The presence of the girl in the warm light made his pulse quicken. So alone, so vulnerable.

Forbidden.

He wanted her. A primal hunger stirred within him. His need was like an electrical charge passing through his body. The others paled in comparison to this perfect creature of the woods.

The others . . .

Oblivious to the sweat that flowed from his pores, he touched his trembling fingers to the coarse mat of his beard. Airy forest specks floated in the golden rays of light that slanted through the tall pines.

Ripples died away in the pond as the girl stood quietly, wringing water from her long blond hair. Pure. Innocent. Maddening. He thought his heart would burst.

Celia—no, not Celia, he told himself sharply. Celia was from long ago, from another lifetime almost. Celia was dead.

The girl in the pond was Tobie. Tobie, lovely woman-child of this quiet place, this remote, secluded temple. *Forbidden*. But this, too, could change.

She dove under the water with a graceful arching of her body, legs straight, toes pointed. She surfaced and, surrounded by light, totally uninhibited in her naked state, she made her way lithely to shore.

His legs trembled as he watched. His breathing became hoarse, ragged in his own ears.

She stopped abruptly, staring directly at him.

He was deep enough into the shadows of the forest to be invisible to her, yet, like a wary buck, he froze. Could she feel him watching her?

When a slow smile appeared on her radiant face, he thought his heart would seize. Was the smile for him? Had she known all along he was there?

She crouched, picked up something from the ground and tossed it several feet. A tree squirrel scampered forward, snatched the bit of food, then stood on its hind legs, eating the morsel. When it finished, it chattered as if talking to the girl.

The sound of her soft laughter carried to the watcher in the woods. With a swing of her arm she sprayed the ground with trail mix from a plastic bag, peppering squirrels and chipmunks that had appeared out of nowhere to feed.

Secure in her belief that she was alone and unobserved, the girl lay down on the flat, sun-warmed rock. After fanning her wet hair out, she stretched her arms above her head and closed her eyes.

Holding his breath, the big man crept forward.

ONE

Roberta Paxton smiled into the camera, her nervousness gradually dissipating. She glanced into the monitor and saw herself; an attractive woman with light chestnut hair, more red than brown under the bright studio lights, looking confident and self-assured. *Don't get too confident, Robbi, he's poised and ready to pounce.*

The host of *Public Events,* Bradley Stevens, was on a roll. A notorious flirt on and off the camera, Brad had a special knack for dragging sex into every conversation no matter how banal the topic. Although harmless, cute even, his every conversation was laced with sexual innuendo and double entendres. As a frequent guest on his show, Roberta could now hold her own. He no longer had her stammering and blushing like a giddy ingenue, though it didn't stop him from trying.

"Let's see . . . here's an event I personally look forward to every August," Brad said. "The tenth annual Discover Dinner Dance sponsored by the Silver State Women's Center. Now, there's a dance anyone can attend, socially incompetent or not. Right, Roberta?"

"You're always welcome, Brad."

He mouthed the word "ouch" as she gave the date and time.

"We've been talking with Roberta Paxton, assistant director of the SSWC, a local organization to aid abused women." Brad casually laid a hand on her knee. She shifted smoothly out of his reach. "Thanks, Roberta, for coming today. It's always a pleasure to have you"—he paused a beat, then—"on my show."

They broke for a commercial.

Roberta breathed a sigh of relief as she worked to remove the microphone clipped to the lapel of her blouse.

"Here, allow me." Brad leaned over, took hold of the clip. His cool fingers fumbled intimately against her skin.

"I can do it."

"Just about got it." His tone was serious, but she caught a mischievous glint in his eye before he lowered his head again. "Your boyfriend still in New York?"

"Umm." Robbi saw a bald spot at the top of his head, the flesh stained a dark brown to match his hair. Shoe polish? She quickly looked away before the urge to laugh got the best of her.

Under his breath he said, "Stick around, we'll go to lunch afterward."

"Can't."

"A drink?"

"Can't."

He gazed into her eyes. "A little clinching in the elevator, then?"

"Your wife should hear you," she admonished him lightly.

"Phyllis and I are separated."

"Yeah, sure." Roberta brushed his hands away and unclipped the microphone herself.

"Really. Would I shit you?"

"In a minute."

"Hey, I slept on the couch last night. That should count for something—besides a stiff neck."

Roberta shook her head. "You're hopeless, Brad." She stood. "Gotta go. Thanks again for the airtime."

"Thank me over a drink, Red."

She laughed, gave him a quick kiss on the cheek.

He grinned. "We're on?"

"No."

He looked dejected. "Ah, so cruel. But then, gorgeous redheaded women with sexy green eyes are notoriously cruel."

And cute balding men with Shinola-brown scalps are notorious flirts. This time thinking about the shoe polish made her chuckle aloud.

She bit down on her lip and hurried off.

Outside, on a late June afternoon, it was no cooler than under the burning lights of the studio. The shelter, a two-story brick house on a quiet tree-lined street, stood in the heart of Reno in a neighborhood very similar to Roberta's own in Sparks. She parked, made her way down the long driveway to the side entrance, then knocked. The upper half of a woman's face appeared at the windowpane. Bolts clicked and clanked. Sophie Bennett, cxecutive director of the center, opened the door.

"My, my, my, but our star PR lady certainly looked stunning on the tube today," Sophie said. "I thought that old lecher was gonna gobble you up—live and in color, and it being an afternoon show and all. But then, that's why we give you all the glamorous jobs while the rest of us make do with the tedious fare."

"If you think it's so easy, next time you go on."

"I'd have littl' Brad crying 'uncle' in no time."

Roberta scrutinized her friend. Late fifties, steel-gray hair cut short like a man's. Nearly six feet tall, a hundred and ninety pounds, Sophie could be commanding and authoritative. She wore skirts, bright makeup, and lots of chunky jewelry. More than once, she admitted, she'd been accused of being a queen in drag.

"How's everything here?"

"All's quiet. The kids especially."

"That's a bad omen," Roberta whispered, following Sophie down the basement steps. "Whenever the kids are quiet, I get nervous."

"Bite your tongue. Negative thoughts not allowed."

Footsteps thundered overhead. Several children yelled, arguing over something. Laughter and angry cries shattered the quiet.

"Ah, there, that's better," Roberta said, moving into her office. "Now I can relax and get to work."

"What kind of day do you have tomorrow?" Sophie asked, standing in the doorway.

Roberta tossed her purse in a drawer. She began peeping under folders and pamphlets on the cluttered desktop, looking for her calendar. "There's the presentation in the morning at the library"—she found the calendar—"let's see, then that appointment with the Delta guy about donating round-trip tickets to Hawaii for the drawing. The usual. Why, what's up?"

"It's time to do some hard-pedaling on funding for the new facility. Bring your legs, little one. You can be very persuasive."

"My legs or me?"

"Do we care?"

"I want to be admired for my mind."

"And I want to be admired for my body." Sophie struck a model's pose, her large belly stretching the knit of her skirt. "Funny how these things work out."

Robbi smiled.

"Tomorrow." Sophie started down the hall, stopped. "Oh, I almost forgot. Donald called."

"Oh?"

"He said he'd try again later in the week, unless you wanted to call him. But don't try after five, his time—or was it our time?—his time, that's right. He has a dinner meeting. So I guess it's too late now, it's already after six in New York."

"Did he say why he called?"

Sophie shook her head. She came into the office, sat on the edge of the desk. "He sounded good. Confident. Tried to sell me some zero coupon bonds, whatever the hell that is. So how's he doing? What's the name of that brokerage firm he went to work for?"

"Stradford and Powers Securities. He's doing great. It's been only six months and he's knocking 'em dead." Roberta leaned back in her chair. "Six months . . ." she said absently. Had it been that long already? She felt a strange tugging deep inside. Donald Bauer, her steady guy, unofficial fiancé, lover—or whatever the hell they called them these days—had been offered a job he couldn't refuse. She had been the one to insist he go, and within a week Donald had packed up and flown east, leaving a big hole in Roberta's life.

"Still planning on joining him?" Sophie asked. "You haven't said much about it lately."

"We agreed on a year. If he didn't like it, he'd be back. Otherwise I move to the Big Apple."

"Long-distance relationships are a bitch." Sophie squeezed Robbi's arm affectionately, then crossed the room to the door.

"I'll have to call him. We've both been so busy. And the time zones, y'know?"

"Yeah, I know." Her friend smiled empathically, then disappeared down the hall.

Roberta sat at her desk, opened her file drawer, and pulled out several fat folders. To the sounds of laughter and children's footsteps thumping overhead, she started on her paperwork.

Several pages into the file, Roberta heard children crying. Fearful cries. She looked upward to the main floor. Something told her the cries were not coming from anywhere in the shelter. They were coming from inside her head. She squeezed her eyes shut and covered her ears. The sounds swelled. An image flashed across her mind's eye. Two children huddled together, crying.

"Go away," she whispered.

The remainder of the afternoon flew by. At five P.M. Robbi called home to tell Angela she was on her way. As she drove home she thought of her house guests.

Two days before, Angela had fled her husband to seek shelter at Roberta's. Offering her own home was not normally an option, but Angela and her first husband, Lee, had been friends of Roberta's since high school. Roberta was godmother to their two children, Mikey and Carey.

Three years after Lee died in a skiing accident, Angela had married Sam Braga, a railroad engineer with a short fuse. The beatings began on a regular basis shortly after the honeymoon. No less than five times over the years, Angela had been treated at the emergency room with injuries ranging from contusions to broken bones. The last time she'd come away with a dislocated shoulder and several loose teeth. Unlike most batterers, Sam wasn't into booze or drugs; rarely touched so much as a glass of beer. His high was rage, and he was fast becoming addicted to it.

Roberta turned onto her street. Half a block down she pulled into the driveway of her house. *Her* street. *Her* house. Pride filled her at the sight of it. Last year, just before Donald left, she had taken her savings and bought the small two-bedroom house on Euclid. Tagged a "dollhouse" and "fixer-upper" by the realtor, it fit her income. But the neighborhood was good, and the open floor plan promising. The best part of having her own home was in fixing it up the way she wanted it. She spent her evenings renovating the interior. The weekends found her bargain-hunting for furniture and household accessories. With Donald gone, the nights and weekends seemed to stretch endlessly.

After parking in the garage at the back of the lot, she walked down the driveway to the side entrance. The sun shone in her face. She kept her gaze down. Suddenly a strange sensation crawled over her, the sensation of being watched. Something flickered behind her eyes; a nebulous image of children huddled together, crying.

At the back door Roberta glanced through the window into the kitchen. Mickey and Carey sat at the table, coloring. Such good kids, she thought. Quiet, polite, almost too good. *Kids afraid to be kids.* Again she had a gut feeling of being watched.

Instead of going in, Robbi continued down the driveway to the front. She stopped at the sidewalk. As far as she could tell, there was no one inside any of the cars parked along the street.

She shaded her eyes with her hand and took one last look. Nothing. Nothing out of the ordinary. No more odd feelings. No images. With a sigh she picked up the newspaper, plucked a dandelion out by the roots, then headed back to the house.

The rich smell of cake baking, a smell not customary to her house in the heat of summer, surrounded Roberta the moment she opened the door. She inhaled deeply.

"What's that god-awful smell?" she asked.

Carey ran to her, threw her arms around her legs. "Aunt Robbi, we're making brownies."

Robbi bent, peered through the window in the oven. It was cool and empty.

"Not there," Mickey said, pointing with a black crayon at the microwave oven. "We're nuking them."

"A celebrity in our midst." Angela walked into the kitchen, her arm in a sling. "Saw you this afternoon. We taped it. You were great. He rattled you just a tad this time."

"If he can't rattle me a tad, he won't invite me back."

"What a sleaze."

The timer on the microwave buzzed. Carey ran to take the brownies out.

"We walked to the store," Angela said. "Cabin fever drove us out. I bought some groceries. Whenever you're hungry, I'll start dinner."

"Let's go out," Robbi said. "It's too hot to cook."

The kids jumped up, excited.

"Pizza, burgers, tacos, liver pâté, snails. What sounds good?"

"Pizza!"

"Shall we try that place in the square with the video games?" Roberta said. "I have this roll of quarters that's burning a hole in my pocket."

The kids cheered.

TWO

Cindy Brewer, a resident at the shelter, was going back to her husband, Neil, and Roberta knew it.

That morning Cindy had asked Roberta to drive her to the fast-food restaurant, "just to talk to him for a sec," Cindy said. "No way am I going with him. No way."

In the stuffy, airless interior of her eight-year-old Jeep Cherokee, Roberta tried not to stare at the couple who were embracing intimately by her right front fender. The young bride was quickly relenting.

Robbi sighed and looked away, feeling a sense of futility. Ten minutes earlier she had pulled into the parking lot of the Jack-in-the-Box with a frightened battered wife; she would drive out alone. It was as simple as that.

Reaching for the window knob, she hesitated. If she rolled it down, they might think she wanted to eavesdrop. She cursed softly under her breath, pressed the back of her hand to the moisture gathering on her upper lip and forehead, then glanced at her watch. She wished she had one of Sophie's crossword puzzles to help pass the time.

Neil handed Cindy a bouquet of pink roses wrapped in green florist tissue. She smiled, and the smile would have been radiant if not for her swollen, purplish eye and the fat lip with its row of ragged black stitches underneath. He grinned, squeezed her shoulder, seemingly oblivious to her injuries. Then he mumbled something and glanced at Roberta.

Robbie watched Cindy approach. She lowered the window.

Cindy leaned down and gave her a lopsided grin. The delicate flowers and her vivid, battered facc seemed at odds with each other.

"He wants another chance," Cindy said passively. "He promised to stop drinking. I think he's really sorry this time."

Robbi looked at the husband. Neil Brewer was a high-level executive, a handsome, charming fellow. A man with expensive toys, such as the late-model Corvette he'd driven up in.

Their gaze met for a brief second before Neil turned away.

Cindy cleared her throat. "Thanks for bringing me over, Roberta."

Robbi nodded solemnly. "If you need . . ." But she was speaking to the hot, dry air, for the young woman was already walking toward her husband.

Good luck, Cindy.

Robbi turned the key in the ignition, grinding the starter. Before pulling out onto McCarran Boulevard a dreadful scnse of foreboding enveloped her. She gripped the wheel, rolled to a stop and, with her knees shaking, tried to take stock of the situation. The sound of children sobbing rang in her ears. A vision of Mikey and Carey huddled together, their faces distorted from crying, flashed across Roberta's windshield. She realized it was the same vision she'd had the night before in her driveway. *Angela and the kids are in trouble.*

She spotted a pay telephone at the corner, left the car, and hurried to it. As she fed in coins and dialed, the sky went dark. A bank of thunderclouds had moved rapidly across the sun; the wind chilled her bare arms. She shivered, hearing a low roll of thunder far away. On the second ring the phone was answered. Robbi heard children crying in the background.

"Angela, it's me. Are you okay?"

"Roberta, thank God you called! Sam's out front," Angela's voice, charged with tension, blurted out. "He's trying to get in!"

How the hell had Sam found them so quickly? "Hang up and call the police—dial 911. I'm on my way. Don't let him in. No matter what, don't let him in!" She slammed the receiver in the hook and ran to her car.

As she sped down McCarran Boulevard, another vision flashed behind her eyes. Blood. Bright, crimson. *Her own blood.* She jerked the steering wheel and the car swerved. A horn blasted to her left.

Tires squealed when she made a sharp turn onto her street. The passing houses blurred in her haste. As she turned into the driveway, she saw Sam on the porch, his face framed between hands pressed to the window in the front door. Thank God he hadn't managed to break in. Where were the police? She had talked to Angela nearly ten minutes ago.

Robbi screeched to a stop halfway down the drive, rushed from the Jeep, and quickly ran to the back door. She saw Sam round the corner of the house, charging toward her. She barely made it inside, slammed the door, and engaged the lock before he rammed it.

Robbi dragged a kitchen chair to the door, tilted it under the doorknob as he rammed against it. With her hands covering her ears, she backed away.

In the dining room she found the children huddled together in a corner, crying. The *vision*.

Robbi knelt, hugged them both, then gathered them up and led them to her bedroom.

Angela rushed in, clutching a fireplace poker. She looked both relieved and apologetic when she saw Robbi. "I'm sorry, Rob."

"It's not your fault."

"He's been banging on the door like that since you called." She wrung her hands, wincing from the pain in the shoulder he'd dislocated. "I thought he'd give up and go away, but now I know he won't. He's over the edge. Nothing can stop him when he gets like that."

"Did you call the police?"

She nodded, looked around helplessly. "Where the hell *are* they?"

Roberta turned back to the kids. "Mikey, there's a lock on the door. Lock it if you have to? Understand?"

He nodded.

Sam called out his wife's name in a tortured singsong tone. . . . "An-gela. *An-gela.*" Stanley calling out to Stella in *Streetcar*.

From her purse Robbi took out a tiny key. "Wait

here," she said to Angela. She strode into the living room, straight to a slim secretary desk against the wall, and unlocked it. She pulled open a drawer and lifted out the revolver. It was loaded. Behind her Sam was banging and calling out. Making sure the safety was on, she replaced the revolver and closed the drawer.

With her back ramrod-straight, displaying grit she didn't feel, she strode to the entry. Her insides quaked and she felt sick. *No trouble, please. Not with the kids here. Not in my own home.*

The burly man watched her approach, his face devoid of emotion. Her heart thumped heavily.

The normally bright room with its floor-to-ceiling windows, floral-print chintz, natural wicker and latticework, suddenly dimmed, turned cool and gloomy as a cloud shut out the sun.

Through the closed door she said calmly, "Sam, this isn't going to settle anything . . . you're scaring the hell out of the kids."

"Open . . . this . . . door." He kicked the door. Robbie jumped, sucking in her breath. He began to pound on the window inset. Suddenly a denim elbow crashed through the pane. A hand reached in and began to fumble with the chain and dead bolt.

Robbi tried to push his hand back out. He grabbed her wrist and sawed it across the remaining shards of glass. She cried out and wrenched her arm away, watching in horror as the flesh opened and blood oozed out. She backed up toward the desk.

Angela appeared in the arched doorway of the hallway, her hand against her injured shoulder, her mouth and eyes open wide in fear.

Sam flung the door against the wall, his presence

filling the space. He looked around quickly, then made for his wife. Angela froze. He punched her in the stomach. She went down on her knees without uttering a sound. He grabbed a handful of her thick, dark hair and yanked on it.

Robbi rushed at him, but, as if she were a mere gnat, he easily flicked her away.

On unsteady legs she ran to the desk, pulled out the drawer, her fingers leaving smears of blood on the handle, and grabbed the gun.

"Stop it!" she screamed.

Sam turned to Robbi and pointed a finger at her. "Stay out of this, you meddling bitch!"

Angela was on the phone, dialing, when Sam lunged at her. He pulled the cord from the wall, twisted it around Angela's throat and pulled it tight.

Robbi's chest felt tight, her vision blurred. Shaking violently, she raised the gun. *Do it. Do it. Do it. He was going to die today, and she knew it. She had seen it. There was nothing anyone could do to stop it.*

The children appeared at the couple's side, crying, begging for him to stop hurting their mother. Mikey began kicking his stepfather, screaming and slapping. Sam momentarily abandoned his attack on Angela and turned to the boy, grabbing him around the throat, holding him at arm's length.

"I'll break your neck, kid," he snapped at the boy. Then he whipped around and faced his wife. "Is that what you want, bitch?"

Mikey coughed, struggled.

Angela moaned deep in her throat. She turned to Roberta. "Stop him, please! For God's sake, stop him!"

Roberta's mind screamed, *Do it!*

Do it . . .

She watched in horror as the gun slipped from her leaden fingers and dropped to the floor.

Angela lunged for it. On her knees, the gun in tremulous hands, she aimed it at her husband.

"Let him go," Angela whispered.

"You think you can shoot me? Huh?" When she failed to answer, he added, "You're so fucking stupid. How many times have I told you, you are so *fucking* stupid." He pushed the boy away and took a step toward Angela. "Gimme that."

Angela pulled back. The sharp click as she cocked the gun stopped Sam momentarily. Then he charged.

Angela closed her eyes and squeezed the trigger.

Robbi looked from Angela to Sam, staring in disbelief as blood appeared at the waist of Sam's blue denim shirt. He looked stunned.

Angela stared into his eyes, lost, scared. Then she cocked the gun and shot him again, square in the chest. He dropped to his knees, teetered there a moment before toppling over on his side on the braided rug, lifeless.

Robbi moaned, squeezing her eyes shut. She heard the gun drop to the floor, she heard distant thunder and a sad mingling of sobs. And finally she heard the wailing sound of sirens.

THREE

When the police arrived minutes later, Roberta freaked out. She screamed at the two officers, accusing them of reducing the complaint to low priority because it was a domestic battle. She blamed them for the dead man in her house. In the end it was Angela and the children who calmed her down by embracing her, whispering consoling words to her.

They took Sam Braga to the morgue, Angela away in cuffs to the county jail, and the children placed with welfare. Roberta went to the hospital for the cut on her wrist.

Back at home, Sophie Bennett took over. She called a glass shop to repair the broken window, straightened the house, and cleaned up the blood—Roberta's as well as Sam's—while Roberta soaked in a warm bath. After tucking Robbi into bed with a glass of warm Chianti, she put the telephone in her lap.

"Call Don," Sophie said. "You wanted to call him, so now's the time."

Tears sprang into her eyes at the mention of Donald.

Somehow thinking about him made her realize how vulnerable she was. Six months earlier he had been there for her. A solid shoulder. Someone to turn to for support.

She was scared. In a series of visions she had seen it all; brief but vivid, accurate. The children crying, her own blood, and finally Sam's death.

As she dialed, Sophie backed out the bedroom door. She blew Robbi a kiss and waved good-bye.

Robbi waved back. Then Don was on the line.

She told him about her experience.

"Jesus, Rob," Donald said, "you could've been killed. Are you sure you're okay? You say you were cut?"

"A few stitches, that's all."

"Babe, if this doesn't convince you to get a normal job, I don't know what will. This was bound to happen. You're dealing with violent people. They're crazy."

"Don, she's my friend. Angela's my friend."

"Well, sure, but—dammit to hell, I really wish I could be with you right now. But I—I don't know how I'd swing it."

"It's okay."

"I guess you could fly here," he said tentatively. Then with a bit more gusto, "Yeah, sure. That's what you could do, come to New York . . . a visit. You might as well have a look at the place before you decide to move here."

"That sounds good, Don. I'm really tempted."

And she *was* tempted. She needed him. She needed a male she could be entirely female with, someone she loved who loved her in return.

"Well, think about it," Donald said. "I've got an

unbelievable workload, but—well, shit, if you feel the need to get away, just give me a call. Better yet, let my secretary know. She'll take care of all the arrangements."

Robbi didn't respond.

"Rob, are you there? Rob?"

"I'm here." She faked a yawn. "Don, the doctor gave me a shot to settle my nerves. I guess I'm not with it. Getting sleepy."

"Well, good, good. Lie down. Rest. I'll talk to you later. Love ya, honey."

Pause. "Yeah, me too." She slowly hung up the phone.

Despite the sedative, it took her a long time to fall asleep.

That night she dreamed about her dead brother.

FOUR

Angela spent the weekend in the county jail. Monday morning she was released on bail to return to her own home. The children, however, remained wards of the state.

After visiting Mikey and Carey in a foster home, Roberta sought a court order to have the kids released from welfare into her temporary custody.

The day of the arraignment, Roberta called Calvin Tanner, Angela's attorney.

"Cal, what's the charge?"

"Open murder. There was a smoking gun and a body."

"But it was my gun. It was a clear-cut case of self-defense."

"Not quite so clear-cut, I'm afraid. She told the police he wasn't coming after her when she fired the fatal shot."

"Calvin, you and I both know that the way he was going he probably would've killed her. Maybe not at that moment, or even that day, but eventually." Yet

Roberta realized there was no "eventually" for Sam. His time had come and she had known it well before it actually happened.

"Let's hope the grand jury sees it that way too," Calvin said.

That afternoon in a conference room at Harrah's Hotel just minutes before she was to address the Junior League—over Sophie's heated objections—Roberta Paxton suddenly and without warning, like a flash flood gushing down a crusty wash, broke down and sobbed. Sophie sent her home and insisted she take the rest of the week off.

At home, as she attempted to lose herself in yard-work, Roberta was forced to take stock of the situation. The doctor had told her that the shock of Sam's death could have a delayed effect on her. Consciously she hadn't been thinking about the incident, so the weepy outburst had been as much a surprise to her as it had been to Sophie. But she knew the human mind worked in mysterious ways, and hers was trying to tell her something.

Crouching at the flower bed along the side of the driveway, she rammed the trowel under a particularly stubborn weed and tugged with her other hand. The weed broke, dropping her on her bottom, hard.

"Damn, damn, damn," she moaned miserably, then burst into tears for the second time that day. On the warm concrete, still gripping the weed, arms hugging her legs, face buried between her knees, she sobbed, oblivious to the neighbors and playing children.

She needed to get away. She hadn't taken a vacation

in years—hadn't wanted one. Where would she go? To New York to see Donald? Somehow she sensed that a part of her problem had to do with Donald. What would she find in his new world? And was she ready for the answer?

"Mom," Roberta said tentatively into the phone, "is it okay if I come for a visit?"

A pause. Roberta sensed her mother's perplexity. "What's happened? What's the matter?"

"I just need a little time away from . . . from . . ." Tears stung her eyes. Then she was telling her mother about Angela and Sam.

"Come today—now," her mother said. "I'll send Hanley for you."

"I'll drive up. Tonight, after dinner."

"Come sooner if you can. I wanted to see you on your birthday, and now I will. We'll have a little party."

"Don't go to any trouble. I'm really not in a celebrating mood." She hesitated, then: "Oh, Mom, don't tell him I'm coming."

"Sweetheart, you can't avoid your father."

"I've been doing it for years."

The sun was just setting over the mountains when Roberta turned off Highway 267 onto a narrow paved road flanked by enormous evergreens. The air was cooler in this scenic valley in the Sierra Nevada less than a hour's drive from Reno. Roberta inhaled deeply, the crisp scent of pine filling her head. She loved it up there. If it weren't for her father, she'd go every weekend. But he was there, a blemish on the otherwise pleasant picture. Seven years ago her father, Cameron Paxton, had retired from his psychiatric practice in Reno and moved his family to this mountain wilderness. A short time later he suffered a stroke. Although he was an invalid now, his movements restricted, his presence cast an ugly shadow over the large ranch house.

Several minutes later, through the tall trees, she made out the sprawling ranch-style house with its brass lamps, used brick, and white pillars and posts.

As Robbi approached the curve in the long circular drive, the front door opened and a young girl rushed out of the house and jumped down the steps, arms pinwheeling to keep her balance. The girl ran towards her down the gravel drive, her long blond hair swirling around her oval face. Beneath a pair of skimpy green shorts and a narrow pink tube top, she was as golden as a toasted almond.

Roberta smiled, a pleasant glow warming her insides. Coming out to meet her was her thirteen-year-old sister, Tobie.

FIVE

That first night, Roberta, her mother, and her sister had sat up in the rustic kitchen drinking Cokes, munching on popcorn, and talking. Sometime in the wee hours they wound down and gave in to the contagious cycle of yawns. Roberta had the guest room on the opposite side of the house from her father's room. It was easy to pretend he didn't exist, nearly as easy for her as it was for him.

In the morning Roberta helped Tobie feed her pets in the rear yard. The menagerie consisted of two rabbits and their litter of bunnies; three cats, Clarice, Bonnie, and Snowman; and two ducks. Then there were the wounded wild animals. A stellar jay—pried from the mouth of Snowman—and a young yellow-bellied marmot shot with a BB gun. These Tobie would nurse back to health, then turn loose.

"Tomorrow's your birthday," Tobie said.

"Let's not dwell on it, okay?"

"Thirty's not so old . . . is it?"

"If you have to ask, then it's old."

"Well, you're not old. In fact, tomorrow after the party I want to show you a secret place. Nobody knows about it but me."

"Where is it?"

"Tomorrow." Tobie's expression was laden with intrigue.

"No trail blazing or mountain climbing, I'm out of shape."

"Maybe you *are* too old." Tobie grinned. "We'd better just stick around here. Sit on the porch swing and blow bubbles."

"I wouldn't mind."

"Oh, c'mon, Robbi," she whined softly, "it's a special place. We'll ride double on Madonna."

"Okay, okay."

Tobie knelt before the rabbit cage, poured food pellets into the bowls, then brushed her hands together. "God, I'm starving. This housekeeper makes the best egg and salsa burritos."

"She cooks Mexican food? He always hated Mexican." They spoke of their father in the pronoun.

"He still does. But she cooks it special for me and Hanley. Oh, don't worry, Robbi, he's already eaten. I peeped in the window and saw him in bed with the lap-tray."

A brown and white bunny buried in a cloud of rabbit fur crawled over a mound of siblings. Robbi reached into the hutch, lifted it out, and snuggled it to her face.

"I know I can't avoid him forever, but I'm not ready for a confrontation just yet." Robbi blew on the soft fur. "Do you think he knows I'm here?"

"Sure. He knows everything. He'll stay away just long enough to give you a false sense of security, then he'll come rolling in, real quiet like, and totally bum you out."

"How can you stand it?" Roberta asked.

Tobie shot her sister a guilty look. "It's better, y'know . . . since the stroke. He's just as mean, but he can't get around as much now."

The cats complained, rubbed against the two sisters, then scratched at the bag of Cat Chow.

Tobie scooped out three bowls. "Rob, when you have a premonition, or whatever it's called, what do you see?"

Roberta had told her sister that she'd known of Sam Braga's death before it happened. Although she and Tobie were seventeen years apart, they shared everything, never shocked or critical of the other. Tobie was one of the few people privy to Roberta's rare and infrequent flashes of clairvoyance, a phenomenon that Robbi had repressed for so long she almost forgot she had it until it hit her right between the eyes.

"Just flashes, honey. I get cold . . . and scared."

"I wish I could do that. See things like that."

"Be careful what you wish for—"

"I know, I may get it."

Robbi draped her arm over Tobier's shoulder, squeezed. The light scents of fruit filled Robbi's head. "Jeez, is that you who smells like a fruit salad?"

Tobie giggled. "Yeah. Coconut mousse and watermelon bubble gum. Oh, and peach lip gloss."

"No wonder animals love you. They think you're dinner. And you're making me hungry. Let's eat."

The housekeeper cleared away the breakfast dishes.

Tobie had gone off to spend the day at the beach with her best friend, Pam, and her family. With her gone, the spacious room seemed limitless and deadly quiet. The entire ranch-style house with its score of rooms took on an eerie emptiness.

Lois Paxton sat across from Roberta at the formal dining room table, slowly sipping a cup of herbal tea. Roberta noticed deep furrows in her brow, the squinting of her eyes.

"Headache again, Mom?"

"Still," Lois replied, rubbing the base of her skull. "Just the tail end of one. I wonder if I'll ever stop having these damn migraines."

"Go lie down till it's gone."

"I'd rather visit with you. It's not often you stay with us."

"I'll be here for a couple more days. We'll have plenty of time to talk."

"I know, but—"

Roberta cut her off. "I thought I'd go riding this morning. With Tobie gone for the day, I can have the horse to myself."

"Well, in that case, while you're out maybe I will lie down for a bit. Have Hanley saddle Madonna. And when he's done, send him in to tend to your father, will you?"

Outside, she crossed the yard to the stable, looking for Hanley Gates. Hanley, the Paxtons' caretaker, had been with them the seven years they had lived there. Although Roberta knew him only slightly, her sister was very close to him. For Tobie he served as the father figure she so desperately needed, a position her own father scorned.

Hanley wasn't in the stable or the tack room. As she neared his bungalow, she saw him through the open door. He sat on the edge of a bunk, hunched over, a hand working absently through his hair, splaying the wispy gray strands up and out, staring at something in his other hand.

Gravel crunched loudly beneath her shoes, yet he failed to hear her approach. She stepped up on the low stoop. As she raised a hand to knock, she wondered about his age. He had one of those timeless faces; he could be anywhere from fifty to seventy. At that moment he looked the latter.

She tapped on the door frame.

He looked up, confusion clouding his eyes, then slow recognition. He greeted her with a timid smile.

"Roberta. For a minute there I thought it was Tobie."

"She's gone for the day."

"Yeah, I know."

He quickly rose to his feet, his back straight, shoulders squared, and with that simple motion his age seemed to reverse.

"I was jus' wool-gathering." He waved a yellowed snapshot, then slipped it out of sight on the dresser top. "My wife, Em, and grandson. Em died a long time ago."

"I'm sorry."

He looked away, nodded. "Had a daughter too. She died before my Em did."

"Are you close with your grandson?"

He shrugged, looking solemn. "Naw. Lost track of him. Got the wanderlust like his mama." Then he smiled, a broad grin that crinkled his eyes. "Got my hands full right here with your little sister. That one can't sit for a minute. And always wanting to know 'bout everything."

"I'm glad you're here for her. She really cares for you, y'know? It's always Hanley this, Hanley that."

Hanley seemed embarrassed by her comment. He shrugged again. They stared at each other for several awkward moments.

He smiled and quickly crossed the room to the door. "What can I do for you?"

"I'll be taking Madonna out . . ." Roberta began.

"Well, sure, sure. I'll saddle her for ya."

"That's okay, I can do it. My mother needs you inside."

"Well, let me get you lined out." He reached for a canister of snuff and, with his long wrangler legs, strode through the door and toward the stable.

Hanley helped Roberta saddle the horse. As he led Madonna out of the stable, he stared intently at the sky.

"Looks like we might get a summer storm," he said. "You be careful you don't get caught out in it. Head back the first sound of thunder."

Robbi heard a harsh voice raised in anger coming from the house. She felt her stomach knot.

Her father's voice made her cringe.

Hanley quickly handed the reins over to Roberta. "He don't like to be kept waiting."

Halfway to the house, he called over his shoulder, "Keep an ear open for that thunder."

A mile or so from the stable, Robbi slowed the horse

to a walk. It had been a long time since she'd ridden, and she realized she was pulling too tightly on the reins. Irritably, Madonna sawed at the bit until Robbi loosened the tension.

She had been thinking about her father. Why was he so damn unpleasant, not happy unless he was brow-beating someone? She swallowed the anger, forced herself to calm down. Hadn't she come to this pristine wilderness, away from the city and the pressures of her job, to unwind and rejuvenate? Breathe in the crisp, clean air, the woodsy scent of trees and grass? Fill your lungs and head. Enjoy, she told herself.

Finally allowing Madonna the reins, Robbi let her body relax. Looking around, her eyes feasting on the verdant landscape, she attempted to identify the different types of pine trees by the shape of the cones, at the same time chiding herself for not bringing something, a satchel or bag, in which to collect pine cones.

Sometime later she came to the wire fence that marked the southwest boundary of the property. She was in a deep-wooded area that butted up to land once crowded with logging camps. She crossed a small creek, no more than two or three inches deep. The echo of the horse hooves clopped over wet stones and moss, splashing water on Roberta's jeans.

A half mile farther, a sudden chilling gust of wind blew dust and debris into her face. She turned her head away, rubbing her eyes. The temperature seemed to have dropped twenty degrees in just minutes. She tilted back her head and looked over the tops of the tall aspen trees, their leaves quaking silver and green in the wind. The sky, which an hour before was more blue than gray, was now entirely obscured with a gloomy mass of clouds. Thunderclouds.

A quarter-size raindrop hit the back of her hand. Then another. Then she was being pelted with large drops.

The horse snorted, pranced nervously. Robbi flicked the reins and leaned forward. Madonna, needing no more encouragement, turned her head in the direction of home and broke into a trot, following the fence downhill.

Within moments a torrent of water beat at her, obstructing her vision. Roberta knew that the hard, dry ground beneath them could soak up only so much water before it began to run off, taking pebbles and pine needles with it.

The sudden force of the storm surprised her. Already soaked to the bone, she shivered from the cold, relentless rain. It stung like bits of gravel. Where was the thunder Hanley had warned her to listen for? How far was she from the house? She was uncomfortable but not overly concerned—not yet. The horse knew its way home, and as long as they remained a team, she'd get there. She prayed Madonna wouldn't bolt, throw her, and run.

She reached the creek that she'd crossed earlier, but instead of the six-foot-wide rippling stream, it was now an angry rivulet, surging with muddy, debris-littered water. Madonna balked, refused to cross.

Roberta sat stiffly in the saddle and took stock. The swollen creek ran perpendicular to the barbed-wire fence, cutting through it. They had no choice but to cross the creek.

Robbi dismounted and, taking the reins, she stepped into the roaring water. The water pulled at her ankles.

She teetered, her heart pounded. Rocks cut into the bottom of her running shoes. She pulled on the reins, coaxing Madonna to cross with her. A scene flashed in her head, nearly blinding her. A scene of a river, a wide river. A gray concrete bridge. A small hand desperately gripping a bush. Screams, rendered silent by the raging rapids. *Ronnie . . . ?*

In a panic, Roberta slipped, fell to her knees. She cried out. The water pushed and pulled, threatening to drag her along its muddy course. She grabbed onto a stirrup, pulled herself up. Holding tightly on to Madonna's neck, Roberta nudged the animal until it clattered across to the other side. She buried her face in the horse's neck, gasping for air, waiting for her heart to steady.

Ronnie . . . so long ago, yet still so painful. The sight of the rushing water had triggered her memory.

After several moments she pressed on, deciding to walk the horse rather than ride. The ground, like the creek, had become unstable. Flashfloods were common to this area. She worked her way down a rocky ravine, the rain beating against her face, her feet slipping beneath her. After going only a short distance, Robbi found herself at the edge of a steep projecting mass of rock and twisted pinion pines. She stood shivering alongside the burned-out stump of a large pine tree, its roots exposed beneath the edge of the crag. Madonna shifted, moving in behind her. Suddenly the ground gave way under her feet. A scream ripped from her throat as she, the horse, and the huge stump plunged forward off the rugged edge. Over and over she tumbled, crying out as the rocks drove into her body from all directions. Pain burst in her head.

Everything became still. Even the rain eased. Robbi opened her eyes. Lightning flashed, followed by a low rumbling. *There's the thunder Hanley spoke of.* A little late now. Then she closed her eyes and drifted off to the sound of horse hooves, muffled by the sodden earth, disappearing into the distance.

After an indeterminable amount of time Robbi came around. She lay on her stomach, her head turned to one side. A patch of velvet moss cushioned her cheek, but the pain in her head was intense. She wove in and out of consciousness. Her legs and arms felt like dead appendages. Was she paralyzed? She couldn't say, but she knew for certain she was going to pass out again soon. It hurt too much to endure.

The rain felt good. She moved her tongue forward, pushing bits of grit from her lips. She tried to lift her head, and it seemed to explode from within.

She slowly opened her eyes. Over the droning of the rain she heard twigs snapping. Someone was out there. Thank God, someone was coming for her.

"Here . . ." It was merely a whisper. "I'm . . . here . . ."

Between the thin boughs of young saplings surrounding her, Roberta saw a woman in a transparent white dress running through the woods. The woman seemed to glow. *What a delicate thing the mind is,* Roberta thought. *She's not really there. There's no woman running through the forest in the rain.*

The woman came within several yards of her. She stumbled and fell to one knee, crying out. Angry criss-cross scratches covered her legs. Her bare feet bled. Around one slender ankle something glittered in the dim light, reflecting into a puddle under her foot; a gold and silver ankle bracelet.

"Help me." Roberta forced out the words.

The woman turned her face toward Roberta. In her eyes Roberta saw terror—sheer unequivocal terror. The woman in white jerked her head from side to side as though looking for something, then she abruptly rose and continued to run.

"No, don't . . . don't leave. . . ." Roberta sobbed the words, watching her go.

Suddenly from out of nowhere a large man appeared. The running woman screamed. He chased her, caught her by her long blond hair. He pulled her around to face him. Again the scream, like the long shriek of a train whistle in the night.

Roberta, horrified, looked on.

The man hugged the woman to him as she struggled and repeatedly struck out at his face. She squirmed out of his grasp and began to run again. A huge fist shot out and knocked her down. His hand circled her throat and he lifted her off the ground, feet dangling, thrashing. The man trembled with rage. His face twisted, became monstrously cruel beneath a beard and sopping masses of hair. The muscles in his arms bulged from the tremendous tension he exerted in the strangulation of the woman.

Roberta's vision blurred, then cleared, blurred again.

The thrashing stopped, yet, for what seemed like an eternity, he continued to hold the limp, rag-doll figure off the ground by her neck.

An involuntary moan escaped Roberta's lips.

His head snapped up; alert, listening.

Her pulse crashed at her temples, sending a renewed

surge of pain through her injured body. She tried to move but was powerless to budge.

He released the woman. She crumpled at his feet. His hand swiped across his eyes as he turned in Roberta's direction. He took a step, stopped, and glanced down at the dead woman, then looking back toward Roberta, he began walking her way.

Behind the thin saplings she tried to make herself small, invisible. Her throat locked. Her mind screamed. Mercifully, she blacked out.

SIX

Sounds. Ordinary, everyday sounds. Traffic in the street, soles on linoleum, metal clinking against metal, a toilet flushing. All quite normal sounds.

Pain. It rode her body in waves, one following the other, rising, cresting, crashing; never ending.

Blackness. Not a glimmer of light anywhere. With the blackness came a feeling of unreality, of timelessness and despair—utter despair.

The universe consisted of pain, sound, and a black void. There was something else . . . a strong smell of damp earth.

The nebulous voices:
"Robbi, darling, can you hear me?"
"Roberta? Roberta?"
"Okay, honey, we're just going to turn you over."
"Can she hear us . . . ? Little one, can you hear me?"

The voices were distant sounds, drowned out by pain.

She wove in and out of the dreams.

Running, running, so tired. Still she ran, mired in the denseness of the night. She ran through the black forest, the stinging rain pelting her, the eyes chasing her. Eyes, glowing and feral. Gaining on her.

"Robbi?"

Watermelon. Coconut. Peaches. Tobie? Tobie, turn on the light.

"I think she can hear me . . . hear me . . . I know she can . . . can . . ."

Tobie, I'm here. Keep talking. Don't go away. Would the daylight never come? She tried to choke down the rising panic.

Where am I?

I want to see . . . *Please, let me see!*

And as if in answer to her desperate plea, images began to form. Smoky monochromatic images. Roberta strained to see, grateful for any impression, greedy for the drab, indistinct picture developing before her.

She was in the woods. Rain stung her face. To each side of her she caught flashes of trees, blurred images in the grim light as she raced pass them.

The storm.

Her fall down the ravine.

Of course. Of course, that explained it. She was *dead.* She was dead and in a state of limbo in some vacuum in time.

But could she be dead and feel so much pain?

She tried to move but couldn't. Panic rose again. What was wrong? Was she paralyzed? Tied down? A spirit without physical energy?

Suddenly another image flashed across her mind. An image of a running woman surrounded by a torrent of rain. A huge man choking the woman to death. The man turning toward Roberta . . . coming after her.

At that moment Robbi gave in to the panic and cried out, her mind desperately urging a helpless body to react—to fight. Never before had she known such terror and anguish. She thrashed out, screaming.

Instantly hands were holding her, voices shushed, and she felt the sharp jab of a needle. The image disappeared, leaving her to struggle with the black void. As her senses began to dull, despite the dreaded darkness that had ruthlessly clawed at her before the vision, she experienced a ray of hope. She was Roberta Paxton. She was alive. She was in a hospital and she'd had a nightmare.

"Miss Paxton? Roberta? Can you hear me?" the deep baritone voice asked.

Robbi had been staring into space—black space—listening to the sounds, seeing nothing. She had regained consciousness hours earlier, drifting in and out, but had not called out to anyone. She just listened, trying to stay calm.

"Roberta, if you can hear me, please answer."

"I can't see," she said softly.

Scratching sounds of a pen to paper. "Well, hello. How do you feel?"

"I can't see," she repeated.

A gentle hand covered hers. "Can you see anything? Light, shapes, colors?"

"Nothing. Black. Sometimes red spots, flashes."

"Um."

"Who are you?"

"I'm Dr. Newton. You're at Washoe Med. Now it's your turn. Can you tell me your full name?"

"My name is Robbi—Roberta Paxton."

"Address? Phone number?"

She told him.

"What's wrong with my eyes? Why can't I see?" She put cool fingers to her eyes and pressed lightly.

More scratching. "Roberta, you had a bad fall. You've been comatose for nearly four days. Aside from a concussion, you have several cracked and bruised ribs, a sprained ankle, contusions, and abrasions. No internal damage. Nothing broken. You're a very lucky lady. At first we thought you were paralyzed from the waist down, but within twenty-four hours you regained complete mobility. That gives us hope, and reason to believe your sight will be restored as well."

"When?" she blurted out anxiously.

"I don't know that, Roberta." His hand patted her. "Maybe tomorrow . . . maybe next month."

He lifted her hand. "The cut from the broken glass. It's healing nicely. We'll get these stitches out in a day or two."

Blind. She was blind. What would she do? How could she take care of herself? Her job, what of her job? Don't think about it now. *I'm alive. I came out of a coma. My body's on the mend.*

"We want to do a few more tests now that you're

awake. But tomorrow will be soon enough."

"Doctor, the horse? Did it survive?"

"I don't know. Your mother will be here in the morning. She comes every day. I'm sure she'll have answers to all your questions."

The horse. The storm. The man and woman. Robbi doubted that her mother would answer *all* her questions.

SEVEN

Through the heavy blackness Robbi smelled the subtle aloe, and she heard the ticking of her mother's old Bulova wristwatch as she sat by the side of the bed talking.

"The horse had to be put to sleep, honey," Lois Paxton said quietly. "From what I understand, Madonna broke her leg in the fall. She was able to get back to the house, but . . . Well, let's not talk about that now. I'm just so glad you're alive. There were a few crucial days when we weren't sure *you'd* make it. You came out of the coma, yet there was still a chance you'd be paralyzed and blind—" Her words stopped abruptly, she squeezed Roberta's hand hard, making her flinch. "You're going to be just fine. Just fine. You'll recuperate at home with us. Hanley and Tobie can help. We'll have that birthday party you missed."

"That's one birthday I don't mind skipping."

"Nonsense. Oh, I saw your friend Angela in the parking lot. What's happened with her? Did she get her kids back?"

"Her hearing was yesterday and the case was thrown out. Something about a 'no true bill,' whatever that means. Anyway, she's free and she has her kids back. That's all that matters. Her parents want her to move to New Mexico, near them. She's leaving as soon as she can pack up."

"She's a nice lady, Angela is. She seems so devoted to those children."

"She is. I'm going to miss them."

"Have you been up yet?" her mother asked.

"No."

Robbi felt the sheet being lifted.

"Your poor legs were all black and blue. But the bruises are fading." Her mother patted her knee, then tucked the sheet around her again. "Sweetheart, someone wants to say hello."

Among the mixed scents in the room, Robbi caught a whiff of smokeless tobacco. A familiar male voice accompanied it. "Hello, Robbi, you gave us quite a scare."

"Hanley. Hi. I hear you saved my life."

"Got you out of the rain anyway."

"Thank you."

"Was the least I could do. Warned you to listen for the thunder, but don't s'pose you got the chance. Got bushwhacked by the storm, did ya?"

"Bushwhacked is the word."

"When Madonna come back without you, we figured something bad happened. I followed her tracks and found you out cold in the woods."

"Hanley, did you see anyone else out there?"

"Anyone else?"

"A large man . . . with a beard?"

"No, Miss, nobody else.

"Are you sure?"

"Sure as I can be. Why?"

"I thought . . ." She let the words d
head. "Nothing."

The soles of his boots shifted. "Well, I jus
wish you well, Robbi," Hanley said. "Mrs. Pax   I'll
go on down and pull the car around to the front."

Roberta and Hanley exchanged good-byes. She listened to his booted steps go out the door.

Suddenly the scent of watermelon mingled with coconut overpowered her. Robbi raised her head, breathed in. "Tobie?"

"How'd you know I was here?" her sister said.

"Hanley chews, but I don't think he's taken to chewing watermelon bubble gum"—she sniffed—"or wearing coconut mousse. Had my mouth watering."

"Boy, you have a good sniff detector."

Robbi smiled, took Tobie's hand. She hesitated before saying, "Tobie, about Madonna—"

Her sister squeezed her hand. "It was an accident. It wasn't your fault, Rob. Okay?"

"Honey, what was that about someone else out in the storm?" her mother asked.

Now was the time, Roberta told herself. She had to tell someone. "Mom, Tobie, listen, I saw—jeez, how do I say this? Something bizarre happened in the woods that afternoon. The man I asked Hanley about, I . . . I thought I saw him kill a woman."

Silence.

"It was raining hard, but . . . but I swear I saw this man chase down a woman and then . . . then he strangled her."

her arm. "Darling, did this happen
after you fell?" her mother asked.

Robbi knew what was coming. Although it had been a long time since the other tragedy, she knew they hadn't forgotten. "After."

"Honey, you hit your head. You were unconscious when Hanley found you. The mind plays tricks on us."

"You mean *my mind* plays tricks on *me.*"

"I didn't say that, Robbi."

"But you meant it."

Her mother said nothing to dispute her words.

"Robbi, in the past couple years I've been all over those hills with Madonna and I've never seen anyone," Tobie said. "I've never run into anyone else. No one lives around there."

Roberta sighed. "I guess it's possible I was hallucinating. I hope so anyway. Everything was sort of dreamlike. It hurt so bad . . . and I couldn't move."

"Oh, baby," her mother said. "When I think of you lying out there in the rain, injured and alone, it makes me sick. I couldn't stand it if anything happened to you or Tobie. I just couldn't stand it . . . not again."

"I know, Mama. It's okay, I'm all right." She squeezed her mother's hand.

After everyone had gone, Robbi tried to sleep. Just beneath the wound on her forehead a pulse began to throb. Within an hour she had her first headache.

She felt cool fingers on her chin, moving her head from side to side. "Open your eyes wide." The doctor's scent filled her nostrils; soap, talc, starch, and, when he spoke, the sugary ingredients of a breath mint. "Good. Good."

Several feet to her left, she heard a strange stirring sound.

"Dr. Newton, what *is* that noise? That rustling sound?" She pointed toward the source. "I've been hearing it all day."

"Oh, you must mean the balloons. The air currents have them rubbing together. Looks like a birthday gift."

"Who are they from?"

A moment later he read, "From the gang at the office."

She felt disappointment. Sophie had collected her mail. Nothing had come from Donald, not even a card. Had he forgotten her birthday?

"Roberta, your sense perception, does it seem more acute to you? Taste, smell, sound, touch?"

She considered a moment, then replied, "Yes, very much so."

She heard a pen scratching on paper. "Still having the headaches?"

"Yes."

"How often?"

She shrugged. "Every other day. Usually with the nightmares. The pain wakes me up."

"Roberta, I'd like to call in another doctor. I don't think we should overlook anything concerning your blindness."

"What kind of doctor?" she asked, knowing full well what his answer would be.

"A psychiatrist."

Damn.

EIGHT

Roberta sat up in bed, listening to the passionate yet soothing sounds of the mandolins of Harry Geller. The Gypsy music came from a small cassette player on her lap.

She adjusted the earphones. Having no concept of time, she wondered how long before Dr. Reynolds would come. Their appointment was for one o'clock.

At the thought of a visit from the psychiatrist, Robbi's insides cramped. A *psychiatrist.* How could she have let herself be talked into seeing a psychiatrist? *For the blindness,* Dr. Newton had said. *There's a good chance the problem is psychosomatic.* By reputation only, she knew Reynolds. The reports of his work were admirable. She'd heard he was somewhat eccentric—something about a passion for collecting and restoring old cars—but what did she care about his hobbies as long as he could cure her? If her father could restore her vision, she'd let *him* treat her, that's how desperate she was.

Her father had been a psychiatrist, and the power

he'd wielded—more accurately the power he wielded because of his profession—had been inconceivable.

When she was nine, not long after Ronnie died, her father had taken her to the state mental institution, to the children's ward. Leading her by the hand, he had proudly showed her the facilities, the grand tour. The first floor housed incapacitated diapered children in cribs. Each floor thereafter proved more disturbing than the last. She had been frightened by the intense stares of the young patients, by their compulsion to follow her, to touch her, to try to eat anything they came in contact with. She had begged to go home, petrified he would leave her there. The nightmares haunted her for years.

When the tender strings of "Czardas" came to an end, Robbi felt the tears that had suddenly welled up spill over her lower lashes and flow down her face. She brushed at them impatiently. She couldn't give in to the music today. She had plenty to feel sorry about, and one day soon she'd take advantage of it and just let go—let the tears gush while she sobbed her heart out—but not today. At least not until after the shrink had come and gone.

Earlier, one of the nurses had combed her hair, working it into a French braid in back. Although Roberta had refused makeup, the nurse had added a touch of blush to cover up that "ol' hospital pallor and bring out those marvelous cheekbones."

"Two Guitars" began, one of her personal favorites. The sweet romantic music filled Robbi's head with visions of purple nights and Gypsy campfires. She leaned her head back and let it take her away.

Before the song was over, Robbi strongly sensed

another's presence. The room seemed to lose a measure of space. She detected a faint odor of aftershave. Despite the music filling her ears, she heard sounds of breathing, of fabric rustling. She kept her eyes closed and waited. After many long moments Robbi asked, "Is someone there?"

"Your hearing is very keen," a male voice said.

She opened her eyes to more darkness, pulled off the headphones, and lifted her head. "Dr. Reynolds?" she asked cautiously.

"Yes. It's one o'clock, Ms. Paxton." The voice was closing in. "I believe we have an appointment."

He had been silently watching her. For how long? She felt a flash of anger at the invasion of her privacy.

"My hearing may be good, Dr. Reynolds, but my inner clock needs some development." A tightness crept into her voice.

As if reading her mind, he said, "I would have announced myself, but you seemed so captivated by what was coming from the cassette player, I was reluctant to intrude."

His voice was soft and soothing—a true shrink's voice.

She shut off the tape player and waited.

"Dr. Newton tells me you had a blow to the head."

"That's correct." Crisp, stuffy, not her usual casualness. A defense mechanism. She was on guard. Could she ever trust a shrink after her father? She could remember his threats. *Be careful, girl . . . there's a room for you there, Roberta. . . .* If her own father questioned her sanity . . . ?

"Have you always had such keen sensory perception?"

"No."

"Interesting."

"Did Dr. Newton tell you about the nightmare?" she asked.

"He didn't tell me anything except that you had a serious fall and woke up blind."

She heard a scraping noise and then his voice came from a lower position than before. She guessed he had pulled up a chair and was sitting.

"I'd like to hear about your experience, if you'd care to talk about it."

How much should she tell? Go slow. Too little is safer than too much. Robbi wet her lips and began. She told Dr. Reynolds about the accident. She neglected to tell him that while she lay on the rain-soaked ground, injured and unable to move, she saw a man choke a woman to death.

When she finished, he laid a hand on her shoulder and talked of post-trauma and depression. He talked of strength and support.

"Married? Children?" he asked.

"Not yet. My fiancé lives in New York." She smiled. "He wanted me to visit him there, but instead I chose to go to the mountains. Poor choice, I'm afraid."

"Ever been to New York?"

"No, but I'll be moving there soon. Donald's a stockbroker on Wall Street."

Why am I telling him this? she wondered. She realized she had a profound need to talk about Donald, about a life before the blindness. Bringing up Donald gave her a sense of normalcy, of a time when problems were easily fixed or fixed themselves. She was going to be all right. Think positive. Don loves me, she told herself. She was certain he'd be sitting at her bedside that very moment, offering his love and support, if he knew she was here.

Dr. Reynolds said he would return in a few days, or sooner if she needed him, then he was gone.

When she was alone, a gut-wrenching pain doubled her over. *Donald didn't know she was in the hospital because he was too damn busy to call.*

Oh, God, how would he react when he found out she was blind?

Before opening the door of his '55 T-bird, Jake Reynolds paused to look up at the fourth floor windows of Washoe Medical Center. He located Roberta Paxton's window by the shiny bunch of balloons clustered to one side, the sun reflecting off their metallic casings.

The coma, blindness, and nightmares could very well be psychosomatic. Trauma induced. She had come out of the coma, therefore she could regain her sight. To dream of a storm would be in keeping with this sort of trauma, and dreams of being pursued were not uncommon.

He knew of Roberta Paxton from a newspaper account. She had witnessed the killing of a man by his wife shortly before her accident. At this point it was impossible to say for certain if the nightmares and the killing were related, though a strong possibility existed.

He found himself wondering about her fiancé. If ever there was a time when a woman needed the special man in her life, it was now. Yet he was in New York. What kind of a man was he? If Jake were this guy Donald, he sure as hell wouldn't be three thousand miles away on Wall Street. He'd be here at the bedside of the woman he loved.

She was the one.

From a small cocktail table in the rear of the room, Joseph Eckker stared at her trim back as she sat alone at the end of the littered bar, sipping a straight shot of whiskey.

At 3:20 in the morning the place was nearly empty. The bartender leaned against the back of the bar, his tattooed arms folded across his chest, lost in an old *Rockford Files* rerun on the television. The young blonde stared down into the drink, her hands around the glass, a long, thin cigarette smoldering between her fingers. An old woman dropped a coin in the jukebox and made her selection. The bartender turned and glared at her.

Eckker finished his beer, rose, and with measured steps moved to the bar. From the jukebox Tom Jones asked, "What's new, pussycat?"

The blond woman turned when she sensed someone behind her. Her gaze swept upward until she was staring into his face with large blue eyes, red-rimmed and smudged with mascara. She had been crying.

She turned back to the bar, lifted her drink, and sipped.

He sensed her fear. She had no reason to fear him.

"Another?" he nodded at her drink.

She shook her head.

He eased onto the stool next to her. She was very pretty. He liked looking at her.

Her eyes darted nervously to the bartender. Then she glanced at him. He smiled. She turned on her stool, offering him a stiff back.

He placed a hand on her shoulder, leaned down, and whispered in her ear, "Too pretty to be so sad."

She pulled away, trying to dislodge his hand from her shoulder.

"I'd never make you cry."

She vehemently shook his hand away and jumped from the stool. Without a word or a backward glance, she grabbed her purse and strode off toward the back of the bar. He watched her enter the ladies' room. As he slid off the stool, he looked around. The bartender, with his back to him, was engrossed in the TV program. The old woman had passed out at the bar, her weathered face a sponge for a puddle of spilled beer.

He went out the front door, stood on a sidewalk littered with cigarette butts, tourist coupons and cocktail glasses, and looked up and down the deserted street.

He walked to the end of the building, then turned left into the alley. Within moments he heard heels clinking along the pavement, coming his way. He stood in the shadows, waiting.

A waist-high barricade of black plastic trash bags lined the curb. Opposite them, she was walking briskly. He quickly moved to intercept her. She turned, saw him, and stopped cold.

He was within a foot of her when she spun around toward the street and started to run. The bags tripped her up. She fell into them as he reached for her. The expression on her face changed from fearful to feral. She brought her hands up, the fingers clawlike.

He moved in, pinning her to the trash bags, his

massive hairy hand closed around her throat.

"I won't hurt you," he said low in his throat. As he squeezed, she clawed at him, raking long furrows of skin from his hands and wrists. He squeezed until she ceased to struggle against her bed of black plastic bags—

Robbi jerked awake in the darkness. She was sitting upright in the hospital bed, gulping for air. Icy sweat stung her eyes and she rubbed them. Moaning now, she rocked back and forth.

The nightmare faded rapidly, but the ominous vision closed around her with suffocating clarity. The large man, the woman, the trash bags. What did it mean?

Robbi clutched the sheet, brought it to her stinging eyes. She wiped one eye, then the other. Though barely visible in the dim light of the hospital room, she realized she was staring at a white sheet held in long, tapered fingers.

Her own fingers.

She opened her eyes wide, straining to see. A pale moon glow reflected off a chrome paper towel dispenser across the room. The balloons in the window—four of them—shifted softly, catching the light. The large clock on the wall read 3:32.

Roberta sucked in a deep breath.

She could see again.

NINE

Margaret Winston opened her eyes and stared into a glaring light. She quickly closed them. Taking a few moments to get her bearings, she opened her eyes again, more slowly. A bare bulb hung from the ceiling in the middle of the tiny room. Where the hell was she? How had she gotten here?

As she looked around, she began to recall things she didn't want to recall. The bar. The big man with the black eyes. *Oh, God, no.*

Her hand went to her throat. It felt tender both inside and out. It all came back to her in a rush. He had jumped her outside the bar, choked her into unconsciousness, then brought her to this place.

She sat up quickly. She was fully clothed in the casino black and whites, her black high heels on the floor at her feet. Her nylons were snagged on both legs but still mostly intact.

She swiveled around, taking in her surroundings. The room was approximately five by six feet. She sat on a narrow army cot covered with a lavender chenille spread. The walls and ceiling were a mosaic of various carpet scraps, a straw mat fit corner to corner on the floor. Adhered to the walls with masking tape were pages torn from magazines. Three pictures: a mountain lake, two deer grazing in a golden meadow, and a single dewdrop rose.

She reached out and pulled back a corner flap of carpet on the wall. Behind it she saw a layer of Styrofoam. Styrofoam was used for insulation. It could also soundproof a room. She'd learned that from Sonny. Her boyfriend, Carl Masser—she called him Sonny—was a carpenter. *Sonny.* They'd had a fight last night after she'd gone home from work. To punish him she had stormed out of their apartment and ended up at the Stardust, a bar she hung out at before she met Sonny. *Oh, Jesus, Maggie, you really did it this time.*

Beyond the small room she heard scratching. The door opened and he ducked down and came through. His huge bulk seemed to choke the tiny space.

Margaret's heart slammed painfully in her chest.

The man remained hunched over, the back of his head touching the angled ceiling. He looked around the room as though seeing it for the first time, then his gaze settled on her. He smiled that same lopsided smile.

"Time to eat."

Margaret only stared.

"Come."

"I wan"—Maggie's voice cracked, partly from fear and partly from the physical trauma to it—"to go home."

"C'mon." He stepped away from the doorway.

Maggie stood, began to slip a foot into one shoe.

"You won't need those."

She walked ahead of him through the door. Her legs shook. Any minute she expected a blow to the back of her head. She had to crouch down, walk crablike to an even smaller door at the end of a short, dark passage. He was right behind her as she entered a main room.

She straightened. It became clear to her that she had been kept in the closed-in stairwell. She started toward the staircase, a sense of urgency giving her wobbly legs the strength she'd need to climb.

He held her back. "No." He pointed to a small Formica-topped table.

Margaret wanted to scream. If she opened her mouth just a tiny bit, a blood-curdling scream would rush out and paralyze her with fear. She pressed her lips together and allowed the big man to propel her, on leaden feet, to the table. From out of nowhere he produced a limp bouquet of wildflowers. She took them, held them in a death grip.

They were in a basement of some sort. She saw old furniture, a wood stove, things that failed to register fully in her numbed brain.

She heard him saying something about fixing the place up . . . she only had to tell him what she liked . . . anything she wanted . . . wanted . . . wanted . . .

She sank down on a plastic and chrome chair, exposed strawlike stuffing prickly through her thin blouse. In a daze she watched him open a can of Campbell's chicken noodle soup with the blade of a Swiss army knife. He poured the soup into a tin coffee mug and put it in front of her. He pushed a spoon to her.

Maggie stared at the cold soup. Pale chunks of hardened fat floated on the surface.

"Where . . . where are we?" she asked quietly.

He smiled. "Home."

Despair overwhelmed her. The wildflowers slipped from her fingers.

TEN

The next two days Robbi spent more time out of bed than in, savoring the wondrous gift of sight. She read, watched TV, or stared out the window at the towering Sierra Nevada. She marveled at inconsequential things: traffic on Mill Street and jetliners taking off and landing at Reno Cannon International. The fluffy cottonwood seeds floating through the air and the pigeons on the ledge just outside her window gave her hours of pleasure.

The regular visitors to Room 411—her mother, sister, Angela, Sophie, and the staff from the shelter—surprised her with a belated birthday party. She was an exuberant guest of honor, eager to talk, laugh, but even more eager to go home.

The battery of tests, CAT-scan, EEG, and others, taken after she'd come out of the coma, showed nothing out of the ordinary. Her mood, already excellent, grew jubilant with word she was free to leave the hospital.

She sat up in bed, applying the last of her makeup. It

felt fantastic to be able to put it on herself, then to actually *see* the results in a mirror.

The phone beside her bed rang.

"Hello?"

"Robbi?"

"Yes?"

"It's me, *Donald.*"

"Donald?"

"Don't tell me you've forgotten my voice already?"

"I—"

He didn't wait for an answer. "Christ, Robbi, why didn't you call, or have someone call, and tell me about your accident?" His tone hurt, scolding.

"I'm okay now. How did you find out?"

"I kept getting your damn answering machine. I finally called the center," he said. "Sophie told me. I couldn't believe it."

Robbi couldn't believe it either. Why had he waited so long to call Sophie?

"Well, I'm okay now," she said. "Just about to go home, in fact."

"So tell me . . . what happened?"

After she told him and he had fussed appropriately, they spent several minutes talking about mutual friends, then current events.

"So, Don, what've you been doing . . . besides working?" she asked.

"Well, there's a few of us who hang out together. Conrad, Wayne, Tom and Kar. A great bunch of people. Can't wait for you to meet them."

"Kar?"

"Yeah, Karen. She's an interpreter at the U.N. Helluva head on her shoulders. Most guys would be intimidated by her."

"Not you?"

"A little at first." He cleared his throat. "But hell, I don't have to impress her. Oh, hey, I got that big account I've been working on. Busted my butt, but it paid off. Last weekend I zipped over to the Cape to close the deal. The guy put me up at his estate. Jeez, Rob, you should've seen this place. Ten thousand square feet, gold inlaid pool. I thought I was at Hearst Castle. I kept wondering where those little velvet ropes were . . . y'know, that keep people off the carpet? Babe, this could mean a lot of money for me—for us."

"Congratulations. Did you celebrate?"

"Sort of. But we'll celebrate together when you come up. Someday soon yours truly will be eating at classy places on a regular basis. I won't deny it, babe, I love this kind of life. Love the pace. I bet you will too."

"Ummm," she responded.

"Honey, I'm sorry. What a jerk I am. Talking about classy restaurants and estates and there you are laid up in the hospital." He spoke softly. "I'll make it up to you soon. Promise."

After that the conversation waned, the pauses became more frequent, lasted longer.

"Don, I have to go," she lied. "The nurse just came in. I suspect she's here to do something unpleasant to me."

"Roberta, if you want I . . . uh, can fly out to Reno, or at least . . ." His words, feeble, trailed off.

"Thanks, Don, but no. We'll save our money and meet somewhere in between. We'll make it a vacation. I still haven't had one yet."

"Hey, sounds good. You take care, huh? Love ya,

babe," he said.

"Me too."

For several minutes, with the receiver hugged to her chest, Robbi sat quietly. Sophie's words came back to her. *Long distance relationships are a bitch.* You bet, babe.

As she reached around to hang up the phone, her elbow bumped the water glass and tipped it over. She grabbed for the glass which spun away from her fingertips on the wet table. She swore under her breath.

"Good morn—" a voice began. Then, "Oh, here, let me get that for you."

Twisted around in the bed with her back to the door, Robbi paused. She recognized the voice of Dr. Reynolds immediately.

He pulled tissues from the box. "It's tough enough when you can see what you're doing," he said, mopping up the water.

He didn't know she could see. No one had told him.

"Doctor, I'm sorry . . . I—" She stopped herself. Turnabout was fair play. "Thank you," she said, sitting back and staring straight ahead. "I must've made a real mess."

He gathered more tissues and caught the flow before it went over the table's edge. "When I was a kid I spent a few days in the hospital with an eye injury. I'm lying there, both eyes bandaged, can't see a thing. The nurse brings my breakfast, runny oatmeal and a bowl of overripe blueberries, puts a spoon in my hand, and leaves. *That,* Roberta, was a *real* mess."

From the corner of her eye she watched him. He was taller than she imagined, at least six feet. She guessed he was in his mid-thirties. Though his voice was not deep, she'd expected a much older man. He had light brown hair, sun-streaked nearly blond in front, swept to one side of the high forehead. The hair at the back of his neck was somewhat long and curly. He was wearing stonewashed shorts, a green polo shirt, and gray Avia sport shoes. He dressed like no shrink she knew.

When he straightened, she quickly averted her eyes. She felt him openly staring at her as she focused at a point on the opposite wall.

"There," he said. "No harm done."

She smiled, blinking.

"So how are you today, Roberta? You look . . . very nice."

"Thank you. I'm better."

"Headaches? Nightmares?" He was looking at her intently, studying her. She began to feel uncomfortable under his intense scrutiny.

"Gone," she said.

"The headaches or the nightmares?"

"Both."

"Oh? Well, that's interesting. When was the last?"

"Two days ago. Actually, the day you came."

"Really? Perhaps I can take credit for that," he said, grinning. He leaned in toward her, his head moving from side to side as he continued to observe her.

She smiled. "Somebody should, so it might as well be you."

"I wish I had more patients like you," he said, pulling back. He turned and stepped to the window. With his hands in his pockets he rocked on his heels as he stared outside. "There's still the blindness. Of course, there's more than a good possibility it's psychosomatic."

With his back to her she took the opportunity to

look him over. Strong profile, good posture and physique. Then she tipped her head and forced herself to stare at a point beyond his head.

He turned to her again. That same intense stare.

She looked directly into his clear blue eyes. "Do psychiatrists always dress so casually for appointments?"

A heavy silence filled the air as he stared back. Then he said evenly, "Only when the doctor thinks his patient can't see him."

"I'm sorry. That was rude of me."

His smile was slow to form, but when it did it was broad and friendly. He shook his head as he moved back to the side of her bed, laughing good-naturedly. "We're even now."

She smiled. "Good."

A lock of hair fell onto his forehead. He brushed it back. "That's great news. When?"

"The same night. I had a headache and a nightmare. When I woke up I could see again."

They stared at each other. Robbi could think of nothing more to say.

"Well," the doctor said finally, "I guess you won't be needing me anymore."

"No, I . . . I guess not."

He offered his hand, said good-bye, then moved toward the door. He paused. "Roberta, if you ever need to talk, call me." And he was gone.

ELEVEN

The cold rain beat against Roberta's face. Her joints ached and her ankle throbbed unmercifully, yet she couldn't stop. She ran through the dense woods, her heart pounding, her breath ragged in her throat. Branches reached out, impeding her escape. Over her shoulder she heard something huge crashing through the brush, gaining. Two burning disks glowed in the untamed forest. There was no escape, absolutely no escape.

She bolted upright in bed, her legs churning under the damp sheet. She moaned softly.

Her eyes darted around the room, its familiarity instantly calming her. She buried her face in her hands and moaned again. The running nightmare was back. Since leaving the hospital three days before, she had slept soundly. Now it was starting all over again. What did she expect? Miracles? It was only a nightmare. It would go away with time.

A commanding thirst forced her from her bed.

Minutes later in the kitchen, as she stood at the open

door of the refrigerator, a plastic bottle of ice water in her trembling hands, a tiny pinprick of pain stabbed in her forehead. Images began to take shape before her eyes.

Moonlight sparkled on the pond's mirrored surface. In a long white dress she glowed ghostlike—a wood nymph. Her lovely hair now hung in dull, limp, tangled ropes. Eckker wanted to see it shine again, like that night in the bar where they met.

Standing at the pond's edge, he handed Maggie a sliver of soap. She stared at it as though it were something alien.

"For your hair," he said.

She looked from the soap to the pond to him incredulously. "It's freezing."

He reached out to touch her hair. "Make it shine again."

"I won't go in unless you leave."

"I have to stay . . . to protect you."

"I'm not afraid."

He folded his arms over his chest, a set expression on his face.

An animal screamed deep in the woods. Sounds of something scurrying in nearby shrubs made her jerk involuntarily. He saw fear in her eyes.

"I want to go back."

"Your hair. Wash it."

"Turn your back, then," she said.

He hesitated, watching her, then he slowly pivoted his large bulk until his back was completely to the pond.

Several moments later he heard the rustle of fabric, then water sounds. He pictured her wading out to her waist, lowering herself until the water covered her nakedness.

Thinking of nakedness made him think about her, Tobie, the one who unknowingly shared the pond with him. The young, innocent one.

He turned his head and looked for Maggie.

In the long white dress she was swimming, pulling herself through the water with strong, silent strokes.

With unhurried steps he walked to the bank, pulled off his boots, and waded out to his thighs. Then he pushed forward and began to swim. The freezing water puckered his skin, though he scarcely noticed its coldness.

Her once-smooth strokes turned choppy when she realized he was in the pond, not far behind her and rapidly closing the distance. She had nearly reached the other bank when he caught up to her. He felt the movement of the water as her feet kicked frantically beneath the surface. His massive hand closed around an ankle.

She cried out, twisted around, sputtered, spitting water.

He stood, pulling her up with him. She screamed and flailed out at him.

"Quiet. Quiet, Maggie, you'll—"

She shrieked, the sound stabbing into his brain like needles.

"I won't hurt you," he said. "Don't be afraid."

"Let me go!" Then she screamed again. "Oh, God, let me *go!*"

Her shrieks were spoiling the sweet peacefulness of the pond. His pond. Echoes of her cries rushed up and down the mountain. His mountain. Desperation raced through his body like a flashfire. It consumed him. Angered him.

She was hysterical. Out of control.

He pushed her under to silence her. She broke free, her head cleared the water, and she screamed loud and long before he pushed her back under again. He leaned over her, his body weight pressing down. Why wouldn't she stop? She was acting crazy. He pulled her out long enough for her to fill her lungs with air before pushing her back under.

The futile struggles of her submerged body beneath his hands confused him, yet he felt a strange elation. He lifted her up. She gasped, threw her arms around his neck, and clung to him tightly. She was through screaming. Everying was going to be okay. He tenderly brushed back the wet hair from her face.

"Shhh, shhh, Maggie." His hand awkwardly patted her heaving shoulder. "I won't let nothing hurt you."

The brightness of the moon filled his eyes.

Robbi stared at the soft light. Her eyes focused and she realized she was staring at the bulb inside the refrigerator. In the dark kitchen she stood with the ice water container in one hand, the door handle in the other.

Pain in her head pounded like a hammer against an anvil.

What was happening? That was no dream, no nightmare, and certainly no hallucination. A vision of some kind. Not the premonitions that had been a part of her life in her early childhood—the portents of death—

Grandma Paxton, her best friend, Trudy, and just recently, Sam. And there was *Ronnie.* Just thinking about Ronnie made her heart ache and tears fill her eyes. With an effort she managed to push the memory back into a crevice of her mind.

In a dream, or what she thought to be a dream, she had seen a blond woman attacked in an alley by the large man. A chilling gut-feeling told Robbi that this man was the same one in the forest who had killed the woman in white.

In the dry summer air she shivered violently.

TWELVE

Sophie Bennett drove the dilapidated Chevy down Plumas Street. Over the loud roar of the muffler she hollered out. "What can it hurt? Robbi, she can tune in to you. Tell you if the guy's for real or not."

"Who's going to tell me if *she's* for real?" Robbi replied.

"Take my word for it." Sophie pushed the tortoise-shell frames of her glasses up on her nose. "She's a damn good psychic, little one. She told me to lose Leonard before he caused me major grief. Do I listen? Two months later Len borrows a grand and I never see him again."

"What else did she tell you?"

"She said I was going to move. Which I did. That I'll be moving again. Which I am."

"Most people move."

Sophie stopped at a red light and turned to stare at Robbi. "She also said a good friend of mine would have an accident and land in the hospital."

Robbi felt a chill skip down her spine.

"What did you tell her about me?"

"Not a thing. Why would I—hey, little one," she said quietly, "paranoia doesn't become you."

They rode in silence the rest of the way. Sophie pulled to the curb at a large modern apartment complex and shut off the engine. The car backfired, then died.

"Here?" Robbi asked, surprised.

"What did you expect? A tent? A sideshow wagon? A haunted house? Get going. It's on the ground floor. Number nine."

"Aren't you coming too?"

"Can't. Interference," Sophie said, starting in on one of her endless crossword puzzles. "She might get our signals crossed."

Robbi reluctantly left the car. Inside the complex she made her way down the row of red lacquered doors to the end unit. She knocked lightly. Her first encounter with a psychic had her jittery and feeling a bit foolish. Would her mind be an open book, every private thought exposed? Although Robbi was certain she had a degree of spiritual sensitivity—the premonitions—she'd always played it down, dreaded it actually, not wanting to develop the powers or even confirm them.

She was about to turn away when the door opened. A tiny woman in her late sixties wearing a chartreuse caftan edged in purple velvet, purple pointed-toed sultan slippers, and a white turban, looked up at her through milky eyes. Robbi's nervousness turned to embarrassment. Certainly she had expected some sort of mystic motif, but not a costume quite so obvious. A *turban,* for God'ssake. *Sultan footwear.* There was absolutely no way she would be able to take this woman seriously. And from now on Sophie's ability to give advice was also seriously in question.

The medium smiled, showing small white teeth. "Roberta Paxton, right? Come in. Come in. I'm Wanda Zimmer. You're early, or I'm late. Come and sit a minute while I finish." After depositing her client on a firm brocaded love seat and handing her a dish of Hershey Kisses, she quickly disappeared.

Robbi took a Kiss, released it from the silver wrapping, and slipped it into her mouth. Letting it dissolve on her tongue, she glanced around the oblong living room. It was sparsely furnished with inexpensive modern pieces in green and biege, the walls stark white and bare. The personal touch in the Zimmer apartment was achieved through the jungle of potted and hanging plants and the riotous assortment of African violets and geraniums. She saw none of the new age paraphernalia—candles, incense, crystals—that one associated with fortune-tellers.

Within minutes Wanda Zimmer was back wearing khaki pants, a safari-print cotton blouse, and brown loafers. Her short, damp gray hair had been worked into waves on top and sides.

Roberta laughed to herself. The turban had only been a towel, the caftan a housecoat, and the pointed shoes a pair of slippers.

"There, that's better," Wanda said, taking a chair across the room from Robbi. "Tea? Coffee?"

Robbi smiled and shook her head.

"Then let's begin." The psychic closed her eyes.

Robbi shifted on the love seat. "What do I—?"

The woman put out a hand to silence her. Robbi closed her mouth, cleared her throat, and stared at the small figure who sat stiffly in her chair.

The milky eyes opened, stared fixedly at a spot on the wall just above Robbi's head. Wanda began to speak rapidly, interrupting herself when something more important, more pressing, seemed to come to her. She spoke of challenges, of Roberta's need to work with others in a helping, caring manner. Twenty minutes into the reading, she said, "You've had a terrible accident, but you're mending well. You're very strong. You will need your strength for the challenges ahead."

Robbi's heart palpitated.

"You are sensitive, extremely sensitive in a psychic way. Yet you are limited. *Potent,* oh, my goodness, yes, yet limited. This is not new to you, though you have no idea why the power is yours or how to use it. Right?"

"I'm not sure—yes," Robbi whispered.

"Do you know him?"

Robbi came forward abruptly. "Who? Know who?"

"The man who is psychically linked with you."

An icy claw clutched at her stomach. "No, no, I don't know him. Can you tell me who he is?"

Wanda closed her eyes. She swayed slightly. After a few moments she said, "I don't like him . . . he's bad. I'm unable to pick up much except that he is there—there with you somewhere on some other plane—and he's no good."

"Why is he there?"

"I can't say."

"Is he real, or a figment of my imagination?"

"I can't say that either. He's real to you."

"I have to know who he is, what he wants with me, why I see him. I *have* to know. Please, Mrs. Zimmer, help me. At least one woman has died."

Wanda crossed the room, sat on the love seat, and reached out, touching Robbi's hand. She closed her eyes again. "I sense these women—these victims. They are lost angels. I sense they were once a part of this planet. They are lost and crying out to be found . . . to be free to go on with their journey."

"They? I saw only one killed. Then it's true? This man has killed more than once?"

"I don't know. They could be souls from your own past lives. I have no way to tell." She sighed deeply and repeated, "My dear, I have no way to tell. But I can say this, you must be very careful."

"I'm in danger?"

"Yes," she said quietly. "I don't like to frighten people, but I feel you must be warned. You are in *grave* danger."

"From this man?"

"Yes."

"When?"

"Soon."

"Well?" Sophie said. She had driven to Virginia Lake and parked in the lot facing the water. A steady stream of joggers passed by.

"Well what?" Robbi answered.

"Well, what did Wanda say?"

"She said I would meet a tall, dark, handsome man and we would run off to Shangri-la and have two point five children and live happily ever after. Isn't that what they all say?"

She met Sophie's peeved glare before turning away

to look out the window. Robbi said in a disquieting tone, "That's what I hoped she would say. Instead, she scared the shit out of me and then sent me away with instructions to not darken her door again."

"Are you exaggerating?"

"Not by much."

Roberta related the reading. "Someone's going to die. It could be me."

"You know what?" Sophie said, her voice tight. "I made a big mistake sending you to Wanda. The woman's obviously losing it. Hey, we'll go to another psychic. I hear there's a good one in Virginia City, I—"

"No more psychics."

For several long moments both were lost in their own thoughts, watching the ducks and geese bob for thrown bread pieces in the lake and on the lawn to their right.

Roberta sighed. "I made another mistake. My mother called this morning and I confided in her."

"You told her about the vision?"

Robbi nodded. "She didn't believe me when I was little, and she doesn't believe me now. She wants me normal, like other people. She wants me to move in with them."

"She's afraid for you."

"I guess."

Jake Reynolds typed from a stack of notes at his elbow. Directly above, a stellar jay screeched angrily, and to confirm its displeasure, a bird dropping hit the keys of his typewriter with a wet plop. Jake cursed, threw an empty plastic glass at the limbs of the spruce where the jay sat. Another squawk, the glass hit the deck and bounced off into the bushes.

Jake went inside, grabbed a handful of paper towels, returned to the typewriter, and dabbed at the green mess. Damn jays. If anyone needed therapy, it was the jay. Always angry, always taking it out on the world below.

The cordless phone on the redwood table rang. His Reno calls were transferred to the lake house.

"Yes," he said.

"Dr. Reynolds, there's a Ms. Paxton on the line," Carolee, the receptionist at the medical plaza, said. "Shall I put her through?"

Jake's pulse quickened. More than once he'd found himself thinking about the intriguing woman from the hospital. He wondered how she was doing. "Roberta Paxton?"

"I don't know. Shall I ask?"

"No. Put her through." A series of clicks and a woman's voice was on the line.

"Dr. Reynolds, my name is Lois. I'm Roberta's mother."

Jake stifled his disappointment. "Yes, Mrs. Paxton, what can I do for you?"

"My daughter mentioned that you had come to see her when she was in the hospital."

"That's right."

"She seemed to like you, Doctor. There aren't many doctors in your field that she likes or trusts."

"I'm flattered, Mrs. Paxton."

"I wondered, Doctor, if you'd consent to follow up on her, so to speak?"

"She hasn't lost her sight again, has she?"

"What? Oh, no, nothing like that. Her vision is fine, her normal vision, that is. It's the other vision that has me very concerned, Doctor."

"Other vision? I'm afraid I don't follow you."

"My daughter seems to be seeing things. Hallucinations. She's always been very inventive, especially as a young girl, her father was quite abrupt with her, insisting she not talk about—she's not a liar, it's just that . . . well, it's my belief she's under too much stress. The shooting, then the accident, all on top of a very heavy workload."

"I see."

"Can you see her?"

On hiatus from private practice, writing a book on the battered woman syndrome, he had initially consented to see Dr. Newton's patient because of her involvement with the center, although they'd never gotten around to discussing their mutual interest.

"I'll be happy to. Have her call my receptionist at the office and set up an appointment."

"I'm afraid that could be a problem. I rather doubt Roberta will consent to see you on a doctor-patient basis. You see, she doesn't have a very high opinion of psychiatrists."

"In that case, I don't see how I can help her."

"As I said earlier, she seems to like you, Doctor. Perhaps you can see her in a nonmedical setting. Socially, so to speak. Naturally, the matter of your fee will be taken care of by me."

"Mrs. Paxton, I can't—"

"She claims to have witnessed a killing in the woods moments after her accident."

"A killing?"

"A woman. She swears she saw a barefooted woman running around in the woods. A man was after her . . . killed her. It was all so wild. But to hear Roberta talk, you'd almost have to believe her. She was so descriptive. The woman—the one murdered—was wearing a long white dress and, supposedly, an anklet."

"An anklet?" Jake's heart skipped a beat. "You mean an ankle bracelet?"

"Yes, I guess. But none of that matters because she didn't really see anything like that. I'm sure she imagined all of it. The blow on the head, the—Dr. Reynolds, she needs help."

"Mrs. Paxton, I . . ."

"Think about it, won't you, Doctor?" And then she was gone.

The jay screeched again. Deep in thought, Jake was oblivious of the racket. How many women wore an ankle bracelet? Jake had known only one.

THIRTEEN

At Radcliff's deli, Robbi moved gingerly in the long line, absently staring at the assortment of food through the window of the cold case.

"Miss Paxton?"

She turned, and directly behind her stood a smiling, clean-cut man. He wore blue slacks, a yellow shirt open at the collar, and a grayish blue sport coat. She smelled the same mild aftershave he'd worn at the hospital. The handsome psychiatrist with the nice knees.

"Dr. Reynolds, hello."

"Good to see you up and about."

"Thanks. Ankle's still a little tender . . ." She raised the cane. "But I'm not complaining."

"Back to work already?"

She nodded. "Takes my mind off"—she coughed, looked away—"off the aches and pains. Hope you're not in a hurry." She indicated the slow-moving line. "They're always shorthanded here."

"I'm not in a hurry. I try to make any waiting time productive time."

"Oh, how so?"

"I watch people. I write speeches. . . ." He shrugged. "I talk to pretty ladies in front of me."

Robbi smiled, moved forward. How pretty could she look? She was too pale from the weeks in the hospital. She hadn't slept well in ages, and the July heat soon drained what little energy she had each day. Today she was wearing her favorite skirt and blouse, but both were wrinkled, damp in places. And her hair, pulled up in back, was rapidly coming loose, strand by crimpy stand. The doctor, however, looked cool and crisp. Air-conditioned office—*oh, to have such luxury.*

"More important, I was raised with four sisters. In my case patience became mandatory for sanity and survival," he said. "So how's everything with you? No more headaches?"

"No," she said too quickly.

"How about the nightmares?"

"All gone." She awkwardly stepped forward, bumped the man in front of her.

An attractive woman Roberta's age stopped to talk with the doctor. Robbi turned forward, focused on the food in the cold case. She could hear the conversation between the two, something about a dinner honoring a best-selling author, a regatta at the lake, and a score of names frequently heard in the local media—the state's movers and shakers.

Robbi felt the doctor's gaze on her as she inched along, trying her damnedest not to eavesdrop on their conversation but losing the battle. A party invitation was extended to him. She surmised the doctor was unmarried.

When her turn at the counter came, she paid for her order, gathered a bag in each arm, turned to the doctor and, without interrupting the woman who had been talking nonstop, smiled, then mouthed the word "bye."

She had gotten only a few steps outside the deli when Dr. Reynolds caught up with her.

"You look like you could use some help," he said, relieving her of the larger bag. "Can I give you a ride back to work?"

"As much as I'd love to get off my feet and out of this heat, I'm supposed to be getting some exercise. It's just a few doors down."

"Then I'll walk with you."

She noticed he was empty-handed. "No lunch?"

"Nothing appealed to me."

She held the small bag in her left hand and the cane in her right as they walked north to the main office of SSWC.

"Do you ever eat lunch out?" he asked.

"Rarely. We take turns going for sandwiches."

"You're quite involved with your work, aren't you?"

"I guess."

"Were you always this enthusiastic? Or has it increased since the accident?"

"Are you asking if I've suddenly become immersed in my job to take my mind off something else?" she said warily.

"No, I'm not. But have you?"

She stopped in front of the brick building and reached for the bag in his hand. "Thanks for the help. I have to go. They're waiting."

"I'll take it in."

"No, that's all right. I can manage from here."

"You don't care much for psychiatrists, do you, Miss Paxton?"

"Before his stroke, my father was a practicing psychiatrist."

"Yes, I know. I've read several of his papers. Dr. Paxton's a brilliant man, but that doesn't answer my question."

"It would be unfair of me to judge an entire profession by one man," she said evenly, conscious of her evasiveness but unable to stop herself.

"It would."

She reached for the doorknob.

"Miss Paxton, I'm researching a book on battered women. I wonder if you could give me a hand. You'd be doing me a tremendous favor, and perhaps I can help you in turn."

Robbi looked at him, distrustful. "Help me? What makes you think I need help?"

"I meant with the center. Donations, time, anything I can do."

"I don't know. I—"

"Tomorrow I'll be at my place at Tahoe. Come up for the day. It'll give you a chance to relax, take in some sun and mountain air. I really think you'll enjoy it."

Could she work with him, trust him? Dr. Reynolds was like no psychiatrist she'd ever met. If he was working on a book about domestic abuse, they certainly had something in common.

"All right. I'll come."

"Great," he said, a smile brightening his face. He backed up. "I'll call and give you directions."

The rest of the day her work took a backseat to thoughts of the doctor. Who was he? What kind of man was he? Images of his smile, so captivating, played across her mind.

FOURTEEN

Roberta cruised the narrow street slowly, taking in the quiet solitude of the evergreen-shaded lane. The sharp scent of ponderosa pine reached inside the closed car as cones and needles crunched under the tires of her Jeep Cherokee. Straight ahead, like a mirror reflecting the clear blue of the sky, lay the deep, icy waters of Lake Tahoe.

On the phone that morning Dr. Reynolds had given her directions to his summer place at Incline Village. His lake-front house was to the left, within yards of the sandy beach of Crystal Bay. A neighborhood dock moored several powerboats and a sailboat. In the driveway sat a classic white T-bird.

She found the doctor on a large wooden deck that faced the lake. At a picnic table covered with books and papers, held down by fist-size rocks, he sat barefooted behind a manual typewriter, wearing a navy blue tank shirt and white tennis shorts. A stack of papers balanced in his lap.

She climbed the steps to the deck.

"Hi," he said, smiling as she crossed to him. "Thanks for agreeing to drive up."

"It's certainly no hardship." Her gaze swept the landscape appreciatively.

He dumped the papers onto the table, rose to his full six feet, and stretched.

He had the body of an athlete. Solid, though not too muscular. Good, strong legs, looking even more tan in contrast to the white shorts. A tennis physique, she thought. Waterskiing for certain, since he lived right on the lake.

At a smaller table with a striped umbrella he pulled out a lime green director chair for her.

"Relax," Jake said when she sat. "Take a half dozen deep breaths while I play host." He went inside.

Robbi took his advice and filled her lungs with the clean mountain air. She looked around at the assortment of evergreen trees surrounding the house. In the yard, clusters of wildflowers in purple, red, and blue complemented the greens. He returned minutes later with a tray bearing two mugs of coffee, a plate of sliced pound cake, bowls of whole strawberries, brown sugar, and thinned sour cream.

"Goodness," she said.

"I want this to be as painless as possible," he said, putting down the tray and sitting opposite Robbi.

"You're doing all the right things." Robbi sipped the coffee, pleased by its rich, nutty flavor.

For several minutes while they drank coffee and ate, they engaged in small talk about the area. Mesmerized, Roberta watched a bright parasail, its two riders soaring high over the water behind the speedboat that towed it.

Jake refilled their cups.

"I'm into the chapter on the battered woman's syndrome as a legal defense," Jake explained. "I've plenty of the dry material, statistics, trials, and such. I could use some insight, personal and general, and an anecdote or two."

For the next hour, without using names, Roberta related one case history after another. When nothing more came to mind, they took a break. Jake brought out fresh coffee.

He leaned back in his chair. "The nightmares you spoke of in the hospital, tell me about them."

Her guard went up. She had agreed to help him with his research, and now he was asking about the nightmares again.

With her thumb she rubbed away the light lipstick mark on the rim of the coffee mug. "Dr. Reynolds—"

"None of that 'doctor' stuff. Please, it's Jake."

Despite the picturesque surroundings, his casual attire, and his attempts to make her feel like a guest, she had the discerning feeling that this little tête-à'tête was between a doctor and his patient. All the directors at the center were trained as counselors. She was no stranger to the techniques of therapy. He observed her without being obvious. He listened carefully to what she said, the underlying nuances in particular. He didn't miss a beat.

"The nightmares are still with you, aren't they?"

"I can't afford you, Doctor."

"This is between friends."

She stared silently off into the distance. Should she tell him? Why was he so eager to get inside her head? Occupational involvement, perhaps. Could an artist take in a spectacular landscape without a desire to capture it on canvas? Before him sat a woman whose mind was filled with mysteries—unexplored.

"What happened that day in the woods, Roberta?"

After a long pause, she said, "I saw something . . ."

"Go on."

"I'd rather not."

"Tell me about the dream, then."

"I'm being chased through the woods on a rainy night." And with that admission, despite her reservations, she found herself powerless to remain quiet.

"Man or beast?"

"Man. A man-beast."

"And?"

"And I dream of a man who holds a woman against her will."

"Where does he hold her?"

"In the woods. In a cabin, I believe."

"Does she know him? Are they married?"

"No, he abducted her. I mean, in my dream, he forcibly took her."

"From where?"

"From an alley outside a bar."

Jake dipped a strawberry in the sour cream, then twirled it in the brown sugar. He held it up and stared at it. "What does she look like?"

"Long blond hair. Fair skin. Slender."

"Any distinguishing marks or features?" he asked.

She shook her head.

"Jewelry? Rings, pendants, that type of thing?"

"Jake, it's only a dream." Why did she sense his questions went beyond mere curiosity, to the point of interrogation.

Jake rubbed the end of the pen along his eyebrow as he stared out toward the lake. "The day of your accident, what did you see in the woods?"

"You don't give up easily, do you?"

A corner of his mouth lifted in a smile.

"Everything was pretty murky . . ." On the table Robbi formed a small mound of brown sugar with a forefinger. "I'd fallen, hit my head. The rain was pouring down and I was just coming around . . . everything was hazy. . . ."

"Tell me what you saw."

She glanced at him, looked away. "A man, a very big man, chased down this woman and . . . and he strangled her."

Jake shifted around. "How far from where you were?"

She contemplated. "About eight to ten yards."

"Then you couldn't have seen her very clearly."

"Before he caught her, she'd run within just feet of me."

"Could you describe her?" Jake asked. "And him."

"She was slender, with long blond hair. He was large, six-feet four or five. Black hair and a beard. A mountain man."

"You've described the woman in your dream."

"And the man," she said. "Jake, if what I saw that day was real, a woman was murdered. If it wasn't real, then—"

"Assuming it was an illusion—"

"Ah, the psychiatrist speaking," she asked tightly. "Shoot for the screwed-up head first. Dismiss it as hallucinatory. The doctor neatly files it under trauma, burnout, or a dozen other psychological buzz words, and we're off and running."

"Roberta, I'm only trying to—"

She stood. "I'm not your patient, Doctor. I agreed to help you with your research, not become your mental guinea pig."

Without another word she turned and left the deck.

In her rearview mirror, as she drove off, she saw the doctor standing in the middle of the road. Behind him whitecaps broke the smooth surface of the lake.

FIFTEEN

Hot excitement throbbed in his blood, racing through his veins as he stealthily moved from tree to tree along the back of the ranch-style house. It was dark. Moon shadows crossed the yard to angle sharply up the rough wood siding. The fragrant scent of night jasmine filled the air. A cat meowed, rubbed against his ankle. Eckker pushed it away with his foot. Crickets chirped. Another cat's meow joined the first. They weren't afraid of him. The big man was no stranger to them.

He had to see her; it couldn't hurt anything to just look at her. He would have his look, then go.

He usually got his way. He learned early in life to take what he wanted. But there were still certain rules. He had survived the streets. He had survived his crazy mother—who struck out first and asked questions later, only to strike out again—and her rotten, worthless men. And in the end she'd gotten hers.

The window was dark. Disappointment dropped over him like a heavy shroud. He had to see her. A glimpse and nothing more. He looked around, considered circling the house, checking other rooms. He moved forward. The light came on. His heart jumped in his chest. He slipped back into the shadows.

Dressed in a white bathrobe, the girl strode into the room. She moved to the full-length mirror and stood before it, soberly contemplating her image.

Pulling her hair up on top of her head, she tilted her head this way and that, assessing the effect. She smiled, frowned, pouted, then leaned in, partially closed her eyes as she lightly placed her lips to the mirror in a chaste kiss.

The man in the shadows absently kneaded his bunched hands against the coarse fabric of his pants.

The young girl leaned back, stared at her face for several moments longer, then she put her palms over the nubby terry cloth at her chest and pressed upward, creating a slight cleavage at the V of the robe. Her fingertips closed around the bodice and gingerly pulled the two pieces apart, exposing small, budding breasts with swollen dusty rose-colored nipples.

With the side of his face pressed to the rough wood of the house, he watched her from the corner of his eyes. His breathing came heavy, raspy. His gaze burned into her, consuming her.

SIXTEEN

The group, six in all, sat in a loose circle on orange plastic contour chairs in a conference room in the Medical Plaza. They met one morning a week. To Jake's left a boy, bushy red hair shaved close to his head on one side, doodled on his palm with a Marks-a-Lot pen as he spoke.

"No one's gonna find those guys guilty. Christ, they're a famous rock group. They got more money than God."

"Do you really think they put subliminal death messages in their songs?" A pretty girl named Beverly, who sat directly across from Jake, asked. "I mean, why would entertainers want kids—their fans—to kill themselves? Who'd be left to buy their albums?"

The group shrugged and mumbled.

Jake glanced at Beverly. She was staring at him with a strange, faraway gaze and a hint of a smile, as if they shared some personal secret.

He quickly looked away. There was one in every group. That one teenage girl who came on to him in this, her advanced exercise in the seduction of the older professional man. More than once in today's session he had inadvertently looked up to see her miniskirted legs crossing and uncrossing, exposing flashes of creamy inner thigh and peachy lace. Five years earlier seventeen-year-old Belinda Sardi had been the group femme fatale. Thinking of Belinda made him think of Roberta Paxton. She claimed to have seen a woman murdered in the woods. Could there possibly be a connection?

A fat, unkempt boy blurted out, "My grandmother's dumping me back on my mom."

"She's threatened that before," Jake said.

"This time she means it. She snagged some old fart. She's moving him in and me out."

"Good for her," the girl on Jake's right said. "Grannies need lovin' too."

The fat boy glared at her.

"Well, since it's an ongoing issue that so far has remained unchanged," Jake said, "let's just see what happens."

"Dr. Reynolds," Beverly said. Her leg lifted, slowly crossed over the other. "My mother wants to know if I can have private sessions with you?"

One boy whistled under his breath, another snickered.

"I'll talk to her about it." In a pig's eye, Jake told himself. He stole a glance at the large school clock on the wall. He was due in court to testify for the prosecution on an insanity plea murder trial. "Anything else, ladies and gentlemen? If not, I'm going to set you free for the day. I have to be at the courthouse in half an hour."

The kids shifted, stood, began gathering their things. Within several minutes they had all filed out, all but Beverly.

"Dr. Reynolds, since you're going to the courthouse and I'm going there, too, maybe you could give me a ride?"

"Sorry, Beverly, can't do." He put on his suit jacket.

"If you're not ready to leave now, I can wait."

"The reason I can't is that I'm your doctor, you're a minor, and you're a very pretty girl who likes to play games."

"Sometimes I forget you're a doctor. You're really cool." She stepped in closer, emanating a robust exotic scent. "Don't you like games?"

"Not that kind. I'm not eligible to play. Sorry." He picked up his attaché folder, tucked it under his arm, and strode out of the door.

Fifteen minutes later on the steps of the Washoe County Courthouse, Jake pressed through the crowd of demonstrators for the heavy-metal rock group. He struggled to pull open the main door and quickly entered.

In the middle of the wide marble vestibule, talking to a woman with a baby in her arms, was someone Reynolds had been thinking a great deal about since he'd last seen her at the lake a week earlier. He recognized her instantly by the light chestnut hair with its red highlights, her statuesque posture and the cane she absently twirled, like a baton, in her fingers. She patted the woman's shoulder, lightly touched the baby's cheek, then turned and headed toward Jake.

Her face devoid of emotion, Roberta was eye to eye with Jake when she focused on him for the first time.

She quickly looked away and pushed through the door. The chants of the demonstrators poured in as she rushed out.

He watched her work her way gingerly through the crowd on the steps until she was gone. The enigmatic Roberta Paxton undoubtedly had his attention. How could he get hers?

Robbi used her forearm to stop a rivulet of perspiration making its way down her temple to her jaw. It was nine P.M. and hot. Wearing shorts, a midriff top, her masses of hair twisted and clipped on top of her head, she stood barefoot in the laundry room, putting new vinyl on the walls. Earlier she had juggled the washer and dryer to the center of the small room.

As she smoothed a strip of pink and sea-green vinyl on the wall, she heard a car stop in front of the house. She eased a bubble out to the edge and took a final swipe with a damp sponge.

The doorbell rang.

Through the kitchen window she saw Dr. Reynolds's white sports car at the curb.

He was the last person she wanted to talk with. After seeing him at the courthouse that afternoon she'd felt uneasy, anxious. It was hard to explain, and she knew it sounded irrational, but somehow he made her feel disconnected and out of touch with reality. Her father had that same effect on her.

She went to the front door, unlocked the dead bolt, and opened it.

"Hi," he said. He had changed clothes. The suit replaced with jeans and pullover shirt.

"Hello."

"Saw you today at the courthouse . . ." He let the words trail off.

She remained silent. What did he want with her? Why the great interest?

"I should have called first." He turned his head, looked down the street. "I guess I was afraid you'd hang up on me. I just want to know how you're doing? If you're okay?"

She rested her head against the open door, waited a moment longer than she said, "I'm fine, Dr. Reynolds."

He stared at her solemnly. "You took off rather abruptly the other day. I made you angry and I hadn't meant to. Seems I may have overstepped my bounds."

She managed a smile. "Well, I may have overreacted." With the sponge she rubbed at vinyl paste on her fingers. "I'm wallpapering. I guess I better get back to it. In this heat everything dries pretty fast. Thanks for stopping—"

"Wallpapering? I did a little of that in my college days. Yeah, rather enjoyed it too."

She stared at him.

"That's an offer to help, for what it's worth."

What the hell. She'd be a fool to turn down a strong back and a pair of hands. Sophie was right, paranoia didn't become her.

She opened the door for him. As she led the way into the kitchen, she made furtive tugs at her short blouse. In the sink a strip of wallpaper lay soaking. Robbi lifted the paper from the water, folded it, and slipped it into a plastic bag. From another bag she pulled out a wet strip, unfolded it, and moved to the wall in the laundry room. Jake followed.

They squeezed in behind the dryer. He held the paper while she climbed a stepstool. She aligned the border to the ceiling and together they smoothed the paper onto the wall. They worked side by side without speaking until the strip was up.

"We deserve a break," Roberta said. She stepped down. "Iced tea okay?"

"Perfect."

She filled two tall glasses with ice and sun tea. They took their drinks into the laundry room.

"How's the book coming?" Robbi stepped on the stool again and lifted the paper he handed to her.

"Pretty good, thanks. Your input was a big help."

In the limited space they shared, she was acutely aware of his arm brushing along her bare leg, the wiry hair tickling, rousing tiny shivers in her. Each time his skin made contact with hers, an image flickered behind her eyes. *Trees, a horse, the sound of crying*—mere flashes, yet she saw enough to know they were related to that incident in the woods. She tried to shake it off.

"Roberta?"

She peeled back a corner, realigned it carefully. "Hmmm?"

"I need your help."

She looked at him quizzically.

"It has to do with what you saw at the time of your accident."

"I don't understand." Another flash. This one crystal-clear. *The woman in white running through the forest.* Robbi blinked to erase the image.

"Do you have any idea who those people were?"

"Assuming it really happened?" she said with a tinge of sarcasm.

"Either way, Roberta, I'm not judging you or making evaluations."

Robbi pressed the sponge to the paper so hard, milky water ran down her arm and the wall. What the hell was his problem? Why was he so concerned about what she saw—or had imagined she saw? Nothing had changed. He was a psychiatrist. She couldn't confide in him. Especially not about her clairvoyance.

Jake's arm pressed against her calf as he reached for another strip of wet paper.

The pink and green pattern of the vinyl in front of her became a forest of gray, brown, and green.

She heard the woman scream. She saw the tall, bulky man squeezing the life out of her. After lowering the body to the ground, he turned and started toward the forest of saplings, where Roberta lay helpless in the mud. A voice echoed through the woods. The killer paused, glanced around uncertainly, turned back to her—everything went black.

The bright wallpaper swam into view for a moment, only to evolve again into the grayed hues of the forest.

With rain pounding at him, the man carried the woman's body close to his broad chest. He stopped, knelt, and carefully lowered her to the ground. He reached out and pulled a dead, dry, reddish spruce tree to one side. Beneath the fallen tree lay a bleached and weathered plank, its color blending with the soil around it. With his booted foot he lifted the plank, revealing a circular shaft lined with sheets of corrugated metal. A short distance down the hole was black. A dank odor wafted upward. The smell of death.

The man turned back to the woman. He tenderly removed the white dress and the delicate silver and gold chain from her ankle, then he lifted the body and gently lowered it down into the pit. A streak of lightning brightened the landscape. For an instant the stark light illuminated a grisly tangle of limbs and hair far at the bottom of the hole.

For the past several moments Jake Reynolds had carefully observed Roberta. When he'd reached for another strip of paper, he had touched her leg. She began to sway. He called her name, yet she gazed straight ahead with a look of fear and revulsion on her face.

When he put his arms around her and lifted her down from the stool, she didn't resist. In the cramped quarters, the dryer on one side, the wall on the other, he held her. Her breath quickened. He could feel her heart beating rapidly.

Jesus, where was she? Jake gazed down into her face, a face whose loveliness was even more apparent in her trancelike state. His arms tightened around her waist.

Suddenly she shuddered, then moaned low in her throat. A moment later, eyes clouded with confusion, she stared at him.

"Are you all right?" he asked.

She gently disengaged his arms and stepped back. "I—I felt dizzy for a moment," she said, her voice breathy. "I guess I'm still pretty weak."

He waited.

She smiled, looked away. "Well, I think I better give it up for the night," she said. "Thanks for the help. It would have taken me hours to do this much."

She was dismissing him.

They said good night at the back door.

Several minutes later, in his car at the corner stop sign, Jake let out his breath. Dammit, his main objective for dropping in on her had been to learn as much as possible about the woman in the woods—the woman with the ankle bracelet. He had gotten nowhere there.

But the trance? That was no fainting spell. She'd had some sort of vision. Her mother had hinted at something. Psychic?

Roberta was certainly being cautious. Her distrust of shrinks was obvious. He suspected that if she discovered her mother had asked him to treat her surreptitiously—something he would never undertake—it was all over.

He didn't want it to be over. She intrigued him. Thoughts of her occupied his mind, and not all those thoughts were platonic. More than once that evening in her laundry room his libido had surfaced just watching her on the stool. When she'd reached above her head, her short top had inched upward, exposing the underside of her full lace-and-satin-clad breasts. Time and again his arm had brushed her bare legs. And finally, when she was in his arms . . .

Forget it, he told himself. In a few months she'll be married and living thousands of miles away.

But then again—

An alarm far in the recesses of his mind went off. How long had it been since he'd allowed himself to become involved emotionally with a woman? He knew exactly how long. Three years. Since Susan's death.

He rammed the gearshift into first, grinding gears, then pressed down hard on the accelerator. Slamming on the brakes, he barely avoided hitting the pickup entering the intersection. The driver laid on his horn. Jake cursed and drove away.

Roberta sat in a tight ball in the floral wing chair, wrapped cocoonlike in the quilt from her bed. Although the house was still warm, she couldn't shake a chill that racked her body. An hour had passed since Jake had left.

A deep pit with more than one body. How many? Three? Five?

Oh, God. Had the killer seen her? He had been moving toward her when she blacked out. Was it possible that Hanley, coming after her, calling her name, had scared him off? Was the killer looking for her right now, to silence her?

Roberta shivered.

A slight throbbing continued above her eyes. Absently rubbing it, she tried to visualize the killer. No clear image existed in her mind. Brief flashes, fragmented. A large man with dark hair and beard.

The throbbing over her eyes intensified. She rubbed it again, vaguely conscious of it. Suddenly fear stabbed her. What if, just by thinking about him, she was able to link with him psychically?

She felt a queasiness in her stomach.

What was he doing now? The pain grew. *Had he hurt the latest woman he'd abducted? Would he strangle this one as well?*

A thought came to her. During a clairvoyant episode, could she in some way communicate with the victim?

And then she knew she had to try.

She willed herself to go to him. The pain drilled deeper into her head. Think about him. Think about her. The headache intensified, making her weak, sick. She would feel herself becoming weightless, then firmly grounded. Again and again she attempted it, stopping when the pain became unbearable, only to try anew when it eased. An hour later, physically exhausted, mentally drained, she gave up and went to bed.

As she lay in bed, she decided there was no way in hell she could do this alone. She had to confide in someone.

Jake was nothing, absolutely nothing, like her father.

SEVENTEEN

The top of Robbi's head felt warm in the sun. She shook her hair out, leaned back on her palms, and sighed contentedly. "I should be working. Not sitting in the sun being a bum."

Jake lowered himself beside her on the dock. He handed her a fishing pole, the line already in the water. "We have rules around here. Today's rules are, number one, no talk of work. Can't even think about it. Number two, the guest may not catch more fish than the host."

She took up the slack on the line. "Sounds fair."

"Besides, you did your work for the day. You appropriated me as a program speaker for the dance next week," he said, rummaging around in a tackle box getting swivel, hook, and sinker for his own line.

She found herself staring at him, thinking how attractive he was. She suspected he was watching her as well, but with his eyes hidden behind the mirrored sunglasses, she couldn't be sure.

That morning Roberta had shown up unexpectedly

at Jake's house at the lake. She'd found him in the carport tinkering under the hood of a gleaming black '40 Ford pickup. His slow, warm smile when he saw her approaching had produced a strange, sweet wrenching in her stomach.

Now, a half hour later, she felt relaxed, content, as though she'd been going there for years. She shifted her gaze and stared at the Hyatt Regency resort spread out along the shoreline to her right. A speedboat on another part of the lake and the perpetual shriek of a jay were the only sounds to break the stillness of the morning.

He loaded his own hook with red salmon eggs, then cast it into the water. After peeling off his polo shirt, he leaned against the corner piling, facing her.

"Why did you come up here this morning?" he asked.

"To find out why you keep popping into my life."

"Do I?"

"It certainly seems that way."

"Synchronicity."

Roberta turned a puzzled face to him. "Enlighten me."

"I believe we were meant to meet. We may each have pieces to a puzzle. Fitted together, they could form the whole picture."

"That's rather philosophical for a psychiatrist."

He made no comment, but his lips stretched into a tiny smile.

"What pieces do I have?" she asked.

"I'll know when you tell me."

"So very cryptic. How will I know what it is that you want to hear?"

"Tell me everything you can remember about the

man and woman in the woods. The woman in particular."

The incident in the woods. *Synchronicity?* That was exactly why she had come to him, to talk about that day. A chill passed through her.

For the second time she told Jake all she could remember.

He had listened without interrupting, his head nodding occasionally. But when she finished, he seemed disappointed.

"That's it? Think."

She started to shake her head, then something flickered in her mind. She'd forgotten about the ankle chain. From the time she told her mother and sister about it until the other night when she'd seen the killer removing it and the white dress from the body, she'd completely forgotten about it.

"An ankle bracelet."

He leaned forward eagerly. "Yes?"

"From my perspective I saw it clearer than the woman herself. It was gold and silver and there was something dangling from it. A charm."

"Could you make out the charm?"

"No."

"Are ankle bracelets popular among women?"

"I don't know anyone who wears one."

"You'd forgotten about seeing it. What jogged your memory?"

"Is this one of the puzzle pieces?" she asked.

"A very big piece."

Her stomach twisted. Last night, after much soul searching, she had decided she would tell him everything. If he believed, as her father had, that she was a liar seeking attention, she would just march to her car, drive away, and not look back.

Robbi ran fingers through her hair, pulling it back from her face. A pinprick of pressure worked above her eye. "I saw it again in a vision. Last night."

"A psychic experience?"

She nodded, then studied his face for signs of disbelief, disapproval, and saw none.

"How long have you been sensitive?"

"As far back as I can remember." Then she told him about the flashback vision of the deep pit in the woods.

"A pit," he said, when she had finished. "With other bodies. Christ."

"That's what I saw. I can't say if it's real or not. I went to a psychic after my accident. She spoke of lost souls . . . *angels*. She spoke of a man—a bad man—who was linked to me. She said I was in grave danger."

"From this man?"

"Yes."

"It sort of ties in with your visions, doesn't it?"

"Frighteningly so."

"Okay." He gave the rod a tug, reeled the line in a few feet. "Tell me about your clairvoyance. What's your opinion?"

"From what I've read on the subject, I seem to possess the three main types of ESP. Telepathy, clairvoyance, and precognition. Telepathy, however, hasn't played a part in this drama."

"You mean you're not tuned in to either the victim or the killer?"

"That's right. It's merely information related to me. Sometimes only in flashes, other times it plays out longer." The pressure grew, spread across her forehead. She pressed fingertips to her temple. "The psychic said my ESP abilities were potent, yet limited."

"Can you see images at will?"

"Apparently not. Last night I exhausted myself trying. No luck."

"Roberta, that isn't something you should attempt on your own. It can be dangerous."

She nodded, glanced away.

He pointed at her fishing rod. "You're getting a bite. Quick, set the hook before it gets the bait."

She gave the rod a short yank, felt the drag as the hook set. A moment later she landed a small rainbow trout.

"Good eating size," Jake said, gently removing the hook. "A couple more like these and we'll have our lunch."

She laughed, the retreating pressure above her eye gone, forgotten.

Jake, his chair tipped back to rest on the wood siding of the house, sat on the deck at the small round table amid the remnants of their grilled-trout lunch and watched his guest through the silver lenses of his sunglasses. Roberta was picking a bouquet of wildflowers across the yard.

He thought her a very alluring woman. Exquisite even, though he couldn't say why. From the moment he'd set eyes on her in the hospital, a blind woman with no makeup, wearing a plain gown and stereo headphones, something tugged at him. The sunlight coming through the window had presented a fascinating illusion, bathing her in a radiant, pearly aura. She had looked so . . . he wanted to say bewitching, but felt ridiculous just thinking it.

Who and what was this woman with the strange knowing eyes? She had visions, nightmare visions. Reality seen through extrasensory means.

She returned to the table, a bunch of pink and purple sierra primroses in her hand. He watched her pour water into a plastic cup and arrange the bouquet.

"Question," Jake said, pointing to the chair opposite him.

She sat, fussed with the wildflowers.

"You say you've been sensitive all your life?"

"It started when I was about three. I had . . . three or four experiences in my early childhood."

"What did you see?"

"Are you going to scrutinize me through those glasses?" she asked evenly.

He pulled off the mirrored glasses and laid them on the table.

"I saw the deaths of my grandmother, my best friend, and my . . . my brother." She cleared her throat. "Then nothing until three weeks ago, when Angie killed her husband, Sam."

"All deaths?"

She nodded, looked away. "You were going to tell me about your piece of the puzzle." She seemed eager to change the subject.

"In a minute. Tell me about the abduction in the alley."

Roberta explained that that particular vision came to her in dream form. "But later I had a vision—the one at the pond—and it was the same woman from the bar."

"Are you familiar with the bar? Any idea where it is?"

"No."

The wind came up and they moved inside. In Jake's rustic living room, among the knotty pine and leather, the potted trees and driftwood-mounted bromelaids, he and Roberta sat on a sofa upholstered in a Pendleton print of red, gold, and turquoise.

Without looking at Roberta, he said, "So he selects a woman, snatches her off the street, and takes her to where he lives. Why?"

"He's lonely?"

"But he kills them."

"Yes. You're the professional, what do you think?"

"It's possible he's lonely, seeking a companion. It's also possible she cannot live up to his expectations. He may have a certain role model in mind, a role no woman can realistically meet. If he's a psychopathic killer, the act of killing is his principal objective and his methods and motives will be known only to him. He's going to kill again if he hasn't already."

"God, for some insane reason he's linked to me. Either I'm supposed to stop him or I'm in line . . . as a victim. If that's the case, then . . . then . . ." Her words died away. She buried her face in her hands.

Jake wanted to go to her. He wanted to fold her into his arms and hold her tight, comfort her. He wanted to, but he held back. Instead, he said, "I'll have someone at the police department check this out . . . see if there're other women reported missing."

"Other women? Do you know of one?"

"A patient of mine. Missing since mid-June. She's blond, slender, and wears a gold and silver ankle bracelet."

"My God."

"On my insistence her mother reported her missing. As far as Mrs. Sardi's concerned, Belinda took off alone. You see, she was a chronic runaway. I've had her in group since she was sixteen. Family problems mostly. Peer pressure. No father, mother wrapped up in other things."

"But you don't think she left town willingly?"

"No. She was twenty-two, no longer a kid. She started coming to me on her own six months ago. She really wanted to get it together. And dammit, she was doing just that. At our last session the patient sitting in my office was a woman with a focus, a future. She'd been working for a radio station for six months and had just gotten a promotion and raise. She wanted to go into broadcasting, was planning to enroll at UNR in the fall." It occurred to Jake that Belinda Sardi was probably dead, her body lying in a pit with other hapless victims. No one would know she was dead. No one would mourn her.

"Why don't we just go to the police and tell them everything?" Roberta asked.

"Because they won't believe you. What crime? Where are the bodies? They're overworked as it is without throwing something conjectural their way. Did you report what you saw on the day of your accident?" he asked.

He caught a flash of compunction in her eyes before she looked away without answering.

"It probably would have served no purpose unless,

of course, you can pinpoint the area where the bodies are hidden."

"Not likely," she said. "There are thousands of acres of wilderness up there. And I can't be sure that what I saw that day was actually happening right in front of me. It's possible they were miles away."

"Well, one thing is certain. If this man is really out there, we'll find him. After all, you have a direct pipeline to him. As long as he doesn't know you're eavesdropping, sooner or later he's bound to give himself away."

EIGHTEEN

Roberta sat at her desk at the center, staring out the window. Her mind wandered, and even the simplest task was an effort. If she were able to completely immerse herself in her work, then and only then did the man in the woods recede to a remote place in her mind.

The phone rang, startling Robbi out of her grim reverie. She snatched up the receiver, eager for any diversion.

"Hello. Is this a bad time?"

"Jake?" Her stomach fluttered.

"Yes. What's your schedule like? Can you break away?"

"To do what?"

"I thought we'd cruise around. See if we can locate that bar."

Robbi glanced at her watch. Four forty-five. Before he'd called, trying to concentrate on anything had been an effort; it'd be impossible now. "Meet me at my house in half an hour?"

* * *

Robbi stood on the sidewalk, waiting. A light breeze tugged at the hem of the dress's pleated skirt, threatening to rush underneath and billow the whole thing about her hips. She held it down with splayed fingers.

Jake's white T-bird pulled up to the curb. Robbi quickly opened the car door and climbed inside.

"No cane?" he said.

"Nope. Too much of a crutch. Gave it up, cold turkey."

He shifted gears, pulled out, and merged with the traffic.

"Great car," she said. "Looks brand new. Even smells new."

He smiled. "I restored most of it myself. Kind of a hobby of mine."

He was wearing jeans and a button-down shirt, the sleeves rolled up. He looked exceptionally attractive in blue, the periwinkle matching his eyes. She caught the scent of his aftershave, a subtle, clean fragrance that made her think of a boy in college whom she'd had an intense crush on. They had never dated, had never really talked to each other for that matter; his name escaped her now, yet something in her stomach stirred.

Five minutes later they stood on Fourth and Lake streets. Robbi had a strong feeling the bar in her vision was situated within the downtown casino district. They would leave the car in the parking lot and cover the area on foot.

"Are you sure you can manage?" Jake asked. "We might have to cover a lot of ground."

"I've been walking every morning. As long as we don't go too fast."

Within the first hour they covered the area from Lake to Virginia, the city's main drag. By seven o'clock

Roberta, her foot beginning to ache, was having serious doubts that the bar existed beyond her dreams.

"There's an alley on the other side of the river," Jake said. "If it's not there, then we'll break for dinner."

Robbi nodded, shouldered her purse, and walked on. They crossed the Sierra Street bridge; the courthouse was on their left. As they neared the alley, she slowed. There was something here, she could feel it. A tightness at the back of her scalp sent a chill down her spine. She hung back.

Jake watched her.

She stopped at the mouth of the alley and turned toward the street. The garbage bags were no longer there, but she saw them nonetheless, stacked at the curb, black and bloated.

Hesitantly, Robbi moved to the dark metal door of the bar. She looked up at the neon sign. STARDUST LOUNGE.

Jake followed.

"Let's go in," she said with a slight tremor in her voice.

The air inside was unbelievably dense. It crowded around her oppressively. The room was dark, illuminated only by recessed lighting behind the bar and candles glowing in red glass holders on a half dozen tables. Robbi stepped to the bar. She took hold of the first stool to steady herself, her fingers digging into the vinyl back. The room seemed to whirl and rock crazily. So adversely affected by the place, she was certain the man in her visions had to be near.

Jake squeezed her arm reassuringly. "What, Roberta?"

"This is it," she whispered.

Robbi glanced toward the corner. A man and woman, both blond, sat at a video table, playing. An old woman shuffled into the room from the dark hallway and climbed onto a barstool. Robbi had seen her playing the jukebox the night of the abduction. The bartender mopped the bar in front of them, waited.

Robbi ordered white wine, Jake a beer. He pulled a stool out for her.

"The bartender and that woman at the bar were both here that night," she said under her breath.

A moment later the bartender was putting drinks down on paper disks. Red-eyed dragon tattoos on his arms twisted and squirmed.

The old woman lifted her beer and drank. "We need some mood, Chappy. Plug the box in, why don'tcha?"

The bartender ignored her.

Jake struck up a conversation with him. They discussed the merits of the As and Giants. Finally the bartender said, "You folks new to the Stardust? Don't remember seeing you in here."

"We're looking for someone. Maybe you can help."

"Maybe."

"Pour one for yourself," Jake said to the bartender, pushing two tens toward him.

The bartender grinned, showing purple gums. He poured a shot of Jack Daniel's, then popped the cap on a Coors. The money disappeared.

"Name's Chappy. Who you looking for?"

"A woman with long blond hair. Pretty. Early twenties," Jake said. "She was in here a week or two ago."

"You asking about the one the cops been asking about?"

Robbi and Jake exchanged looks. Jake nodded.

Chappy tossed back the shot, gulped at the beer, then stifled a belch. "Came in after work with friends once in a while."

"Her name?"

Chappy shook his head. "Don't usually bother with names. Put the face and the drink together, that's all that counts."

"What did she drink?" Roberta asked.

"Wild Turkey. Neat. Could hold her liquor too. There's not many a woman can down straight shots like that and not fall on her butt."

Roberta's heart was beating hard. In her mind's eye she saw the woman sipping from a shot glass at this bar, sitting in the same seat where the old woman now sat. Roberta lifted her gaze and met the hard stare of the old woman.

"Did she work around here?" Jake asked.

"Wore black and whites. That says casino. Dealer, that'd be my guess."

"Which club?"

He shrugged. "Wasn't real social. In fact, I was surprised to see her in here after her not coming in for so long. She was down in the dumps that night. A fight with the old man probably. Been crying, looked like. I learned long ago to stay clear of the crying ones. They latch onto a sympathetic ear and, man, you can't shut off the waterworks."

"Was she alone?"

"Yeah. Some guy tried to pick her up, but she wasn't having any."

Robbi's fingers dug into Jake's arm.

"Wasn't her type, huh?"

Chappy shrugged. "She was way outta his league, that much I know."

"In what way?"

"Lowlife. Creepy. 'Member Charles Manson?" Robbi and Jake nodded. "Don't need to say more."

"He looked like Charles Manson?"

"Well, no, but he had that *look*. That Ramirez guy in L.A.—the Night Stalker—same thing. That 'devil made me do it' look. Ultra weird."

"Can you describe him?"

Chappy stared at the floor and pulled on his long nose, thinking. "Average size, I'd say. Hey, man, I can't put features to the face. I remember what he drank though. It was well whiskey. Drank it neat, like her."

Roberta wasn't satisfied with his answers. The man in her visions was big, very big, that much she knew, and he had been drinking beer.

"Chappy, you're so full of shit," the old woman said. She turned to Robbi and Jake. "He was a big bruiser. A giant, pert near. Hair all over the place. And he drank Miller draft, same as you and me, son."

"You talking about that guy in the corner? He never hit on her," Chappy said.

"Sure he did. You was too busy watching *Rockford.*"

"A drink for the lady," Jake said, laying more money on the bar. "Make it a double."

The woman saluted him with her empty glass.

"And how would you know," Chappy responded sarcastically, "you was passed out cold, I remember that."

Jake and Roberta left the bar when the argument between the two began to get heated. Outside, Robbi paused, staring across the one-way street to a building on the corner. The courthouse. Police cars lined the curb. She shook her head incredulously. *Did this man fear nothing?*

"I don't know whether to feel good or bad," Roberta said.

"Feel good. Your mind's a window, and as long as you can see through it to this man, she has a chance." Jake stared at the courthouse. "Tomorrow I'll do some checking. Find out who she is."

Jake offered her dinner, but Roberta was exhausted and wanted to go home. After making certain she was safely inside her house, he promised to call the following day, then he drove away.

At twilight, in her nightgown, Robbi sat on the edge of the bed holding the receiver to her chest. She debated whether or not to call Donald. It would be close to midnight in New York. She felt an overwhelming need to talk to him, to make contact. She dialed. The line rang five times before it was picked up. A woman's voice, low, sleep-filled, mumbled a hello.

Robbi paused. "Karen?" she asked softly.

"Ummm . . . yeah, whozis?"

Roberta heard Don's muffled voice in the background. She pressed the disconnect lever, then gently cradled the receiver.

She turned off the light and, feeling as if she were swimming underwater, crossed the room and cracked the window. A light went on in the house across the street, outlining the silhouette of a cat sitting on the sill. Maybe she should get a cat. A low-maintenance pet. They were quiet, ate very little, and were fiercely independent. Cats were companions. Before Donald had left, their relationship seemed to have mellowed to companionship. They had been pulling apart gradually for a long time. She thought of a piece of taffy, stretched to a thin strand, never quite breaking apart but no longer able to come together again.

It was she who had encouraged him to move to New York. Within just six months he was achieving his goal of success, had made new friends, and had adopted a new and more exciting life-style. Would she have fit in, she wondered.

She returned to bed, threw off all the covers, and crawled beneath the crisp sheet.

She fell asleep reflecting on the boy in college whose bracing aftershave made her think of Jake. Or was it the other way around? Since she couldn't remember what the college boy looked like, the two men melded, became one.

NINETEEN

Outside the room, with his ear pressed to the door, he could hear her speaking softly, "Sonny, oh, Sonny, please find me."

Eckker turned the key in the lock and twisted the knob. The door opened. The overhead light burned. A surge of anger shot through him. He'd asked her not to turn it on unless it was absolutely necessary. Power was generated from large surplus batteries charged by a diesel generator. The generator was noisy and he used it only sparingly. He'd given her a flashlight for auxiliary light. Why didn't she do what he said?

She sat on the edge of the cot in a white dress, staring at her bare feet. The dress had come from the makeshift closet in the main room. An assortment of women's clothes, some stolen from clotheslines and some left behind by previous companions, were now hers. The black skirt and white blouse she'd worn when she came to live with him hung on a hook in the closet. She seemed to like the white dress best.

He had also gotten her the female toiletries she'd

asked for; some were new, some not. He refused to get her cigarettes.

"I have a surprise."

Without lifting her head she glared up at him.

"Come."

"Why do you lock the door?" she said woodenly. "You say you want me to be happy, but you treat me like a prisoner."

"You're not a prisoner."

"I want to go home. My friends and family must be worried sick about me."

"This is your home. You're not trying." He grinned. "Come. The surprise."

She slowly stood.

Eckker took the flashlight from the floor and flipped it on. He reached up, took hold of the burning light bulb and twisted it, scarcely feeling the searing heat.

He led the way out through the closed-in stairwell to the main room.

The items sat on the floor in the middle of the room. He had stolen a yellow floral bedsheet from a clothesline in Truckee. The little phonograph player he'd had hidden away just for this purpose. Women loved music. A shoebox held over a hundred records from Sinatra to the Beatles. He hated that hard rock stuff, it made his head hurt. There was a hand mirror and vanity set. He'd washed the brush and comb. They looked like new.

She approached slowly, knelt. With a stiff forefinger she poked at the objects as if they were full of cooties.

"A bedsheet," she said sourly.

"To make curtains . . . for the windows." He pointed

to the narrow paneless rectangles toward the ceiling.

"And how will I do that?"

"I have thread . . . needles."

She tossed the sheet aside. "I don't sew."

He bit down on the inside of his mouth. His vision blurred slightly.

Lethargically, she sorted through the 45s. "Some of these aren't too bad," she said without enthusiasm.

He smiled. He plugged the record player into the extension cord, then turned it on.

She made a selection, then put it on the turntable.

He recognized the singer instantly. Johnny Cash. She'd chosen a slow one. He preferred the fast to the slow. "Folsom Prison Blues." Why'd she pick that one? It had bad memories. He didn't need a reminder.

Halfway through the song he looked at Maggie. On her knees, her arms hanging listlessly at her sides, she stared blankly at the bare wall as tears streamed unchecked down her face.

He chewed the inside of his cheek until a sharp, coppery taste filled his mouth. His huge hands balled into fists. The light in the room seemed to dim, turn sanguine.

He heard her sob.

He leapt up. A hand shot out to the record player. The stylus screeched across the 45 as he grabbed it from the spinning turntable. Using both hands, he twisted the record until it was nothing more than a distorted black lump. Then he savagely threw the warped record across the room. He snatched up the shoebox of 45s and hurled them against the wall.

Red flashes danced before his eyes.

She just wasn't trying.

TWENTY

At six P.M. Robbi stepped off the elevator on the sixth floor of the Medical Plaza and crossed the wide corridor to the Truckee Meadows Medical Group. Jake Reynolds, M.D., was the third name down.

She opened the door and entered. The receptionist desk sat vacant. Robbi crossed the rich blush-tinted carpet to the open door of an office and looked in. Jake stood at the window, staring out at the city.

She cleared her throat.

He turned, saw her, and smiled. "Hi. C'mon in. Your timing is perfect. My last patient just left."

"I thought you were on hiatus?"

"I have a few patients I see once a week, plus a group." His hand swept the room, indicating a number of chairs in several groupings. "Have a seat."

Robbi chose one of two club chairs arranged around a sofa.

Jake lifted a manila envelope, came around from behind the massive desk, tugging at his necktie to loosen it, and sat in the other chair. He handed her the envelope.

She looked at him questionably.

"Missing women. Police reports and pictures. There were four in all, but I threw out two for obvious reasons."

She held the envelope in her hand, staring at the names but not seeing them. She forced her eyes to focus and read: Belinda Sardi and Margaret Winston.

Astonished, Robbi looked at Jake. "Margaret! That's the one he has now. Maggie. He called her Maggie." She opened the flap and tentatively pulled out the forms. Two photographs fell into her lap. Robbi lifted them, looking from one to the other. Her heart raced furiously. Breathing deeply, trying to calm herself, she stared at two faces from another dimension.

"Are they the ones?" he asked.

"Yes." She looked down at the names of next of kin. "If my intuition is correct, I can't help the Sardis. Belinda's already dead."

Jake was silent. He moved to the window, looked out as though reflecting on her words.

"Belinda was your patient. I'm sorry," she said.

He nodded.

She scanned the other report. "Margaret is the one from the Stardust Lounge. It says here Carl Masser reported her missing. Who is he?"

"Her fiancé."

"I've got to talk to him."

"Mr. Masser is under suspicion in the disappearance. If she turns up dead, he'll be a prime suspect."

"It's not him. I know it's not."

* * *

Jake followed Roberta to her house, where she parked her car and got into his. As he drove south on Rock Boulevard he glanced over at her. Roberta stared straight ahead, a faraway look in her eyes. On her lap sat the envelope with the police reports and pictures, her fingertips absently playing over the surface. Is she trying to psychically tune into one or both of them, he wondered.

Just looking at her caused something inside him to twist and pull. She was a lovely woman, growing lovelier every day. Although theirs was not a doctor-patient relationship, there were still professional ethics to consider. Roberta was under a certain psychological strain. And try as he might, whenever he thought of Roberta in an intimate sense, another woman had a way of creeping into the picture. Susan—bright, beautiful Susan—utterly psychotic. He still hadn't completely gotten over her or the tragedy of her death. He doubted he ever would.

On the main street of Sparks' Victorian Square, Jake pulled up to the construction site of a new casino. Presently in the steel-girder-and-concrete phase of construction, the two-story building would soon sport a Victorian façade in keeping with the town's overall concept.

Jake parked in the dirt lot behind the building. They left the car, moved across the dusty lot.

"It's seven o'clock, what time do these guys quit work?" Roberta asked.

"We're in luck, looks like they're on overtime."

Sounds of hammering, sawing, and the *tat* of the concrete and screw guns echoed in the hot July afternoon. They ducked under a suspended scaffold and entered the back entrance, but before getting five feet in, someone yelled.

A man with short legs and a portly belly hurried up to them. "Hey, you can't go in there without a hardhat," he said.

"We're looking for Carl Masser. Is he around?"

"Yeah, he's the super. Stay out there," he said, pointing to the way they came in. "I'll get him."

Jake and Roberta walked to a shoulder-high stack of sheetrock. Several minutes later a well-built man in his early thirties, wearing tight, dusty 501s, a blue knit tank shirt, brogans, and a shocking yellow hardhat came around another part of the building. He approached, a quizzical expression on his face.

"Carl Masser?" Jake asked.

The man nodded.

Jake introduced Roberta and himself.

"Mr. Masser, do you have a minute to talk?" Jake asked. "It's about Margaret Winston."

"Maggie?" Something desperate flashed in his eyes. "Yeah, sure. Let's get off the site." He turned, calling out to the man who had stopped them. "Dilly, I'm outta here. Send the men home in an hour." He removed the hardhat, ran fingers through his thick black hair, then tossed the hat to the man.

Masser led the way to a bar across the street called The Gang Box. If the name didn't give it away for a construction crew hangout, then the dusty clientele, hardhats since replaced by billed caps with lumberyard and building material logos, did. The dozen or so men openly watched Roberta as she crossed the dim room and took a seat at an empty table. A miniskirted waitress appeared with an icy bottle of Dos Equis and placed it in front of Masser.

"Thanks, Barb," Masser said to the waitress. He downed half of it in one long pull.

Roberta and Jake declined a drink.

"Either of you related to Maggie?" Masser asked.

"No."

"You from the cops?"

"No."

"Then who the hell are you?" Masser looked from Jake to Roberta. "What do you want?"

"We'd like to talk to you about her."

"Yeah? That's what you said before. Here I am. So talk."

"Mr. Masser," Roberta began, looking at the ceiling, "this is going to sound really bizarre . . ."

He tipped his head, waiting.

"I've been having visions . . . psychic visions, and I think your fiancée is in them."

Masser stared at her, incredulous.

"I think Maggie's been kidnapped. That she's being held captive by a man . . . a very big man with a beard—"

Masser turned to Jake and asked, "What'da *you* do?"

"Psychiatrist."

"She your patient?" He jerked his head toward Robbi.

Jake tensed. "Look, Mister—"

Then Masser laughed, cutting Jake off. "*Bizarre,* she says? That's fucking crazy." His eyes were hard as he turned back to stare at Roberta. "You took me away from an overtime job for this? You think this is funny—a kick in the ass? You don't honestly expect me to believe this crock of shit?"

Jake stood, took hold of Robbi's arm, and said, "Come on, let's go."

She put her hand over Jake's, stalling. "He's keeping her somewhere in the mountains."

"Oh, yeah? Well, with the entire Sierra Nevada range at our back door, she should be a cinch to find."

"Roberta . . ." Jake said, urging her up.

"She was taken from an alley near the Stardust Lounge. I don't care if you believe me or not, I saw it."

"Jesus fucking Christ," Masser said, shaking his head, his expression unreadable.

Roberta was halfway to her feet when Masser stopped them.

"Hey, wait," he said quickly. "What you just said about the Stardust—look, give a sec to digest this, okay? You come waltzing in telling me my girl's been snatched by some big, bearded dude and your proof is a—what did you call it—a vision? I'm a wreck. I'm trying to cope with Maggie's disappearance, I'm on overtime with the club, the cops are leaning on me. I can't sleep or eat. I'm running on caffeine, booze, and sheer tension. Then two complete strangers pop up out of the blue and throw stories of the strange and unexplained at me—now, how the hell am I supposed to react?"

"I know," Roberta said. "I don't understand any of this myself, Mr. Masser."

"Carl. It's Carl." He ran an impatient hand through his hair. "Shit, I don't believe in this psychic mumbo jumbo, but I'll tell you something—at this point, if it gets me closer to Maggie, or sheds some light on what happened to her, I'd believe in flying saucers. So far the cops haven't come up with a damn thing. I—I don't know what to do. I'm going outta my fuck—oh, hey, I'm sorry, Miss Paxton. Excuse my language, I'm not thinking straight." He pointed to her chair. "Talk to me. Please."

Jake and Roberta sat again.

"Do you know the Stardust Lounge?" Jake asked.

"The bar on Sierra? Sure. Before we met, Maggie used to stop there after work sometimes." Carl turned to stare at Roberta. "What was she wearing that night?"

"A white blouse and black skirt. She was smoking one of those long, thin cigarettes that are popular now. She drank whiskey neat."

"You weren't in the bar that night? And you didn't know her before she disappeared?"

"I never laid eyes on her. I was a patient in the hospital the night she disappeared."

"Washoe Med," Jake added. "She'd had a serious accident and was recovering from it."

Carl seemed paler. He stared at Roberta, his face an intricate pattern of emotions. "What the hell's going on here? Why you?"

"I don't know."

"What can I do? Tell me what I can do to help," Carl said, leaning forward.

"Did she say anything to you about someone watching her, following her? A big man in particular?" Jake asked. "Did she give you any indication that she was afraid?"

"No," he said, shaking his head. "She works swing shift at the Golden Club five days a week. Eight to two. Blackjack dealer. Came straight home. We didn't get to see a helluva lot of each other. I have to be up at five. I'd usually try to listen for her, y'know, to make sure she got in okay."

"You live together?"

"Yeah."

"Did she come home that night?"

"Obviously not. Damn," Masser said, clunking down the bottle, "there's nothing I can tell you that I haven't already told the cops."

"Is there anyone we can contact?" Jake asked. "Friends, relatives?"

"Sure, I can get you names and numbers." Masser turned to Robbi. "Tell me what you see. Tell me everything."

"Carl, I can't tell you much more than what I've already said. It's not clear to me exactly what's happening."

"Has she asked for me?" he said softly.

Robbi glanced at Jake, then looked down and shook her head. "But," she said quickly, "that doesn't mean she hasn't. I don't see and hear everything. Bits and pieces."

A frown veed Masser's brow. "What's he doing to her? Tell me what he's doing to her."

Robbi blanched. This was one reason Jake had been reluctant to let her talk with Masser. He'd anticipated the questions, knowing the difficulty Roberta would have responding to them.

"Carl," Jake began, "Roberta's under a great deal of stress. This is very hard on her. You understand she can't answer questions like that . . . here . . . now."

"Okay. Okay." Masser pulled a red grease pencil from his back pocket, tore a cocktail napkin in half, and scribbled a phone number on it. He pushed it across the table to Robbi and handed her the pencil and the other half of the napkin. "Could I have yours. Please."

"I think—" Jake began.

"It's all right, Jake." She wrote out her home number.

Masser signaled the waitress for another drink.

Robbi stood.

Jake and Masser rose.

"I have a vested interest in this," Masser said. "The missing woman happens to be my fiancée, remember? We were supposed to get married at the end of the job. I'm about to go outta my mind with worry. The cops are doing nothing." He turned to Roberta. "You're my only link to her. You can't pop into my life, tell me Maggie's been kidnapped, then just say adios."

Roberta looked up into Masser's strong-boned face, a face that now looked about to crumble. "I wouldn't do that. We'll talk. Soon."

They left Masser in the bar and stood outside on B Street, the setting sun burning into their eyes. Jake put on his mirrored sunglasses and Robbi held a hand to her forehead, screening the bright rays.

"You don't know a damn thing about him," Jake said, his voice sounding tight. "Be careful, all right?"

Roberta faced him, a strange, enigmatic expression on her face. "I don't want to go home yet. Can we talk?"

TWENTY-ONE

With their backs to the sun, they strolled east along B Street. A slight breeze whispered against Robbi's face. A hansom carriage conveying tourists through the town square passed them on the cobbled lane. Robbi quietly took in the sights. Trees, shrubs, and bright flowers, black wrought-iron lampposts, spiked railings, and white lattice gazebos made up Victorian Plaza. Ahead she could see the new amphitheater filling with people.

A dull ache in her ankle made her slow her pace. Jake noticed, offered his arm. They entered John Ascuaga's Nugget, made their way through the teeming casino to Trader Dick's and took a booth in the cocktail lounge away from the band.

Roberta's mind kept returning to the women in the photographs and the visions. Something gnawed at her, something that Jake had brought up a few days before.

"You asked me once if I could be clairvoyant at will," she said.

"You said you couldn't."

"I'd like to try again."

"Tomorrow?"

"I'll be tied up all day in a rummage sale for the center, but tomorrow night's okay. Can you come over around eight?"

"Eight it is."

They waited to be called for dinner. Robbi sipped the wine, her second, or was it her third? Whatever, the alcohol was taking effect. With the band playing mood songs, she felt relaxed and warm all over, more relaxed than she'd felt in a long, long time.

"Robbi, tell me about the other experiences. The ones when you were young."

She toyed with a cocktail napkin. "My grandmother was the first. She lived in Rhode Island, nearly three thousand miles away. I couldn't have been more than three at the time. I saw her fall down the cellar steps. I don't remember the details or if I told anyone about it. There was a funeral. Years later I learned she'd broken her hip in the fall and died of exposure on the icy concrete floor. I often wonder, had I said something about what I saw, could she have been saved?"

"Christ, Roberta, you were just a baby. Who would have believed you?"

"Yes, you're right. Next was my best friend in first grade. Peggy had leukemia. I knew she was going to die. Everyone knew it. One day I was in the school lunchroom and suddenly all the activity around me stopped. I saw Peg in her bed with her family gathered all around. I watched as she took her last breath. She died at noon that day."

Jake laid a hand over her trembling one. "And your brother . . . ?"

The mention of Ronnie brought back that crushing feeling in her chest. She felt her throat constrict. "Ronnie drowned. It was an accident. He—" Roberta blinked back the tears that abruptly sprang into her eyes. "I can't . . . I can't talk about Ronnie. Not now anyway. Too much wine, I'll be blubbering."

"I understand," he said. "Only visions of death?"

She nodded. "Once or twice after that, when something would flash across my mind, I ignored it . . . wouldn't let it develop into anything. I managed to repress it—whatever it was. I didn't understand it, and I sure as hell didn't want it. Eventually, I stopped having the visions. Until Angela, that is."

Jake's hand squeezed hers. She looked over at the man who'd been a companion for the past four days. His gaze met hers and locked. He stared at her with a veiled look that told her nothing, yet made her tremble inside. In the flickering candlelight, his eyes were deep, hypnotic. She returned his stare, seemingly powerless to break contact. She felt something in a hollow part of her glow faintly, embers that had lain smoldering. She was being drawn in by the sheer heat. Mesmerized.

The maître d' appeared, informed them their booth was ready.

Robbi was jolted back to awareness. She looked at Jake for some sign that he had felt something of what she'd felt, but he was already standing, buttoning his suit jacket and gazing around the lounge.

* * *

Jake forced himself back to his present surroundings with the ease of dragging a bucket underwater. For a moment he was completely, utterly lost. Lost? Where? He couldn't say. Only that it was a very erotic place, warm and fleshy and moist, filled with a specific woman's scent—and a specific woman. This evening was proving difficult. And only a moment before, her soft voice relating things personal and obviously painful, he'd wanted to draw her into his arms and hold her tenderly.

Over dinner she asked him questions about himself. He told her he grew up in a large house in a small town in central Kansas. The only boy of five kids, fourth in the birth order. Their mother died of a viral infection when he was seven, recasting his three older sisters into a single-parenting role.

"What was it like having three sisters mother you?"

"Heaven and hell. But I had male support. My father and grandfather."

"What did your father do for a living?"

"Both he and Grandpa were wallpaper hangers. They had a business together."

Roberta laughed lightly. "So that's where you got the experience when you were in college."

"Right."

"Happy family?"

He smiled. Aside from losing his mother, his childhood had been idyllic. When he spoke of his carefree childhood and wholesome family, Jake saw something in her eyes—envy, a quiet longing.

"Tell me about you," Jake said.

She talked eagerly about her young sister, spoke briefly of her mother, yet said nothing of her father, her childhood, or her fiancé, the Wall Street Wonder.

"What about your father?"

"Are you trying to spoil this pleasant evening?"

"I met your father about eight years ago at a luncheon. He was the guest speaker."

"What did you think of him? Not the psychiatrist, but the man?"

"Intense," Jake said, watching her closely. "Angry."

She smiled cryptically, then smoothly maneuvered the topic back to him.

By the time they had finished dinner and stepped out of the casino into the plaza, it was nearly ten. The sky to the west, above the ragged, midnight-blue mountain peaks, glowed a luminous shade of ultramarine. At night, with the old-fashioned streetlamps glowing and the dazzling casino lights, the town looked like a movie set. A Dixie band with strumming banjos and clinking tambourines accompanied a barbershop quartet in the large gazebo bandstand directly in front of them.

Roberta leaned into him as they walked back to his car. She was slightly inebriated, which he found charming. Usually nervous and uptight, she was at ease tonight. Her smile, quick to come, lit up her face. This was the real Roberta Paxton. Or, he surmised, as close to what her personality had been like before the accident and all the tumult it had evoked.

He wanted the real Roberta Paxton. Wanted her with a profound ache.

On the ride home, Jake was quiet, almost pensive. She stole glances at his firmly set profile and wondered if he was upset with her for drinking too much.

At her door, unwilling to end the evening, she said, "Jake, let's try the ESP." She had her key in hand, trying to fit it into the lock with rubbery fingers.

"What? Now?" he said.

"Yes, right now."

"It's late."

"I'm not tired. I feel good."

"You feel good because you're tipsy." He spoke in a flat tone.

"So what if I'm tipsy," she said defiantly. "It's been a long time since I've been tipsy, or relaxed or . . . or . . ." She let the words die away.

"Or what?" he asked quietly.

She shrugged. "It doesn't matter."

"We'll work on it tomorrow night," Jake said, helping her insert the key in the lock.

Pushing the door open, she turned to step up onto the threshold when her ankle, weak from walking in the plaza, gave out. She felt herself falling, reached out abruptly. Suddenly strong arms were around her waist, twisting her around to face him. He held her against him with her back pressed to the door frame.

"You okay?"

"No . . ." she said softly, putting her arms around his neck, leaning into him.

His arms tightened around her. And then she was staring into his eyes, eyes that seemed to harbor a feverish glint. Not sure who made the first move, though she suspected she did, her eyes closed and she felt his lips on hers; at first light and tender, an instant later they were hot and moist and alive with a fierce energy.

Devour. He would devour her and she found herself

inflamed with the very idea of it. The intensity of their passion startled her. So swift, so forceful. What had been building between the two of them these past weeks had reached volatile proportions. She wanted him. Wanted him now before she could think about it.

He moaned, then abruptly pulled away from her.

Robbi opened her eyes and stared at him, questioning.

He shook his head sadly, reached out and tenderly touched her jaw with the tips of his fingers. He lifted her into the entry, turned, and was gone.

She sank to the floor, her legs too weak to hold her.

At the corner of Roberta's street, at the stop sign, he gripped the steering wheel and shook it viciously, then laughed ironically. It seemed he spent a lot of time at this miserable stop sign, contemplative time, time spent easing the pressure in his crotch.

She had a guy in another part of the country. Over six months separated. Undoubtedly she was lonely, perhaps longing for a man's touch, but definitely intoxicated and therefore not in full control of herself. Tonight she wanted him. But tomorrow, sober, she would probably regret everything. It had been up to him to draw the line.

So what was he, for chrissake, the policeman of logic and emotion?

He laughed again. Only one other time in his life had he felt such wanting. Such obsession.

Oh, God, he was in trouble.

TWENTY-TWO

When Jake entered the lake house the phone had rung a half dozen times. Wiping engine grease from his hands, he answered.

"Dr. Reynolds, it's Lois Paxton."

"Mrs. Paxton, how are you?"

"I hope I'm not disturbing you. I . . . I'm calling about my daughter, Roberta."

Jake's stomach twisted at the mention of her. An image of her in his arms, her body pressed to his, played across his mind. "Yes?" he said through a tightness in his throat.

"Well, I want to thank you for seeing her and, of course, to . . . to find out how she's doing?"

"Mrs. Paxton, I'm afraid there's been a misunderstanding."

"You're seeing her, aren't you?"

"Your daughter does not want professional help from me or from anyone."

"No one knows that better than I. Her father, you see, he—well, it doesn't matter. I won't take up any more of your time. I know you tried and I thank you for that. Please send me a bill, Doctor." A click and the hissing line told him she had disconnected.

He considered calling her back, then decided to leave it be. He should have made it clear to her in the beginning that he had absolutely no intention, for any amount of money, of treating her daughter on the sly.

Roberta Paxton did need help. But psychiatric help? Again he thought of Susan and felt that familiar ache.

Susan. Five years ago, at the age of thirty, Jake met Susan Calla, a psychological assistant, at a seminar in Reno. She was beautiful, intelligent, and the most sensual woman he'd ever encountered. He embraced her. Became *obsessed* with her. Blinded by a consuming love lust, he overlooked or made excuses for the subtle signs of emotional instability that had gradually begun to surface. After moving in together, the barriers fell away one by one. Daily the chronic lying, the tantrums, the paranoia emerged. When he suggested she get counseling from one of the staff doctors, she refused, and at that point seemed to go off the deep end. He tried to break it off. She sank deeper, threatening suicide if he left. *Fatal Attraction* personified. For two endless, roller-coaster years he remained trapped in a web of sex and sickness, his own sanity teetering precariously on the edge. His own sanity . . .

Jake stared out the window at the shimmering turquoise lake and willed himself out of the past. There was nothing he could do for Susan now.

But he might be able to help Roberta. It was impossible to shut her out of his thoughts. Images of her haunted him. A thrill shot through him just thinking about seeing her that night.

* * *

Roberta struggled with the cumbersome box on her way out the kitchen door. The phone rang. She backed up to the table, put the box down, and answered.

"Darling, did I wake you?" her mother said in her soft voice.

"Hello, Mom. No, I was just going out the door. A rummage sale for the center."

"You work too hard, honey."

"I like being busy. It keeps my mind . . ." Her words died away.

"Off your problems?"

Robbi said nothing.

"Now, please don't get upset, but I was talking to a very nice doctor the other day and I happened to mention your problem. She was quite interested and said as much. Perhaps you could tell her yourself. Her name is Panaski. Claire Panaski."

"What kind of doctor, Mom?" she asked, knowing the answer.

"Psychologist, I believe."

"Mother, I don't need a shrink."

"You need to talk to someone. I don't know what went wrong between you and Dr. Reynolds, but I'm sure you'll like Claire—"

"What about Dr. Reynolds?"

"Oh, dear, I—honey, I know you hate it when I butt in, but you did say you liked him. And I wouldn't have called him if . . ."

Roberta felt a tightness in her chest. "You asked Jake to treat me?"

"Well, we did discuss treatment. Of course—"

"You actually paid Dr. Reynolds?"

"Not yet, he hasn't sent the bill. I just spoke to him."

Roberta sank down into a chair. She swallowed; her mouth felt dry.

"Honey, don't be mad at me. I've been worried about you. I only want to help."

"I know."

"Would you like Dr. Panaski's number?"

"Maybe," she said absently. "Not right now, Mom."

"Well, I won't keep you. Good-bye, dear."

She waited until her mother had hung up before she angrily slammed the receiver on the hook. *So the doctor believed her, did he? Theirs was no doctor-patient relationship, no sir.*

She shook her head, laughed dryly. No wonder he kept his distance. Ethically, professionally, she was off limits. Last night, after throwing herself at him, he had responded impulsively, only to gain control when he realized that a quickie at the door wasn't worth jeopardizing his practice.

What else was a lie? Belinda Sardi? Had he used a missing woman as an excuse to gain her trust?

Embittered tears welled up in her eyes.

The phone rang again. Roberta gave herself a moment, then answered.

"You're late," Sophie said.

"Sorry, it's been one of those mornings."

"Well, gatemaster," Sophie said, "if you value the lives of your friends and coworkers, you'll step on it. There's a crazed rummage-sale mob out here and you, little one, hold the keys to the building."

"I'm on my way."

* * *

At eight that evening Jake knocked on the door of the small house a second time. He rang the bell and resisted the urge to peer in the windows. Roberta wasn't home. As he turned away, he heard the front door open. He turned back.

She stood there, radiant. From a window at the rear of the house the setting sun provided a startling backlight. Through the white gauze sundress, the curve of her waist and her long legs were silhouetted sharply. She wore leather sandals, the thin straps laced around her ankles. Her light reddish-brown hair was down, loose, the long spiral strands a fiery, glowing cloud about her head. Large gold hoop earrings caught the light, sparkled.

The only word to describe the way she looked standing there with the rosy light caressing her from head to toe was heavenly.

"Hi," was all he could muster.

She stared at him with an expression that at first he thought impassioned, then decided it was apathetic, and finally realized it was both. Did she already regret their display of passion at the door the night before? The memory for him was quite pleasant, but then, he didn't have someone waiting for him in New York.

She stepped back, opening the door to allow him to enter.

Jake crossed the threshold, sensing the tension.

"Why the charade?" she said, softly closing the door.

There was definitely something wrong. "I don't understand."

She kept her back to him. "My mother called me this morning." Smooth, cool. She turned, leaned against the door, and added, "Don't hesitate to send her a bill. She and my father can certainly afford it."

His heart sank. *Aw, shit,* he groaned inwardly.

"Roberta," he said evenly. "I think we should sit down and calmly discuss this. I told your mother that—"

"Oh, spare me," she cut in, pushing away from the door. "Save the shrink crap for your patients . . . your *real* patients."

He stared at her for a long moment, then, "Roberta, we—"

"Not *we.* I've been alone in this all along, haven't I?"

The doorbell rang. Roberta turned and opened the door.

Carl Masser, his thick hair shining blue-black, his tight Levis and polo shirt free of sheetrock dust, the construction boss now movie-star handsome, stepped into the entry.

A surge of resentment shot through Jake.

"Hello, Roberta . . . Dr. Reynolds."

Jake nodded, turned to Roberta. He stared into her large green eyes, searching for the right words.

Carl cleared his throat, held up a ladies wristwatch. "I brought Maggie's watch. Hope it'll do?"

"Can we talk a minute?" Jake said. "In private?"

"No." She opened the door wide. "Thanks for coming," she said casually.

"Roberta, I think I know what you're planning to do, and I wish you wouldn't."

"Good-bye." She waited at the open door, avoiding his eyes.

Jake wanted to shake her. She was going to attempt to connect with the victim through clairvoyance. If she wouldn't let him guide her, then she should have the good sense to let him find someone else who was qualified. There were so many things that could go wrong.

"Dammit, Roberta, you've got to listen to me." Jake's voice became gruff.

She whirled around and strode from the room. He heard a door closing in another part of the house.

Carl stood awkwardly in the entry.

Jake turned to him. "Don't let her do it," he said tersely.

"Do what?"

"Anything using her ESP."

"What can happen?"

"Just about anything."

"I'll tell her."

"Carl, this is serious, *damn—fucking—serious."*

"Okay, okay."

Jake glared at Masser a moment longer, then shook his head and left.

He walked hurriedly to his car, looking like a man in complete control. As he passed Carl Masser's silver and black GMC pickup, he resisted the urge to smash his fist against the tinted windshield.

TWENTY-THREE

Roberta heard the front door close. She stood at the window in her bedroom and, through a gap in the drapes, she watched the doctor climb into his car and drive off. She inhaled deeply, held it, then exhaled with a rush. A moment later she joined Carl in the living room.

Carl didn't ask and Robbi didn't volunteer anything about the weird exchange at the door.

She opened a beer for him and poured a glass of iced tea for herself.

"That's as strong as it gets?" Carl asked, nodding at the tea.

"For tonight anyway. I'll need a clear head."

"You planning to go into a trance?"

"Something like that. Does that bother you?"

He shrugged. "Your doctor friend seemed to think it was . . . well, risky. Is he right?"

She shrugged, crossed the room to stand at the window. "I suspect the doctor wanted to be included. If he can't play, he doesn't want anyone else to play."

"Roberta, I don't know you, and I don't know much about séances or any of that psychic stuff, but I have a feeling it isn't a game."

"No, you're right," she said somberly. "It isn't."

"I must be nuts to go along with this. But, fuck it—sorry—but it can't hurt to believe, can it?"

"You don't have to do this."

"Yeah. Yeah, I do." He lifted the beer bottle. "Maybe I shouldn't be drinking either."

"One won't matter." She smiled. "Actually, you may need it."

"Now you really got me nervous."

"I want to try to go to Maggie tonight."

Something incomprehensible flashed in his eyes. Fear? Suspicion? Wariness? Then it was gone, and he was gulping down the beer.

"You're right, I do need this." His strained voice was followed by nervous laughter.

Robbi sat in a wing chair, removed her sandals, then put her feet up on the matching ottoman. She looked up at Carl. He was standing in the same spot, the beer forgotten in his hand, staring blankly at her. "Carl, sit down. Anywhere."

He backed up to the sofa and sat, his eyes never leaving her.

"Tell me something about Margaret."

"She hates to be called Margaret," he said with a thin smile.

She smiled back. "Go on."

"Well, she looks a little like you, except her hair is blond." He took a quick pull on the beer. "Guess you mean personal stuff, huh?"

"Whatever you care to tell me."

"She has a nice voice. A real nice voice. She's always singing along to the songs on the radio."

"What kind of music does she like?"

"Country. Crossover mostly." His voice turned quiet, reflective. "But she'll sing to anything, damn near anything. And she can bake a mean rhubarb pie. Funny," he said, chuckling, "she's a terrible cook, terrible. But nobody can touch her in the pie department."

He was sitting with his elbows on his knees, leaning forward, the beer bottle cradled in both hands between his legs. He stared at his shoes.

She waited.

"She was—*is*—crazy about animals. When she was a kid she raised a chicken as a pet. Can you believe that? There's nothing dumber than a chicken . . . unless it's a cow. Then she had a three-legged dog, a one-eyed cat, and a crow that couldn't fly. But that was Maggie, always favoring the underdog." He paused.

"Sounds like a nice person. She reminds me of my little sister. She loves animals too."

"Yeah." He finished the beer, peeled at the label on the bottle. "What do you see in . . . in these visions?"

How much should she tell him? Until she knew him better, it was wise to say very little.

"I see a woman who looks like Maggie being kept against her will. The visions are more or less flashes, images."

"Did he rape her?"

"As far as I can tell, no."

He looked down at his shoes again, nodded.

"It's getting late. We better start." She held out her hand for the wristwatch.

"When you called and asked me to bring something personal of hers, this was the first thing I thought of. She wore it all the time till it busted."

She took the watch, then sat back. The crystal was cracked. "Did Maggie wear any jewelry? Rings, chains, pierced earrings?"

"Her ears weren't pierced. She said just the thought of having holes through her earlobes was enough to make her sick. No rings either. We were gonna go shopping for her wedding set when I finished this job. I usually get a bonus if the job comes in ahead of schedule. Does . . . the woman you see wear jewelry?"

Robbi shook her head.

"What should I expect?" Carl asked.

"I'm going to try to go into a relaxed state—" She chuckled dryly. "Hell, Carl, I don't know. I've never done this before. We play it by ear, okay?"

He stared at her.

"Probably nothing will happen." She cleared her throat, inhaled deeply. "Ready?"

He responded with a feeble smile.

Robbi closed her eyes. Her thumb rubbed across the webbed glass. She felt something. Her fingers tingled, as if they had fallen asleep and were just awakening.

Outside she heard the muted sounds of traffic, of kids laughing in the neighborhood. Ice settling in her glass was the only sound in the still room.

In the dark, airless space of the stairwell, just outside the small door, sweat gathered on Eckker's body, soaking the coarse hair on his chest and back. An acrid taste filled his mouth. He felt an ache low in his gut, moving lower. His need grew.

She was only feet away, inches actually. The key to the dead bolt felt icy in his hot, trembling fingers. He turned it in the lock, heard the tumblers clunking softly. He wiped sweaty palms on the legs of his pants, opened the door, and stepped inside.

She sat on the cot, her back pressed into the corner, a rigid ball of white and gold.

He had to take the hanging light bulb away to teach her a lesson in conservation. But he had left her the flashlight—the light now anemic from constant use. It glowed from her hands, pointing upward and casting long, broad shadows. The flashlight beam listlessly floated across the carpeted ceiling and walls to center on his face.

He smiled.

She seemed to bury herself deeper into the wall. The beam of light moved down the front of his body. It stopped at his lower torso where, beneath the khaki fabric of his pants, she saw his need.

A look of horror marred the pretty features of her face.

He took a step forward and reached out for her.

She whispered, "No."

He took her arm and gently but firmly pulled her from the cot. Her body resisted, but she was feather light as he backed out of the room with her. She kept whispering no over and over.

A static excitement raced through his body. The strange odor came and suddenly he was confused. Shimmering waves of light filled the closed-in stairwell. *Not now,* he begged to himself, *not now!* Any moment now he would lose it entirely. The seizure full-blown.

Agitated, unable to control himself, he ruthlessly shoved Maggie back into her tiny room and slammed the door shut. Through the closed door he heard her sobbing, then he heard only the roaring in his head as he gave himself up to the convulsions.

One moment Roberta was staring at the watch in her hands and the next moment wild images flashed behind her eyes. A bright kaleidoscope of colors and shapes whirled through her mind in hysterical animation. A rushing filled her ears. Roberta felt as if she were being sucked into a vortex, whirling helplessly, gaining velocity, the dazzling impressions growing brighter, louder until she wanted to scream. Hysteria. Chaos. *Stop! Stop!*

Everything stopped.

Black. Silent.

No perception of time, space, direction.

No feeling, senses dead.

A vacuum without sound or movement.

Nothing.

Nothing.

Roberta was paralyzed with fear. Where was this place? Why was she here? Would she ever get out?

TWENTY-FOUR

It was pitch-black. Joseph Eckker pulled himself up from the dirt-packed floor, his weak, sweat-drenched body still a prisoner of the violent muscle spasms. He leaned against the small door in the stairwell.

When he was again able to think rationally, he was relieved that Maggie was in the safe room. She wouldn't have known what to do for him. It would've scared her to see him like that. All his life people had shied away from him because of the fits. Kids in school and at the state detention had teased him, until he got too big to be teased. No one teased him now.

Roberta endured. The vacuum remained absolute. The blackness reminded her of her blindness. Time did not stand still, but seemed to crawl slowly, endlessly. She wondered how long she had been frozen in this empty space; when she finally returned to her physical self, would she be surprised to discover that only a few minutes had elapsed?

If she returned to her physical self.

Soon she felt a vibration, a tingling. Though she was unable to see it, she sensed, by a sensory mechanism in her mind, that her arm was pushing through the oppressive void. A hand took hers.

Roberta tried to pull herself forward. A rushing sound. She felt motion again. She had a strong feeling of falling, then she slammed into the body pulling on her hand. Masculine arms held her securely.

She opened her eyes to find herself standing and in the muscled arms of Carl Masser.

She moaned. She felt dizzy, sick to her stomach.

Carl lowered her into the chair. He knelt in front of her, an odd expression on his face.

"How long?" she managed to say through an incredibly dry throat.

"Thirty, forty minutes. It seemed like a lifetime."

Robbi looked at the clock. Six past nine. They had begun the experiment at eight-thirty.

"What happened?" he asked. "What did you see?"

"Time in a bottle. Like the Jim Croce song."

He looked confused. "Did you see Maggie?"

She shook her head. "No. I'm sorry, Carl." That she hadn't connected with Margaret Winston gave her a sinking feeling. Was Maggie already dead?

"What now?" Carl asked.

She closed her eyes, rubbed her temples. "I don't know. God, I don't know."

"You looked whipped. Listen, you get some sleep. I'll leave now, get outta your hair." He headed for the door. "Tomorrow, we'll get together tomorrow." Then he was gone.

Exhausted, she went to bed, but sleep was a long

time coming. Flickering scenes stole into her head. Superimposed over images of Jake making passionate love to her in a grassy meadow, she saw nightmare pictures of women in long white dresses crawling from a pit, their lost and mournful cries raining down on them.

TWENTY-FIVE

Eckker had taken Margaret into his woods, careful to stay clear of man-made landmarks. With pride he showed her the wonders of the forest. The creeks, the thimbleberries—ripe and falling from the vines—the delicate ferns, the field of wildflowers. He had found several kinds of mushrooms, explained how to tell the edible from the poisonous. He pointed out the animal burrows, rattlesnake hiding places, tracks of a bear. They had even seen a black bear high atop a rocky plateau. A mere speck without binoculars, but its presence had visibly shaken her.

They headed down the slope as the last trace of twilight brushed the sky. Darkness crept through the trees melding with the shadows. Until the bear sighting, she'd been unimpressed, sulky even. She was still sulky, but fearful now.

He had shown her the beauty all around them. How could she not fall in love with it? Her dislike for his way of life, for the very mountain, made her a bad choice for a companion. And it continued to get worse. Each day she became more sullen, hostile even.

She was such a disappointment. *Like all the others.*

It would take a special woman, a woman with grit, a woman who loved the wilderness, a woman not too set in her ways. A much younger woman maybe. The first two had pretended to be happy, but in the end he knew. The third one had cut her own wrists and bled to death in the safe room. And the last one had fought him constantly, making his life a living hell. And now Maggie. Moody Maggie. If only she'd try. There was only one person who loved the mountain as he did. But she was forbidden.

Thinking of Tobie brought on the *need.* He looked at Maggie ahead of him on the path. She was so inferior, but she was all he had.

He put his hand on her shoulder. She turned, saw the lust in his eyes. A look of revulsion flashed across her face.

"Not here . . . please," she whined. "It's dark. I'm afraid."

"Hurry then."

It was completely dark when they returned to the church. The starless night, black and solid. Rustling sounds stirred the bushes. A bird screeched. He sensed her fear. She was afraid of the dark, afraid of the wild animals, afraid of everything.

They entered the church, crossed to the rectory. He lifted the trapdoor. Waited. She held back.

"Let me go home," she said quietly.

"Home?"

"For a visit," she rushed on. "One day, there and back . . . please."

"Why?"

"There are things—personal things I'd like to have. Books, pictures, things like that."

"I'll get them for you."

She seemed to blanch at his suggestion. "No. I'm the only one who can get them. I have to be the one to go."

"You'll get your stuff and come right back?"

"Yes. Yes," she pleaded, then began to cry.

"And when you come back, you'll stop all this crying?"

"Yes, yes, I swear."

He stared long and hard at her, then nodded. He ushered her down the steps.

"When?" she asked eagerly.

"In the fall. When I go for winter supplies."

Her face crumbled. "The *fall?*" She pulled her arm away. A look of sheer hatred on her face. "You're lying. You don't intend to take me anywhere. You liar!"

"Quiet." He pulled her down several more steps.

"You filthy liar!"

He stopped. "Go then," he said, pointing upward.

She twisted to look up at the opening above. A yearning sprang into her eyes. She looked back at him, wary, mistrustful.

He marched down the steps to the living quarters, leaving her on the stairs. He sank down onto the worn overstuffed chair and waited. The stairs groaned. Above him floorboards creaked. By the squeaks and moans in the weathered wood he was able to follow her path. She had traversed the aisle and was now in the church's vestibule.

He sat, listened. There was nothing for the longest time.

He heard creaking again. Footsteps. The squeak of a

door. She had made a decision and he knew what it was.

He raised his eyes, looked up to the top of the stairs. She stood there, trembling uncontrollably. A moment later she was down the stairs. Without looking at him she rushed across the room, stooped to enter the space under the stairwell, and disappeared. The sound of her wretched sobs filled the barren lodging.

He smiled.

He got to his feet and headed for the stairwell.

TWENTY-SIX

Roberta opened her eyes to bright sunlight. She sat up abruptly, confusion clouding her mind, and looked at the clock on the nightstand. Nine past nine. Groggy, she climbed from the bed, struggled into her robe, and made her way to the kitchen.

As she filled the coffeepot with tap water, Robbi vacantly stared out the window above the sink. Light flickered before her eyes. An image flashed across her vision. She stared at the plum tree at the back of the yard. Suddenly a tall pine tree replaced it. Through the pine's spiky boughs she saw a building. It was a natural wood structure with double doors. A single window in the shape of a cross stood above the doors. A church.

The doorbell rang. The massive pine dissolved and she was again staring at the deep purple leaves of the plum tree.

A church in the woods.

Roberta's pulse accelerated. Could it be so easy? How many churches could be nestled in the pines?

The doorbell rang again. Through the living room

window she saw Carl Masser at the door. She'd forgotten about him.

She tied her robe, let him in, directed him to the kitchen and, trying to tame the mass of spiral strands falling into her face, she told him about the vision.

"It was a church in a forest of pines."

"There's a lot of forest up there," Carl said.

Pouring coffee into a filter and sliding it into the coffeemaker, she said, "But how many churches with a window above the door in the shape of a cross?"

"It's something, that's for sure."

"I'm going to get dressed. Interested in going for a ride?" she asked.

"Church hunting?"

She nodded.

"Hurry."

They crossed the state line into California. Robbi drove. She had decided that her parents' house was a good place to start. She would revisit the spot where she'd had her accident.

For the past fifteen minutes Carl had talked nonstop about Maggie. "Shit, would you listen to me. I'm making her out to sound like some kind of saint. She's no goody-goody. She has a temper. You don't want to get her riled."

Robbi saw a woman in an alley, fingernails bared, prepared to fight a giant. Then she remembered a sobbing, frantic woman, nearly drowned, clinging to her captor.

"She smokes too much. We fight about that sometimes. She promised to quit." He looked out the window, then added quietly. "Maybe she already has."

Carl continued to speak of Maggie. After a while, Robbi began to feel as if she'd known her for a long time. No longer was she a nameless victim without background or personality. She came alive through Carl.

They left the freeway and entered Truckee. She pulled up to Watts' Feed and Grain and General Store.

Inside the cool interior, with its array of farm tools and potpourri of cloying smells of fruits, vegetables, and grain, Roberta selected a couple of packs of watermelon bubble gum and a dusty bottle of Chardonnay. As the woman behind the antique cash register rang up her items, Roberta asked about local churches, showing her the pages torn from the phone directory.

"Miss, if it's around here and it's got an address, I'd know about it. There's nothing that's not on that list there."

"Well, thanks anyway," Robbi said, turning away.

"Say, you wouldn't happen to be related to the Paxtons off 267, would'ya?"

Robbi turned back. "Yes. I'm Lois's daughter."

"Thought so. That little sister of yours is a spitting image, 'cept for the hair. If she follows in your shoes, the local fellows are gonna be tripping over themselves to be near that one."

"I hope not for a few years. She's only thirteen."

"You going out to their place?" she asked Robbi.

"Yes."

"Give my regards, and tell Hanley we got that brand of snuff he ordered."

"I'll take it to him," Roberta said, reaching back into her purse.

Back in the Jeep, they drove out on Highway 267, then turned onto the narrow paved road. As she pulled up the circular drive to the sprawling ranch-style house, she heard Carl whistle softly under his breath.

"Nice, huh?" she said.

"Your old man connected with the mob?"

She smiled. "He was a doctor. A psychiatrist."

"So you were a spoiled rich kid, huh?"

She laughed lightly.

Carl started up the front steps to the massive double doors.

"No, not that way. Round the back. I always feel like I need an engraved invitation to pass through those doors."

Carl stared at her, an odd expression on his face, but he shrugged, reversed his steps, and followed her. At the back of the house they passed the stable, chicken coop, and Tobie's animal hospital and pet menagerie. The gray, wooden door to the kitchen was as austere as the front door was baroque.

Robbi leaned down and peered through the window alongside the door. A woman she'd never laid eyes on before stood at the island, cutting up a whole chicken. The woman saw them. With a stern expression she hurried around the island, the cleaver still clutched in one bulky hand, and jerked open the door.

"What you want? Who send you?" She glared from Carl to Robbi. "You not allowed back here."

"I'm Roberta Paxton. My folks live here."

The woman tilted her head, squinted some more, then said in that same gruff tone, "Nobody say you coming." She stepped back for them to enter.

"Nobody knew."

She went back to the chicken, whacked at it. "You stay for supper?"

"Yes, thanks."

The woman snapped the joint between the leg and thigh, then hacked the two pieces apart. "Nobody tell me."

Robbi put the wine in the refrigerator, then motioned for Carl to follow her.

She found her mother at a mahogany desk in the library, going over a stack of bills. At her elbow was a calculator and checkbook.

"Sweetheart," Lois said, rising and going to Robbi, "what a surprise."

"Is it a bad time? You have other plans?"

"No, of course not. You'll stay for dinner. It's just chicken. Chick, chick, chick, like every other Sunday of the year."

"That's why I came."

"Well, good." She squeezed Roberta's hand. "Now, who's this nice-looking young man standing here with you?"

Roberta introduced them. They shook hands, exchanged hellos.

"How long has the new cook been here?" Robbi said.

"Pomona came while you were in the hospital."

"What happened to the other one?"

"Oh, they tend to come and go."

"I don't wonder," Robbi mumbled under her breath, thinking of her father's disposition.

Her mother took her arm and led her from the room. "Let's get something cool to drink and then we'll sit down and talk."

With a pitcher of iced tea the three settled down in

the closed-in air-conditioned porch. In the evening, after the sun set, the windows lifted to allow the cool westerly breeze to flow through. The air now caressing Robbi's face, bringing goose bumps to her arms, was manufactured and cold.

Hooves clopping on earth sounded in the yard.

"That'll be Tobie," Lois said. "Home from the hill."

Several minutes later Roberta heard the back door open and close. Hushed voices. Then Tobie, dressed in shorts and a halter top, rushed into the sun porch.

"Robbi!" Tobie squealed. "I saw your car on the road, so I turned Prince and headed straight back. You must have read my mind. If you didn't come today, I was going to hitch a ride into Reno to see you."

Robbi met her halfway. The sisters hugged, then pivoted till they were back to back. They stood straight, waiting.

"Mom?" Tobie said, reaching up to measure for herself.

"Almost," their mother said. "Tobie, I swear you've grown an inch or two since the last time."

"If you don't stop growing, you're gonna tower over me," Roberta said.

"I don't want to be any taller than you. I think you're the perfect height."

"Tobie," Lois admonished. "We have company. Why don't you go put some clothes on."

Suddenly Tobie appeared self-conscious as Robbi introduced her to Carl.

"So this is the future heartbreaker?" Carl said. "Truckee High, look out."

"My sister's a regular wood nymph," Robbi teased.

"There's no one around here to see me," Tobie said

quietly. She sat on the three-legged stool, her chin resting on her knees, her cheeks flaming.

"Prince. That's the new horse?" Robbi asked.

"Yeah. C'mon," Tobie said, vaulting to her feet. "You have to see him, he's beautiful."

Robbi signaled to Carl to follow. As they walked through the house, Tobie whispered to Robbi, "What about Donald?"

"What about him?"

"Does he know about Carl?"

Robbi squeezed her sister's hand. "Carl's not a boyfriend," she whispered back. "This is business. We'll talk later."

The horse was magnificent. A black Arabian stallion, over fifteen hands high, with obvious good bloodlines.

"How old?" Robbi asked Tobie.

"Going on eight."

"Looks spirited."

"No, he's real gentle. Take him out." She handed Robbi the reins.

"I don't know . . ."

"Oh, please, you'll love him. Go on, Robbi, try him out."

Robbi mounted. Prince was a bigger horse than she was used to riding, and she felt slightly apprehensive. She felt his energy, his power beneath her legs.

"Roberta," a voice called out.

Roberta turned to see Hanley crossing the yard toward her.

She smiled, waved.

"If your sister told you that horse was gentle, don't you believe a word of it," he said, looking stern. "He knows only one speed, *breakneck.*"

Tobie ran to Hanley and wrapped her arms around one of his, skipping to his long strides. He patted her head affectionately. Robbi observed the exchange between her sister and the caretaker. How lucky she is, Roberta thought, to have him around in her formative years. She wished she'd had someone like Hanley to fill the void when she was growing up. Maybe that's why her sister seemed so happy and carefree.

"Hi, Hanley. I brought you something from town." From the breast pocket of her shirt, she took the canister of snuff and gave it to him.

"Why, thank you, Robbi." He reached into his pocket.

"Put your money away. It's the least I could do."

He nodded, grinned. "How ya feeling now?"

"Good, thanks." Roberta shifted in the saddle. "Carl, this is the man who saved my life when I was hurt in the woods."

Masser and Hanley shook hands. "When that horse come running back to the house, its leg broke bad, I had a hunch the little lady was in trouble. Madonna was a gentle mare and real sure-footed. This one," he said, stroking the horse's muzzle, "he can be a devil."

"He acts like a real killer," Robbi said, smiling as the horse nudged the man warmly. "But thanks for the warning. I'll be careful."

Tobie pulled on Carl's shirt-sleeve. "C'mon, I'll show you my animal hospital."

"Got any snakes?" Carl asked, obediently following.

"Timber rattlers. I'll let you hold them."

"You're kidding?"

Roberta chuckled as she watched the two stride toward the backyard, then she glanced at the house and paused, became somber. Through a ground floor window she caught a glint of light, the sun reflecting off something metallic. And then she realized what it was. Her father's wheelchair. Her father sat in it and he was staring at her, his face a stony mask.

She looked away, pulled on the reins until the horse pivoted. "I'll just take him to the edge of the woods and then back."

Prince was already moving, prancing backward, waiting for a command. She applied light pressure to his sides. He trotted several yards, cantered for a few more, then, with little encouragement from her, he shifted gracefully into a smooth gallop. In no time they were out of the yard and into the sparse copse of pine and aspen at the rear of the property, the horse easily maneuvering through the trees. She let him have his head, trepidation all but gone now as he sprinted lithely on a preordained course. Suddenly they were out of the trees and racing across the meadow toward another denser copse of trees in the distance, grass and wild-flowers melded together in a brilliant collage.

She heard a clap of thunder and her heart froze. She looked at the sky. *Not a cloud.* A heavy scent of sodden earth bit into her nostrils, and her skin became clammy, wet from the humidity. *Not a cloud in the sky.* The thunder rolled this time, long and ominous. The skin on her forehead felt tight, as if a steel band, encircling her head, were being tightened centimeter by centimeter. Her stomach quaked.

Roberta pulled hard on the reins. Prince tossed his

massive head, protesting. She continued to pull back until the horse, snorting, rearing up, slowed his pace and at last came to a full stop.

The thunder cracked, a deafening explosion reverberating in all directions. *Not a cloud, not a single cloud.* Her pulse raced; she couldn't draw a full breath. Sick to her stomach now, the bile rose into her throat, choking her. She tightened her legs around Prince.

The horse shot forward, galloping toward home in a stiff gait, his head whipping back and forth. She realized she still had the reins pulled tight, the bit cutting into his mouth. She relaxed her hold and the horse continued to carry her farther away from the dark forest beyond the meadow.

She began to breathe easier, and although her stomach remained queasy, no longer did she feel the urge to throw up. The invisible band around her head gradually eased.

Scarcely twenty yards into the trees behind the house, she stopped. The cool canopy of the trees instantly revived her. She sucked in the crisp, sweet air.

She pulled the tails of her chambray shirt from her jeans and wiped the sweat from her face and throat. She tucked her shirt in, then tipped back her head and stared at the clear sky through the treetops. Not a cloud. No thunder, no lightning, no storm. It was all in her mind.

The only explanation for what had happened as she approached the dense forest was an anxiety attack. Anxiety with a capital A.

A panic attack.

As if she didn't have enough to worry about.

TWENTY-SEVEN

Steaming bowls of chicken and dumplings, bright green peas with pearl onions, gravy, biscuits dripping with honey butter, and a cranberry mold graced the Paxtons' formal dining room table.

Tobie sat alone on one side of the long table opposite Robbi and Carl. Lois occupied the end seat. Much to Roberta's relief, the spot at the head of the table was without a place setting, vacant.

"So, Roberta," Lois said, "tell us what's happening at the center. Will they have that dinner dance again this year?"

"Next week," Robbi said.

"Robbi, can I come to Reno and stay with you before school starts?" Tobie asked.

"I'm working on it, Tobe. Maybe a week in August. Okay?"

"Can we go to Circus Circus one night and play the carnival games? I've been practicing darts and—"

"You won't be tossing away my money on asinine

amusements," a gruff voice muttered from the arched doorway.

"Pomona," Lois said quickly, "a plate for Mr. Paxton."

Cameron Paxton, in his wheelchair, was pushed into the room by Hanley. "It's the same as gambling—worse." The words were garbled and thick with saliva.

Pomona hurried from the room, returned with a plate which she placed in Lois's outstretched hand. Lois filled the plate and gave it to Pomona to take to the man at the head of the table.

"We thought you would be eating in your room tonight, Cameron," Lois said timidly.

He stared hard at his wife. "This is my house. I want a place set in this spot"—he tapped a bony finger on the table in front of him—"at every meal, whether I eat here or not. Is that clear?"

Lois nodded.

The bastard, Roberta thought. Suspecting she might not stay if she knew he'd be present, he waited until they were all seated before he appeared at the table to spoil their dinner. Again.

Paxton's gaze meandered indolently from person to person at the table as Hanley tucked a linen napkin into the open throat of his shirt.

"Cameron, this gentleman is Carl Masser, a friend of Roberta's," Lois said.

"How do you do, sir," Carl said, holding his napkin and half rising.

"I've been better," Paxton said.

Roberta toyed with the peas on her plate, kept her eyes down. Carl lowered himself back into the chair and looked around uneasily. She should have warned him about her father.

Paxton stabbed the piece of chicken with a fork and held it up, inspecting it. "There's blood at the bone. I don't care for blood and veins and gristle on my chicken. I don't care for thighs." He let the piece drop onto his plate. Peas skittered across the table.

"I'm sorry, Cameron, I thought it was the breast," Lois said. She turned to the housekeeper. "Pomona, find Mr. Paxton a breast." To her husband she said, "Would you like it cut away from the bone?"

He glowered at her, saying nothing.

"Remove the bone, Pomona. Please."

While the housekeeper went about her task, Paxton again surveyed those in the room. "You were having a discussion when I arrived. Continue."

"Robbi was telling us about the dinner reception coming up for the women's center," Lois said. She turned to Roberta. "Go ahead, dear."

With reluctance Roberta began. "Well, the center is—"

Her father cut her off, directing a question to Carl. "Mr. Masser, what do you think of all these whiny organizations that are popping up? Women's this and women's that. I say crybabies, the whole bunch of them, hiding behind the skirts of the law."

Carl cleared his throat, glanced at Robbi.

"Young man, do you hunt?" Paxton said.

"Yes, sir."

"I'll have to show you my gun collection. Done any elk hunting lately?"

"Not in a while, sir, I've been pretty busy with my job."

"What is it that you do, Mr. Masser?"

"Construction, sir. High-rise buildings, mostly. I'm super for . . ." Carl's words died away when he saw that the man, instead of listening, had turned away and was addressing his caretaker in a hushed voice.

The room became deadly quiet. The only sound was the dragging of Paxton's fork across his plate. He ate heartily. Finally he turned to his youngest daughter. "You been caring for that animal of yours?"

Tobie nodded.

"If I find that you aren't, it's gone. No second chances. Do you hear me?"

"Yes," Tobie said quietly.

"I don't intend to replace a horse for you every couple of months"—his gaze fell on Roberta—"due to negligence."

"It wasn't Robbi's fault," Tobie snapped, darting a look at her father.

"You show respect, young lady, or I'll shoot the damn thing myself."

Tears welled up in Tobie's eyes. She muttered something that sounded like "excuse me," tossed her napkin on the table, then ran from the room, a sob escaping her lips.

Hanley, sitting in a chair by the door, rose partially, hesitated, then sank back down. His white-knuckled hands clenched into fists as he watched Tobie exit.

Paxton turned to Carl. "A family of women," he said. "Weak sisters all."

Roberta caught an exchange of glances between Hanley and her mother. His sympathetic, hers disconcerted. Then Roberta felt a gentle touch on her knee. Her mother's pleading eyes seemed to say, Please don't interfere. You can walk out, but we have to live with him.

Robbi bit down on the inside of her lip, forcing herself to keep quiet.

The room was uncomfortably silent.

The invalid lowered his utensils. "Hanley, take me out. I prefer the solitude of my room to these damn silent stares."

Hanley wheeled him out.

After dinner Robbi and Carl found Tobie in the stable with her horse. Tobie insisted Carl take Prince out.

Sitting on the rail fence alongside the stable, they watched the horse and rider disappear into the trees. Robbi reached into a paper bag, brought out the bubble gum, and handed one package to Tobie.

"Watermelon! Cool. He'll have a cow if he sees this. 'Gum chewing's for sluts.'" Tobie mimicked her father.

"I remember." Robbi unwrapped a square and popped it into her mouth. "I doubt he'll ever change."

There was nothing more to be said on the subject, so they each opened another square of gum and popped it into their mouths. After an appropriate amount of silence, when they worked at chewing the sugar from the gum, Tobie blew a practice bubble, then cleared her throat.

Here it comes, Robbi thought, *the Tobie Paxton third degree.*

"So if he's not a new guy, then what is he?" Tobie, staring off in the direction of the forested slopes, asked softly as if they'd been talking about Carl Masser all along.

From experience, Robbi knew it was useless to be evasive. "His fiancée is missing. I'm trying to help him find her."

She turned to stare at Robbi, her eyes large and inquisitive over an enormous pink bubble. She sucked it back in. "Yeah? Like how?"

"It's a long story."

"I got lots of time."

"Can you keep a secret?"

"If you say 'Tobie, don't tell,' it'd take truth serum to get it out of me. You know that."

Robbi told her sister about the visions and the missing women.

"Wow," Robie exclaimed in a rush of air when Robbi had finished. "That's incredible. You're so lucky to have the power, or whatever it is, to see this stuff."

"This isn't fun and games, Tobe. It's serious." She thought of the death premonition. Then she remembered the dream, the nightmare of being chased through the woods. An urgent desire to leave, to get as far away from there as possible, rushed over her. It couldn't come true, could it? Everything had to be just right. If she stayed far from the woods on a rainy night, then it couldn't come true.

Tobie sat quietly a moment, staring off into the distance. "Sometimes I think maybe I have it."

"Have what?"

"A little of the Roberta Paxton 'inner sight,'" Tobie said, seeming to like the idea. "Maybe it runs in the family."

"What do you feel?"

Tobie became solemn again. "I'm not sure, but sometimes when I go into my room, it feels weird. Like my privacy's being invaded. Like somebody's in there watching me. And even when I'm out riding I can feel eyes on me. Does that sound totally wacko?"

Roberta managed a smile. "You're asking me?"

"I read a sci-fi story once about two sisters who could read each other's minds. Wouldn't that be cool if we could do that?"

Robbi put her arm around her sister's thin shoulders and squeezed.

A pulse pounded in Eckker's temple. From the edge of the treeline he watched the dark-haired man on horseback cut through the woods. Then he turned his attention to Tobie and the brunette sitting on the rail fence. The brunette had been riding the black horse in the forest. His forest. He didn't like strangers traipsing all over his mountain. If they got too close . . .

Jake sat in the small room that served as his office in the condo. He leaned back in his swivel chair, his feet propped on his desk, and spoke into a compact tape recorder. He reviewed certain passages, made notes, then resumed. From Roberta's descriptions of the killer's environment, mannerisms, and general make-up, Jake attempted to work up a psychological profile.

Roberta, as the receiver, was able to see the man as no other could. No other who lived to tell about it, that is. In the two visions she had seen a childlike man, eager to please, become out of control when angered—

angered to the point of murder.

Was this man a recluse, squirreling himself away in his mountain retreat, having little or no contact with the world in general? Was he impotent? Incapable of normal sexual relations? Did he derive sexual release from killing his victim?

There were so many details that only Roberta knew, points he hadn't asked her about. She had turned away from him, unwilling to let him explain the misunderstanding regarding her mother. She needed him, and he certainly needed her. He had to find a way to regain her trust.

He checked the time. Eight forty-five P.M. He looked up her number, lifted the receiver, then dialed. Before it could ring, he hung up. Go to her.

As he gathered his notes he came across the latest draft of his manuscript. He paused, shuffled through the pages with a sense of guilt. Several weeks before he'd been bursting with enthusiasm, working at a furious pace. And now . . . now it seemed so far removed, as exciting as the survival instincts of the earthworm.

He tucked the folder under his arm and headed for the door.

"Your old man's a real jerk," Carl said on the drive back to Reno.

Roberta stared straight ahead at the road.

"I like the rest of your family though. Your sister was shitting me about the rattlers." He looked over at her. "Robbi, did you . . . pick up on anything out there? Y'know, sense any vibes concerning Maggie?"

Their eyes met. She shook her head.

Conversation became sporadic, and finally ceased as Roberta and Carl neared her house. For the past several miles Robbi had been thinking about Jake. Where was he right now? What was he doing? Then, from a block away, she spotted his car parked in front of her house. Her pulse quickened.

"Company," Carl said.

Jake sat behind the wheel. He glanced over and their eyes locked for a split second before Roberta pulled into the driveway. After shutting off the engine, she looked in the rearview mirror and watched him walk up the drive.

Roberta and Carl Masser met Jake at the side entrance. Before he had a chance to say anything, Roberta invited him in.

The kitchen was hot and stuffy. Both men accepted a beer. Roberta poured herself a glass of Chardonnay. They sat at the kitchen table with the tinkling wind chimes filling the void.

"Roberta . . ." Jake began.

"Were you taking money from my mother to treat me?" she said with a tightness in her voice.

"No, I'd never do anything like that. She called me but—"

"And the woman with the ankle bracelet—Belinda—she was really a patient of yours?"

"Yes, of course."

She stared him straight in the eye. "You should have leveled with me in the beginning."

"I know."

Carl glanced from Roberta to Jake, looking uncomfortable.

Poor Carl, Robbi thought, conflict surrounded him today.

"Robbi and I went to her parents' place," Carl said. "She thought—"

"I had a vision of a church," she cut in brusquely. A restless energy had her on edge. "A church in the woods. I think that's where he's keeping Maggie."

"Any luck?" Jake said.

She shook her head. "We really didn't look. Not yet anyway."

The chimes tinkled.

"There's a breeze," Robbi said. "We could use some air." She started to rise, stopped, her hands flat on the tabletop. Her eyes became fixed on the window above the sink. She realized then the reason for her nervous energy. Something was about to happen.

TWENTY-EIGHT

Margaret lagged behind the big man on a narrow footpath that cut through thickets of manzanita and buttonbrush. The full moon, a luminous orb low in the sky, followed along.

She wore the long white dress and a pair of thin-soled shoes resembling ballet slippers—the only shoes available to her. When she stepped on a sharp pebble or twig, she made a tiny, involuntary cry. Her mood was dismal and promised only to get worse. Nearly three weeks had passed since she'd been taken prisoner by this madman who called himself Joe. Reflections of Sonny and her former life filled her waking hours, depressing her beyond all rationality.

Lately he had been as sullen as she, leaving her locked away in that cramped room for longer periods of time. The flashlight batteries were nearly dead. Without the light she would die.

Last night when she'd begged to go home, he'd told her to leave. The bastard knew she was afraid of the dark, afraid of the wilderness and what was out there, especially at night. He knew she couldn't go, and his smugness when she'd come crawling back made her want to scream, to strike out at him. And then he had come to her, violating her. For the first time she seriously considered killing herself.

And now here they were, on another of his tiresome nature pilgrimages. When would he get it through his ugly, thick skull that she would never take to this god-forsaken place.

She slowed, deliberately being difficult, refusing to share even a tiny fragment of his enthusiasm. To the left of the path a bush of wild pink roses grew. He stopped, picked a small bouquet, and pressed it into her hand.

She threw them on the ground and turned away.

From the corner of her eye she saw him bend down and pick up the roses. His blunt fingers caressed the petals tenderly.

"She doesn't see your beauty," he mumbled to the flowers. Then he crushed the roses in one massive hand, the tiny needle-sharp thorns burrowing into his palm.

She looked at him, feeling a prickle of fear.

For the longest time he stared at her, saying nothing. There was something obscure in the black eyes. Inflamed, frightening.

He held out the hand with the crushed flowers. Pin-pricks of deep purple blood rose up from the embedded thorns. "You don't want to try."

She attempted to turn away again.

He grabbed her arm, pulled her around to face him.

"I hate it here!" she cried. "I want to go. God, let me go!"

"Go," he said in a deadly calm tone. "*Go*. Get off my mountain."

Panic rose. "I don't know the way."

He squeezed her arm. She cried out, tried to wrench free.

"I won't share my mountain with you. Get off."

"Lead me down."

He laughed harshly.

She looked around frantically. "How? Which way?"

"The dress and shoes . . . leave them." He reached for her.

She stumbled backward. He could never allow her to leave this mountain alive. He was going to kill her. Suddenly she realized how desperately she wanted to live.

"I want the dress. It belongs here . . . for her." He advanced toward her. "Now or later, it don't matter."

She backed up. A mournful wail escaped her lips. And then she turned and ran.

"Roberta?" Jake said softly.

She stared out the window above the sink, then slowly lowered herself onto the chair.

"What's happening?" Carl asked.

Jake raised a hand to silence him.

Roberta's eyes flickered rapidly. She was seeing something no one else in the room could see.

Eckker waited ten minutes. Maggie had been out of sight for some time, but in the dark, and with her flimsy shoes, the going would be slow. The sound of her crashing through the manzanita, scrambling over broken limbs and bits of loose rock, had eventually died away as well. All was quiet now.

He couldn't let her leave the mountain. She had brought it on herself. She could've been happy here, but she just wouldn't try.

He began the hunt.

He moved to his left—the direction Maggie had chosen once she thought she was out of sight and sound—and forged through the brush confidently. He knew these woods. There was no place she could hide for long. No way for her to escape.

He moved forward. Stopped. Listened. No hurry, he had all night. Forward. Stop. Listen.

It was dark now. Darker inside the canopy of trees, but the moon's stark rays filtered through the branches. Her white dress would practically glow in the dark.

A twig snapped. Movement to his right. Something shuffled out from beneath the low boughs of a ponderosa pine. It was only a raccoon, its eyes fiery in the metallic light of the moon. Eckker had begun to turn away when Maggie came crashing out from a nearby tree. She passed so close he could have reached out and stroked the soft cotton of her dress. He feigned a lunge, missed, going down on his hands and knees in a bramble patch. He looked up to see her veer off to the left.

Just where he wanted her to go. The closer she got to the shaft, the less carrying he would have to do once he caught her.

He followed. She would run again, blindly, without thought, with only sheer terror driving her onward.

Twenty minutes later, tracking only by sound, he continued to pursue. Then all was quiet again.

He paused, listening.

He pictured her buried deep in dense undergrowth, her breathing labored, her heart pounding. This time she would not come out. He would have to find her. She would die before she'd run another foot. She would die . . .

He crossed the footpath and there in the recess of a giant boulder, underbrush filling the crevice, he saw something bright. A bit of white fabric.

He stooped, lifted the hem by two fingers, and began to pull slowly. He waited for the resistance, but there was none. He gave an impatient yank. The dress dangled limply in his fingers.

He whirled around just as the thick log came down hard against the back of his neck and shoulder. He stumbled and fell. He turned to see her running naked into the trees.

He had underestimated her. She had continued to run, to fight back. Although no match for him, she'd finally taken a stand. The hunt continued.

The sight of her pale body stayed within view of his sharp hunter's eyes. She ran blindly, keeping to the path. Within a quarter mile of the pond, he caught her. She cried out as his hand shot forward and grabbed her shoulder, spinning her around. By her throat he lifted her from the ground, her bare legs thrashing, kicking. Soon she lost consciousness.

Effortlessly, he heaved her over his broad shoulder, then carried her the short distance to what would be her final place on earth.

At the shaft he hauled away the fallen tree, then lifted

the wooden plank. The rank stench coming from the hole sobered him.

She regained consciousness as he reached for her. The sight of him brought the terror back into her eyes. The smell of death from the deep hole turned her into a feral beast. She twisted, beat out at him.

"Sonny!" she screamed out. "Sonny, oh, plea—!"

Eckker held her by the throat, squeezing, excitement growing in him as she struggled in vain. He squeezed until she resisted no more.

TWENTY-NINE

The ghastly image gradually faded. Roberta blinked, sucked in a sharp breath, then slowly let the air out as her body went limp. On the tabletop she laid her head in the circle of her arms. Her heart continued to hammer madly in her chest.

Jake knelt by her chair and stroked her hair, then enfolded her in his arms. She felt safe there, breathing in the clean smell of pressed cotton and a light scent that she'd come to recognize as his. She closed her eyes, blanking out everything else for the moment. Soon she would have to dredge it all up, relive it. She had no strength for it now.

"What happened?" Carl's voice betrayed his trepidation.

"Give her a minute," Jake said. He tucked a strand of hair behind her ear. "You okay?"

"I think so."

Carl handed her a tall glass of water. "It was Maggie, wasn't it?"

Unable to meet Carl's fervent gaze, she looked away

and nodded.

He stood staring at her anxiously. Robbi instictively squeezed Jake's arm.

"So tell me," Carl said, his eyes boring into hers. "Goddammit, tell me!"

"Knock it off, Carl," Jake said, "You're scaring her."

Carl knelt on her other side. "I'm sorry, Robbi. It's just—look, what did you see? Jesus, you've gotta tell me, please."

She wet her lips. "They were in the forest. She got away from him and ran. He chased her."

"Did he catch her?"

"I—I don't know," she lied. "That's all I saw—her running from him."

"You said a name," Carl said. "You yelled out a name. Why?"

"She called for someone named Sonny."

"Oh, Jesus!" Carl said in a groan, slapped at his thigh, spun around. "Oh, Jesus Christ almighty." His broad chest heaved in and out. He glared at Jake, then Roberta, his expression unreadable. "That's her nickname for me. Nobody knows that. I don't let her use it in front of other people."

Robbi glanced at Jake.

"Jesus, it's true then." He paced the length of the room, spun around. "If you didn't see him catch her, then maybe she got away."

Robbi didn't respond.

"It's possible, isn't it?"

Roberta felt a crushing weight on her chest. She nodded.

"Did you see anything that would tell us where they

are? Anything at all?" Carl asked, his voice charged with excitement.

"No. No more than before," she answered helplessly. "I saw a forest . . . trees."

"Christ, if she managed to get away from him, then she has a chance. Oh, God, she's a smart lady, she'll find a way out, I know she will." Spinning on his heel, he crossed the room, his strides long and stiff. "I gotta get home in case she manages to get to a phone." He jerked open the back door and rushed out, leaving it open behind him.

They both stared at the door.

"He killed her," Robbi said softly.

Jake slipped his hand into hers.

"I couldn't tell him. I just couldn't tell him."

"I think he knows, he's just not ready to face it yet. You probably did the right thing."

"Oh, God, Jake. It was awful."

He rose, closed the back door, then reached for the wall phone. "I'm calling the police."

"Will they believe me?"

"There's only one way to find out." He dialed, spoke several minutes, gave Roberta's address, then hung up. "I talked to someone named Avondale. He's on his way."

Jake came back, stood behind her, and began to massage her shoulders.

She brushed the hair back from her face. In a quiet voice she said, "He chased her down, caught her, then carried her to this place, this deep hole in the ground, and then . . . then—" Robbi felt the tears burning her eyes. She forced them back, came to her feet. "I'd like to take a very hot shower," she said. "I . . . I feel . . ."

"Go. I'll get the door when he comes."

She crossed the room, paused at the doorway, turned, and said, "I told Carl she'd gotten away from him. Jake, he *made* her run. It was a game to him."

Detectives Avondale and Lerner sat in Roberta's living room. For the first half hour Officer Kathleen Lerner, a striking blonde with a deep tan, in her mid-twenties, had let her partner do the talking.

"You say this man abducts women off the streets, holds them against their will for a time, kills them, then deposits the remains in a hole somewhere out in the desert?" Detective Avondale said, looking from Jake to Roberta.

"Mountains, not desert," Robbi said.

"Which mountains?" Lerner asked.

"I don't know. I assume somewhere in the Tahoe National Forest."

Avondale cleared his throat, glanced at his partner. "Do you see this sort of thing often? I mean, have you had these supernatural sightings all your life?"

She nodded tentatively. "Very infrequently, though, until the accident last month." Robbi, in a pair of gray workout tights and a pink tank top, her wet hair pulled back loosely at the nape of her neck, sat on one end of the sofa yoga fashion. Jake sat on the other end.

Avondale grunted, wrote in a notebook. "It's your belief that two women who the Reno PD have on file as missing persons may be victims of this man?"

"Yes."

Avondale sighed. "We've got this problem."

"My credibility as a psychic?" Robbi ventured.

"Naw, we've worked with psychics in the past. Right, Lerner?" He turned to his partner.

She smiled, sat up straight. "And quite successfully too. No, the biggest problem is the absence of a body. Until there's a body, there's no proof of homicide. No proof even of foul play. Granted, women have vanished, but they could be anywhere . . . safe and sound. If I'm not mistaken, the Sardi girl was a chronic runaway. I understand her own mother—"

"Filed the report after I insisted," Jake finished for her. "She didn't run, I know it." He told them about his missing patient and the ankle bracelet.

Lerner leaned forward. "Now, there's something. If that ankle bracelet turns up in someone's possession—well, you see what I mean?"

"I see."

Lerner went on. "Or, Miss Paxton, if you can pinpoint this area where you think he's dumping the bodies, we'll go out there with dogs, metal detectors, whatever it takes. Other than that, I'm afraid our hands are tied. Without witnesses to an abduction, without a body or physical evidence, without a confession . . ." She shrugged helplessly.

"I can't pinpoint anything yet. Wait—I saw a church. One of those small, wood frame chapels common around the lake." Robbi described it.

"We'll check it out." Lerner stood, brushed at a strand of blond hair.

Avondale unfolded his long frame from the wing chair. "Call us if you get anything new. We'll work with you."

Robbi showed them out. As she silently stood in the

entry, it all came rushing back to her. The scene in the woods, Maggie running for her life. Her death.

She leaned against the wall, the palms of her hands pressed to her face. Strong arms wrapped around her, pulled her close. She buried her face in the crevice of Jake's throat.

"She's gone. Jake, she was right up here"—she tapped her forehead—"and I couldn't do anything to save her."

"Roberta, stop it. There was nothing you could do."

"I *lost* her. Goddammit, I lost her." The sobs came, at first tentative, mute, then unconstrained. Carl's loss was hers as well. She had known Maggie, in her head, in her heart. A little part of her died with Maggie that night.

Jake lifted her, carried her to her bedroom and gently placed her on the bed. Moonlight illuminated the room with a quicksilver eeriness, glinting off the chrome-and-white-enamel bed.

She clung to him.

He disconnected the phone on the nightstand, slipped off his shoes and, fully clothed, stretched out alongside her. She curled around him, trying to lose herself in the warm, firm security of his body.

She was so tired. Jake stroked her comfortingly. After a indeterminable amount of time she felt herself finally drifting off.

Sometime later in the night, in a deep sleep, she dreamed of Jake, saw his clear blue eyes staring into hers. The color began to change ever so gradually until she was staring into black cyes, black as chips of flint, superimposed on blue, glaring at her maniacally.

Robbi's eyes flew open. She bolted up, a cold sweat

covering her. *She had seen his eyes mirrored in the eyes of a dying woman. Black demonic eyes.*

Jake wrapped her in his arms again. He whispered words of comfort in her ear and gently rocked her trembling body until she fell back into an exhausted slumber.

THIRTY

Monday morning Roberta woke to find herself alone in bed. Sensing another's presence, she rolled over. Jake, in a wrinkled shirt, holding a steaming cup of coffee, stood in the doorway, watching her.

He smiled.

"Hi," she said.

"'Morning." He started toward her. The doorbell rang. He paused. "Shall I get it?"

"Please."

"You might have some explaining to do. What if it's your mother?"

"It'll serve her right. Besides, I lead a much too sheltered life."

He crossed to the nightstand, set down the mug, then left the room.

Normally a morning person, this day she could hardly drag herself from bed. Her sleep had been anything but restful.

"It's Carl," Jake said from the doorway as she headed for the bathroom.

"What's he doing here?"

"I'm afraid it's my fault." Jake crossed to the phone, connected it. "I shut off the phone last night."

"Tell him I'll be out in a minute."

"I have group this morning," Jake said. "Will you be all right?"

"Yes. I'll call you later from the office. Jake . . . ?" She watched him turn again. "Thanks."

He smiled, nodded, then left.

As she dressed she thought about Jake sharing her bed and holding her in his arms all night. Jake, just by being there, had helped to soften the horror of the nightmare. Then she thought of Carl waiting for her in the other room, and a heaviness invaded her chest. Everything she'd been trying to bury these past hours resurfaced.

She found him pacing in the kitchen. His eyes were red-rimmed and bloodshot. When he spoke, the stale odor of alcohol reached her.

"What am I going to do?" he said quietly.

"Carl . . ." She felt sick. She had to tell him. She had to tell him what she saw, whether it was real or not. She stared at him, trying to find the words. "Carl, I—"

"Look, now's not a good time. I tried to call but no one answered. I wanted to make sure I caught you before you left for work. I hafta get back to the job now, but if you have something more to tell me, something you didn't say last night . . . well, we could meet later . . . for lunch."

She paused, then, "There's a deli next to your construction site. Do you know the one I mean?"

His expression froze. He nodded.

"Twelve-thirty okay?" she asked.

He stared at the floor, nodding his head woodenly.

Several minutes later as she backed her Jeep out onto the street, she saw Carl sitting in his pickup, staring out the windshield, his face devoid of expression. She felt a tremendous knot in her stomach.

Carl sat in the leather recliner that Maggie had given him for his birthday, the TV remote control in his hand. He stared absently at the screen, flipping from channel to channel indiscriminately, his thoughts on Maggie.

He lifted the beer to his mouth and drank until it was gone.

"Maggie, I haven't given up. Don't think I've given up. I'll find you, babe. Damn right. I'll find you if it's the last thing I do." He crunched the can, let it fall to the floor.

The big tomcat jumped up in Carl's lap. It purred, watching him warily with large yellow eyes. The cat rarely came around Carl. Conan was Maggie's misfit, one of an endless line of misfits that she'd taken in.

"Hey, guy, you gotta be awful damn lonely to seek comfort from me," Carl said. He reached out and scratched the tom's backside near its stubby tail. Carl remembered the morning he'd started up his pickup and nearly pissed his pants when he heard the damn thing screeching under the hood and saw orange fur flying to hell and back. Fan blade. Within an instant Maggie's long-tailed cat turned bobtailed. He'd really gotten hell for that one.

"Miss her too, don'tcha?"

The cat kneaded Carl's stomach, purred louder.

"I haven't given up on her, ol' guy. No way. No fucking w—" Carl's voice caught.

He hugged the cat to him, buried his face in the long fur, and cried.

At the deli Carl looked no better than he'd looked at her house that morning. He looked worse.

Jake had called, offered to go with her, but she had declined. She couldn't expect him to hold her hand through everything. She agreed to have dinner with him that night.

Carl brought a beer to the small table where Robbi sat.

She opened her meat loaf sandwich, lifted out the lettuce, and added catsup.

"You should eat something," she said.

"Yeah, maybe later." Carl dropped into a wooden chair. He gulped down half the beer before setting the bottle on the table.

She pushed half a sandwich toward him.

He smiled weakly, ignored it, and looked around the deli restlessly. His gaze came back to her. "He killed her, didn't he? I mean, that's what you saw?"

"Carl, I'm . . . I'm so sorry."

He didn't seem to hear her. He finished the beer and continued to swallow long after it was gone. He stared at the quartz wall clock, mesmerized, as though the vaulting second hand was beyond his comprehension. Then he laughed, a deep, humorless laugh. "Christ, we don't know for sure if Maggie's dead. I mean, you go into a trance and see someone who looks like my girl being killed by some psycho. Shit, you could be on drugs and I'm about to tear myself up over an hallucination." He chuckled this time, shook his head like it was a good joke on him. "There's no way we can be sure anyone was killed last night, especially Maggie."

"That's right, Carl." She avoided his eyes.

"Right." He slammed down the beer. *"Right!"*

Robbi touched the back of his wrist, consoling. He snatched at her hand. "You called the police?"

"Yes. Two detectives came out and took a statement."

"Did they believe you?"

"I don't know. They'd like more than what I had to offer. I have nothing concrete. Even if we find him, without evidence we have very little. One of his victims wore a gold and silver ankle bracelet. Now, if that turns up . . ."

Carl stared off into the distance, apparently deep in thought.

"Carl . . . ?"

"We had a fight that night. It was over something . . . something so goddamn stupid I can't even remember. She stormed out and I let her go. Can you imagine how that makes me feel? The last time I lay eyes on the woman I love, we're screaming at each other." A tear dropped on the tabletop. "I didn't tell her I loved her. I didn't tell her good-bye. I—" His voice cracked.

Robbi felt tears form in her own eyes.

Both his hands now held hers. Gazing down at them, he stroked her fingers pensively. "Robbi," he said softly, "help me."

"Oh, Carl . . ."

"Help me find her. I can't stand to think of her lying in a filthy hole with God knows how many other rotting bodies."

Robbi closed her eyes, saw the shaft and the tangle of limbs, and quickly opened her eyes again, nauseated. She pushed her half-eaten sandwich away.

"He's going to kill again, and you know it. Someone else's girl will end up in that hellhole, food for the worms."

"Carl, please," she said, tossing her paper napkin over the now-revolting sandwich. The psychic's words came back to her—*Lost angels . . . lost and crying out to be found . . . to be free to go on with their journey.*

"Someone's got to stop him," Carl said.

"I'm not even sure what he looks like."

"Let him know who you are. Give your identity away. If he knows there was an eyewitness to his crime, he'd hafta shut you up. We'll get the S.O.B. when he comes after you."

Roberta's heart leapt into her throat.

"Oh, that's great, Carl. And if he finds out who I am and comes after me, a lot of good I can do you, or anyone, if I'm dead."

"I won't let him get near you."

"How are you going to stop him?"

"I'll move in with you. I have a gun. You'll be safe."

"Don't ask me to do something like that."

"It won't be forever. Robbi, please, I'm begging you." There was such despair in his eyes, his voice. But he was asking too much. Much too much.

She rose abruptly, grabbed her purse, and hurried away before he could stop her.

When she returned to the center there was a message to call Gladys Sardi. Belinda Sardi's mother? Robbi sagged under the weight of so much anguish. In her job she saw pain and suffering daily. But while under the roof of the shelter, the residents were afforded a certain measure of peace and well-being.

There was nothing she could do to help Belinda or Maggie now. And what could she offer Gladys Sardi and Carl? The answer was obvious. She could give them an opportunity to bury their loved ones and get on with their lives as best they could. But there was only one way to do that. He would have to be caught. And to catch him she would have to put herself in jeopardy—offer herself and wait for him to come after the bait. A heavy price.

She picked up the phone, started to dial the Sardis' number, then put it down again. Not now, she told herself. She needed time to gather her strength. So much was happening at once.

She made it through the remainder of the day, her mind occupied with the business of the shelter. The committee meeting ran on and on, finally ending at eight P.M. Among the debris of fast-food wrappers littering her desk, she was finally alone in her office.

Roberta rubbed her temples, trying to ease the pounding in her head. She needed an aspirin, she needed sleep, she needed a vacation from all this. She called Jake and begged off on dinner, saying that she was going straight home to bed.

"Roberta, you need a break. Listen, tomorrow take the day off. Come with me and a group of kids to the lake. I could use an extra hand or two."

"Jake, I—"

"No excuses. I'll pick you up at nine in the morning. Beach clothes." He hung up before she could protest.

Before going home, Robbi, concerned for Carl Masser, dug his number out of her purse and made a call. There was no answer.

She locked up and left.

Carl Masser continued to drive slowly, hoping the rising dust from his pickup wouldn't be noticed. Right after lunch with Roberta he had driven out to the Paxton estate, though he steered clear of the main house and its occupants. It took him relatively no time to locate a wide logging road that cut through the forest into the mountains.

From this dirt and gravel road were dozens of narrower roads shooting off like fingers, crisscrossing one another. Each one ultimately ended in dense trees, steep gorges, or streambeds. He had spent the entire afternoon driving up and down unused logging roads. Occasionally he explored a hiking trail which either circled back to the main road or petered out after so many yards.

Nearing nine o'clock, as daylight gave way to dusk, Carl sat parked just off the road, wondering what to do next. He was hungry and thirsty, not to mention frustrated. He cursed himself for rushing off like an idiot without thinking to bring supplies—water at least. He had found several tiny streams and had drank until his stomach hurt, but that had been hours before and he was dry again.

The last vestiges of light faded. A few minutes more and it would have been too dark to see the faint but distinct cloud of dust down the road. Carl sat up, forgetting his thirst, and watched an old battered pickup slowly pull onto the gravel logging road and move away in the opposite direction. The pickup had turned off from a road he'd investigated earlier and had determined a dead end.

When the truck was out of sight, Carl slipped on a Windbreaker and took down the Remington 30-06 rifle from the gun rack in the rear window. From the toolbox in the bed of the pickup he lifted a sheetrock knife and dropped it in the pocket of his nylon jacket.

On foot he cut across the rocky terrain to the smaller road, then followed it for a quarter mile to a wide, dry flat creek. The road continued again some twenty feet upstream. About a mile farther up the mountain, Carl followed tire tracks to a shelter formed from solid rock and manzanita. Under the natural canopy he found blotches of darkened earth. He squatted on his heels, took a pinch of dirt, and sniffed it. Motor oil.

Adrenaline raced through his veins. From above, by plane or chopper, the old pickup would be visible. Carl searched for and located what looked like a deer trail through the manzanita. He crashed through it, unmindful of the spiny branches.

It was nine sharp when Roberta pulled into her driveway. Someone sat on the front steps reading a paperback by the dwindling light. She recognized her sister immediately.

Tobie ran to Robbi, hugged her. "Hi," she said.

"Hi. How'd you get here?"

"Caught a ride in with Hanley about three."

"Why didn't you call?"

"Didn't want to be a pest. I got water from the hose

and plums from the tree in the back. And I had my book."

"Well, aren't we little Miss Resourceful." They went inside arm in arm. "It's great to see you, Tobe, but I'm afraid I'm going to be very poor company tonight. I'm zonked."

"That's okay."

"Better call Mom and tell her you arrived safe and sound."

"She has one of her headaches."

"Oh." Robbi pulled her blouse out of her skirt and unbuttoned it as she moved toward her bedroom. "There's a six-pack in the fridge. Help yourself."

"Beer?"

"Root beer." She undressed to her underwear, went into the bathroom, and began filling the tub. "If you're hungry you can toss a TV dinner into the microwave. It's all I have."

Several minutes later Tobie came into the bathroom. She sat on the hamper, flipped the pop top on the root beer, then said, "Can I stay awhile, Rob?"

Robbi, washing her face, looked at her sister in the mirror. "You mean now instead of August?"

"Yeah, and longer than a week?"

"Oh, Tobe, I don't know what to say. Any other time I'd be thrilled to have you. But things aren't too good right now. In fact it couldn't be worse." Robbi sensed danger and she didn't want her sister involved. Tobie was better off at home.

The girl stared down at the A&W can in her hand. She pressed her lips together, a halfhearted nod followed.

"Next month," Robbi said. "For two weeks, at least.

Movies, Circus Circus, the mall, we'll do it all. Promise."

Tobie grinned. "Oops, there's the buzzer on the nuker." She hurried out. "Is it okay if I turn on the TV and eat in the living room?"

"Sure." Robbi shut off the tap, poured a generous amount of Epsom salts into the water, stripped off her underwear, and climbed into the tub. She settled down with a deep sigh, her head resting on a folded towel.

THIRTY-ONE

Through the gray haze of cigarette smoke, Joe Eckker watched. The blonde sat alone at the end of the bar, dropping quarters into a video poker machine. Every so often she looked up, her cool gaze sweeping the room as if watching for someone.

Lifting his beer mug, he closed his eyes and drank deeply. When he looked back toward the bar he saw a shimmering aura surrounding the woman. The aura began to rise from her in radiating waves to spread throughout the entire room. The strange odor came. Friction danced along nerve endings. The familiar warning signs.

He rose quickly, knowing that soon he would feel confused, agitated. No one could see him like this. They'd think he was crazy. They always thought he was crazy.

He strode toward the back exit, down the long dark hall. He burst through the door into the alley only moments before his powerful muscles were gripped by the violent, relentless spasms—

* * *

Robbi gasped, sputtered as her throat filled with water. She was drowning.

She threw herself forward in the bathtub, coughing, trying to clear her lungs. She inhaled greedily, felt her throat open at last to receive the air. Clutching the side of the tub, she laid her face against the cool white porcelain and breathed in tight, ragged breaths.

She looked up to see Tobie standing in the doorway, her face anxious.

"Robbi, you okay?"

"Yeah. Just took in a little water."

Tobie came into the room, sat on the hamper again. "You had a vision, huh?"

Roberta nodded, but volunteered nothing.

After several long moments Tobie said, 'You had a vision about Ronnie once, didn't you?"

Just the mention of her brother's name made her heart ache. "Once."

Tobie sat on the floor, her back against the hamper. "How come our own father doesn't like us?"

Roberta sighed. How many times had she asked herself that same question? She thought she knew why he hated *her,* but she would never understand his indifference to Tobie. "I think he loved Ron so much, that when he died, all his love died with him."

"Does he blame you for Ron's death?"

Roberta considered the question for a long time. "I don't know." But Roberta blamed herself.

The Jeffrey pines gave off a sweet scent of vanilla. If

not for the full moon, the forest would have been impenetrable. Nearly an hour had passed since Carl had left the natural carport to follow the deer trail. His search had turned up nothing.

Again he cursed himself for the fool he was. Rushing off without provisions had been the dumbest thing he'd ever done. But hell, he told himself, there was nothing rational about this whole fucking mess. His woman disappears. An amateur psychic tunes into it like it was *As the World Turns,* then tells him Maggie's been killed just when he felt they were getting close to finding her.

Carl continued on, blazing a new trail, no longer eager or confident. It was impossible at night without a light. How did he expect to find what he was looking for in the huge forest? He'd be lucky to find his way back to his truck.

Fifteen minutes more, that's all. Then he'd give it up for the night. Tomorrow, with the proper provisions, he'd return, comb every inch of this range.

Eckker had come to in the alley, his back against the rough stucco exterior of the building. Two male cats squared off at his feet, hissing, then wailing in that god-awful, mournful cry of challenge. He kicked out at them. Instead of sending them off, the sudden movement surprised them into combative action. They rushed at each other, screaming; fur flew in clouds.

He groaned, shimmied up the wall until he stood, his knees weak, his head pounding.

The cats had separated again. They glared at each other, guttural moans low in their throats. He moved toward them. The closest cat, an immense gray tabby, divided its attention between the giant lumbering toward him and its tan adversary. The man growled. The two cats scattered in opposite directions.

He rubbed his large, callused hands over his face.

It was over for the night. After a seizure, control was gone. He could turn into a wild man. He'd try another night.

He headed for the parking lot and his truck.

That's it, Carl told himself when he tripped over an exposed root and pitched forward in the dirt. *Pack it in.*

On his knees, through the seemingly endless line of vertical trees just ahead, Carl saw a solid rectangular mass. With his breath coming in deep gulps, he leapt to his feet, then jogged ahead until he was close enough to see a wooden structure nestled snugly in the pines.

Staying within the shelter of the trees, Carl worked his way around the building. At the front, above double doors, he made out a large wooden cross.

"Jesus," he breathed. Jesus Christ almighty, Roberta was right. Here in the woods, miles above her parents' property, was the church she'd seen in a vision.

He quietly moved from tree to tree, taking it in. The north side of the structure was gone. The roof sagged, large portions missing, open to the stars and treetops. The interior a mere shell.

His heart raced. Robbi had seen a church, and it was there, not much more than a façade, but a church just the same. His excitement turned to despair. If the church was real, then was Maggie's death no less real?

A sudden rage consumed him. The sonofabitch. The filthy sonofabitch couldn't kidnap his woman, kill her, then expect to get away with it. No fucking way.

The one in the old pickup was the one he had to reckon with. The bastard was gone now, no doubt to look for another unwilling companion for his mountain retreat. Carl had to get inside his living quarters. There was, after all, a slim chance Maggie was still alive. He tightly gripped the rifle, patted the sheetrock knife in the pocket of his Windbreaker, then cautiously approached the old church.

Inside the dilapidated ruin, behind the altar, it took Masser another twenty minutes to find the trapdoor in the wooden planks of the floor. On the first step was a flashlight. He flipped it on and descended the steep staircase. Within minutes Carl was down in an airless, sparsely furnished basement surrounded by the rank odor of unwashed bedding and decaying food.

It took him only a few minutes to make certain the place was vacant. The squat door cut into the stairwell stood open. Carl waved the flashlight beam inside. Another door at the back of the stairwell, at the high point, was also open. Carl ducked, went in.

He stood hunched over in the tiny room at the end. An army-issue cot with a lavender spread took up most of the space. Pictures torn from magazines hung on carpeted walls. The room, Carl realized, was meant to look homey, feminine. It was the most depressing room he had ever seen. *Maggie's room.* Carl swallowed over a vast lump in his throat.

He quickly returned to the main room. In a makeshift closet he found women's clothing. Alongside a soiled white dress, a black skirt and white blouse hung on a hook. Carl stiffened, backed away.

Several footlockers sat along the east wall. He hurried to the nearest one and lifted the lid. He laid the rifle on the floor and began to rummage through the items. It was filled with men's winter apparel—longjohns, wool socks, and plaid shirts, stocking cap and gloves. The second footlocker held women's things. A straw hat with a wide brim, a vanity set—mirror, comb, and brush, toiletries. The brush contained strands of long blond hair.

Feeling sick to his stomach, Carl dropped the brush and was about to close the lid when the beam caught a reflection. In the corner of the locker something metallic glinted. Carl lifted out a bracelet of gold and silver. A tiny silver star charm dangled from it.

There was something about a bracelet. What? Robbi had said the woman before Maggie had worn a bracelet. No, not a bracelet, but an ankle chain. Excitement raced through him. *This was proof!* This was the evidence Robbi spoke of in the deli.

"Oh, Christ, Robbi, you were right," he muttered aloud. "You saw it! You really saw the fucking bastard do it!"

A huge black boot stepped on the rifle at Carl's feet. A hand the size of a medicine ball reached down and snatched the ankle bracelet from his fingers. Carl instinctively lunged for the rifle. The man grabbed him in a chokehold.

The big man squeezed. "Who's Robby?" he growled in Carl's ear. "What did he see?"

Bright spots danced before Carl's eyes. The man was choking him. Carl grappled to get to the sheetrock knife in the pocket of his jacket. The rifle was out of reach. His only chance was to get the knife.

"Who's Robby?!"

The man was crazy! His arm was cutting off all the air and Carl was unable to utter a word. His neck felt about to snap. He struggled, his mouth opening and closing in desperation as he fought to stay conscious.

Abruptly the pressure eased. He was still being held in the headlock. Any moment the choking could resume. Carl sucked deeply, filling air-starved lungs. At the same time his fingers closed around the handle of the knife.

"Talk! What does he know?"

Carl felt his other arm being wrenched up behind his back. He screamed out in pain.

"She . . . saw everything, you . . . crazy *bastard!*" Carl blurted out. He inched the knife from his pocket. "You killed Maggie—" Carl's arm shot out and took a wild swipe at the side of the man's neck with the knife. The man jerked back. Carl felt coarse whiskers along his knuckles. There was a measure of resistance as the triangular blade sliced through something.

A low bellow, an inhuman sound, erupted from the big man. He wrestled the knife from Carl's hand and, with a ferocious spark in his black eyes that made Carl's gut twist painfully, he drew the blade across the front of Carl's throat.

"What's her name?" the man whispered hoarsely.

But Carl would never tell. He was incapable of telling. Blood and air whistled out of the severed larynx and trachea. In a matter of minutes Carl lost consciousness. Death followed soon after.

* * *

Eckker disposed of the man's body in the shaft with the others. Then he found Masser's silver and black pickup. As he drove the truck to the Truckee airport—where he would abandon it in the parking lot—he thought about this bad turn of events. According to the dead man's Nevada driver's license his name was Carl Masser. He must have come for Maggie. But how did Masser know where Maggie was?

Robby? Who was Robby?

He thought hard. Someone . . . this Robby, had seen him kill. When? Who? Maggie or Belinda? Then he recalled that rainy afternoon in the woods. Maggie—no, it was Belinda that time. Belinda had gotten away from him at the church. She had given him quite a chase. An hour later he had caught her near the east boundary, and it was there they had shared their last moments together. He forced his mind to concentrate on that particular part of the hunt. Belinda had been in sight the entire time. At one point, just before bringing her down, he'd seen her stop and stare at something on the ground, but only for a moment, then, with him close behind, she'd raced on a dozen more yards. End of hunt.

Eckker squeezed his eyes shut tightly. Now he remembered. He'd heard something in a stretch of saplings just below Cutter's Ridge—the cliff had partially given away in the steady downpour. A wounded animal, he'd guessed. Before he could investigate, he was interrupted by the sound of someone approaching. Not wanting to be discovered, he'd quickly retreated.

Robby? Robby who? Masser knew. He hadn't meant to kill Masser. He'd lost control. In one of his black rages he'd slashed the man's throat before he realized what he was doing.

It was his temper that always got him in trouble. If only people wouldn't cross him . . . wouldn't give him reason to snap like that.

He thought of Celia. Sweet, beautiful Celia with her long blond hair and innocent blue eyes—his first love. He'd been sixteen, nearly twenty years ago, but the memory was still so fresh, so vivid. He had found her all alone at the lake that afternoon. He still loved her even though she had been responsible for the eighteen months he'd spent on the detention farm. He offered her another chance, but she'd struck out at him, called him names, threatened to have him locked up again. He couldn't bear being locked up, he loved the open spaces too much. So he'd snapped. Even now, after all those years, he still thought of Bluegill Basin as their place. He hadn't been back. But Celia was still there, tied to an anvil in the deepest part of the lake . . . waiting.

Eckker pulled to the side of the road. He emptied out Masser's wallet on the seat of the pickup. Sorting through the credit cards and paycheck stubs, he found half a cocktail napkin with a name and number written in red pencil: Roberta Paxton 555-2441.

Roberta Paxton. *Robby.*

THIRTY-TWO

Roberta, with Tobie sharing her bed, slept fitfully. The running nightmare played over and over in her head. At midnight, so as not to disturb her sister, Robbi took her pillow and moved to the living room couch. The dream continued throughout the night, leaving her exhausted by morning.

Roberta called Sophie, told her that her sister was in town and she was taking the day off. Then she tried Carl again. No answer. She'd call again that evening.

Over a breakfast of toaster waffles, canned peaches, and coffee, Robbi told Tobie about their proposed day at the lake.

"Hurry and eat, Jake will be here soon," she called out on her way into the bedroom.

Into a tote bag she stuffed a change of clothes, a couple of swimsuits, Windbreaker, sunscreen, and some toilctries.

"Who's Jake?" Tobie asked, entering the bedroom.

"A doctor I know."

"Is he cute?"

"Judge for yourself."

"He's cute. I can tell by your voice and the spacey look in your eyes," Tobie said. "What about Donald?"

Robbi paused. Should she tell her sister that her relationship with Donald was probably over? She snapped the tote bag closed. "You ask too many questions."

A few minutes later, when the yellow school bus arrived filled with nine outpatients of St. Mary's Hospital and several parents, Tobie and Roberta boarded.

As the bus headed for the freeway, Jake introduced everyone. Robbi noticed that some of the children were without hair—a side effect of chemotherapy; several of them were missing limbs, but all of them appeared bright-eyed, energetic, and ready for a day at the lake.

For Robbi, the day turned out to be special. The children marveled and exclaimed over every little thing. Some fished with Tobie, others were taken on boat rides by Jake, and the less ambulatory sat with pails and shovels along the sandy shore. On the beach under a vast rectangular canvas tarp suspended on poles, they ate deli box lunches.

At six P.M. the group boarded the bus for the journey back to Reno. Jake, Roberta, and Tobie stayed behind. They stood in the road and waved back at the kids in the belching, backfiring bus until it turned the corner and disappeared.

As a gentle breeze rippled the lake's surface and stirred the leaves of the aspens, they climbed into Jake's vintage '40 Ford pickup and started off around the lake.

They took Highway 28 to Kings Beach, then cut off north on 267, the road to the Paxtons'. The three filled the tiny cab. The stick shift lever rose out of the floor and Robbi, no matter where she put her legs, seemed to be in the way when Jake shifted gears, which he did often on the curvy two-lane highway. They both pretended not to notice, but the charged air in the cramped quarters was palpable.

They reached the house by seven-thirty. Lois Paxton, just rising from her bed, the worst of the migraine over, asked that they occupy themselves until she had dressed and could visit with them.

With the sun low in the sky, Tobie brought Prince around, and when Jake and Robbi declined to ride, she mounted him bareback and took off, leaving them alone in the yard.

"So this is where you had your accident?" Jake asked.

She stared toward the trees. "Out there somewhere."

"Feel like taking a walk?"

Robbi held back. "Not really."

"Then we won't."

"What you mean is that we *should.*"

"Sometimes it's best to confront the fear before it gets a real foothold."

"How'd I know you'd say that?"

His smile was reassuring.

She began to walk in the direction of the meadow. "We'd better hurry; it'll be dark soon."

Atop a large boulder Joe Eckker lay on his stomach, staring at the reflection of the setting sun in the water.

She was late. It occurred to him she might not come at all.

He had to see her.

He scrambled down from the boulder. At the bottom he paused, listening. Somewhere far below could be heard the echo of hooves. He started down the mountain.

As Robbi and Jake made their way through the woods, Robbi's heart occasionally skipped a beat. She repeatedly pushed thoughts of the recurring nightmare away. Jake was with her, she'd be okay. There were no clouds, no chance of rain.

She tried to lose herself in conversation. She told him about her vision in the tub the night before; told him she suspected the killer had been stalking another woman before having a seizure in the bar. It was dusk when they reached the meadow.

Robbi stopped at the edge of the tall dry grass and stared toward the copse of trees on the other side.

"What do you feel?"

"From here? Nothing more than a little apprehension." She pointed straight ahead. "It happened somewhere across the meadow, deep into that forest. I can't say where exactly."

Jake looked to the horizon, the jagged outline of the mountain. The sun had already set though it was still light.

"We better head back," he said.

Robbi gratefully turned and led the way.

On the walk back they were unusually quiet. Every now and then Robbi stooped to pick up a pine cone, examining it first before deciding whether or not to keep it. She explained to Jake that she collected them for craft making.

When she could carry no more, Jake began to gather them. As they neared the rear yard, the lights from the house visible through the trees, several cones fell from her overloaded arms. She bent to pick them up and more tumbled out. She laughed as she retrieved one, only to lose two more in the process.

"What we have here is the case of the monkey with his fist in the jar. He traps himself out of sheer greed, refusing to open his fingers and let go of his meager cache."

"Here, I can remedy the greedy-monkey dilemma," Jake said. He dropped his armful of pine cones, pulled is knit shirt over his head, laid it out on the floor of the forest, and filled it with the cones. Robbi deposited hers on top. He brought two ends together to make a satchel. "There's room for more," he added.

Robbi looked around. A large ponderosa pine stood to her left. She circled the tree, searching. As she reached for a prickly cone, a rustling noise made her pause. A tiny dormouse scurried out from a mound of leaves and ran over her foot. Startled, she cried out and rose abruptly, only to be seized from above by low-hanging boughs.

She grabbed at her hair, trying to free the long strands.

"Here, hold still," Jake said in an amused tone, reaching up to work at the branches.

Standing very close, he manipulated gently to loosen her hair. She felt a radiating warmth from his naked torso.

She wobbled, her feet unsteady upon a network of exposed twisted roots.

"Hold on to me," he said softly into her ear.

She put her hands on his chest and felt curly, fine hair beneath her palms; heat pulsated into her fingertips. He smelled manly; he smelled of the sun and of the forest and of the lush natural elements surrounding them.

When the last trapped strands were free, he seemed reluctant to move away. His fingers, like the tree branches a moment ago, became buried deep in her thick hair.

He pulled his head back slightly to look into her eyes. In the remaining twilight she watched the pupils of his keen blue eyes grow large; his eyelids grew heavy, closing. She leaned into him as he used his body to press her against the broad tree at her back. His lips, when they met hers, were warm and supple.

The kiss was deep, sweet, and searching, their lips alive with a current that sang through her body and made her heart trip rapidly. Her mind reeled with the sensations of the moment. His smell, his taste, his warm skin beneath her hands. The only sound was the rushing of her pulse in her ears.

His mouth seared a path to her throat, his hands brushed over places that had suddenly sprung to life, places that cried out to be caressed, commanded, triumphed over. Her body grew warm, matching the incredible heat of his bare skin that penetrated her layers of clothes to her aching breasts beneath.

She wanted him. Here, now, on a bed of pine needles and maidenhair ferns, the warm night air permeated with the earthy aroma of all organic life around them.

Somewhere behind them a dry branch snapped.

Within yards of the house he came across two people leaning against a tree, embracing. Stunned, Eckker pulled up short. Tobie with a lover? Impossible! She was *his*. Rage exploded within him. If he couldn't have her, nobody could. He would charge them, tear them to pieces, beat them with his fists until they were nothing but bloody, fleshy pulps.

He advanced several yards in a blind fury before the clopping sound of hooves echoing through the woods stopped him cold. He listened a moment, his pulse racing.

Tobie?

Jake's lips came back to hers, his hands reached under her shirt to caress her feverish skin. He inched her shirt upward until flesh met flesh. She'd never made love in the woods before. The thought filled her with a tingling anticipation. A delicious ache throbbed in a feverish core low in her abdomen.

The steady beat in her body migrated to her head. She heard it pounding in her ears like the hoofbeats of a horse, felt the ground beneath her feet vibrate. It slowly dawned on her that was exactly what she was hearing—the hoofbeat of a horse—Tobie's horse.

"Yoo-hoo. Hello?" her sister's voice called out.

Without releasing her, Jake loosened his hold on Robbi, allowing her shirt to slide down. His mouth nuzzled her ear as he said, "She's a sweet kid, but I hate her."

She laughed lightly. His mouth covered hers, muffling the sound.

The hoofbeats were deafening, the clatter diminishing gradually to a prancing tattoo.

Robbi and Jake turned their heads to see Tobie astride the black stallion. She glanced at them, looked away, a shy smile on her face.

"Oops," Tobie said. "Sorry. Mom sent me out to get you, Robbi. I could tell her I couldn't find you."

Jake smiled and stepped back. He took hold of Robbi's hand and pulled her away from the tree. Together they went to where his shirt was spread on the ground. Robbi tossed several pine cones on top of the others, Jake lifted the makeshift satchel, and, without a word, they headed back toward the house, the horse and rider following.

Jake dumped the cones into the bed of his pickup, then shook out the shirt and put it on again. Robbi took him around to the back door and they went in through the kitchen. She plucked pine needles and chips of bark from his shirt.

"Looks like you've been rolling in the forest," she whispered.

"Don't I wish," he whispered back as they joined her mother in the living room.

Lois Paxton insisted they stay for one cup of tea. She smiled as she glanced from her daughter to Jake, as if pleased they were seeing each other again. Yet nothing was said on the subject. Forty-five minutes later Jake and Roberta said good-bye and left.

In the truck, halfway down the long driveway, Jake looked over at Robbi. He laid his hand on her thigh and gave it a slight tug. Robbi slid over close to him. He shifted gears and as he did so the backs of his fingers brushed maddeningly along the inside of Robbi's bare thigh.

"Come home with me," he said.

Her answer was to press his hand down on her leg and to lay her head on his shoulder.

He shifted again, his hand caressing her inner thigh.

She shivered.

The old pickup followed at a discreet distance.

THIRTY-THREE

At Jake's high-rise condominium, Robbi stood in the middle of the living room and took in the surroundings. The furniture was modern. Glass, brass, and leather in a color scheme of off-white, black, and gold. Here and there a bit of bright peacock blue emerged. Large paintings by Vasques Q. in strong, bold hues of black and white accented the light walls.

While Jake fixed drinks, Robbi took her time looking at wall photos of Jake and his family and their two-story frame house. The front porch, the old fashioned kind right out of *Mayberry R.F.D.*, with its porch swing and wicker chairs, seemed to be a favorite spot for family picture taking. Dates, in five-year increments, were inked in at the bottom. The earliest showed five females and three males. Jake, skinny as a stick, was the only boy child. Roberta felt a strange tugging in her belly. She moved on to the next photo. Now only four females on the porch—the mother had died. In each successive photo the children grew, became adults, had children of their own. The last picture was dated the spring of the present year. Eleven adults and over a dozen kids crowded on the porch. A reunion.

Roberta crossed the room and let herself out onto the balcony. Four floors up, the view of the tree-lined river and the downtown buildings caught her breath. With a full moon reflecting on the river and the casinos brilliantly lit, the view was spectacular.

A cricket chirped in the brush below. The night air smelled of grass and juniper. Roberta leaned on the rail, listening to the rushing river. Sparks of white flashed where the water broke over the jutting rocks and logs.

"Sure you're not hungry?" Jake asked, coming up behind her. He handed her a glass of chilled white wine.

She shook her head, took the glass, and thanked him. "Are you?"

He smiled that boyish smile and moved his head slowly from side to side. "Not for food."

He set his glass on the rail and turned to her. She followed suit. They melded into each other's arms, their lips meeting in a stirring kiss that seemed to pick up where the kiss in the woods had left off. Within minutes Robbi's smoldering passion, passion that on the drive home had been kept alive by his exploring hand on her thigh, was rekindled.

Jake pulled away and silently led her into the deeper shadows of the balcony. He reached inside the sliding glass door and flipped a switch that extinguished all the lights. Across the river, twinkling lights reflected brightly in the moving water. Jake slipped his feet out of his shoes, then he crossed his arms, took hold of his shirt, and peeled it off.

"I like watching you do that," she said, low in her throat.

"Taking off my shirt?"

"Ummm."

"Sounds like I do it often."

"Ummm," she murmured, nodding her head.

He gingerly tugged at her T-shirt. "Show me how it looks."

Staring into his eyes, Robbi took hold of the hem of her shirt and, gathering it in her fingers, slowly pulled it up and over her head. She rested her wrists on top of her head, letting the shirt drop to the floor.

Jake stepped closer. "That was nice." He brought his hands up as if to caress her breasts, but instead he stroked the insides of her raised arms. His fingertips went as far as her elbows, then traversed back down, under her arms, along her sides, to pause at the waist-band of her shorts.

Robbi's fingers went to the catch at the front of her bra, snapping it open. She parted the silk cups, arched her chest to loosen the straps from her shoulders. The bra dropped to the floor with her shirt.

Jake gazed down at her. His hands gently cupped her breasts, his thumbs lightly brushing across her nipples. He leaned down, kissed them, his tongue tracing their contours, their texture, tasting, teasing.

She sighed.

He took her hands in his and backed up, pulling her along until they were inside the condo. Scarcely clear-ing the threshold, he caught her to him, the crisp hair of his chest tickling her sensitive breasts, and kissed her again.

His hand slipped between their bodies and undid the

button at her waist. Then he unzipped his own jeans. He knelt on one knee, removed her canvas shoes, then carefully pulled down her shorts and panties; she stepped out of them. His hands caressed the backs of her knees, her thighs, her buttocks.

Roberta coaxed him up. She wanted to be held by him, to feel his hot skin flush against hers. Then they were kissing again. She loved his kisses. They were tender, lingering, urgent, and fiery.

He buried his fingers in her hair, said her name softly.

She tugged at his jeans.

Jake stripped off the rest of his clothes. He lowered her to the thick carpet. Again his mouth sought to drive her mad. With an urgency she failed to understand, she wanted him inside her. Deep inside her as one. It was essential she experience the bonding of their bodies, the mingling of their energies and escalating passion now, before it was too late. Too late? Too late for what? She pushed the unformed thoughts away. *Now,* it must be now.

She reached for him, stroked the solid, rigid length of him.

"Oh, Jesus." It was a half sigh, half moan.

He supported himself above her as she opened herself to him. He entered her. Slowly, filling her up. Looking into his eyes, she saw a primordial hunger, a hunger for her that served only to heighten her own desire. Intense. A look that seemed beyond desire, closer to anguish, pain. Where was that faint smile? That teasing glint? What was it about a man whose usual contenance was playful—boyish almost—what was it that made the awakening passion in his eyes so damn sensual? When he looked at her in that way, that soul-searching, erotic way, it was as though she could see the two of them making love in the reflection of his eyes—his mind's eye. She wanted to cry with sheer pleasure, the sheer agony of it.

Slowly he moved inside her, slowly and rhythmically. He continued to look into her eyes. She marveled at his face, his eyes were soft, loving, yet the muscles in his jaw tense, as though he struggled with an inner tumult. They shared, she realized then, the same sharp joy, the same pure torment.

She had never felt this degree of passion or pleasure. It was something she had not even allowed herself to imagine, so inconceivable was the ecstasy.

His hand moved from one breast to another, caressing. Pinpoints of pleasure spirited about wherever he touched. They moved together now, matching rhythm, as though they were one, had always been one. Gradually the rhythm increased until he was thrusting into her, his strokes long and swift. His breathing quickened; her breath came in sharp gasps.

She had a vague sense of a storm building inside her, gusts swirling and battering at her soft, tender places. She heard the rumbling, crashing sound of thunder in her ears. An amassed electrical energy gathered. She closed her eyes and saw flashes of light, strokes of charged power streaking throughout her body. *Lightning.* Would it snake down, penetrate her most inner core, burst her asunder? She welcomed it. It was the only way she could possibly endure this relentless onslaught.

And when his urgent, driving motion forced the raging storm inside her to erupt into a devastating climax, she cried out, clinging tightly to him. His mouth was kissing hers savagely. An instant later he was pulling her to him, his throbbing merging with hers in the eye of the tempest.

Afterward she felt drained, so tired she could scarcely move. She had survived the storm. She felt like a survivor often does, reverent, grateful, and purged, with a new meaning for existing.

Jake kissed her, a sweet kiss filled with tenderness. Then he rose, helped her to her feet, and led her into the bedroom. They slid beneath the sheets, embracing.

Robbi felt herself slipping away into a gossamer world of serenity.

Eckker grinned. Roberta Paxton, the very woman he had to find, had come to him that evening, had come to his woods. He had only to get his pickup, drive to the Paxton road that intersected the main highway, wait, then follow them back to Reno, to the high-security complex.

Knowing he would not be allowed through the guarded gates, Eckker drove to the park at the end of the block, left his truck, and took the jogging path behind the units. He stood at the river's edge and, on the fourth floor of the six-story building, watched the lovers embrace, partially disrobe in the shadows, then move indoors.

Several minutes later Eckker jogged back to his pickup, an inflamed need gnawing at his gut.

Jake, propped up on one elbow, watched Roberta as

she slept. In the moonlight she was beautiful, angelic. Her hair, a mass of lazy tangles, spread across his pillow. He lifted a corkscrew strand, twisted it around his finger. It was soft, the texture fine. Her skin glowed by the soft light coming from the hallway. Her creamy complexion was the type that changed little from the sun. It deepened like a ripe peach, glowed warm and healthy. He detected a faint smattering of freckles across her nose.

Robbi lay on her side, facing him, the sheet covering only her lower half. Jake caressed her seemingly flawless body with his eyes. She wasn't rail-thin like the model figures of the past several decades. Her body was curvy, full in the breasts and buttocks, slender at waist and legs, her tummy flat. And she was soft, like a woman should be, he thought, lightly stroking his hand along the indentation of her waist and hips. The silky texture of her skin brought to mind their lovemaking of a while ago, and he felt himself swelling with the sweet memory of it. He wanted her again. He longed to kiss and caress her. Yet he knew she needed sleep. There was plenty of time. They had the entire night. He would fix them a snack. He would fill the platform bathtub with water and they would drink iced champagne with strawberries floating in it. They could make love again. Then they would talk. He wanted to know everything about her. Everything.

He realized how little he knew. But what he knew, he admired. And what of her Wall Street boyfriend? She hadn't said a thing about him since the hospital. Was it over?

His hand lightly caressed the length of her torso. She stirred. He leaned down, kissed her smooth shoulder.

She began to squirm; soft mewling sounds came from her throat. She's dreaming, he told himself. What was she dreaming?

A restlessness, a deep irritability gnawed at his nerve endings. Eckker turned this fitful energy toward the blond woman at the far end of the bar. She was there again, just as he sensed she would be. Last night a seizure had sent him running out into the alley, aborting his plan. Tonight nothing would stop him.

On the end stool she sat feeding quarters into the video poker machine. Her mass of golden hair was pulled up into a ponytail to one side of her head, secured by a shiny clip. He didn't care for that, but when he got her home, he'd ask her to let it down. A woman's hair should be worn down about her shoulders, natural, flowing.

He watched her scan the occupants of the bar casually, as if looking for someone in particular. Her scrutiny continued, finally penetrating deep into the dark recesses of the corner of the lounge where he sat watching her.

Her gaze met his and locked.

He smiled.

Detective Kathleen Lerner scanned the bar area of the Zenith Club for the fugitive. A tip from an informant put the California escapee in this bar only two nights ago. Jesus Manuel Gonzales, a.k.a. Chino, was reported to be a regular here. He usually showed around midnight. It was getting close to that now.

Her partner, Avondale, was in the pit shooting pool. Music from a DJ sound system blasted throughout the place. The crackerbox dance floor with its prism of lights was packed. An oldie, "Leroy Brown," beat out from the speakers. Well, she'd had worse nights, she thought. At least she was inside with a cool drink in hand. The music wasn't bad and she'd been lucky on the poker machine.

She chuckled to herself; actually, this was all right. Aside from the fact that she couldn't drink on duty, it was pretty much like her nights off when she did the single scene with friends; danced, played slots, and sometimes sat in on a draw poker or Texas Hold'em game. She was a damn good poker player. Like Kenny Rogers, she knew when to hold 'em and when to fold 'em.

A man asked her to dance. She declined. She sipped her diet Coke and checked out the bar again. In the far corner of the room, through the dusty fronds of a silk palm tree, a big man sat staring at her. Her eyes moved on, then came back, involuntarily, to the man. She was mistaken, he wasn't staring, he was devouring. Something utterly slimy oozed from his eyes, transmitting to her.

His craggy face a mask of granite, he smiled again.

Detective Lerner shuddered and quickly looked away. She twisted her head, looking for Avondale, and felt a measure of assurance when she caught his eye briefly.

Although she didn't look back at the man in the corner, she continued to feel the force of his black eyes on her. She sipped her drink, her throat suddenly dry. No matter how many partners she had for backup, how skilled she was in self-defense, or how heavily armed, that was one hombre she wouldn't want to meet up with in a dark, deserted alley.

Twenty minutes later she watched Avondale finish the pool game and then take a stool at the bar directly opposite her. After four Cokes, Kathleen Lerner had only one thing on her mind now—pit stop. She stared at Avondale until he looked her way. With her eyes she indicated that she was going to the rest room. His acknowledging nod was discernible only to her.

She slid off the stool and started in the direction of the alcove marked REST ROOMS, EXIT. Something compelled her to look in the back corner of the room. The man sat there still, his dark eyes followed her until she passed from his view. She would have to tell Avondale to keep an eye on that one. He looked like trouble.

She clutched her purse closer to her. Through the soft leather she felt the positive, steel bulk of both the service revolver and the handcuffs. Then she was through the door into the rest room and the man in the bar was forgotten.

While finishing up in one of the stalls, she heard the door open, footsteps, then the door of another stall close. She flushed, left the stall, and went to the sink. She heard the bolt release on the occupied stall. She shook the water from her hands, reaching for a paper towel, and, as she did, she looked into the mirror. He stood there, a massive figure in a dark jacket and pants.

Two things about him initially shocked her senses. His immense size and the look in his eyes, a giant with intense black eyes. The smile made him all the more menacing.

"What the hell do you think you're doing in here?" she said.

He moved toward her, that insane grin on his bearded face. "I want you to come with me," he said quietly. "I won't hurt you."

"Get out of here," she said, trying to keep the hysteria out of her voice.

She opened her bag, reached inside. He was on her instantly, a huge hand clamping over the entire lower half of her face, his other arm pinning her arms to her side. She struggled, trying to use the self-defense moves that could bring down an antagonist larger than herself. The man was too big, the advantage clearly his. He lifted her off the ground. She kicked, her high-heeled shoes met unyielding bone; he seemed oblivious to pain.

If he intended to rape her, he would have to loosen his hold, reposition her, and then she'd have him.

He did the unexpected. He pushed through the door into the dim hallway and, as if she were a weightless mannequin, he carried her down the hall to a back door. Her muffled cries were lost to the blaring music.

The policewoman knew what was beyond that door. An alley. Beyond the alley, a parking lot. She and Avondale had checked it out days earlier. *Avondale!* her mind screamed. *Where the hell are you!*

He crashed through the door into the night air and kept going. Down the alley toward the parking lot.

No, she couldn't let him get her in his car.

Her entire body went limp. The sudden slack forced him to pause and reposition the now-dead weight in his arms. She took her best shot and dropped to her knees, at the same instant she drove her arm upward into his groin. Without waiting for his reaction, she scrambled backward, reaching into her purse and pulling out both gun and handcuffs. The cuffs she let fall to the ground, the gun she aimed at him and said, "Police. Freeze!"

"Bitch!" He grabbed the front of her blouse and pulled her to him. His other arm drew back, the hand a bulky fist, then it came at her like a gigantic hammer—

In the circle of Jake's arms, Roberta squirmed and moaned. The long, sleek muscles of her body jumped, bunching tautly.

More moaning.

This was no ordinary dream, Jake thought, pulling her unresponsive body closer to him.

THIRTY-FOUR

The woman cop dodged, causing his fist to drive through empty air. Eckker cursed.

In the dark, narrow alley the policewoman began to scream.

His hand clamped over her mouth savagely. He felt something cool and hard press into his stomach. He twisted, heard the explosion, then felt a burning ache tunnel into his side. She had fired a round, the percussion muffled by his own flesh. Something warm and wet mushroomed beneath his shirt. Blood.

She'd shot him. The bitch had shot him. He found that remarkable.

They scrabbled in the alley, both slipping on the slick rivulet of water running from the building toward the sewer grate.

He wrenched the gun from her hand and dropped it into the pocket of his coat. She screamed again, snatched up the handcuffs, and on hands and knees managed to crawl to the side of the building. He grabbed her.

A door opened opposite them. A small Oriental man dressed in chef's whites peered out. He advanced a step, uncertainly.

"Get outta here," Eckker growled, averting his face.

The small man disappeared inside, the door closing resoundingly after him.

As quick as lightning the cop managed to secure one wristband of the handcuffs to the handle of the steel door.

He smiled, thinking she had in mind to cuff him to the door, and it was going to be interesting to see her try. But instead of attempting to clamp the other band over his wrist, she brought it to her own, the sound of the serrated teeth crunching like steel jaws as she squeezed it closed.

She had handcuffed herself to the metal door. With her other hand she grabbed the bottom of her purse and slung it, scattering the contents every which way across the dark alley.

A rage surged up in him. The ache in his side burned. No one had ever beaten him. He could cut her hand off at the wrist, rip her arm out of its shoulder socket, crush the bones in her hand until it was mush, no longer an obstacle against the circle of steel—but he didn't want her now. She was a cop. She was everything he hated.

His hand loosened from her mouth, then inched downward to circle her throat. She opened her mouth to scream, but within moments the paralyzing constriction to her vocal cords rendered her speechless. Nothing more than a pathetic squeak escaped her lips.

He squeezed and squeezed.

Staring down into her saucerlike eyes, he squeezed

until all emotion dissolved, leaving only two blank, glazed circles of icy blue-green glass.

The Power. The power to eliminate what was worthless, what served no good purpose. He could spare a life or he could take it. It was so easy. He blustered in the power radiating through his loins, making his heart thump like one wild beast triumphant over another. She'd been a cop and she'd shot him and now she was nothing.

Clasping the woman's limp body to his chest, the stainless steel handcuffs clinking against the metal handle, he hauled her dead weight up.

"Where's your power now?" He lifted the lifeless woman's face. "What good's your badge or gun now?"

The door across the way was flung open. The small Oriental and another even smaller man, brandishing a meat cleaver, stared.

"P'lice come now," one called out in a shaky voice.

A siren warbled in the distance. Eckker swung around to the plate metal door to which the dead woman was handcuffed, the light from the Chinese kitchen making it a bright mirror, and glared at his own reflection.

In the shiny chrome of the door his face was captured cruelly, indelibly, like a tintype portrait. Those piercing black eyes burning—

"Robbi—Robbi, wake up!" She heard him calling. Felt him shaking her. Slowly, Roberta dared open her eyes. She was in a dim place, diffused light came from a doorway—*not the doorway in the alley, don't let it be that doorway.* She raised her head and looked into

Jake's gentle blue eyes.

Robbi threw her arms around Jake's neck. "Ohhh, God, Jake, he killed her. The woman from the bar . . . it was Detective Lerner. He killed her."

"What? Are you sure?"

"Yes. Yes! She's dead. He killed her." She moaned, tightening her arms around him.

"Where?" Jake flipped on the bedside lamp. He grabbed the phone and dialed.

"I don't know. An alley."

Into the receiver Jake said, "I've got to talk to Detective Avondale. This is Dr. Reynolds. I know he's not at the station. Find him and patch me through to him. It's an emergency. It's about his partner, Lerner. She may have been killed." The muscles in his back tightened. "Yes, yes, Reynolds. My number is 555-9007. Tell him Roberta Paxton saw it."

He hung up, turned to her. "They'll find him and he'll call." He pulled on a pair of sweat pants.

Roberta shivered.

Jake pulled the blanket from the bed and wrapped it around her, then he left the room. A minute later he returned with a snifter of brandy and handed it to her.

She sipped slowly; the burning path the liquor made going into her stomach warmed her.

"What happened," Jake asked.

Before she could answer, the phone rang. He snatched it up, listened a moment. "Yeah, she saw it. A vision. Not more than five minutes ago." He handed the receiver to Roberta.

"Miss Paxton, Avondale here." His voice was highly charged. "What did you see?"

"He strangled your partner in an alley."

A long pause, then, "Can you come down here—to the crime scene? I can't leave. I'll send a car."

She looked at Jake. "He wants me to go there. He's sending a car."

Jake took back the phone. "I'll bring her. Where are you? No. She only knows it was in an alley. She doesn't know where."

THIRTY-FIVE

At one-thirty A.M. Roberta, dressed in jeans and a sweatshirt, entered the alley with Jake. A uniformed policeman held up the yellow tape that was used to cordon off the area. They ducked under.

Avondale rushed over to them.

The body was still there, handcuffed to the door, just as she'd seen it in the vision. Roberta tried not to look.

Over the next half hour Avondale had her reenact the events as she'd seen them.

"You think he was shot here, where this water is?" Avondale asked. She nodded. "Damn. Most of the blood would've been diluted or washed away. You smoke?"

When she told him no, he bummed a cigarette from one of the crime scene investigators.

She pointed at the stainless steel door. "That's where I saw his reflection. The light came from inside the door across the alley."

Avondale crossed the alley and pounded on the opposite door. "Police! Open up!"

The door opened cautiously, an inch at a time. A tiny man poked his head out. Avondale pulled at the door, exposing the man. "Is this the man you saw?" he asked Roberta.

"One of them."

Avondale looked back at the door on the other side of the alley, the bright metal sharply reflecting Roberta and Jake's image. He pressed his lips together, puffed out his cheeks, and nodded.

"Don't go anywhere," he said to the cook. "I wanna talk to you and anybody else in there."

At two, Jake, Roberta, Avondale, and a police artist sat in a large booth inside the Zenith Club. Earlier the customers and employees had been given a basic description of the killer. Those who did remember seeing a large man with dark hair and beard that evening had never seen him before. He was not a regular to the club. Everyone had been sent home and all the lights turned up.

"Are you certain she was the one who handcuffed her own wrist to the door?" Avondale asked.

"Yes."

The detective clasped and unclasped his long fingers, then patted his breast pocket. "Anyone got a cigarette?" The police artist offered him his pack, lit one for him. "Thanks. We—Lerner and I, were both over there sitting at the bar. She signaled she was going to the head. She didn't come back."

"You didn't wonder . . . ?"

"She wasn't gone that long. Six, seven—ten minutes tops."

"Who made the call to the police?" Robbi said.

"Anonymous. No doubt someone from the restaurant across the alley."

"Would she have gone out into the alley with him?" Jake asked.

Avondale shook his head. "No, not without letting me know. She was bushwhacked. You saw where the rest rooms are . . . out back by the exit. That's probably why she handcuffed herself to the door. She figured I'd"—his voice cracked, he dragged on the cigarette—"I'd be along any minute to back her up."

The police artist cleared his throat, glanced at his watch, then tapped the Identi-Kit on his lap.

Avondale sat forward. "Ready to give the composite a try?"

She nodded. Before speaking, she sat up straighter, brushed her hair from her face, then closed her eyes.

Her eyes quickly opened as a spark of fear ignited in her. If she concentrated too intensely on him, she might just find herself joining him in whatever endeavor he was presently engaged in. His kidnap attempt had failed. Would he continue to prowl tonight, seeking prey, or give it a rest? Go home and lick his wounds?

"Miss?" the artist queried.

Robbi drew in a long breath. She closed her eyes again. "He's very big. Tall, large, though not fat."

"Height? Weight?"

"Six-five at least. Two hundred and eighty pounds."

"Like a professional wrestler?" the artist asked.

"In size, but not bulk. I don't see the muscle. He's just a very large man. Big-boned."

"Go on," Avondale prompted.

"His face is angular, rugged. His hair is black, short, and thin on top. He has rather full lips, what you'd call blubbery. Long teeth. He has a full beard . . ." With her fingers she indicated whiskers high on his cheeks and under his chin. "Not long, but untrimmed, mountain man-like."

"Sounds Neanderthal," Avondale said.

"Sort of. His eyes—it's his eyes that are so terrifying," she said in a quiet voice. "They're deep-set in shadows, heavy brows that meet above his nose. The eyes are pitch black."

The charcoal whisked over the sketch paper.

"And?" the artist said.

"That's about it. He has large hands with coarse black hair on the fingers."

The artist turned the pad around for Robbi to see.

She stared dispassionately at it. Everything about the composite was on target. The hair, beard, full lips, just as she had described. The eyes, she realized, could belong to anyone.

"The eyes are all wrong." To the artist she said, "On TV, the late movie, they sometimes show old horror movies—"

"Vampire movies . . . Bela Lugosi?"

"Exactly," she said carefully. "Exactly."

The artist set to work again, the bit of charcoal scratching and scraping on the paper, his strokes urgent, determined.

He turned it around for her to see.

She felt the hair at the back of her scalp rise. "Yes," she said so quietly it sounded like a hiss.

The artist turned it around for Avondale to see. The detective shook his head. "I don't remember seeing him, but it doesn't mean he wasn't here." He cleared his throat, his pen poised for writing. "Tell me about the bullet wound."

Robbi was thankful for the change of subject. Without hesitation, she touched her left side. "Right there."

"Unless it was a flesh wound, our guy will be looking for a doctor to treat that wound."

"I think the bullet went through his body and came out," Robbi said. "I saw blood on his back."

"I'll have forensic scour that alley for the slug." He scribbled frantically. "The bullet didn't knock him down? He didn't black out?"

"No. Nothing like that. I'd say he was more surprised than hurt."

"Jesus," Avondale said under his breath.

Robbi became conscious of a dull ache at the base of her skull. She hoped it was nothing more than the strain of the evening and not the signal for another vision. She rubbed her neck.

"I think Roberta's about had it for the night, gentlemen," Jake said, standing.

They left the booth.

"Now, you're pretty sure that the man you saw tonight is the same man who killed—who you think killed those other women?" the detective asked Roberta.

"As sure as I can be."

"After we met the other night, I did some checking. I called around up to Tahoe. It seems that last summer a young woman disappeared from Sand Harbor. She was at one of the outdoor Shakespeare performances they have up there in August. In the middle of a thousand people, she just up and disappears."

"Any others missing?"

"Still checking." Avondale took the sketch from the artist. "Okay. We'll circulate this."

It was nearly three A.M. when Jake and Roberta walked out into the crisp early morning air. The body was gone, but the crime scene investigators were still going over everything, gathering evidence.

"Stay with me tonight," he said.

"I think I'd be more comfortable at home."

"Then I'll stay at your place."

She leaned into him as they walked, grateful for his sensitivity.

THIRTY-SIX

Roberta awoke at her usual hour. She vaguely remembered Jake kissing her good-bye and mumbling something about lunch. With only three hours sleep, she felt groggy, disoriented, and dead tired. She had dreamed of Carl Masser, Carl wandering aimlessly in the woods calling for Maggie.

Roberta called the center. After giving Sophie an abbreviated account of the previous night's activity, she informed her she'd be in late.

"We've a lot of catching up to do," Sophie said. "And I don't mean with work. I wanna hear everything. Holler when you come in. Oh, by the way, Donald's been looking for you."

Donald? Shit. Donald's timing was rotten. Well, she'd deal with him later.

"Get some rest," Sophie urged. "G'bye."

Robbi managed to sleep another two hours, though she awoke feeling no more rested. Grudgingly, she opened her eyes to the bright summer day. There was so much to think about, none of which was pleasant—

except for Jake.

Minutes later she stepped into a steaming shower. Standing under the needle-sharp spray, the water cascading over her face and hair, she tried to force away all but the memory of Jake's lovemaking. But try as she might, her mind refused to release the image of the dead woman cuffed to the metal door. She shook her head to clear it, and succeeded only in replacing the mask of death with the hideous face of the killer; those black eyes bored into hers. A wave of nausea washed over her.

As Roberta reached down to shut off the shower, the light in the room suddenly dimmed. With the water beating down on her back, Roberta jerked her head around. Through the shower curtain she made out an obscure figure silhouetted in the doorway. She froze, the blood in her veins icy, racing. Before getting into the shower, she had made certain both doors were locked. No one else had a key.

Anxiously, she looked around for something to use as a weapon. Plastic shampoo and conditioner bottles, a sea sponge, and a pumice stone—*Christ.* The figure moved closer.

Acting instinctively, Roberta simultaneously reached up and twisted the shower nozzle as she yanked open the shower curtain. The water shot out into the room, hitting the intruder in the face. He yelled, a string of curses followed.

From the sink she snatched a can of hair spray and sprayed wildly, aiming for the face, eyes.

"Robbi! What in Christ—!" a drenched Donald Bauer blurted out as he lunged for the shower and quickly shut off the water.

He turned to her, his face questioning.

The silent scream at the back of her throat became a painful knot. Anger erupted, canceling the intense terror of a moment before. Her heart pounded; she felt lightheaded.

"Donald, you . . . you dumb, stupid ass, you . . . you—*Don't you have any goddamn sense?*" she said as she sank to her knees in the tub, gripping the porcelain edge.

"Ah, words I've been longing to hear all these lonely months," he said, shaking water from his arms and hair.

"How—what . . . what in God's name were you thinking?" She turned, glared up at him.

"Hey, babe, I'm sorry." Donald knelt and began pushing the wet hair from her face. "I only wanted to surprise you. I guess I wasn't thinking. I forgot they still show *Psycho* reruns."

"I c-could have h-hurt you," she sputtered, water from her hair running into her mouth. "If I'd had my gun, you could be lying there dead this very minute."

"I'm sorry. Baby, I'm sorry. I tried to reach you yesterday to tell you I was coming in this morning. I talked to Sophie. Then I decided to surprise you. I used my key. C'mon—get out of there." He helped her out of the tub, covered her with a towel.

"You're soaked," she said. The entire front of his shirt and slacks were wet. His short dark hair glistened with beads of water.

"Yeah." He pulled his shirt from his pants. "Is my robe still here?"

She hesitated. "In the closet."

He left the room and returned moments later with

two matching terrycloth robes. He began to undress.

"I'll make coffee," Roberta said, quickly slipping past him and out the bathroom door.

"Hey, hon . . . Rob?"

She sensed his eyes on her back as she hurried down the hallway toward the kitchen. Her mind worked frantically. God, what was she going to do? Donald was the last person she'd expected to see—although he was a sight more welcome than the alternative, and she shuddered at the thought. What absurd timing. Last night with Jake . . .

Well, now that Don was here, the matter would have to be settled. She had made up her mind that it was over between them on the night Karen, his friend the U.N. interpreter, had answered his phone. And now, with Jake in her life—damn, dammit all.

Maybe Don had come to break it off face-to-face? Of course, that was it. Lord knows he hadn't been attentive lately. He would tell her about Karen and she would tell him about Jake and they'd exchange friendship kisses, promise each other to keep in touch, and get on with their separate lives.

From the hallway, coming toward her, she heard whistling. A tune that sounded like "Oh, Susanna," but knowing Donald it could've been anything.

Standing at the counter, she turned. Donald, feet bare, wearing the terry robe, strolled into the kitchen.

He stopped whistling, grinned sheepishly, and said, "Didn't want to scare you again."

"I don't usually scare that easily," she answered.

"Can we start again? Pretend I just walked in the house?"

She smiled. "In your bathrobe?"

"Pretend. Hi."

"Hi." They stood staring at each other. *He's waiting for me to rush into his arms.*

She turned back to the counter.

As she reached to get the mugs, she felt him at her back. His arms slowly wound around her. She tried not to stiffen.

"Donald . . . ?"

"God, how I missed you," he breathed in her ear. "Until I saw you standing here, that hair, that body, I'd forgotten how gorgeous and sexy you are."

Oh, God. "What do you think of the house? I've put a lot of work into it. Did you notice?"

"Yeah, it's nice." He kissed her neck. "Should have no trouble selling it."

"What about the furniture?" She had spent months going from shop to shop, picking out special pieces, refinishing and reupholstering. "Do you like it?"

"Yeah, sure, it's great. Well suited for the West . . . for Sparks." He cupped her breasts. "Sell the house furnished, babe. I've got a decorator all lined up for our place."

"Donald, we have to talk." She pivoted in his arms.

"Later. I'm sick of talking. We've been talking on the phone for six months. I want to get all tangled up with my girl and just touch and feel and squeeze—no talking."

"We haven't talked that much lately. And I think—"

"Save it." He silenced her with a kiss.

She closed her eyes and tried to respond to his kiss. But after several moments she realized she felt nothing. Absolutely nothing. She might as well have been pressing her lips to the palm of her own hand. She felt warm, pliable flesh, but nothing else. No heat deep inside, no stirring of passion, not even a slight buzz. Guilt. She felt guilt.

Footsteps sounded on the back steps.

She opened her eyes, saw Jake standing at the back porch, his hand raised to knock. Their gaze met and locked.

Roberta's stomach rolled. She pulled away from Don. He followed her gaze to the back door.

Jake lightly rapped at the door.

"Who's that?" Don asked. "Whoever it is, his timing stinks."

Roberta couldn't agree more. The timing was off for everyone today. "It's Dr. Reynolds." She moved out of his arms. "A friend of mine."

"Were you expecting him?"

"Not exactly."

"Why don't you go get some clothes on. I'll see what he wants."

She shook her head, crossed the room and opened the door. "Hello, Jake."

He gave her a thin smile, nodded.

She stepped aside for him to enter. Once inside, she introduced him to Don.

"Don's just come in from the East Coast."

"New York, isn't it?" Jake asked Donald, glancing at Roberta. "How do you like life in the big city?"

"No comparison. Once the city gets into the blood, it's there to stay." Donald, standing behind Roberta, laid a hand on each of her shoulders and squeezed affectionately. "Robbi's going to feel the same, no doubt about it."

Jake turned to Robbi. "I didn't mean to barge in on

you, Roberta, but Detective Avondale called. He tried to reach you, but there was no answer. He wondered if you could take a couple minutes to look at some pictures—mug shots, I guess?"

Donald looked from Jake to Robbi. "Detective? Mug shots? What's going on?"

"He doesn't know?" Jake asked.

"I didn't have a chance to tell him." She saw Jake look from terry robe to terry robe, then nod knowingly.

"Well, give Avondale a call." Jake extended his hand to Don again. "Pleasure to meet you."

"Say, Dr. Reynolds, if you ever need a financial advisor . . ." Don patted the breast of the robe, grinned. "No cards on me. I'll leave some with Robbi."

"Yeah." Jake turned and went back out.

"Jake . . ." Robbi called out as the door closed softly. With an utterly sick feeling she watched him walk down the driveway and out of sight.

Don turned to her. "What was that all about?"

"It's a long story."

"I'll make time."

She poured coffee, then filled him in on everything from the time of the accident until that morning. She left out, however, her relationship with Jake. That would come soon enough. *You tell me yours and I'll tell you mine.*

Share-and-tell time came sooner than she expected.

"What's your relationship to the doctor?" Don asked.

She started to rise. He gripped her arm and pulled her back down. "I thought shrinks were supposed to appear impassive—you know, looked detached as all hell no matter what's going on under their skin? Talk about wearing your heart on your sleeve. Is it one-sided, or has my little Robbi been sleeping in someone else's bed?"

She stared at him. Then looked away.

"Ohh-kay," he said. "So where do we stand? I'm a forgiving guy. People fuck up, get lonely, make mistakes. You've had a helluva month. The shooting, the accident. This killer running loose. You're not superwoman. But look, I'm willing to forgive and forget." He caressed her bare arm. "See, already forgotten."

She realized then how very little she knew about Donald. He was going to forgive her. Nice. What about him? What about his insensitivity, his withdrawal when she needed him most, his affair with Karen the male intimidator.

Roberta laughed a short, dry laugh. "How good of you."

He studied her face briefly. "What the hell's that mean?"

"I think you know. Forgive me? You're going to forgive me?"

"Look, I know I haven't been the perfect fiancé. Lately I haven't called as often as I should have. And I should have come when you were in the hospital. We drifted apart for a bit. Naturally I'll shoulder some of the blame."

She had waited for him to say something about Karen, but it was obvious he had no intention of bringing her up.

"It's more than that."

He raised a questioning eyebrow.

"Karen? Midnight call at your apartment last week? Sleepy Kar answers. Ring a bell?"

A measure of color drained from his face.

"Ohh-kay," she said, leaning back in her chair and hugging herself.

"Robbi, babe, it was only—shit, it was little more than a one-night stand. Hardly worth discussing. Dammit, it meant nothing."

She stood, went to the sink, her back to him. "I'm afraid I can't say that about my relationship. Jake means something to me."

For the longest time all was quiet. At last she heard the kitchen chair scrape on the floor, then the soft sound of his bare feet as he crossed the linoleum. He had left the room.

Robbi sighed heavily. She poured another cup of coffee and sat at the table again.

Five minutes later, dressed in dry clothes, his travel bag over his shoulder, he paused at the doorway to say, "They're a bitch."

She looked at him.

"Long distance relationships." He walked on.

She heard the front door open and close.

If the situation hadn't been so depressing, she would have laughed.

Jake thrust the throttle on the speedboat forward. There was a light chop on the surface of Lake Tahoe, just enough to make the fast-moving boat handle like a car with four flats jouncing at breakneck speed on railroad ties. The pounding felt good.

Icy water sprayed over the side of the windshield,

stinging, soaking him through. That felt good too.

Fools deserved worse. He'd been a top-notch fool. How often did he fall in love? Twice, that's how often. Susan and Roberta. It took falling in love with Roberta to get over Susan. What would it take to get over Roberta?

A lobotomy.

THIRTY-SEVEN

"Little one, can you swing by and get me tonight?" Sophie asked Roberta the following day. They were outside, washing the front windows of the center. "My car's wheezing again. Sounds undoubtedly terminal this time."

Robbi stared absently at the soapy water on the glass as it rapidly evaporated in the late morning heat. Before the fiasco in her kitchen the day before, Robbi had hoped to go to the dinner dance with Jake. She had tried calling him, but reached the answering machine at both numbers. Would he call her? Would he ever want to see her again?

"If you have other plans . . ." Sophie began.

"No," Robbi said quickly. She was no longer in high school, waiting for the phone to ring. This was a job, not a social event. "No, I don't have other plans. I'll pick you up at six."

"You're a sweetheart." Sophie picked up the bucket of dirty water and headed for the back entrance. "When I come back I want an update on Roberta

Paxton. I'm a couple of chapters behind and something tells me our heroine is at a turning point in her life."

Reflected in the window in front of her, Robbi saw a moss-green sedan pull to the curb. Detective Avondale got out, flicked a cigarette into the street, then made his way across the lawn to where she stood on the ladder.

"Good morning." Avondale carried a small plastic shopping bag and a file folder.

"Morning." Robbi climbed down from the ladder.

"Miss Paxton, I have some shots, mug shots, could you have a look?"

Robbi wiped her hands on the back of her jeans, took the four sheets—each containing six photographs—and carefully looked them over.

"No. He's not there."

Avondale grunted. He opened the small shopping bag. "Maybe we'll have better luck here. I have some personal items that belonged to Belinda Sardi. Thought maybe you'd have a look at them, or hold them, or whatever it is you do about these kind of things. Y'know, the vibes and all."

Robbi's stomach tightened. After her experience with the black hole the night she'd held Maggie's wristwatch, she'd vowed never to attempt that again. "I can't, Detective Avondale. I'd like to help, but I'm sorry, I just can't."

"Can't, or won't?"

"I can't connect with the victims. I don't know why, but nothing comes. Nothing positive, that is."

"Couldn't hurt to try, now, could it? Mrs. Sardi went to the trouble to get me these things." He held the bag out to her.

She shrank back. "No."

"Okay, Miss Paxton. I don't profess to know the supernatural psyche and what's dangerous and what isn't. If you say you can't, then you can't, and I respect that." Avondale stared candidly into her eyes. "Police work is what I do, and I'm about to ask you to consider participating in something that could also be dangerous . . . in a physical way."

"You want me to reveal myself to the killer," she stated flatly.

"In a sense, you were a witness to last night's murder."

"There were two on-the-scene eyewitnesses. The men from the Chinese restaurant."

"They didn't see the killer clearly. He deliberately kept his back to them. Now, a clairvoyant observer—hell, it'll get press . . ." He let his eyes finish the sentence.

Robbi broke eye contact, focused on two little diaper-clad toddlers playing in a sprinkler half a block down the street. Just the thought of that man knowing her identity terrified her. There was no doubt in her mind he would come after her. If he wasn't already looking for her.

"Twenty-four-hour police protection. A tracer to monitor your every move. We wire you, just like in the movies." Avondale touched her arm. "Mace, gun, flamethrower, whatever makes you feel safe."

"The policewoman had it all," Robbi said softly. "It didn't stop him from killing her in an alley with people looking on."

The tall, thin policeman shifted, obviously uncomfortable. "You're right, there's no guarantees." Avondale smiled weakly. "For now, Miss Paxton, just consider it. Who's to say that he'd even come after you if he knew who you were? He might sense a trap and run."

"I doubt it."

He gave her arm a squeeze. "Let me know if you change your mind. I'll get out of your hair now so you can get back to work." As he backed up he pointed to a streaked windowpane. "Wadded-up newspaper. The only way to clean glass."

"Oh, Detective Avondale?" She stopped him before he reached the car. "I haven't been able to contact Carl Masser and I'm worried. I've been calling day and night for two days."

"Masser? Isn't he the one who filed the report on the second missing woman?"

"Yes. Margaret Wilson, his fiancée. I told him everything I told you."

"You think he might've gone looking for this gal's killer?"

"He might have."

"I'll check it out."

He waved as he drove away.

"Cop?" Sophie said, returning with a full bucket of clean water.

"Yeah. They want to use me as bait."

Sophie directed a long, hard stare at Roberta. "Little one, don't do it."

"I could be valuable to them."

"You're valuable to us, to the women and kids in the shelter. We don't want to lose you."

Robbi climbed the ladder and went back to washing the window. The squeegee squealed across the clean glass. The sound reminded her of a woman's scream.

She shivered in the ninety-degree heat.

Jake paced his office, flipping through the half dozen index cards. He paused in the practice delivery of his speech for the SSWC's banquet that night.

Should he call her?

He turned, stared at the phone as though it would do or say something to help him decide. The instrument remained rigid and uncommunicative, offering nothing.

He lifted the receiver, listened to the droning dial tone, then replaced it.

The Wall Street Wonder was definitely back in the picture.

Screw it. Don't be a bigger fool.

At this point it was up to her.

THIRTY-EIGHT

On the third floor of John Ascuaga's Nugget Hotel and Casino, tuxedoed waiters readied the Rose Ballroom for the Silver State Women's Center annual black tie dinner dance. In the middle of each round, double-linen-covered table, among the sparkling crystal and silver, stood centerpieces of magenta candles, off-white gardenias, and pale baby's breath.

At six-thirty Roberta and Sophie met the other staff members and volunteers.

Sophie tugged at the clingy material of her red and silver knit dress. "After tonight this dress goes in the donation bin. It's a goddamn creeper, and these silver threads itch like a bitch." She shifted from one high-heeled foot to another. "The shoes I'm losing as soon as the lights go down. They don't make comfortable heels for giants."

"You look lovely," Roberta said.

"*You* look lovely. I look like a Tijuana taxi."

Robbi wore a kelly green, above-the-knee silk dress of simple lines. The straight-across strapless bodice was a panel of shiny satin. Her only jewelry of faux emerald drop earrings sparkled through long spiral masses of shiny hair.

A few early arrivals to the seventy-five-dollar-a-plate dinner milled around the two cocktail bars. Since there were no name cards, Jake would select his own place at one of the three head tables—if he came.

Within a half hour the huge room was crowded. A second glass of Chardonnay was pressed into Roberta's hand by an attorney she scarcely knew. As the man expounded on the virtues of mountain biking, she listened absently, sipped her wine, her gaze involuntarily going to the main doors time and again. At eight-ten Sophie claimed the microphone and announced dinner.

Slowly, throughout the room, the more than three hundred people took their places. Robbi stood indecisively at a head table. Sophie, Valerie, the staff physician, and Roberta, were each to head a separate table. Before Roberta could protest, a dark-haired man in his early forties had pulled a chair out for her. She reluctantly slid into it. While the man introduced himself, she was aware of someone taking the seat on her other side. Her pulse raced. Was it Jake? She dared not look, afraid of appearing too eager. A pungent musky smell of a man's cologne indicated it was not Jake.

The man who had held her chair was Zachary Nether, a representative of the Bank of Western Nevada, one of SSWC's newest and more outstanding contributors.

"What good fortune. I'm to have the prettiest woman in the room as my dinner companion."

Nether's cool gray eyes stared boldly into hers. "And I thought this was going to be just another tedious fund-raiser." His gaze dropped to her bodice.

Robbi smiled self-consciously and turned to the heavyset man on her right who was already digging into the basket of rolls. She introduced herself.

He ripped the dinner roll apart, dropped it on his bread plate, and extended a crumb littered hand for her to shake.

"Bill Sexton. Domestic Abuse Coalition." He leaned toward her. "I hope the meal is halfway palatable. It rarely is at these functions, you know. Of course, the Nugget is renowned for its food. Let's make it interesting and wager on what typc of chicken we'll get tonight. Chicken fricassee, cacciatore, tetrazzini? Chicken in orange, pineapple, or tangerine sauce? Glazed, braised, or honey-roasted? What's your guess, Miss Paxton?"

Offering a thin smile, Robbi shrugged then quickly scanned the room. With the exception of the waiters and busboys, everyone was seated. Her own table was full. She looked at the two other head tables. Sophie had a full one. There was an empty seat beside Valerie.

Where was he? Jake was the sort of man who would fulfill any and all obligations. She knew him well enough to bank on that. How could she have fallen so hard for a man, made love with him, and then lost him all in a blink of an eye?

Carafes of red and white wine were placed on the table. Zach Nether, pouring wine in her glass, took this opportunity to tell her something about himself. In the course of ten minutes he managed to weave into the conversation nearly all of his material assets—both liquid and long-term—his honorary achievements and future aspirations. She knew his type. Good-looking, sexy, and charming. Few women were a challenge. At this stage of his life it was no longer a question of victory, but of time. Although he tried to monopolize her attention, she managed to steal glances at an empty chair at the next table.

Dinner ended and the presentation began. Sophie, as moderator, read off the long list of community contributors. Awards were given, door prizes and raffle winners selected, and then Roberta was called as the first speaker.

At the podium, she scanned the packed room. Jake stood in the doorway. Her heart skipped a beat. She quickly looked down at her notes; the words leapt about on the paper. Her fingers trembled, but she recovered, stated the center's goals, then as she thanked those who had helped support the cause, she was acutely aware of Jake crossing the room to a gesturing Valerie.

Joseph Eckker shifted, trying to make his large frame more comfortable on the contoured oak bar-stool. He felt a deep, throbbing ache in his side where the bullet had gone through his body. He looked down to make sure no blood had soaked through the wadded bandage he'd taped there before going out that evening. The wound had looked angry, red, and puckered, and when he'd poured hydrogen peroxide on it, it had foamed, sizzling like an Alka-Seltzer in water. There was pain, plenty of it, but nothing he couldn't handle. He had remarkable recuperative abilities—like a cat—and would heal without incident.

Eckker's search for Roberta Paxton had stalled. Her phone number was not listed in the directory. He had gone back to the high-rise on the river only to discover the condo belonged not to her, but to a Jake Reynolds. He'd hung around for several hours without luck. He would check it out again later.

Now vigilant, focused, he sat on the hard stool and scanned the dim, smoky rooms, searching for a new companion. From past experience it was his observation that the ones most likely to suit his taste congregated, strangely enough, in bars. He was careful not to frequent the same one more than a few times. And never to return to a place where he had been successful in his quest.

He took in a large area in one broad sweep. He never feared missing her, for like sonar, something went off in his head, instantly alerting him of her presence.

He put the half-full mug of beer to his lips and finished it down. He ordered another, his fourth. He could down a keg of beer, a reservoir of beer, and the alcohol would fail to calm the strange chemical stimulus that raged inside him at this stage. There was no way he could deny himself, refuse to take a new companion. No longer in control of his own emotions, he yielded to the powers within. He was merely a robot, doing another's bidding, and until it was done he did not exist for himself.

His gaze swept to three women entering the front door. He felt an involuntary vibration. There she was. Surrounded by a thick mane of golden hair was the one he'd been waiting for. The one who'd happily share his mountain.

THIRTY-NINE

As Jake crossed the room, his eyes stayed on Roberta. She stood at the podium, looking like a goddess in a bright-green strapless dress. He caught her eye and she quickly looked away.

A woman at a front table continued to gesture to him, pointing at an empty chair beside her. He made his way to her table and, his attention still directed on Robbi, quietly sat down.

A moment later Roberta closed her presentation, gathered her notes, and returned to her seat followed by enthusiastic applause. She sat between two men. Jake was relieved to see that neither was Donald Bauer. The one on her right seemed oblivious to anything and everyone. The other one was a different story. He was leaning toward her, talking in a hushed, intimate way into her ear. A date, Jake wondered, feeling an instant resentment for her handsome dining companion.

Someone nudged him. The woman to his left, Valerie Sanchez, was staring at him.

"Your introduction, Dr. Reynolds," she said, nodding toward a lofty gray-haired woman in a red and silver knit dress standing at the podium.

". . . please welcome Dr. Jake Reynolds."

Amid polite applause Jake made his way to the podium. He opened by telling a "shrink" joke. He had a whole repertoire of them, but chose to tell only one to lighten the mood and to ease his own tension. This was a party of sorts, and he decided his talk would be serious but not glum.

He explained the role of psychiatrist in cases of battered women. Within minutes he had the attention of all those in the ballroom with the exception of Roberta and the man next to her. Whenever Jake glanced at her table he saw the man, his hand on the back of Roberta's chair, talking to her. She whispered back.

He tried to concentrate on his speech.

Eckker stared into the mirror behind the bar and watched the girl approach. She wedged in between two empty stools, her fingers tapping on the bar top to the beat of the rock music while she waited for service.

He shifted on the stool to face her. His gaze traveled boldly over her body. He licked his dry lips, then rubbed the stubble on his face where, only a few days ago, a full beard had been. He felt the fresh scab along his jawline where Masser's drywall knife had sliced him.

She asked the bartender for a glass of water. She pried open a bottle of aspirin and was about to spill some into her hand when, pausing, possibly sensing the intensity of his eyes on her, she turned to look at him.

He smiled. "Wanna drink?"

"No thank you," her tone clipped.

She turned slightly. Just enough to discourage him, yet not so much as to antagonize him should he be a psychopath. She pretended to become absorbed in her surroundings.

"Maybe later," he said softly.

Gripping the aspirin bottle tightly, she took the glass of water, turned, and hurried away.

Roberta smiled politely at the man next to her. Since Jake had taken the podium, Nether had monopolized her with questions about her private life. "Mr. Nether," she whispered, "the man speaking is a friend of mine. I should be listening."

"I'm sure you've heard it all before."

"Please," she hissed under her breath. She turned slightly, full attention forward. Earlier Jake had looked her way, but now his gaze seemed to stop just short of her table.

She ached for him. He looked so familiar, so much a part of her, as though she'd known and loved him all her life instead of only a few weeks. She felt a lover's pride as he stood so handsome in a black tuxedo, speaking eloquently, the eyes of every woman in the room riveted on him.

He closed his presentation, praised the center for its superb work, and, under resounding applause, returned to his seat.

Sophie concluded the program with, "And let the fun begin."

Robbi stood. She would go to him, explain Don's surprise visit. Tell him it was over between Don and her.

Jake stood talking to Valerie. Robbi moved through the milling people toward him, but before she had gotten more than a few yards, someone caught her arm.

"The news people are here from Channel 3," Sophie said, turning a reluctant Robbi and leading her to a throng of supporters where anchorwoman Beth Amsterdam stood talking with a man toting a minicam. "This is live for the newsbreak. Let's do our stuff, little one."

Peering over her shoulder, Robbi looked for Jake. She finally caught sight of him moving toward the exit. Despair washed over her. *He can't be leaving! Not before she had a chance to talk to him, to explain. How would she make it through this night without him?*

She started to go after him, but Beth blocked her way. "We're ready, Miss Paxton. They're patching us through."

"But—"

The anchorwoman jockeyed in beside Sophie and Roberta, the microphone held between them. They stood on the edge of the dance floor. Behind them couples moved to a slow rendition of "Mack the Knife."

As she watched Jake exit through the double doors, a tiny red light blinked on the camera and she wanted to cry.

Eckker divided his attention between the television and the mirror. In the mirror he watched the young woman with the beautiful blond hair at a table behind him. Someone asked her to dance, and she moved out of his vision.

He turned back to the TV. Three women were on.

One of the two being interviewed looked familiar. The newslady was saying, ". . . at the tenth annual Discover Dinner Dance, we're here with Roberta Paxton . . ."

He jerked upward with a start.

On the screen a pretty woman in green with masses of reddish-brown hair began to speak. "Tonight's dance . . ." Abruptly her expression turned bewildered, pained, then suddenly her eyes stared vacantly into the camera—

No longer was Roberta in the ballroom being interviewed for the news. She saw an oak bar, liquor bottles lined up under a plate glass mirror. She saw a TV, and she was looking at herself on the screen. She dropped her gaze and saw, reflected in the mirror directly opposite her, a fierce-looking man staring at the TV.

She heard the anchorwoman identifying her: "Live from the Rose Ballroom of John Ascuaga's Nugget, where Sophie Bennett and Roberta Paxton, directors of the Silver State Women's Center . . ."

Those cold black eyes stared unflinchingly at the TV. A wicked, knowing grin spread across his face.

She thought she would scream.

She watched as he waved away the fresh beer from the bartender, slapped down money on the bar, and abruptly left the stool.

Bright spots flashed in front of her eyes before everything went black.

FORTY

A claustrophobic wall of people pressed around Roberta, solicitous, curious. Someone placed a glass of water to her lips, another waved a flat clutch purse like a fan in front of her face. She lay on the carpet at the edge of the dance floor, her head on Sophie's lap.

"Should we call a doctor?" Valerie was asking.

Roberta looked at the faces but saw only the threatening mask of the killer. He knew who she was. He knew where to find her. He would come for her, kill her. How long would it take him to get to her? How long had she been out? Panic made her dizzy again, sick to her stomach. She had to get away.

She shook off the hands holding her and came to her feet. With an effort, she broke through the group. From her table she grabbed her purse, then rushed out of the ballroom. Zach Nether caught her by the arm.

"Roberta, where are you going? Wherever it is, I'm right with you."

Shaking her head, she pushed him away.

Unsteady in her high heels, she raced down the stairs

to the main floor. She rushed to the rear of the casino. At the exit she paused to dig her car keys from her purse, then she was pushing through the glass doors, impatiently plowing through a knot of people coming in.

The headliner show had just ended and valet parking was swamped. Jake stood outside under a violet lit portico and waited for the attendant to bring his car.

To his left a flash of bright green caught his eye. He turned to see a woman with reddish hair running across the street to the parking lot. Roberta?

What would make Robbi run out of a party as if the devil were after her? A fight with her dinner companion? Another vision?

What should he do? Try to catch her before she reached her car? Wait for his car, then drive to her house, assuming that would be her destination? Go back inside and ask her coworkers why she'd run off? Or ignore the whole thing and get on with his life?

He saw her climb into her Jeep, start the engine, and speed away, tires squealing.

Jake stepped to the valet booth, shoved his parking stub under the glass, and demanded his keys. An attendant had already gone for his car.

Jake paced, his gaze directed toward the valet lot. *Dammit, where the hell was his car?*

On the way home her mind raced. It would take her less than five minutes to get her revolver, change clothes, and throw together a few things. How long would it take him to find out where she lived? Her phone number was unlisted, and it was certain no one at the center would tell him—unless they were forced.

Oh, God.

Her first instinct was to go to the police. Avondale would be thrilled by this new development; he'd love to use her to get to the killer. She shuddered violently. No, no way in hell would she take that chance. She could still see the look on that monster's face when he realized who she was.

For the protection of the workers at the center she had to tell the police, but she didn't have to tell them where she was. Let Avondale stake out the house and the shelter. She would be long gone.

She turned into her driveway and slammed on her brakes at the back door. After shutting off the engine and lights, she took several moments to control her breathing. She was hyperventilating, on the verge of passing out again. Cupping her hands tightly over her mouth, she inhaled slowly until the lightheadedness eased.

She looked around. The long drive to the street was deserted. To the right of the Jeep was the tall dense hedge between her neighbor's yard and her driveway. A light wind had shadows dancing all around her. She opened the car door and listened. Leaves skittered along the concrete. A rustling sound had her heart pushing up into her throat. The wind wasn't that strong. The hedge behind her stirred. In the side mirror she saw a large figure moving behind the Jeep. Then the view in the mirror became totally obliterated.

Roberta tried to close the door, but it was jerked open, the handle ripping from her grasp. The man reached in for her. She tried to scramble backward, to get to the passenger door. Her arm was seized cruelly. She screamed as he hauled her, kicking, from the car.

A massive hand covered her mouth. His other arm wound around her waist. Too hysterical to take stock of the situation, she turned on the big man, fighting for her life. He pinned her arms to her sides as they struggled at the back of the Jeep.

Suddenly they were both bathed in a flood of light. The big man loosened his grip just enough for Roberta to push at him. She spun away, falling against the side of the house. Jake's car shot up the drive and hit the assailant before he could reach her again. The man flew across the hood of the T-bird and tumbled over the front fender to the passenger side of the car. The car came to a screeching halt within inches of her Jeep.

Terrified, adrenaline pumping like crazy, she looked around for him. He was there on the other side of Jake's car. He would rush her again any second.

Jake hopped out of the car. He swooped down, grabbed one of the scalloped bricks used to trim the flower bed, and, waving Roberta back, he ran around behind the car, brick raised.

Roberta saw him bend down.

"Jake," she whispered, "is he dead?"

"Gone," he answered.

When Jake started toward the tall hedge bordering the neighbor's property, she cried out, "Jake, *no!* Let him go!"

Robbi rushed into his arms, trembling, gasping for breath.

Silently, with an arm securely around her, Jake pulled open the passenger door. "Hurry, get in."

"I have to get some—" But she didn't finish the sentence. She realized there was nothing as important as getting away from there, and as quickly as possible. Her worst nightmare had come true—the killer knew about her and he wanted her dead.

From his condo Jake phoned Avondale and told him the killer had come after Roberta. He briefly explained the circumstances.

"Dammit, we need to talk to Miss Paxton. Is she there with you?" Avondale wanted to know.

Jake looked down at Roberta sitting on the floor in her party dress, legs crossed in front of her, hugging her knees.

Roberta held out her hand for the phone. Jake gently touched her cheek before handing it to her.

"Detective Avondale?"

"Miss Paxton, you can't—"

"Just listen. He was in a cocktail lounge. The bar was large and had a good-size dance floor with a sound system, no band. The bartender wore a white dress shirt and black bow tie. The place was full of neon signs, you know, the kind that beer and liquor companies use for advertising. It had oak decor, high tables, and stools."

"What was he wearing?" Avondale asked.

"The same dark jacket—sports jacket—and a plain dark T-shirt. He was clean shaven and looked much younger without the beard."

"How young?"

"Late thirties."

"Miss Paxton, come down to the station and have a

look through the mug shots, if—"

She gently pressed the cradle buttons and handed the phone back to Jake.

"Am I being foolish for not letting Avondale protect me?"

"If he's not a blithering idiot, he'll assign some plain-clothes to secure the complex. He knows where you are."

"Do you own a gun?" she asked.

Jake shook his head. "Sorry."

"Oh, God," she moaned, burying her face in her folded arms. "What's happening? And why is it happening to me?" She laughed dryly. "Why me? Why me? Poor littl' Robbi," she finished in a cynical tone.

Jake was silent.

She raised her head, looked at him.

He stared at her for a long moment. Then, in a pensive tone, he said, "There's a guy from New York—"

"It's over."

He waited.

She gave him a thin smile. "It looked pretty bad, didn't it, that scene in my kitchen?"

He shrugged, then nodded.

"He came unexpectedly. We—Jake, I'd rather not go into it right now, but I want you to know that what you saw was our first and only embrace while he was here, which, incidentally, was less than an hour. I didn't . . . we didn't . . . it's over."

Roberta stared up at him. He stood in the middle of the room, tall, his hands in the pants pockets of his tuxedo, the black cummerbund emphasizing his narrow waist. An expression of profound compassion filled his handsome face. She let her gaze take in all of him.

"Do you know how handsome you look in a tuxedo?" she said, her voice low. "When I saw you come through the ballroom door, I said to myself, Now there's an incredibly sexy man."

"Yeah?" he said softly, as though she hadn't changed the subject.

"Yeah." She smiled.

"You're a sucker for a guy in a tux?"

"Not any guy."

He went to her, offered her his hand, then slowly pulled her to her feet.

Her hands stroked the satin lapels, then moved inside his jacket to stroke the satin of the cummerbund. The hook opened and the pleated band fell away.

His hands cupped the sides of her face, fingers sliding through her hair. He kissed her, a soft, sweet kiss that only made her yearn for more. She felt a fluttering in her stomach that soon, with kisses that became hot, hungry, and probing, burned lower in her body.

He shrugged out of the jacket, let it fall to the carpet, slipped off his shoes. She unbuttoned his crisply starched shirt and helped him strip it off. She bent, kissed his dark nipples until they hardened, running her fingers through the fine curly hair between them.

Wearing only the black dress pants, Jake swung Robbi into his arms and carried her into the bedroom, where he placed her on the bed. He took hold of her hips and pulled her to the edge. The hem of the satin dress slid up to the apex of her legs; her feet touched the floor. She opened her smooth, stockinged legs and he moved in between them. Supporting his weight on his elbows, he lay on top of her, kissed her throat, her chin, then found her mouth. Within minutes their kisses were feverish, urgent.

He raised his upper torso, extending his arms out on each side of her and looked quizzically into her eyes. She put her arms above her head and stretched seductively beneath him. Her breasts were round and full above the strapless bodice. He pulled down the side zipper, folded back the bodice until an entire breast was exposed, then caressing with cool fingertips, he bent his head and took her nipple into his mouth.

She sighed when he moved to the other one, sucking, nibbling with his lips. She squirmed beneath the exquisite weight of him, his hardness apparent through the layers of clothing.

His hand went between them, undid his slacks, worked them down, and then he was naked above her. She wanted to feel his flesh against hers. She wanted to be naked, absorbing the heat and sexual vibrations from his body. She sensed a magnetism, like static electricity, drawing, yet unifying the heat and energy from both of them, making every nerve ending tingle deliciously. He stroked her thigh at the very fringe of her desire.

When she whispered his name, he maddeningly slid down the length of her body. At the edge of the bed, on his knees between her legs, he pushed her dress up to her waist, then he rolled down her pantyhose inch by inch, kissing the skin as it became exposed to his lips and tongue. Her long legs trembled. As he freed her feet, Robbi pulled the dress over her head and tossed it aside.

"Please . . ." she whispered. "Please, Jake, hurry."

He came back up, pulling her up with him until they were both entirely on the bed. He kissed her, his tongue slipping like liquid fire into her mouth at the exact moment he entered her. A flashfire of heat surged through her body, meeting at the nucleus of her being, melting.

He was gentle, yet erotically savage as he moved within her. Their fervor mushroomed, and she sensed that they were as one. Synchronized in everything—pace, breathing, moans—she knew exactly where he was, for she was there as well. Within an instant of her exhilarating, throbbing rush of ecstasy, she felt a pulsing inside her as his release surged forth. He spoke her name as she cried out.

Afterward they lay quietly in each other's arms. Even with disaster at the brink of her consciousness, Roberta felt a sense of peace and well-being.

Would it always be like this, this wonderful, this profound? Naturally there had been others before Jake, but none had touched the core of her as he did. No one had ever strived to please her as he did. His tenderness, coupled with an almost ruthless sexual abandonment, strongly bonded her to him in a way she didn't understand, though she suspected that trust and love had a great deal to do with it.

She drifted between sleep and awareness, content in the arms of her lover. A little germ of fear flickered somewhere in the recesses of her mind, but she had only to snuggle closer to Jake, feel his arms tighten around her, and the fear remained nothing more than a benign smoldering ember.

FORTY-ONE

Roberta awoke to the sound of birds chirping, water rushing along in the river below, and the rich smell of coffee brewing. She rose up on her elbows and looked around. The drapes were closed, the room cool, dark, and shadowy. The clock read 7:46. She was alone in the room.

She stretched, for the moment feeling glorious, content. She was at Jake's; he was somewhere nearby. The killer knew nothing of Jake. He would never find her here.

A door closed softly somewhere in the condo.

"Jake?"

No response.

Swinging her legs out of bed, she lowered her feet to the floor and, holding the sheet across her torso, looked around for something to wear. Jake's starched dress shirt hung on the doorknob. She crossed to it, slipped it on, catching a nostalgic whiff of him in the cloth. The stiff material felt abrasive against her tender nipples.

"Jake?" she called again, leaving the bedroom.

She wandered down the hallway, opening doors, calling softly. A guest room, a large bathroom with a platform tub and an oversized shower, a small den with a desk surrounded by built-in shelves loaded with leather-bound books, and the living room stood empty.

She padded barefoot into the kitchen, where water trickled from the faucet and down the drain.

She turned off the water, looked around. On the stark white countertop and floor tiles she saw tiny flecks of crimson. She knelt, touched a large wet drop on the floor. Blood?

Where was Jake?

Her throat constricted painfully.

Jake?

That monster knew nothing about Jake, nothing about this condo. How could he know? Where was Jake? He wouldn't leave without telling her. Immobilized by fear, she crouched motionless, rubbing the blood on her fingers.

Something moved behind her. She felt a light touch at the back of her head. Robbi gasped, leapt to her feet and spun around, a strangled cry in her throat.

Wearing only a pair of tennis shorts and deck shoes, Jake stood in the middle of the kitchen, his hand out, a bewildered look on his face.

"Oh, God, Jake." Robbi flew into his arms. "I thought I was alone. When I saw the blood and then felt—"

"I broke a glass . . . cut my finger on it," Jake said, holding her face to his chest. "The only Band-Aids I have are in the first aid kit in my car. Hon, you're shaking. I'm sorry."

"I thought he'd found me. That he'd hurt you and . . ."

"He's not going to find us. There are places we can go. He won't have a clue. He can't read your mind. Right?"

"No. But Avondale suspects I'm with you, and Avondale wants him out in the open. . . ."

"That's stretching the probable a bit far. He'd have to make your whereabouts public, and I honestly don't think, in all good conscience, that he'd do that."

Robbi chewed her lip apprehensively.

"Speaking of Avondale, I saw him downstairs. He wants to talk. I told him to give us a few minutes."

"Do I have time to shower?"

Jake kissed her forehead, lifted her chin until she was looking into his eyes. "You have time to do anything you want."

She smiled.

He parted the dress shirt, slipped his hands inside, and gently caressed her breasts. "You're so beautiful," he said in a husky voice. He pulled her to him and kissed her.

She clung to him tightly for a moment, then reminded herself, "Avondale."

Several minutes later Robbi was in the double shower stall when Jake poked his head in the frosted door. "He's here. I found some things for you to wear, they're on the bed. We'll be on the balcony when you're ready." Then he was gone.

She put on the clothes Jake had laid out for her. A pair of gray sweat pants and a black tank top. Around the deep scooped neck and armholes, Robbi's braless breasts were exposed more than she cared for them to be. She took up the slack by tying a knot at each shoulder. She shook out her wet hair and ran fingers through it. Without her purse, she had no makeup. She pinched her cheeks to give them a measure of color, then went out to the balcony.

Avondale sat in a lounge chair, Jake leaned on the railing. After Robbi was seated, Jake handed her a cup of black coffee. Her hands trembled, spilling traces of it.

"Miss Paxton, relax. I know you're scared, and with good reason. The last thing we want is to put you in any further jeopardy. We intend to use a policewoman who looks like you, a decoy, to draw him out. We do, however, need permission to use your house and car."

Relief flooded through her. "Yes, of course," she said eagerly.

"We've got stakeouts at your house, your office, and the shelter. He won't get through, I can guarantee that."

She nodded. "I—we don't plan to stay in town."

"Where are you going?"

"I don't know."

"Miss Paxton, granted this isn't easy for you, but we still need your help. If he's inadvertently sending you messages telepathically, it's important we know. I don't know much about this parapsychology stuff, but if it's anything like radar, it might be effective only within a certain range."

Robbi, knowing little more about parapsychology than Avondale, couldn't deny his theory.

"I won't go far and I'll let you know where I'll be."

"Appreciate it. Now . . ." Avondale ran long thin fingers through the deep waves of hair, patted his breast pocket. "Either of you happen to have a cigarette I can borrow?"

They both shook their heads.

"It's just as well. Since I quit buying them, I don't smoke nearly as much. Expensive habit." He looked at Roberta. "So how do you figure he knew who you were?"

"Either he saw me that afternoon in the woods when he killed Belinda but didn't know who I was until he saw me on TV last night, or—and this is a possibility that makes me shudder to even consider—he's clairvoyant as well."

"Perish the thought," Avondale said with a roll of his eyes.

"There's one other possibility. Carl Masser knew about my ESP—"

"Masser? Yeah. There's a strong link there. Checked it out like I said I would. He hasn't been to work since Monday morning. And no one around his apartment house has seen him coming or going all week. Would you mind giving him a call right now?" Avondale asked.

"Not at all."

Jake brought out the cordless phone and the phone directory.

Robbi found the number and dialed. No answer.

"We'll put out an APB on Masser's vehicle." Avondale crossed his long legs. "Is there more we should know about the perpetrator? Dr. Reynolds tells me he hit him with his car last night. What of his bullet wound?"

"I think he has a very high pain threshold," she said. "But he ran off last night instead of fighting, so his injuries may have slowed him down a bit."

"Let's hope. A guy like that—hell, it wouldn't bother

me if he crawled into a hole and died, case unsolved." Avondale flipped a page on his notebook. "Okay, this is what we've got. He cast his net at Bernie's Saloon on Virginia Street last night. The bartender remembered serving a big, dark-haired man matching the composite. He left early. There've been no reports of missing women in the last twelve hours. If he goes back there looking for someone, we've got him." Avondale leaned forward. "Anything more to do with a church?"

"No."

"Could he be a minister?"

She shrugged.

"Just in case, we're running a check on churches in a fifty-mile radius. So far nothing."

"He could be self-ordained or substituting for another clergyman."

Avondale's head jerked up. "Miller," he said.

"What?"

"Back in the early seventies there was a serial killer name of Benjamin Franklin Miller. Convicted of killing five women. He was a self-ordained minister who preached on street corners and was occasionally invited to preach in small community churches. But damn," Avondale said, shaking his head, "Miller doesn't fit the description."

"Will you run the composite in the media?" Jake asked.

Avondale shook his head. "We'll hold on to it for a bit. Don't want to send him running just yet. I can look into having a chopper crisscross that area, though. Might see something worthwhile."

Eckker took the curved tapestry needle and threaded

it with coarse black thread. With two fingers he pinched the small hole at his side together, then forced the needle into the angry flesh, drawing the thread through. This he did three times before tying off the end and snipping the thread.

He seethed deep inside, to the core of his pain. The bullet wound had been aggravated by the car hitting him. A bruise the size of his open hand covered one thigh. But aside from the fresh bleeding of the gunshot wound and the bruise, he was unhurt.

The steady *chuk-chuk-chuk* of the helicopter caused him to pause and look heavenward. He forced himself to relax. No reason to believe the chopper was looking for him. In the summer, hikers got lost or injured in the mountains. Although he wasn't comfortable with the helicopters passing overhead, he failed to let it panic him like it did years earlier when he first took up residence here. If they hadn't seen anything in four years, they weren't likely to see anything now.

Wiping the bloody needle on his pant leg, he rethreaded, reached behind him, and tried to close the larger opening with his thick, blunt fingers. Unable to see what he was doing, he worked by feel, his fingers sticky with blood and viscous body fluid, the sharp point stabbing but failing to close the hole. Sweat ran down his face, soaked his body. He breathed in grunts, from pain and from the effort of straining to work in such an impossible position. Finally he gave up, folded an old T-shirt, and taped it over the bleeding wound.

She was probably working with the cops by now. But it didn't matter, he would find her and kill her.

FORTY-TWO

The police placed a heavily guarded vigil on Roberta's house. Plainclothesmen were stationed in the metal shed in the backyard and in a van across the street. Inside the house were two officers—one of whom was Roberta's look-alike—and a police dog. The phone was monitored. No one would get near, let alone inside, without detection.

At four A.M. he came out of thin air, smashed out the window in the back door, and stormed in.

Avondale and his newly assigned partner, Clark, parked in the van in front, heard the glass shatter, radioed for backup, drew their guns, then ran across the street and rushed into the house.

Just inside the kitchen door the German shepherd lay dead in a pool of blood. In the hallway was Detective Jackson, semi-conscious, both shoulders dislocated, his right foot crushed. They rushed into the bedroom to find the rumpled bed empty and the window open. Over recorded Gypsy music they heard a man shouting outside.

Avondale and Clark leapt through the window.

"He went that way, through there! He's armed with a lead pipe. He's got Howe!" Holding a hand to his bloody head, the cop from the shed pointed with his gun in the direction of the six-foot hedge that paralleled the driveway. Avondale crashed through it, wincing from the twigs that racked over exposed skin, nearly gouging his eye. He stopped, looked around, his stomach sinking. The neighboring yard was a maze of bushes and trees.

Jesus!

"Clark, get out front, down to the corner," he shouted. "Move it!"

Jesus H. Christ, how can this be? In disbelief, as he ran through the yard to the adjacent lot, listening to his partner's soles slapping on concrete, dogs barking in adjoining yards, and the sound of police sirens in the distance growing louder, he asked himself: *How in the hell could one man, with a bullet hole in him, abduct an officer right under the noses of four armed cops and a trained dog?*

Joe Eckker ran with his unconscious burden, carrying her like a sack of grain through the dark neighborhood, keeping in the deep shadows of the houses. At the third house down he saw a real estate lockbox attached to the front door. He hurried down the driveway to the back. He broke out the pane in the back door, unlocked it, and slipped inside.

He put his burden down, then removed any visible shards of glass in the door.

He lifted the woman and carried her through the house to the windowless hallway. He eased her to the floor. Her thick, beautiful hair spread like a fan over the thin carpet. He sat on the floor, his back against the wall. Blood oozed from the wound in his side. He stroked her hair and felt a stirring inside him. His fingers roved over her like those of a blind man as he caressed her face, her neck, and throat. She moaned, muscles twitched beneath her clothes.

He had grabbed the sleeping woman from her bed. All those morons protecting her and he had beaten them all. A rush of pleasure spread through him. Nothing could stop him. He was invincible. Joseph Eckker was invincible.

The woman jerked violently, pulling away from him. In a reflex action his arm shot out and fingers buried in the mass of hair. She continued to distance herself from him, yet her hair remained in his clawed grasp. A wig!

He lunged forward and tripped her with the lead pipe. She crashed to the floor and he fell on her.

Something was wrong. From his pocket he pulled out a penlight, clicked it on. The woman pinned beneath him had short dark hair, as short as a boy's.

This wasn't Roberta Paxton. He had the wrong one, an impostor. Another fucking *cop*.

Roberta stirred in her sleep. She dreamt of a whirlwind—what her mother referred to as a dust devil—spinning through a Gypsy camp, killing and maiming everyone in its path, carrying off a young man with short dark hair. At the end of its destruction, when the force of its power was spent, the dust devil released all that it had sucked up. The boy was dropped to the earth, bleeding and still.

FORTY-THREE

At 11:09 the following morning Star Realty's top producer of the month, Ernie Riccardi, took the key from the lockbox, opened the front door, and ushered the elderly couple into the vacant house. The stale, musty odor of the closed-up house instantly assaulted his nostrils. He hoped the old folks' sense of smell was as infirm as their hearing—he'd been shouting all morning and his throat was raw as all hell.

The old lady asked the same questions she'd asked in every house he'd shown them. The old gentleman tapped the walls with the knobby head of his cane, bobbing his feeble head. Riccardi figured it was going to be a long day.

When they reached the dim hallway, the woman, in the middle of one of her repetitive questions, stopped first, the others followed suit.

"My goodness, what's that pile of messy rags doing in the house?" she said, stepping forward curiously.

Riccardi felt a jolt, as if someone had smartly whacked him on the back. He grabbed her bony wrist and pulled her back. "Outside," his raw throat cracked. "Everyone outside."

"What the heck—?" The old man peered past the real estate agent, who had turned and was trying to usher them out.

"Gotta . . . call the police," Riccardi whispered.

That was when the old man collapsed, taking the old woman down with him.

From the crowded parking lot of the First Interstate Bank, he watched the brick office building of the Silver State Women's Center across the street. He waited, no longer patient. He was in a state of extreme agitation, the rage swelling, growing insanely, burning and eating at him like the wound in his side. He had only one goal now, and that was to find her. Nothing else mattered.

After leaving the vacant house in the wee hours of the morning, he had returned to the river condo with its dark windows. Reynolds's space in the parking garage remained unoccupied. They had run. Both of them.

But someone inside that brick building knew where she was. A fantasy of savagery played out in his head, exciting him.

At seven-thirty P.M. a woman in her late fifties exited the building, walked around to the west side and climbed into a '74 Chevrolet BelAir. He remembered her from the TV interview. She pulled out and drove away, the faulty muffler loudly heralding her departure. Eckker followed.

Sophie prayed the car would come through again.

Oh, sweet girl, just get me home and I won't ask for nothing more. But she always did. The V-8 ran on six cylinders and a prayer. It coughed, sputtered, and wheezed. At every stoplight she shifted to neutral and pumped the gas, a cloud of black, oily exhaust enveloped everything behind her.

A quarter mile more, sweet-talking all the way, she pulled into the alley at the back of her two-bedroom house on Walnut Street. The car backfired, then died.

She patted the steering wheel affectionately. "You're beautiful."

Sophie was in her house only a few minutes when the phone rang and she was summoned on a crisis call. She grabbed her purse and dashed out the door to the old Chevy. "Please, please, ol' girl," she whispered reverently, "just get me there and back and I won't ask for nothing more." The engine caught immediately. The muffler roared. A black fog billowing out from the exhaust pipe obscured the massive form that passed behind the car and moved toward her backyard.

By the time Sophie had picked up the battered wife and her two kids and settled them in at the shelter, it was dark. This time the car took her to within a half block from home before it stalled out. She slammed the hood with a fist, called it a "piece of shit," then walked home.

Inside the house it was hot, stuffy. In the rooms in front she moved from window to window, opening each several inches, hoping to catch a bit of the cool westerly breeze.

At the open door of the refrigerator she munched

impassively on a roll of summer sausage and sipped from a jar of Clamato juice as she absently stared inside. She rolled the cold jar over her cheek, the condensation and sweat mingling. It was too hot and she had no appetite. She'd take a tepid shower and eat later.

In the bathroom, as she adjusted the shower curtain, she heard a creaking somewhere in the house. From one of the back rooms. She paused, listened. It sounded like the creaky hinge on the door to her bedroom.

She slowly came to her feet. Pinpoints of fear pricked at her skin. Just that afternoon the police had warned the staff at the center that a killer was on the loose and anyone connected with Roberta Paxton was to exercise extreme caution.

The creak again.

Sophie's heart banged like cymbals in her chest. In the mirror above the sink she saw herself, eyes wide, fearful, her face a shiny, slick mask of perspiration.

Sophie tried to remember what Robbi had told her about the man in her vision. He was a giant. Shrewd, determined. A killer. He wanted Roberta. *Roberta was Sophie's best friend.*

Another creak was followed by a loud pounding. Sophie cried out, slammed shut the bathroom door, and locked it.

The pounding went on at the front door. A male voice called out.

"Mrs. Bennett, Detective Avondale from the Reno police. I'd like to talk with you a minute, please."

Cautiously, she opened the bathroom door, looked out, then seeing no impending danger, no looming hulk, she hurried to the front door, parted the curtains, and looked out to see the man who had come out to the center to talk to Robbi the day of the dinner dance.

She opened the door, gave him a shaky smile.

Standing just inside, Avondale told Sophie about the killing of the decoy. He advised her to be on her guard.

"Does Robbi know about this?" Sophie asked.

"Not yet. I was going to tell her, but I've decided to drive up tomorrow and have a talk with the two of them in person."

"Poor Robbi. What a nightmare. Give her my love, won't you?"

"Will do." He turned to leave, then turned back. "You live alone here?"

She nodded.

He looked around in contemplation.

She shivered. "Yeah, I know what you're thinking. Just before you knocked, I was working myself into a nifty case of the heebie-jeebies."

"This guy could scare anybody." He stepped out. "Lock up, ma'am."

She closed and locked the door, then turned and started back to the bathroom.

Creak.

"Whadda'ya, crazy or something?" she whispered aloud to herself. Turning, she grabbed her purse, unlocked the door, and yanked it open.

"Hold it a sec," she called out to the detective as he was getting into his car. She stepped out, pulled the door closed behind her. "You know, I don't think I want to stay here alone tonight. I have this friend, Val, who lives close by. How about giving me a lift?"

FORTY-FOUR

At midmorning Robbi and Jake reclined in lounge chairs on the deck of the Tahoe house. Roberta stared at the hardy bromeliads clinging to a bowl-shaped piece of driftwood that sat on the deck's railing. Beyond the plant she could see the clear blue lake. She thought of Ronnie. Could she ever look at driftwood or a body of water without thinking of her brother?

"Penny for your thoughts," Jake asked softly, caressing her arm.

"I collected driftwood when I was a kid. I was thinking about how, in midsummer, when the water was low, my brother and I would go to the river to gather up special pieces for my collection."

They sat quietly for several moments.

"A nickel for your thoughts," Jake prompted.

She placed her hand over his and squeezed. "Don't you get tired of listening to other people's problems?"

"You're not other people. Tell me about your brother."

"He drowned."

"How old?"

"Eight. We were twins." She felt the pressure of Jake's hand. Again the ache in her chest. Such an old wound. How was it possible it could still be so raw?

She glanced at Jake, looked away, cleared her throat, then began to talk. Tentatively at first, then to her utter amazement, the words spilled out.

She and Ronnie were so close, practically inseparable. Her brother was sweet, funny, caring, and because she was such a tomboy, able to compete with him in everything, he allowed her to tag along wherever he went.

Roberta began to tell Jake about the day her brother died.

On a bright spring day in April, scarcely a week before their ninth birthday, Ronnie left the house before Roberta arose without a word to her or anyone in the family.

At breakfast, as Roberta sullenly toyed with her Cheerios, an image of fast-moving water flashed across her mind. She squeezed her eyes shut, opened them. The image vanished.

At midday, when Ron failed to appear, Roberta began to worry, along with her parents. Fleeting images of a raging river, swollen from the spring meltoff of snow on the mountain, plagued her all day.

At dusk her father called the police. Two uniformed policemen came to the house. They asked endless questions, took the photograph of Ron from the mantel, and left. Dinner that night was solemn, tense.

Roberta was sent to bed early, and after what seemed

an eternity, she fell into a fitful sleep. She dreamed about Ronnie. In the dream he was walking along the edge of the riverbank, his arms laden with driftwood. He spotted a twisted piece of wood wedged in the crevice of a boulder several feet from the bank. He took hold of a tree branch, bright with new green leaves, and leaned out over a stretch of rapid water. The limb broke, dropping him into the freezing water.

Within seconds he was swept downstream, tossed and tumbled over slick boulders. After several minutes he managed to grab hold of a bush on the opposite shore. The relentless raging water continued to pull at him. He called out, his cries feeble, ineffectual over the roar of the white water. He hung on for some time, then, too exhausted to keep his head above water, he let go. The river took him.

In those few moments Roberta had shared his anguish, hopelessness, and, ultimately, his peace.

She woke up screaming. Her mother held her as she sobbed out her dream.

"Ronnie . . ." she wailed. "He's . . . he's dead."

Her mother shushed her.

The doorbell rang and her mother hurried to answer it. For several endless moments her father stood silent at the foot of her bed, a strangeness in his eyes. Then he turned and left the room.

Roberta followed. In the hall, squatting on her heels, her arms hugging her legs, she peered around the door-jamb at the front door. The policemen stood stiffly, hats in hand. Her mother sobbed. A word now and then drifted to her. River. Body. Bridge.

Roberta crept back to bed, her own tears swallowed by the large, lonely room. Ronnie was dead. She'd seen him die. Her brother had sneaked off to the river to gather driftwood for her collection and had died for it.

The night of the funeral Roberta lay sobbing in her room. Her mother sat on the bed and held her. "Mama, it was my fault. I knew where he was. He didn't tell me, but I knew. I saw it in my head. The river. I kept seeing the river."

"Hush, Roberta. That's nonsense. Don't you ever let your father hear you say that. He'll have you put away with those other poor children at the institution. Roberta, normal people don't see things in their heads like that."

"But Mama—"

"Not a word to anyone," her mother said harshly. "I don't ever want to hear you mention that again. That's crazy talk. You don't want people to think you're crazy, do you?"

Robbi felt Jake's comforting embrace and leaned into him.

"He started drinking after that."

"Your father?"

"Yes. He blames me for Ron's death."

"Why you?"

"Because Ron wouldn't have gone off to the river alone if not for me. Because he thought I knew where Ron was but chose to keep quiet. Because *I* should have been the one to die and not his only son. Because . . . because . . . oh, shit, I don't know." She buried her face in her hands. "I just don't know. All I know is that he's a mean, rotten sonofabitch."

"To you alone?"

She shook her head. "To my mother, my sister, everyone. But it's because of me."

"Honey, you've carried this tremendous burden, this guilt, for over twenty years. I think it's time you finally let it go. It's probably too late for him. But it's not too late for you."

They were interrupted by the loud popping of pine cones crunching under tires, announcing a visitor.

They exchanged wary glances as Detective Avondale, his face a stoic mask, strode across the sandy yard to the wooden steps. He stopped, stared up at them.

"What's happened?" Jake asked.

"I was hoping Miss Paxton could tell me," Avondale said evenly.

Robbi looked from Avondale to Jake, then back to Avondale. "Tell you what?"

"He got another one early yesterday morning."

Robbi sat up straight, her pulse accelerating.

Jake motioned for Avondale to join them. He started to rise. "Can I get you something?"

"No, no thanks, I'm okay." The detective lowered himself into a chair gingerly, like an old man. "We set a trap for him at your place, Miss Paxton. Five armed cops, a K-9, and the . . . the decoy. This maniac—he came crashing through like Godzilla mowing down a Japanese village. Struck down everyone in his path, grabbed the decoy, and . . . off he went into the night."

Robbi took Jake's hand.

"He got away?" Jake asked.

"Yeah. One . . . dead, two injured, not counting the dog."

"The decoy?"

He sighed loudly. "Dead."

"Oh, God," Robbi whispered.

"He killed the decoy—Roberta's look-alike," Jake said, "so he had to think he killed Roberta, right?"

Avondale nodded solemnly. "Miss Paxton, you sure you saw nothing? It happened around four in the morning, yesterday."

She paused, looking to Jake for help. He shrugged helplessly. "I do remember a dream, but not about him. It had something to do with a storm, a tornado, and . . . and a dead boy."

Avondale stared at her. Then he sighed and stood. "More bad news. Carl Masser's pickup was found at the Truckee-Tahoe airport. Airport security figured it'd been parked in the lot for at least six days. CSI is going over it now with a fine-tooth comb."

Jake and Robbi exchanged looks again. A heaviness hung over her, muggy, oppressive, like the air just before a thunderstorm.

In a parking lot at the Hyatt Regency Hotel, Avondale pulled into a space facing the direction of the doctor's house. He shut off the engine, shifted on the seat, making himself comfortable. From where he sat he could see the traffic on Lake Shore Drive. If Paxton and Reynolds's tried to take off to hide elsewhere, there was a good chance he'd know it.

They were both suspicious and wary.

He realized he had handled it badly. The whole fucking thing had been handled badly. Now, after losing two of their own, the department had finally formed a task force. Not one centimeter of the Paxton house or the vacant house, where the grisly remains of

Officer Howe had been discovered, would be overlooked for clues by the forensic team. Each piece of broken glass was being analyzed for fingerprints, each fiber, hair, or particle large enough to be collected was on its way to the crime lab. Yet the only sure thing they had was Roberta Paxton with her mainline to the killer. How long before she'd realize the killer was still after her?

He had lied about the decoy. He'd kept the sex of the dead officer a secret from them. *No contact with the killer,* she'd said. *Just this crazy dream about a boy.*

Christ.

The department, deciding it was too risky to use a woman officer as a decoy, had picked effeminate, five-foot-eight Frank Howe. Only a selected few knew that the bludgeoned nude body found in the vacant house, covered with women's clothing, had been savagely mutilated. Castrated.

In a roundabout way, Roberta Paxton had dreamed about the incident. A tornado—*the killer?*—and the death of a boy—*Frank?* Odd that she would perceive it in such an unorthodox way.

Odd? Shit, it was downright creepy.

Roberta stood on the deck, facing the lake. Jake hoisted himself up on the railing, then pulled Robbi in between his legs. She wrapped her arms around his waist.

"I'm scared," she said.

"If you want to move on, just say the word." Jake gently lifted a long strand of her hair that had caught on her eyelashes and brushed it back.

"I'm so tired."

"We'll stay the night, then."

"Jake, do you think Carl found Maggie's killer? Or that the killer found Carl?"

"I don't know, hon."

Roberta covered Jake's hand. She felt a raised ridge on his palm. She turned his hand over and gingerly ran her finger over the scar. "What happened here?"

"Someone I once loved cut me."

"Tell me," she said quietly.

Jake absently rubbed the scar as he told Roberta about meeting Susan Calla and the chaotic relationship that followed. Then: "After nearly two years of being subjected to her psychosis, I begged her to get counseling. She refused. Out of desperation I threatened to have her committed. It was nothing more than an idle threat, but I hoped it would push her in the right direction. In a blind rage she attacked me with a boning knife."

"What happened to her?"

Jake swallowed, rubbed hard at his palm. "She killed herself . . . used the same knife. She bled . . ." His words trailed off.

She kissed him, light, tender.

They held each other, said nothing for the longest time.

Then, gazing into her eyes, Jake said softly, "I love you."

"Jake . . ."

"So much it hurts."

"That's good." She embraced him tightly. "I hate to love alone."

* * *

Avondale crossed the street to a pay phone. Time to check in with his partner.

Clark came on the line. "We got fingerprints, all kinds of fingerprints. We got blood, two different sources, so one specimen probably belongs to the perp."

"Yeah, makes sense. The bullet wound from the Lerner killing. As far as we know, he never had it medically treated," Avondale said. An involuntary shiver seized him. "Jesus, this guy's something. He's no longer being cautious. He must want this Paxton woman pretty bad."

"Where are you?" Clark asked.

"Incline. I just talked to Paxton and the doctor."

"She have anything to add?"

"Yeah, only she didn't know it. She had no contact with this guy in the usual psychic way. But she dreamed about a tornado and a dead *boy.*"

After a long pause, Clark said, "Scary shit. We're checking with hospitals in at least six states."

"Hospitals?"

"Mental hospitals. With those seizures, our guy could be certified."

The news did nothing to lighten Avondale's dark spirit. A mental case. The worst kind to deal with.

"I'm going to hang around here a little longer in case she tries to run. I'll check back with you in a couple of hours."

Three hours later Avondale again crossed the street and made a call to his partner. An excited Clark got on the line. "Eureka, we made him!"

"No shit?" Avondale said, his own voice high and excited. "Give it to me."

"Joseph Eckker," Clark said. "We're still waiting for

the DNA results, but the fingerprints paid off. No aliases. Thirty-five. Felon. Four years ago he scaled the fence at the Lompoc Federal Penitentiary."

"Escaped?" Avondale said incredulously, patting his empty breast pocket. Right now he'd kill for a cigarette. "That's fucking maximum security."

"He had another con cut themselves out, then took a walk on a foggy night. The other one got caught right away. Eckker had a habit of going on the lam. Five other times from various prisons and correctional institutions. I'm looking at a picture of him right now. Came over the fax. Big dude. And not real pretty."

"Any relatives?"

"Father unknown. Mother murdered by a boyfriend or a john when he was just a kid. After her death he was raised by grandparents on a farm in northern California."

"What would bring Eckker to these parts?"

"I've been asking myself that."

"You have a file on him?"

"A thick one."

Avondale looked around him. The sun had set, yet complete darkness was a ways off. He wanted to know everything there was to know about Joseph Eckker.

"Brief me."

Eckker sat parked on the other side of the lane on Lake Shore Drive, in the opposite direction of the Hyatt Regency Hotel, where the cop had positioned himself. He smiled. At a point in the middle sat his prey, waiting for him.

It had been so easy. He had broken the window and

entered the house of the woman with the noisy car. From her bedroom he'd heard the cop at the door say he wanted to talk to Roberta Paxton in person. He had only to follow the cop.

She was just down that short, narrow lane. Soon he'd pay her a visit.

Avondale clutched the receiver. Clark's information had the hair on the back of his neck rising.

Avondale caught a flash of a white car as it turned the corner at the intersection and disappeared behind a Trailways bus. He whipped around, clanking the receiver against the metal hood of the phone booth. *Were they running? Jesus, he couldn't lose them.*

The car reappeared in front of the bus and Avondale was relieved to see it wasn't Dr. Reynolds classic T-bird.

"I'm going back to talk to Paxton. Check with you later."

The bright flashing lights of the hotel casino across the street seemed at odds with the peaceful pine-dotted splendor of the mountain on which it stood. It was fully dark now.

Avondale went into a convenience store and bought two packs of Pall Malls.

FORTY-FIVE

Jake walked up from the dock in the dark. A hundred yards from the house he looked up to see Roberta at the bay window, watching him approach.

He gripped the flare gun he'd retrieved from his boat. He'd had to resort to a flare gun, but it was better than no gun at all. For the first time in his life he wished he had an honest-to-God gun, something big and powerful like the cannon Dirty Harry carried. Or a sawed-off shotgun, or one of those outlawed assault rifles. Right now nothing could be too big or too commanding.

As he neared the deck, Jake thought he heard the purring sound of an idling car. He slowed, slipping his finger into the trigger guard of the flare gun.

The sound died suddenly. Jake paused, listened, hearing only the water lapping at the boat and dock pilings. He veered off the road and slipped into the woods. With a pounding heart he moved furtively from tree to tree. Midway down the road, parked fully on the shoulder, was a light green car, whipcord antenna catching the light from a house across the way.

The beating of Jake's heart steadied. He felt his muscles relax and he smiled. *Avondale.* He should have known. He was either staking out the place or making sure they didn't hit the road without a forwarding address. The detective's presence was okay by Jake. At least Avondale had a gun with real bullets and knew how to use it.

Jake turned and, as quietly as he could, made his way back to the house.

The utter silence unnerved Avondale. He had cut his engine, and except for the diffused lights of a house in the woods off to his right, it was dark and quiet.

Only a moment before he thought he'd seen someone wandering around in the dark. The sound of a branch snapping to his left had goose bumps popping out along his arms. Another crack, then steps, slow and deliberate. Avondale mashed his cigarette out in the ashtray and pulled his .45 from the halter holster. He opened the door and slipped out, closing the door without latching it.

Someone or something was out there in the trees. Man or beast? As he neared the doctor's house, twigs snapped sharply under his feet. A frog croaked a moment later, and he welcomed the sound. Shadows stood like black giants, crisscrossing one another. Spiked fingers plucked his shirt-sleeves and ruffled his hair.

He stopped, listened, then moved on. The outline of the house and dock materialized through the tall ponderosa pines. He hadn't run into anyone, nor had he heard movement other than his own since he left his car. Probably deer or, with his rotten luck, it'd be a rabid skunk, both ends ready to rip.

Within a hundred feet of the house, still in the shadow of the trees, he looked up to see a light in the living room go on. Roberta Paxton stood at the window looking out. A man came up behind her, his arms reaching around to envelop her. She closed her eyes and leaned into him trustfully.

Avondale watched, feeling guilty about his unintended voyeurism, yet powerless to move. The doctor, his arms crossed at her breasts, nuzzled her neck and kissed her jaw and throat. She turned her head until their lips met.

Avondale felt a faint stirring. When was the last time he had kissed a woman like that? Or even had the desire to? Two years, five years? Hookers cared nothing for kisses. The last woman he had kissed, really kissed, had been in the evidence room at the station. Officer Cortney had followed him in and, taking his icy hand in her soft warm one, had led him to the back of the room, behind the tall stacks, where she had . . .

Robbi turned in Jake's embrace, her arms reaching up to weave into the thick hair at the back of his neck. She felt so secure in his arms. Only a few minutes earlier she had watched as he came up the path from the dock, heading for the house, then suddenly he was gone. Panic had seized her. She had wanted to run outside, calling his name. And a few minutes later, when he opened the door and came in, she'd gone weak with relief. Fear, she realized, was making her crazy.

Now he was holding her, telling her not to be afraid. Telling her that they had police protection whether they wanted it or not and he had a gun of sorts and she didn't care as long as he was with her and then, against her will, she was pulling away, leaving his warm body, leaving her own body and moving backward, backward, backward, seeing Jake and herself entwined in the living room, their images through the window growing smaller with the distancing.

She was out in the woods. She saw a man—Avondale, the cresting waves in his hair catching the light in a serpentine pattern—standing in the trees, staring into the house at her and Jake. What was happening?

Someone else was out there, closing in on the unsuspecting man.

A metal bar rose above Avondale's head, then came down just as the detective whirled around. The bar crashed down on his shoulder. He cried out, staggered. His eyes, filled with agony, met the eyes of his attacker. He tried to raise the gun. The bar grazed the side of his head before smashing down on his other shoulder.

Avondale dropped to his knees, the gun locked in his long, thin fingers. He seemed unsure what it was, or what to do with it. He looked upward again, but did not blink or flinch when the bar came down solidly and with such force that it seemed to disappear into the deep, dark waves of hair. A sickening gurgle came from the dying man. Still on his knees, he fell forward, the gun buried beneath his chest, his forehead resting on the rapidly darkening carpet of pine needles.

Roberta moaned.

Jake held her tight. "Robbi?"

"Avondale," she whispered hoarsely.

"He's down the street in his car. I'll signal him."

"No!" Robbi cried out, grabbing hold of Jake fiercely. "Avondale's dead. He . . . he—oh, God, he just killed him."

"Are you sure?"

"I saw it."

"Then he's here—right here?"

"Yes. Hurry, hurry, we have to get out—now."

Jake snatched up the phone, slammed it back down. "Dead," he muttered.

He doused the lights, grabbed the flare gun, took her hand, and led her to the back door. Before opening the door, he lifted a key from a peg on the wall, pulled Robbi close, and pressed the key into her hand.

"Run for the dock. He'll expect us to take the car. Do you know how to run the boat?"

"I'm not going without you," she said vehemently.

"If we get separated, or anything happens to me, get to the boat and get the hell out of here."

"Oh, Jake—"

"Do it," he growled.

She nodded.

Jake quietly unlocked the door. The ensuing silence was nerve-racking. The killer stalked the house. He was out there, very close. What was he waiting for? Would he charge in, crashing through the door like an enraged beast, or was he biding his time, waiting for them to go out to him?

"Where is he?" her voice near hysteria.

Jake gave her a brief but meaningful kiss, looked into her eyes. "Ready?"

She nodded.

He lifted the flare gun, opened the door, and whispered, "Go!"

Together they charged out. They ran along the narrow path, looking neither left or right, intent on getting to the boat. At the end of the dock she turned, saw the big man crossing the sandy beach behind them.

Jake grabbed Robbi's arm and lowered her down into the speedboat. He threw off the rope, ordered her to start the engine.

She scrambled over the seat, dropped down behind the wheel, and, with trembling fingers, shoved the key in and turned it. The engine roared.

Jake had one leg over the dock ladder when the killer reached him, grabbed the back of his neck, and flung him to the dock.

Jake rolled, the flare gun flew from his hand, then spun along the weathered planks, stopping inches from the edge. Jake leapt for the boat, but a massive arm knocked him back. The giant was on his knees, his long arm stretched out, fingertips brushing at the ends of Robbi's hair.

Jake dove for the gun. The big man threw out an arm, barring his way. He abandoned his pursuit of Robbi and turned back to Jake.

"Robbi, go!" Jake yelled out. "Dammit, go!"

The engine roared. The man turned, arms spread out as though to seize both victims. The killer frantically pawed the air over the boat as it pulled away from the pilings.

Robbi saw Jake's fingers close around the flare gun a moment before he rolled, toppling over the side of the dock into the water.

She cleared the dock, sped straight out toward the middle of the lake, then turned the wheel sharply. Jake was in that freezing water, and soon his body would become numb, making it impossible to swim or save himself.

She looked back to see Jake pulling himself through the water ten feet from the dock, his strokes strong. Her plan had been to circle, come in as close to him as possible, but she'd miscalculated, turned too soon. She realized that the boat, unable to cut sharp enough, would pass within reach of the dock.

The killer stood midway down the ladder, waiting.

Robbi hit the throttle full. The boat broadsided a piling with enough force to jar the dock and throw the big man off balance. He threw both arms around the ladder.

The impact slammed her against the steering wheel, knocking the wind out of her.

Jake, caught between the boat and the giant, flung an arm over the bow and attempted to pull himself up. Unable to help him, she watched in frozen horror as their attacker, looming over him like a tidal wave, caught hold of his ankle, lifting him up and away.

Robbi screamed, grabbed Jake's hand, and held on.

"Reverse!" Jake called out hoarsely.

Robbi pulled back the throttle. The boat hit the dock again, causing the killer to loosen his grip just long enough for Jake to hurl himself into the boat. He landed on his back in one of the aft seats. His ankle was seized again, but now Jake had the advantage of leverage. He kicked out, catching the man squarely in the throat with his heel. A low grunt was the only sign that the blow had any effect on him. And now the massive hand that held his ankle was squeezing, twisting it savagely.

Jake groaned, trying to turn with the force to keep it

from snapping in two. His face was contorted with pain, he struggled with the flare gun, finally bringing it up, and, with stiff fingers, he fired.

A boom, a whooshing brilliant flash, and flying sparks told her that the projectile had hit its mark. Robbi heard something like a growl, followed by a string of curses. The giant raised a blackened, bloody hand with several digits missing. He stared at the spurting wound. Releasing his hold on Jake's ankle, he gripped the wrist of this grotesque, defiled appendage.

Frantically, Robbi thrust the throttle full forward. With a tremendous roar the boat shot away from the dock, leaving behind the howling beast swaying at its side.

He howled in pain and rage. With his arm between the rungs of the ladder, he grasped his bloody wrist and watched as the boat with its two passengers grew smaller and smaller on the lake's black surface.

A moment later he climbed the ladder to the dock. Holding his left wrist tightly to abate the flow of blood, he strode down the dock to the sandy shore. At a point where the sand blended with the mountain soil, he reached down and buried his scorched, mangled hand in the dirt. Two fingers were missing, the little one entirely, and the ring finger at the second joint. After several moments he pulled it out. Powdery dirt and sand thickly caked the flat stumps. He repeated the process until the blood no longer poured from the wound.

On his way back to his truck he wound around behind the house and stared down at the dead cop.

He then went through the open back door into the house. He saw little of interest there until he found her purse. That he took with him.

After docking at the public marina in Kings Beach, Jake, shivering uncontrollably, dropped coins into a pay phone at the 7 Eleven. He placed a call to the Reno PD. Clark, Avondale's partner, came on the line.

Jake told him what had happened.

Clark swore. "You saw him kill Avondale?"

"No. Robbi saw it clairvoyantly. He had parked midway on the lane. He must've walked through the trees to the house. Look, check it out for yourself."

There were a few minutes while this information was being assimilated, then passed on. A moment later Clark said solemnly, "Units are on their way now. Where are you?"

Jake ignored his question. "Any idea yet who he is?"

"His name is Joseph Eckker. He escaped from prison four years ago. We've got every law enforcement agency in a seventy-mile radius, California included, looking for him. If he's hiding out in a church somewhere in the forest, we'll have him in no time. A guy like that can't be invisible."

Invisible? Invincible? Why not? Jake thought ironically.

"Where are you two?" Clark asked again.

"At the moment we're safe. That's all you need to know," Jake said through chattering teeth. As he talked, Robbi stood close behind, trying to warm him by vigorously rubbing the gooseflesh on his arms. "We have a better chance on our own. Avondale led him to us."

"That's bullshit, Reynolds. Come on in. We'll protect you, you have my word."

Jake chuckled humorlessly. "You ever see the movie *Terminator,* Detective?"

"Yeah. But what the hell does—"

"Well, as far as I'm concerned, there's not much difference between that character and the one we just tangled with, except that one's real and one's not. This Eckker character is injured again. He stopped a flare with his hand."

"Dammit, Reynolds, that's all the more reason to come—"

"I'm freezing my ass off out here. We'll keep in touch." Jake hung up. He turned to Robbi, hugged her. "C'mon, let's get a room with a fireplace."

FORTY-SIX

When Eckker had scrubbed away the dirt and sand on his hand, with it went the peeling black shriveled skin. The weeping burns concerned him little, but the raw stumps plagued him. He felt physically lacking, defective. And it was all her fault.

He poured hydrogen peroxide over the hand and fingers, and watched, fascinated, as the wounds erupted into a bloody froth. The stinging intensified his rage.

Lifting the ragged flaps of skin over the raw stumps, he smeared a tallow-colored salve over the wounds, then wrapped his entire hand in clean gauze. Blood seeped through the bandage.

When he finished, he pulled her handbag onto his lap and opened it. He lifted out each item, inspected it painstakingly before putting it aside and selecting another. He found her driver's license and examined the picture in the upper corner. Then from one of the accordion sleeves of plastic that held her credit cards, he carefully lifted out a color snapshot of Tobie sitting bareback on her horse.

He studied both pictures. The two sisters were so much alike.

His pulse raced. He wanted them both.

One would be his to have and hold.

The other one would die.

At noon, Jake and Roberta left Lakeside Lodge and walked to a diner on the main street. Sitting at a table near enough to a window to see outside clearly yet back far enough to not be seen from the street, they ate ham and eggs, drank cup after cup of coffee, and read the newspaper. The composite of the killer, with and without the beard, looking every bit the monster he was, stood out starkly on the front page.

"For the time being we're probably safe where we are. But we have to rent a car. We're too damn vulnerable on foot." He picked up the check and stood. "Ready?"

Robbi absently reached for her mammoth shoulder bag, forgetting again that she'd had to leave it at Jake's. Something worried at her . . . her purse, its contents, left at Jake's.

"Omigod," she whispered.

"What?"

"My purse was inside your house. If he took it, he'd have my address book. It has the names and numbers of everyone I know. Friends, coworkers, family . . ." She let those words die away. *Her family.* They lived nearby. And naturally the first place he would expect her to go would be home.

"Jake, I've got to warn my family."

He dug in his pocket for change, handed her an assortment of silver. "There's a phone by the register."

In the foyer, she fed coins into the pay phone and jabbed at buttons. She was relieved to hear it ringing. It rang and rang. *Answer please,* she said under her breath. She was about to hang up when the line was picked up.

"Paxton residence."

"Hanley, it's Robbi. Is my mother or sister there?"

"Hello, Robbi. How are you?"

"Is everything okay there?"

"Why, sure. It's a good thing you called when you did, else you would've got no answer. I just came in to tend to your daddy. Your mama's down again with one of those bad headaches and your little sis is out wearing out the hooves on that black beast of hers."

"Has anyone been out to the house today? Any strangers?"

"No one's been out as far as I know. 'Course, I've been outdoors all morning. Like I said, I came to see to your daddy."

Robbi buckled under the relief. "Hanley, listen to me. Listen carefully. Someone . . . a man, is after me. I think he might go out to the ranch, looking for me."

"What man, Robbi?"

"He's dangerous, extremely dangerous."

"Why's he after you?" The tone dubious.

"It's a long story and I don't have time. Hanley, I want you to call the sheriff or whoever it is that's law out your way. Tell him to contact the Reno Police Department, a Detective Clark. Have him mention my name."

"Hold it a sec. Reno police . . . Clark," he repeated. "Okay."

"Clark will fill him in on this man, the killer—"

"A killer?" Hanley cut in.

"Yes, a killer. Do you have a gun or a rifle?"

"The place is full of them. You know that. Your daddy has about every kind they made."

"Load one and carry it. When my sister comes home, get her and my mom in the car and tell them to go straight to the police."

"What about your daddy?"

"Yes, of course, him too."

"Your sister just left. I don't 'spect her back for a while."

"Any idea where she went?"

"Not a clue."

"Dammit," she said under her breath. "Just make sure they all leave the house, okay?"

"I'll see to it personally. What's this man look like?"

"Dark hair and . . . he's big. Very big. Don't take any chances, Hanley."

"Robbi, I don't understand any of this. It's all crazy stuff. What's going on? Why is this killer after you?"

"Later, just call the sheriff." There were more questions, but she ignored them and hung up.

Jake had paid the check and was standing behind her.

She ran trembling fingers through her hair.

"They'll be all right." He put a hand to her face. "C'mon, let's get that car."

They stepped out into the bright, warm mountain air.

* * *

On a scratch pad before him, Hanley Gates had scribbled *sheriff, Reno police, Clark*. The number for the local sheriff was attached to a sticker on the base of the telephone. He lifted the receiver again, dialed the number. Two rings later a gruff voice identified himself as Deputy Barr.

Hanley lowered the receiver and let it gently slip back into the cradle. He buried tremulous fingers into his wispy gray hair. "Lord, oh, Lord, what have I done? *What* have I done?"

He absently brushed his hands on the back pockets of his dusty Wranglers, then he sighed and, with a weariness befitting a man of advanced years, he walked out of the room.

Robbi and Jake took the boat back to Crystal Bay. They put in at the public dock and walked to the Hyatt Lake Tahoe. At a Hertz booth just inside the door they rented a car.

"I want to check in with Clark," Jake said.

"I'll get the car."

Clark come on the line. "He was right where you said he would be. Dead."

Jake knew he meant Avondale.

"Anything?"

"No," Clark said. "We're chasing our damn tails."

"Last night you said you knew who he was. Give me some background."

"Joseph Eckker. Thirty-five. Illegitimate. Childhood a real horror. Abusive, prostitute mother. He took to the streets early, stealing, fighting, drugs. At eight he was sent to live with grandparents after his mother was beaten to death by her crazy live-in boyfriend—which, incidentally, he was a witness to."

"Go on."

"Couldn't stay out of trouble. One correctional institution after another. At sixteen he was incarcerated for abduction and assault with intent to commit rape. A model prisoner he wasn't. He got additional time for repeated violence and breakouts, at which he was quite adept. And hard time for brutally killing a cellmate."

The receiver in Jake's hand became slippery with moisture. "Escapee?" Jake asked.

"Four years ago from maximum security."

"Christ."

After promising to check in again later, Jake signed off.

She had pulled the beige Buick Skylark under the portico of the Hyatt where Jake was waiting. He climbed behind the wheel, then drove around to a lot overlooking the lake and a playground. He parked and shut off the engine.

Jake told her what Clark had said.

Roberta rubbed her temple. Nothing he had said surprised her. She knew the man in her visions was capable of anything.

A hundred feet in front of them, at the private beach of the hotel, the sounds of children carried to where they sat. From out of nowhere Robbi detected the sweet scent of watermelon and coconut. Then melodious humming filled her head. Joy enveloped her, a feeling of peacc and innocence. Shimmering water cascaded over her arms. She felt the coolness of it, felt her body light and buoyant, felt smooth pebbles under the soles of her feet and spongy mud between her toes. A horse snorted. She saw trees, quivering aspen leaves. All around her the forest danced with speckled sunlight.

A deadly calm clutched at Roberta's heart.

FORTY-SEVEN

He listened to the splashing sounds and cautiously crept forward, avoiding twigs and pine cones in his stealthy advance to the pond. The horse, sensing his approach, whinnied and pranced nervously. A pair of shorts, T-shirt, and worn athletic shoes lay at the edge of the flat rock. The girl, humming, intent on her water acrobatics, was unaware of his presence or the horse's agitation.

He stopped between two fir trees and crouched down. He watched her, unable to take his eyes from her sweet essence. She was so beautiful. So much like Celia.

She was in his pond. Everything had a purpose. Nothing was mere chance or coincidence. The sound of a helicopter over the ridge broke into his reverie. They were getting too close. He couldn't stay here anymore. It was time to move, to find another mountain and start again. This time he would do it right. Tobie loved the mountain. She would want to live in the wilderness no matter where the mountain was.

But what of the other one, her sister? He rubbed his bandaged hand.

When he found her he would kill her.

Jake felt Robbi's fingernails dig into his wrist. He watched her staring trancelike through the windshield. Her body was beside him in the rented car, but her mind was somewhere else. There was nothing he could do but watch and wait.

She sat stiff, gaze fixed straight ahead, then in a cracked voice she said, *"Tobe . . ."*

She blinked, sighed heavily, seemed to visibly sag, then she was looking around frantically.

"Let's go," she said abruptly.

He started the car, turned to her. "Where?"

"My parents' place. I just saw my sister, Tobie."

It was late afternoon. With the summer tourist traffic it seemed to take them forever to go the eight miles from Incline Village to Kings Beach. They turned northwest toward Truckee.

On the two-lane highway, Robbi reflected on the last vision. She had gone into Tobie's mind, had felt her mood and experienced the sensory sensations around her, just as she had done all those years before when her brother was in the river, drowning. Her sister was the first person other than Ronnie that she had been able to link with this way. Why? What did it mean? Was her sister to be his next victim? Tobie, in the pond, had perceived no danger. *But Roberta had.*

Ten minutes later they arrived at the house. Jake headed to the stable to see if Tobie's horse was there.

Roberta rushed inside.

In her mother's dark bedroom, Robbi used the diffused light from the open door to find her way to the large canopied bed.

"Mom? Mom, are you asleep?" she whispered, forcing herself to speak calmly. "It's Robbi."

"Hmmm? Oh, hello, darling," she answered weakly, and started to sit up. "I was just napping."

"Mom, Jake and I have come to help you leave."

"Leave?" Lois said quietly, matching her daughter's hushed tone. "Leave for where?"

"It doesn't matter. We're all in danger here. I don't mean to scare you, but I want you to get up, dress, and pack a few things. We're leaving as soon as Tobie gets back."

"Roberta, what's going on?" Her eyes showed confusion.

"I'll explain later."

Her mother took her hand. "This isn't one of your strange notions, is it?"

"Later."

She quickly made her way back to the kitchen.

Pomona stood at the sink, filling a copper tea kettle.

"Pomona, have you seen my sister?"

"She ride off like every other day," the woman said without turning around.

"Where's Hanley?"

The woman looked at her now, frowning. "Something not right?"

"Hanley, have you seen him?" Her voice betrayed her impatience.

"He out there someplace fooling 'round."

Robbi crossed the room, flung open the back door,

and ran toward the stable, calling both names. Jake was just leaving the stable. He shook his head.

"Hanley!" She pulled up, pivoted uncertainly. She called out Hanley's name again, her voice nearly a shriek.

The caretaker stepped out of the tack room and quietly stood facing Robbi.

"She hasn't returned?" Robbi asked Hanley.

"No, Miss." He stared out toward the woods. "It's not unusual for her to be gone a couple of hours."

"What's going on here? Why aren't my mother and father ready to leave? Where's the gun I asked you to carry?" she said accusingly.

He shrugged, looking helpless.

What was wrong with Hanley, Robbi wondered. Always so strong and virile, he now seemed old—old and feeble and evasive.

Roberta's chest constricted. Why was he acting so strangely? What the hell was going on?

"Did you call the sheriff?" she asked.

The man continued to avoid her eyes.

"Dammit, Hanley, did you?" she shouted.

His gaze finally met hers. "No, Miss."

Eckker had worked his way around the pond until he was near enough to the horse to stroke it. The animal cast him uneasy glances, fidgeted. The girl was out of the pond and lying on her back on the large flat rock five yards from where he stood.

Excitement pounded in his veins. He'd waited so long for this moment. Thought that it could never be. But everything was changed. He could do as he pleased now. No one could stop him. He'd have to do things differently. There wasn't time to try to gain her trust. That would all come later when they were far away from here . . . on their own mountain.

He moved around the horse and started toward her, no longer mindful of his footsteps. He had nearly reached the rock when she turned her head lazily and opened her eyes.

Shock and terror registered on her face. She sprang upward like a jackknife, quick, yet uncertain what to do or where to go. She attempted to cover her nakedness with her hands.

He advanced on her, saying nothing.

She scooted backward on the rock and tried to make it to the pond. He reached out and grabbed her by the foot. She cried out.

He bent, picked up her clothes, and held them out to her.

She snatched them and held them in front of her.

"Get dressed."

She quickly slipped the T-shirt over her head. He released her foot and she anxiously pulled her shorts on. When he reached for her again she tried to run. She fell on the rock, cried out when she scraped her knee, then she turned and lunged toward the water. He caught her, swung her around. His bandaged hand circled her throat. He squeezed, willing himself to go easy. He didn't want to lose her after so long.

"Shhh, shhh," he crooned softly in her ear. "Don't be afraid, sweet Tobie . . . beautiful Tobie. I won't hurt you. I'd never hurt you."

She struggled, her arms and legs merely jerking in reflex now, then she collapsed.

* * *

"Why?" Roberta asked, staring at the caretaker in disbelief.

Hanley shook his head.

In confusion she turned to look at Jake, who was moving her way. He covered half the distance, then suddenly it wasn't Jake walking toward her, it was *him,* the killer. *The look in his eyes induced sheer terror like she had never felt before.*

The massive, broad hand came toward her face and wound into her long hair. The other hand, wrapped in soiled, bloody strips of gauze, closed around her neck. Her breathing became labored, torturous. She heard harsh gasps and screams that came out mere squeaks.

Robbi gripped Jake's arm, struck numb by the horror of what she was seeing. *The killer's face pressed close to hers. His black eyes seared into hers, his foul breath made her sick as bright lights exploded before her eyes.*

Then he was gone.

"He has her," Robbi, filled with despair, whispered.

Jake held her, a soothing hand in her hair, stroking.

Her mother stood in her robe in the doorway to the kitchen. "Robbi, what is it? What's happening? Someone tell me what's going on here?"

"Mama," Robbi said, shaking all over. "Tobie's in trouble."

"What kind of trouble? How do you know this?"

"I *know* it. Just like I knew Ronnie was in trouble. I see it."

"Oh, darling . . ." Lois began sadly.

"Don't start that," she said sharply to her mother. "You never believed me. 'It's not normal, Robbi. People will think you're crazy, Robbi.' Well, I wasn't crazy then. And I'm not crazy now."

Lois looked to Jake, questioning.

"It's true, Mrs. Paxton," Jake said. "Believe her."

Roberta stormed into the house. In the kitchen she snatched the receiver off the wall and began to dial the number of the local sheriff. Hanley appeared. He pressed the lever, held his hand on it.

Robbi turned on him, shaking with rage.

"Calling the police won't help," Hanley said.

Then Jake was there. "What do you mean?"

"If he does have Tobie . . . he might kill her or . . . or let her die if he thinks . . ."

"What?" Robbi said.

"He won't do nothing unless . . . unless . . ."

"Unless what?" Robbi wanted to shake the words out of him.

"Unless his back's up against the wall. I made him promise he wouldn't bother nobody here." Hanley avoided her eyes. "I told him to stay clear of her. I threatened to turn him in if he did. I never dreamed . . . I—oh, Lord . . ." He shook his head ruefully, his gaze fell on Lois. "I'm sorry, Mrs. Paxton."

Lois laid a comforting hand on the caretaker's arm. "Hanley, please, what is it?"

Robbi felt a scream rising from deep inside. With it she felt fury, frustration, ineptness.

"Who is this guy?" Jake asked.

"He's my grandson."

The room became deathly quiet.

Robbi, disbelieving, recovered enough to turn back to the phone.

"No, please," Hanley pleaded. "First let me tell you about him—about us."

"Why should we believe you? You're a liar. You told me you had no idea where your grandson was." She punched buttons on the phone.

Jake stepped up to her. He took her by the shoulders and said, "Robbi, let's listen to him."

"There's no time," she said.

"We can't afford to go off half-cocked. Hanley knows him. We have to trust him."

She clenched the receiver, wanting to smash it down, wanting to scream and pound her fists against the caretaker's chest. Instead, she inhaled deeply and slowly hung it up.

Jake put an arm around her. "Let's all go into the other room and sit down."

They started out of the kitchen to the front of the house. Hanley moved ahead. "No, not in there. This way. I can talk while I get ready."

Lois, Jake, and Roberta followed him into the large open room that was her father's den and gun room.

Hanley went to an oak case, removed a key ring from his belt loop, unlocked the drawer. After a moment's deliberation, he choose a snubnose .38.

"Joe—that's his name, Joseph Eckker—is my daughter's . . . son. Jennifer was fast and wild. She ran off in her teens, went to San Francisco. We lost track of her then. It wasn't till we learned she'd been killed by some crazy, outta-his-head junkie that we even knew we had a grandson. There was nothin' to do but take him in . . . him being kin.

"He was eight. Emma and me thought we had another chance to raise one right. Guess God didn't agree. Joe was already too tainted. Stealin', fightin', and the likes." Hanley went to a drawer in the tall rifle cabinet, unlocked it, and removed a box of shells. "And he was having these fits, epilepsy, I guess. Any fool could see the boy'd been mistreated."

As he talked he carefully slipped a cartridge into each hole of the cylinder. "Emma took him to church every Sunday and I showed him how to live off the land. For a city kid, he sure took to the woods." He popped open the snaps on his western shirt, slipped the gun inside, under his belt, then closed the shirt. The gun was undetectable.

"Then he got into a little scrap with the law and . . ." The words trailed off.

"He was arrested," Jake said. "For what?"

Hanley looked as if he would not answer.

"I can find out, Mr. Gates." Jake made a move to reach for the phone. "A few phone calls."

"When he was sixteen he took a fancy to a little neighbor gal and . . . when she wouldn't have nothin' to do with him, he . . . well, he forced himself on her."

"He went to prison for rape?"

Hanley looked away. "Attempted rape and assault."

"What aren't you telling us?" Jake said.

"This ain't easy for me, Doctor." Hanley cleared his throat. "Joe spent eighteen months in what they used to call a reform school. A month after he come home, that little gal just disappeared. Some said she run off, some said Joe got even. They never could pin anything on him, though they sure as hell tried."

"What's your opinion?" Jake asked.

"He's my grandson, Dr. Reynolds. I hafta give him the benefit of the doubt."

"What landed him in prison?"

"Same thing. Another gal. He don't mean to hurt them. It's just that he gets disheartened when they don't take to him like he does to them. He don't know his own strength. And he's got a real short fuse."

"So for years you've hidden him somewhere in these

mountains?" Jake asked, incredulous.

"He gets around. Has his own truck. Earns his own money cutting trees and selling cords of firewood. He loves the woods. He's a loner. Never liked being around a lot of people. I figured it wouldn't hurt nothing." He looked at Robbi and her mother.

"Where is he?" Jake asked.

"I can't tell you—for Tobie's own good," Hanley said. "You go marching in on him and he's gonna get mad. I know him, I know what he can do."

"So do I," Robbi whispered.

"I gotta be the one to go. He trusts me. I can find out what he's done with Tobie, and then I can talk to him, reason with him. He respects me. And he knows I can turn him in to the law. But the important thing is finding out where she is. If he gets killed first, we may never find her."

"A church," Robbi interjected, "does he have anything to do with a church?"

"That's enough questions," Hanley said, picking up a skinning knife in a leather sheath, then discarding it.

Robbi stopped him. "Hanley, Tobie's so young and trusting . . . if it comes to blood relation over—"

Anger flashed in his eyes, then disappeared. "I've known Tobie since she was just a pup. She's like one of my own. She's closer than my own. Don't insult me, Roberta."

Insult him? Robbi wanted to strike out at the man who'd allowed this evil monster to practically live with them. But hysterics wouldn't do anyone any good. She bit her lip, looked away, nodded.

Lois Paxton stepped in front of him and spoke for the first time since the scene in the kitchen. "Hanley, what if you don't come back? How will we find him?"

He picked up the Browning semi-automatic .12 shotgun and a full box of shells. "I'll be back."

"Wait a minute," Jake said. "You've got two hours, then we're calling the police."

Hanley paused, nodded. Then he was gone.

On the flat rock he squatted on his haunches, brushed the hair from her face, and looked at her curiously.

Her skin was smooth, flawless, the color of a ripe apricot. Beneath the damp shirt he could make out her thin form. The calves of her long legs were covered with a fine fuzz.

So unspoiled, he thought, quelling the excitement building inside him. She was young enough to mold to his way. The others had been too set in their ways—too worldly.

He lifted her, carried her to the horse and draped her forward across the saddle. Swatches of bright blood stood out on her throat and on the back of her T-shirt. He looked at his left hand and saw his own blood saturating the edge of the gauze bandage. Thinking about the missing digits turned his mood ugly again. Roberta Paxton would pay for that.

He led the horse in the direction of his sanctuary.

FORTY-EIGHT

Hanley pulled off the logging road and parked his pickup behind a thicket of manzanita. He shut off the engine, grabbed the Browning, got out, and headed up the mountain on foot. Storm clouds were amassing to the south. A slight breeze rustled the collar of his shirt.

Thirty minutes later, only slightly winded from the long climb, he reached the pond, skirted around the west end, found the trail, and followed it. Another half hour and he neared the clearing. He quieted his steps.

From the tree line Hanley squinted and stared off in the direction of the wooden structure. Tethered to a quaking aspen was Tobie's black horse. Hanley felt a twisting in his gut.

Staying within the cover of the trees, he made his way to the horse. Prince whinnied, tossed his head at the man's furtive approach. Hanley patted his neck, spoke softly to quiet him. The horse recognized him, nuzzled his shoulder affectionately. "Good fella, good fella," he whispered, stroking Prince's coarse mane. The mane was wet and sticky with drying blood.

Hanley stared at the dilapidated church, the only remaining structure of a tiny logging settlement abandoned at the turn of the century. In a full chokeberry bush at the base of the tree he hid the shotgun. He patted the horse, spit a stream of tobacco juice into the bushes, then started for the ruins, his hand touching the metal bulge at his waist. A scraping sound reached him as he neared the building. Surreptitiously, Hanley circled until he found the source. At the rear of the church the massive, sweaty back of his grandson, bent to his task of digging, presented itself to him. Shovelfuls of dirt formed at his knees. The hole was five feet long and, at this point, no more than a foot deep. Sweat trickled down Hanley's sides. He carefully drew back, then continued to the far end of the building. He lifted the trapdoor and quickly went down the steps, closing the door behind him.

The basement smelled of loamy earth, mildew, and burned coffee. The main room held an assortment of discarded furniture that, years ago, Hanley had supplied.

No one was in the room.

The scrape of the shovel moving through the dirt drifted down to him.

Hanley moved along the walls, tapping, listening for any variation in the sound. Next he moved the larger pieces of furniture and the mattress, looking for a door that meant access to a subcellar.

He was sweating profusely now, his heart banging like a bell clapper in his chest. He listened. The steady scraping went on.

He turned back to the stairs, started up. He paused, stared curiously at the riser. Stepping back down, he moved along the staircase. The space beneath the stairs had been closed in with planks of scrap wood. At the narrow end, almost invisible, a door blended with the planks. Hanley dug his fingernails in a crack and pulled. The door opened.

He bent over and poked his head in. The space was dark. He looked around the main room, saw a book of matches on the table, retrieved them, then went back to the opening. He lit one and held it inside. In the flickering glow of the match, depth was deceptive, but it was plain to see the space didn't run the full length of the stairway. Another closed-off area stood under the high point of the stairwell.

The match went out. Hanley bent down to enter the stairwell. He crab-walked until he felt another door. This one with a dead bolt, its key in the lock. He turned the key; the tumblers clanked softly. The door drifted open.

The dark crowded around him. Hanley's fingers fumbled out another match, struck it. The flame flared so bright he instinctively blinked, lowering his head. When it settled into a steady, soft glow, he looked up.

Just inside the room and to the left, she lay on a small army cot. She still wore the white T-shirt and shorts he'd seen her in that morning when she'd galloped off on Prince. Her feet were bare.

It took him a moment before he could gather enough spit in his mouth to speak.

"Tobie," he whispered.

Her head lolled sluggishly and she moaned. "Hanley?"

The match burned out.

He fumbled with the matches, tore one off.

The vise that clamped over his shoulder nearly paralyzed him. He cried out, sank to his knees.

"Joe . . . it's me, your gra—grandpa," he managed to say through the pain.

"What are you doing here?" Joe said, his tone hard.

"I've come to—"

He was cut off. "Did you bring anyone?"

"'Course not."

"What do you want?"

"Let's talk, son."

Hanley was being pulled back, out of the room, through the angled space. He toppled over, cringed as his foot caught sharply under him, scrambled back on his feet to continue troll-like to the door of the stairwell. He was pitched roughly out into the center of the room.

Hanley stared up at the man towering over him. He was filthy with dirt, dust, and sweat. One hand was covered in a tattered, grimy bandage, black with dried blood. The brown T-shirt stuck to his skin at his waist with another spot of dark blood.

"You were looking for *her,* weren't you?" Eckker said, pushing him back down.

"Damn right I was. Have you gone crazy? We had an agreement. I let you stay up here, you keep away from the Paxtons—especially that young one in there. Lord, boy, she's just a baby."

"She's mine. I'm not giving her up."

"Don't be a fool. I never took you for a fool, Joe."

"I'm leaving this mountain. She's coming with me."

"You can't hide, son. Tobie's sister knows you got Tobie."

"How's she know?"

"She says she saw you."

"You're lying."

"I swear."

His grandson seemed to ponder a moment, then, "It don't matter. I'm gonna kill her. I'll kill anybody who tries to stop me."

"What's happened to your hand, boy?" Hanley asked.

As Eckker looked down at the bloody bandage, Hanley reached inside his shirt, grabbed hold of the gun, and pulled it from his waistband. Eckker looked up. With a wounded growl the big man charged him, grabbing at the gun. Both men had a hand on it. The gun discharged.

Hanley dropped to his knees. Blood saturated the faded plaid shirt. He struggled for air, clawing at the other man's pant leg. A moment later he collapsed.

FORTY-NINE

Tobie tried hard to control the wild beating of her heart. She fought the nausea and lightheadedness. Her throat felt bruised, restricted. Everything was black, airless.

Only a few minutes before she'd heard Hanley call her name. Then a commotion, raised voices, and finally a loud bang. Someone had cried out in pain.

"Hanley?" Tobie whispered in a shaky voice.

Eckker carried the body up the stairs and out into the yard. The sky was overcast now. Patterns of cloud shadows darkened the mountains. The horse, tethered to the aspen, flared his nostrils and snorted.

Eckker lowered the old man into the freshly dug hole. He lifted the shovel and began to toss dirt over the top of him. A sudden burst of excitement charged through his body, fueling his actions. He raced against time, knowing what was coming.

Clumps of earth flew as first the odor, then the

images, assaulted him. He gripped the shovel's handle, his hands sliding down the shaft as he dropped to his knees, the seizure now fully upon him.

Hanley opened his eyes, squinting upward into the gray afternoon light. He tasted fresh dirt, gagged. Searing pain, like a branding iron against his lungs, burned in his chest as he staggered to his feet, pushing dirt away. Sprawled inches from him was the unconscious form of his grandson. Hanley crawled from the shallow grave.

He struggled to stay upright, his steps slow yet urgent as he crossed the yard to the horse. Sweat stung his eyes, blood soaked his clothes. Reaching the tree, he leaned against the rough bark, forcing himself to take shallow breaths. Through a haze of pain he stared at the bloody path behind him.

Prince whinnied softly. With great effort Hanley retrieved the shotgun from the bushes and untied the tether. Then, glancing over his shoulder, he took hold of the saddle horn, and, after several agonizing attempts, managed to mount the jittery horse. Leaning forward, the shotgun across the front of the saddle, Hanley gently urged the horse on.

Eckker fought his way back to consciousness. Disoriented, he looked around the yard, wondering what he'd been doing before the fit came over him. In front of him was the hole. He'd been digging. He had to get back to work.

Sluggishly he rose to his knees, reached for the

shovel. Thoughts of his grandfather flashed in his head. His grandfather? He'd been up here to the church. He'd been in the cellar—snooping. A gun.

Eckker struggled to stand. He'd killed his grandfather and put him in the grave. Now the space was empty.

He looked around, saw no sign of him. A trail of blood led him to the aspen tree where the horse had been tethered. Gone, both of them. Gone to warn the Paxtons.

He cursed. Now he'd have to go after him.

Tobie heard a key in a lock. A moment later, through she was unable to see anything, she felt another's presence.

"Hanley?" her voice a mere whisper. "Hanley, is that you?"

A callused hand stroked her thigh. She jerked, pulled her legs in tightly.

"Who's there?"

"Tobie—" a bottomless voice began.

She said nothing.

"Tobie . . ." As though he simply wanted to hear her name spoken aloud.

"Where's Hanley. I want Hanley."

"Gone."

She began to cry. Deep, hopeless sobs.

The hand grazed a path down the front of her T-shirt, between her small breasts. She shuddered. Who was he? What did he want with her? Where was she?

"We'll leave soon," he said.

She heard the door close and the lock engage.

* * *

They gathered in the gun room. Jake had selected a pump action .12-gauge shotgun. He stood at the desk pushing shells into the loading gate. For herself, Robbi decided on a lightweight .20-gauge single action.

Lois Paxton, refusing even to handle a gun, wrung her hands and paced. She stopped, looked solemnly at her daughter, then broke the long silence. "You saw this man take Tobie?"

"Yes." Robbi slid a shell into the chamber. As though talking to herself, she added quietly, "All along it was really Tobie he wanted; the others were merely surrogates." She turned and faced the French windows, staring out at the rapidly darkening sky. The gun made a sharp cracking sound as she snapped the barrel shut. "I couldn't save Ronnie, but, dammit, I *will* save Tobie."

Robbi shivered. Through the windows of the sun porch she saw sheet lightning flash in the distance. A few minutes earlier, as she and Jake closed the windows in the porch against the gusty winds, everything around Robbi had suddenly gone black. At first she thought her blindness had returned. Then she realized she was not alone in her mind; the blackness dwelled in another place. She'd smelled earth and decay and coconut. Then Tobie's fears had flooded her brain.

Now, able to see clearly again, and Tobie no longer in her head, she said to Jake, "It was pitch black. She may have been blindfolded."

"Any sounds that might give a clue to her location?"

"Nothing. It smelled of earth. It was cool. I'm positive it was underground."

Lightning flashed across the western sky. Thunder followed. Robbi stiffened, remembering the running nightmare. A sudden gust of wind rattled the windows. As the storm clouds increased, the sky darkened.

Lois had gotten dressed and was now sitting rigid on an overstuffed floral-printed chair. She held a small throw pillow to her chest, picking at the fringe, her lap littered with a cottony fuzz.

"I'm calling the police," Roberta said.

"No!" her mother cried out. "You heard what Hanley said. He'll kill her. Listen to Hanley, he knows best."

"But Mom, Hanley may be dead."

"It hasn't been two hours yet," Lois said, her eyes darting from Robbi to Jake. "Give him the two hours."

Robbi looked at Jake. He nodded.

FIFTY

Eckker stood in the shadows of the stable. There had been no sign of his grandfather or the horse on his trip down the mountain.

He looked through the windows of a room at the back of the large house and watched the woman he had to kill.

A tall, good-looking man moved to the window and stood gazing out. Eckker's gut twisted. There was the one responsible for taking pieces of his body. Eckker rubbed the bandaged hand on his pant leg. It would give him great pleasure to annihilate, slowly and with much pain, this man who had deformed him.

From his pocket he took out a Swiss army knife, then went to look for the telephone line to the house.

"Hanley's quarters, where are they?" Jake asked Roberta.

"Out by the stable. Why?"

"This waiting is driving me crazy. Maybe we'll find something."

Roberta gripped the shotgun and opened the screen door. "C'mon."

With the wind ripping at their hair and clothes, they ran across the yard to Hanley's bungalow. The first drops of rain began to fall—fat, silver-dollar-size drops.

The door was unlocked. They rushed inside and, using the weight of their bodies against the powerful gusts, they forced the door closed.

"What are we looking for?" she asked.

"Anything that can shed some light on this . . . this . . ."

Roberta didn't wait for him to finish, she strode across the room to a bureau and pulled drawers out.

Jake pried open a footlocker under the window and began going through it.

"Look here." He sat on the bunk, a shoebox filled with papers, photos, and personal momentos in his lap.

She sank down beside him and gazed at a faded Polaroid snapshot of a threesome—a thin-legged man in jeans and western straw hat, an ebony-eyed woman, her expression stern, and a dark-haired boy who looked fourteen but probably was only eight or nine.

Two newspaper clippings. An obituary: *Jennifer Eckker, 25, died Monday in her San Francisco residence . . . surviving are her parents, Hanley and Emily Gates of Cold Creek, California, and a son, Joseph.*

A two-inch article from the *San Francisco Examiner,* September 9, 1963:

WOMAN BEATEN TO DEATH,
BOYFRIEND ARRESTED

Jennifer Eckker, 25, was found dead in her residence at the Colonial Apartments in the Ten-

derloin. Her live-in boyfriend, Charles Blackstone, was arrested at the scene. Neighbors, hearing the woman's screams, called the authorities, who were unable to respond in time to save her. Eckker's eight-year-old son witnessed her death . . .

Robbi looked at the photograph of Hanley, his wife, and grandson again. The three were standing in front of a white wooden church.

Robbi closed her eyes. Another wooden church materialized in the recesses of her mind.

She heard faint creaks and groans. The walls of the chapel vibrated like a living creature breathing in and out. The ceiling sagged, opened up to the sky.

What did it mean?

"The walls are coming down," Robbi whispered. "The church is falling apart."

Jake took her hands. "Which church. His church?"

"Yes . . ." Robbi saw the parishioners in the chapel waver, grow nebulous as they seemed to break up along with the building. The building was disintegrating. She saw weeds and wildflowers growing inside the empty shell.

"Ruins." She spun around to Jake, grabbed his arm. "Not a church, but the ruins of a church."

"On this mountain?"

Roberta jumped to her feet, charged by the probability.

They ran back to the house through the steady rain.

Pomona had brought tea on a silver tray and was pouring.

"Mom, do you know of any old buildings, a church maybe, around here?"

"I'm afraid I've never paid much attention to the area. Your father is the one who knows this mountain inside and out. Before his stroke he traipsed all over—"

A distant voice shouted Lois's name.

"That's the mister now," Pomona said. "Hanley, he usually put him to bed long ago."

Lois rose slowly, looking weary. "Jake, could you help me with my husband?"

"I think it's time you, Pomona, and your husband left." He took her arm. "I'll help you take him out."

"Wait," Robbi said, stopping them. "Give me a few minutes with him."

"Honey, leave him alone. You know how difficult he can be."

"We have no choice, Mom. He may know where she is."

Lois nodded.

"I'll bring the car around to the back door," Jake said.

"Pomona will show you where the keys are," Roberta said, hurrying from the room.

She had never been in his bedroom in this house, but she had only to follow a *tap-tap* and the string of curses to find the room and her father. At the end of the long hallway stood a pair of white enameled doors.

Roberta rapped lightly.

"Come! Come!"

She opened the door and stepped in.

Caught off guard by her presence, his jaw worked up and down. He recovered. "Lost?"

"No."

"Then leave. Send Hanley."

"In a minute. I—I need some answers."

He looked past her to thc doorway, where Lois

silently stood. "What is this, a circus? Where the hell is Hanley? I'd like to retire, if it's not too much trouble."

Roberta forced herself to stay calm. "Tobie's in trouble."

"Her mother can handle it," he said. "I want to go to bed."

"Cameron," Lois stepped into the room.

"Out. Both of you."

"Dammit. It's no use, you were right," Roberta said to her mother, turning to go. "We're only wasting time with him. I'm calling the police."

Lois stopped her, turned to her husband. "Cameron, this is very serious. Tobie—"

"Is your responsibility," he cut in brusquely. "If she's in trouble, *you* get her out." He swiveled the wheelchair around, putting his back to them.

Lois stood still for a moment, then bore down on her husband, anger twisting her face.

"You listen to me. You have a daughter. She's thirteen years old. Right now, as we speak, a monster of a man has her in some godforsaken place in these woods, and he may kill her. Do you understand? You've been all over these hills." Without taking her eyes from him, she said, "Robbi, tell him what you're looking for."

"A stone and log structure, probably the ruins of a church."

Something in his eyes sparked.

He knew. The bastard knew. Roberta felt a mixture of disgust and elation.

"Tell her where it is," Lois demanded, gripping the wheelchair tightly.

"She'd never find it," his tone cynical.

Robbi ran from the room, oblivious of the tears

welling up in her eyes.

She rushed into the gun room. On a bookshelf she found dozens of regional maps. Pulling them down, she tossed one after another aside until she found the right one.

She ran back into her father's bedroom. Unfolding the map, snapping the crisp paper open, she put it on his lap, grabbed his hand, and slapped it on the face of the map. "Show us."

He glared at her, defiance in his eyes. "Where's Hanley?"

"Dead."

His head jerked up.

"That's right. Hanley's dead, killed by the man who has Tobie. Killed by his own grandson."

He looked from Roberta to her mother; a flicker of uncertainty flashed in his eyes. Then he seemed to deflate before her eyes. He looked down. His hand began to move slowly over the map. He stopped, his palm flat on the paper. Robbi recognized a portion of it as the Paxton land. Then, his hand curled, his shaky forefinger pointed to a spot south of the highway, national forest. "There," he said flatly.

She circled it in ink. "How far from the house?"

"Two, three miles."

"Is there more to the structure than the stone and log shell?"

"A basement."

"Did you know he was there?" Robbi asked.

Her father stared solemnly at her with pale blue-green eyes. He shook his head. "No."

Jake appeared in the doorway. "The car's out back. Ready?"

"Jake, I know where the church is."

"I'll get the sheriff and Clark on the phone," he said.

Robbi watched him go down the hall. She turned back to her father. He closed his eyes, refused to look at her.

She folded the map, wedged it down into the side pocket of her khaki shorts, then turned, hugged her mother. For now they could both savor this moment of victory.

In the hallway Jake stood with the phone to his ear, pressing buttons. He opened his arm and she moved into the space. He tapped the lever on the phone. "This phone's out. Where's another?"

She rushed into the gun room, yanked up the receiver, and listened. A flash of lightning streaked across the western sky. Thunder boomed. The lights flickered.

"Dead," she said, going to Jake. "The storm?"

"Must be," Jake responded, conviction lacking in his voice.

From the kitchen, glass shattered. Pomona screamed. The house plunged into darkness.

FIFTY-ONE

The scream echoed through the large house.

In the dark, Jake fumbled on the desktop for the shotgun, grabbed it, and ran out of the room.

Robbi followed.

They found Pomona standing in the middle of the grayed kitchen, a broken lantern on the floor tiles, kerosene pooling at her feet. She pointed to a window next to the door. "Somebody . . . out there!"

"Are you sure?"

"Yes—no. I don't know. The lights go out and I think I see somebody at the window."

Pomona put a shaky match to the unbroken lantern. Anemic yellow light blossomed outward. She turned the wick until the light brightened and flickered. Black smoke snaked from the glass chimney.

"Be careful of that match. Lower that flame." Jake moved to the window and looked out. "There's no one out there now."

Roberta lowered the gas in the lantern. From a shelf by the door she took down a flashlight and handed it to the housekeeper. "Pomona, tell my mother it's time to go."

Pomona followed the beam of light out of the room.

Robbi brought the lamp to the table, unfolded the map, and spread it out. She and Jake bent over it.

"There's a boundary fence about here." She pointed. "I saw it once while out riding. I think the best way is to head for the fence and follow it up. The map shows a body of water, a small lake or a large pond, just this side of where the old structure should be. It can't be too far beyond that."

"If for any reason we get separated, we'll try to meet at the pond."

Robbi shuddered at the thought. "We won't get separated." She folded the map and put it back in the pocket with the matches and extra shells.

Pomona entered the kitchen, pushing Cameron Paxton in the wheelchair. Lois followed, her face drawn. "I want to stay here," Lois said.

"No, Mom. You'd be alone in the house. You have to go."

"Where will you and Jake be?"

"We're going to look for Tobie."

After securing a rain slicker over the old man, Jake lifted him from the chair. Then, with Robbi at his side acting as shotgun, he carried the invalid out to the car and buckled him into the backseat. The two women got in the front, Lois behind the wheel.

"Lois, keep the doors locked and don't stop for anyone," Jake said. "When you get to Truckee, go straight to the police and tell them what's going on here. Tell them to send every available man."

Jake and Roberta hurried back to the house.

* * *

The horse trod carefully down the slope, its burden shifting awkwardly from side to side. The rider moaned, held his hand firmly against his chest to staunch the flow of blood.

The rider tipped, caught himself, his arms going around the horse's neck.

Prince lowered his shiny black head and continued on, the steady rain beating down on both horse and rider.

Roberta laid the shotgun on the island counter, then moved to the sink to a box of wooden matches on the windowsill. As she reached for the box, a dark figure loomed up in front of the window. The broad face peered in at her.

She screamed.

The face disappeared.

Jake was beside her in an instant.

"It was *him,*" she whispered, backing away.

"Where?"

"There." She pointed.

A moment later there was a powerful thud at the back door.

"It's him!" Robbi shouted. "Shoot him! Shoot him through the door!"

Jake grabbed the .12 gauge and took a stance.

Panes shattered from high in the door, showering them with stinging bits of glass.

Roberta dashed to the island for her gun just as the door flew open, smashing against the water cooler. The

Sparklett's bottle crashed to the floor, sending a cascade of water across the tiles. A figure towered in the doorway, the gray, rainy night a backdrop for the enormous hulk. Still several feet from her shotgun, she realized she had put herself between Jake and the killer.

Robbi froze.

The man lunged at her, seizing a handful of her clothes. She felt her back pocket rip, heard the map and extra shotgun shells spill onto the floor. She twisted away, snatched up the shotgun from the counter, and tried to turn it on him. His hand wrapped around the barrel. Then he suddenly let go, his feet going out from under him as he crashed to the floor in an oily pool of kerosene and water.

Jake rushed around the island, the shotgun aimed at the man on the floor. Just as he pulled the trigger, the man kicked out at the barrel. A blinding flash lit up the kitchen. The blast blew out the window above the sink.

"Run!" Jake yelled.

Roberta hesitated, then tore out the door, the gun banging against her legs. Once outside, she slowed, called out to Jake.

"Get the hell out of here! Run!" he shouted.

With a despairing moan she turned and ran.

FIFTY-TWO

Jake caught a glimpse of Robbi running across the yard toward the woods before he turned back to Eckker. The man, on his feet again, was reaching for him.

Jake lifted the shotgun, pulled the pump back, but before he could finish the action, Eckker grabbed the barrel and wrenched it from his hands. Jake was thrown onto the center island. He rolled over the top and fell off the other side, landing on the abandoned wheelchair. It careened noisily across the room as he came to his feet.

Jake circled the island until he had a nearly clear passage to the back door. He saw Eckker glance at the door, anticipating his next move.

At opposite ends of the island, both men charged for the door. Jake's ankle rapped the edge of the footplate of the wheelchair and, without slowing down, he grabbed the armrest, whirled the chair around, sending it into Eckker. The big man fell into it, a clatter of metal, then both man and chair tumbled over, blocking the exit.

Jake reversed his course and bolted out of the kitchen into the dark house. He heard a clamor, the rattle of metal, what sounded like the wheelchair being thrown across the room. Without benefit of light he tried to remember the layout of the house. He had to find the gun room. He ran through the living room, down the endless hall. Not far behind, he could hear glass breaking, cursing.

Inside the gun room, Jake headed for the rifle cabinet. The first gun he grabbed was a high-caliber rifle, and not certain which cartridges fit it, he tossed it aside. He found a double-barreled shotgun. He yanked out the drawer that held the ammunition, but before he could get his hands on the shells, Eckker charged into the room.

Jake abandoned the gun. There was no time. He struggled with the tall cabinet, pulling it away from the wall. It clipped Eckker on the shoulder as it crashed to the floor between the two men. Jake picked up the swivel desk chair and smashed it through the low windows, jumping out with it. He rolled in the slick, rain-soaked grass, came to his feet, and, without looking behind him, he ran.

Jake ran west, making his way over boulders and around small firs and seedlings. Once in the cover of the trees, he would veer south, find the boundary fence, and follow it up to the pond and Robbi.

After a quarter mile he considered going back to the house for the shotgun. But if Eckker was waiting for him, he was a dead man. Robbi, he told himself, had the single-action .20 gauge. Once he met up with her, the one shotgun would have to serve them.

Deep inside the first wooded area beyond her yard, Robbi shifted westward. She had to find the fence. Without a guideline she could go in circles, lose her bearings, and become hopelessly lost.

She moved along as rapidly as she could in the dark timberland. Tree branches clutched at her, scratching and jabbing; roots and boulders tripped her up, sending her to her knees time and again. Her ankle, where five weeks earlier she had sprained it on this mountain, throbbed unbearably. She tired easily; her muscles and joints screamed with fatigue. She stopped often to catch her breath, to massage aching tendons, and to drink water from cupped leaves.

She reached the barbed-wire fence and the open meadow at the same time. Locating the boundary marker elated her, yet the vast clearing that she must now cross to reach the pond filled her with trepidation. She would be out in the open. If he had a rifle, he had only to aim and shoot.

She braced herself and stepped out. A streak of lightning zigzagged through the clouds, and she froze in a crouch, her heart slamming in her chest. She could wait here for Jake. He'd have to cross the clearing sooner or later, and she'd just sit tight until she saw him. Unless he wasn't coming. If he's dead—no, don't think like that. He's coming.

What if he had already crossed? She had stopped so many times to catch her breath that he might have passed her, might at that moment be waiting for her at the pond.

Oh, God, what should I do? Go or stay?

The decision was made for her. Snapping twigs sounded behind her. Someone else was in the woods. Jake or the killer? It was foolhardy to assume it was Jake. She must cross, and she must do it now.

Gathering all her courage, Robbi set out, her steps swift and long. Thunder rolled somewhere in the distance. The farther she went into the clearing, the faster her pulse raced. At the point of no return, she sped up.

Off to her left another bolt of lightning lit up the sky. Thunder followed within seconds. She sucked in her breath, inhaling water from the deluge beating painfully down on her. It occurred to her that she was the tallest object in the meadow and lightning could strike her.

Trying to ignore the shooting pains in her ankle, she continued to run. Wind and rain battered at her. She kept her eyes to the ground, watching for obstacles and to avoid being blinded by the lightning.

The next streak brightened the entire sky. Thunder exploded within the light. Thunder or rifle shots? Robbi cried out and dropped to the ground in a crouch. Panicked, too paralyzed to move, she trembled, shivering violently.

Do it, kill me! Get it over with! Then she thought of her sister and she knew she had to go on. She forced herself to get up and run.

Coughing, gasping, she felt she would drown from the water being sucked into her lungs. As lethal as combat fire, lightning exploded all around her, the accompanying thunder giving it the gravity due a force so deadly. The woods she raced toward seemed to retreat with each footfall.

Several times she fell, sharp bits of gravel biting into her knees. She scrambled to her feet and rushed on. The wind and rain shifted direction, at her back now, pushing her, urging her onward.

So intent on clearing the meadow, she had entered the woods some twenty feet before she realized it. A tree loomed in front of her and, throwing her arm straight out, she abruptly stopped herself with her hand and shoulder.

She dropped to the ground, her back to the tree, her breath a ragged wheeze.

The rain suddenly eased. Looking out the way she had just come, Robbi scanned the field. To the northeast, with the dark trees as a backdrop, she thought she saw someone crossing. Only by focusing her eyes a bit to one side of the object could she detect the movement. She stared, mesmerized. The form grew. By his massive bulk, she discerned it to be the killer.

She was so tired. Where would she find the strength to go on? She could hide, then shoot him if he discovered her. But she had only one shell; the others lay on the kitchen floor.

Yet, if he failed to discover her and he went on, he was that much closer to Tobie. Better to have him behind her.

Wearily she struggled to her feet. She glanced back once to see the man midway in the clearing, coming at a fast lope. Wanting to cry but swearing instead, she picked up the shotgun, pushed off from the tree, and hurried on, scratching her legs on the prickly manzanita.

FIFTY-THREE

The killer was certain to guess she was following the fence, yet Robbi was afraid to stray too far from it. He knew this wilderness, had roamed the area for years both day and night.

She thought of the night in the woods when he'd turned Maggie loose. Remembered his glee at the prospect of a hunt. She tried to recall his technique and strategy. How did he finally catch her? He'd anticipated her actions. The running, the hiding, the running again until she could run no longer. He had only to look for the white dress.

Robbi looked down at her own clothing. The khaki shorts blended with the surroundings. Her gray athletic shoes, caked with mud and leaves, were dark. But her shirt was white.

She pulled it off, rubbed it in the mud, then put it back on. The mud, acting as insulation, added a degree of warmth.

When a rustling in the brush had her frantically searching for a hiding place—only to realize it was a porcupine—she paused to take stock. Maggie had hidden. Then, like a frightened rabbit, she had revealed herself. He would expect her to do the same.

In this game of cat and mouse, of tactical warfare, hysteria would be her downfall. Only if she continued on in a relatively composed manner to the pond would she have a chance.

One thing comforted her: if he were in the wilderness stalking her, then he couldn't be in that basement with her sister.

She moved on. Several minutes later she approached her destination. The pond was approximately one tenth of a mile in length and fifty yards wide. The barbed-wire fence split the oval body of water widthwise down the middle. Which side will Jake be on?

There was something familiar, yet alien, about the place. Waves of energy rose from the ground into her body, rising in tingling ripples. She took a step, felt what appeared to be solid ground totter beneath her feet. She jumped back, her feet braced apart.

All was still, the ground hard, unyielding. At the outer edge of a fallen pine tree she tentatively put a foot out and pushed. The ground rocked beneath her foot.

The rain, a mere drizzle now, glistened off the dry red needles. She tugged at the tree; it moved. Robbi pulled, hauling it away. Dropping to her knees, she brushed at the layer of sandy wet soil until she felt the wooden plank. Digging her fingers under it, she lifted.

Roberta didn't have to see in the hole to know what was there. The stench overwhelmed her. She gagged, swallowed down the bile that rose to her throat. Over her pitiful retching, she heard him coming through the brush.

She dropped the plank. She had to choose now: hide or fight. The killer was closing in at her back, barbed wire loomed to her left, the pond in front, its rocky bank, running to the right. Frantically she looked around.

Eckker crashed through the brush. He had her trapped. She was ahead of him with nowhere to go. With the eyes of a cougar, he searched the landscape.

She was nowhere in sight. Baffled, he looked around, turning his entire body in a full circle. She had been just ahead of him. He'd seen her cross the clearing. He'd heard the manzanita rustling, then the bits of shale sliding down the ridge just before abutting the rocky bank of the pond. She had to be there somewhere.

He crossed a flat boulder to the pond and looked down. Tiny drops of rain peppered the surface and broke the usually tranquil water into a dark, fragmented pattern. He scanned the pond on both sides of the fence for a swimmer. Except for the rippling water, nothing else moved.

He hurried back to the thicket of manzanita, crashing through it until he reached the shaft containing the bodies. He threw the dead tree aside, bent down, and lifted the wooden cover.

Oblivious of the reek of decaying flesh, he took the penlight from his pocket and peered down into the pit. Nothing had changed. More water filled the shaft, but all was as he'd left it.

He dropped the plywood, scattered a layer of sodden earth, and replaced the tree.

She had never reached the pond. She was hiding somewhere behind him. She was trying to keep him from her sister.

In the dark, with the rain again pouring down, he made his way along the boulders as gracefully as a big cat.

Roberta had no concept of time. It seemed an eternity since she'd lowered herself over the side of the boulder into the pond. The water there was chest-deep. She'd cracked the shotgun, removed the shell, and hidden it in a crevice between two rocks. Then she'd fitted her mouth over the chamber and bent her knees until she was submerged entirely, tightly wedging her body beneath the jutting rock with the end of the barrel just above the surface. She was soaked already from the chilling rain; the pond's water felt no colder.

Her long hair floated on the surface, but there was nothing she could do about it. In the darkness she prayed it would blend with the water weeds that grew along the bank.

There was no way to tell how far the end of the barrel poked above the surface. She kept the gun at a slight angle to the rock. Several times, from sheer weariness, she lowered her arm, but miraculously no water rushed down the barrel.

Her arms and shoulders screamed in agony. Tiny fish nibbled at her clothes. She shivered, more from fear and exhaustion than from the cold. The shiver became a fierce spasm, convulsing her entire body. She felt the water rush into her mouth, its oily taste acrid on her tongue, yet she was unable to stop its course down her throat. She gagged, choked, and with painful racking coughs she shot out of the water, her arms thrashing the surface.

A steely hand wound around her upper arm and yanked upward, pulling her from the pond. Still holding the shotgun, she flailed out with it wildly.

"Robbi!" Jake's voice, hushed yet urgent, whispered against her ear as he tried to hold on to her and keep the gun's barrel from splitting his head open.

She cried out in relief, then clung to him, coughing, sobbing, trying to talk.

He pushed her hair back from her eyes, held her face tenderly, kissed her.

"You're alive . . . thank God," she cried. "Bodies, there . . . under a pine tree . . . oh, Jake, Jake . . ." She coughed, clung to him tighter.

"Shhh, don't think about that now."

She tried to sit up. "We have to hurry."

"Robbi . . . hon, rest a minute." He held her securely, tried to calm her. "Rest a minute."

When the coughing was under control, Jake took off his shirt and made Robbi put it on. Although it was damp, it covered her exposed skin, the layers somewhat cutting the wind and cool air.

"Before we go on," Jake said, "we have to figure out how to do this."

"I want you to take the gun," Robbi said. "Divert him in some way. Get him away from the church. Then I'll go in and find Tobie."

"I think we should stick together."

"Believe me, I'd like nothing more, but I have a better chance to home in on her if she's alone. Do you understand?"

"No, not really."

"Trust me."

"Then take the gun. I'm not leaving you totally defenseless."

"No. He'll come after you and you'll need it."

"What if he goes after you?"

"Then I'll scream, and you can come and save me," she said, touching his face tenderly, ". . . again."

They found the lone shotgun shell, loaded it, and moved on.

FIFTY-FOUR

Eckker filled the footlocker with food rations, clothing, blankets, the first aid kit, flashlight, and anything else he thought he might need. The white dress went in last. If there was time, he would come back for the phonograph and records and maybe the generator.

He carried the footlocker up the stairs and out the trapdoor into a light drizzle. Hoisting the locker onto his back, he started down the path to his pickup.

Jake and Roberta followed the fence up the mountain, then, to be certain they wouldn't bypass the ruins, they traveled perpendicular to the fence for several hundred yards and crossed diagonally back to it, employing a serrated pattern.

Jake carried the shotgun. As they climbed he wondered where one aimed a gun to kill a giant. If he hit him at close range with a shotgun blast and the guy kept coming, his life, as well as the lives of Robbi and

Tobie, wouldn't be worth the powder it took to fire the ineffectual shell.

They were midway to the fence when Robbi put out an arm to stop Jake.

"I think she's close," she said quietly. "I can sense her." She started off again. "Hurry."

In the dark Tobie had paced off the small room. Five by six, cell size. She'd found the suspended bulb in the middle of the room, but when she pulled the chain, no light came on.

Where was she? Who was this creepy guy who'd snuck up on her at the pond and tried to choke her? What did he want with her? He knew her name. He'd called her Tobie. She shivered.

Blanketed by the blackness and the confined quarters, Tobie felt panic rising. She'd heard of claustrophobia, but until now she had no idea how debilitating it could be.

A scream was forming in her throat when the door suddenly swung open. Wan light from an indirect source glowed faintly, illuminating the big man as he entered, shoulders hunched to clear the top of the doorway.

Tobie's heart thumped insanely.

He tossed her her shoes. "Put em on."

Tobie tried not to stare at the commanding giant, yet she found it impossible to look away. He terrified her. A filthy dark stubble made his craggy features even more menacing. His hair, dirty, greasy, burrs locked in, was tangled like a mangy dog. The bandage on his hand was gray with grime, the dried blood black and stiff. The foul smell of him overpowered her.

They stared at each other as she quickly pulled on her shoes.

"You and me, we like the same things," he said in his deep voice.

"I want to go home."

"We're going home. A new home."

He grabbed her arm and took her out of the room, out from under the stairwell into the main room. He looked around as though double-checking for something. Then he led her up the stairs.

Above their heads on the ground floor she heard something thump against the structure.

The man paused, looked upward, listened. More thuds, sounding heavier, coming more frequently now.

Tobie's eyes darted upward. "Robbi?" she whispered.

He started back down, pulling her behind him. "I gotta do something first."

"No!" Tobie screamed. "Robbi, I'm here!" She twisted free, caught him off guard. He stumbled down several steps as Tobie scrambled upward. She reached the trapdoor just as his massive hand curled around her ankle. She kicked out at him. He fell on top of her, knocking the wind out of her. Beneath his oppressive weight, she struggled for air. Frantic now, she bit, clawed, and kicked. He began to shake her. Her head whipped on her neck, cracking against the wooden steps. Tobie cried out, fought harder.

His repulsive face pressed close to hers, his hot breath enveloping her with a nauseating stench.

"Tobie. Tobie, please," he said, "I don't want to hurt

you." But his expression belied the soft words. His eyes were maniacal, his face contorted with rage. "Sweet, sweet Tobie, don't fight me." He continued to bang her head on the steps until light exploded in her head, then nothing.

Jake climbed the steep bank, using his feet, his hands, and at times the shotgun barrel to loosen boulders in his attempt to create a series of mini-landslides. For the most part, the sodden ground hampered the descent of the tumbling rocks.

A moment later a hollow thumping echo floated up the mountain. A boulder or two must have found its mark.

The rumbling grew louder. Behind the church, up the tree-studded slope, rocks and debris tumbled down.

Eckker burst through the trapdoor. He looked around, listened. More rocks descended, thudding against the back of the ruined church, causing what was left of the decrepit structure to groan and tremble.

He cursed. Nothing would stop him. He'd waited too long. He'd had to kill his own grandfather to keep her. He would annihilate everyone on the mountain to keep her. The meddling sister would be the first to go. He would not leave this mountain until she was dead.

He started up the slope in the direction of the rock slide. At the deer trail he knelt, took in the single tracks of a shoe within the thin beam of his penlight. Not the same tracks he'd followed across the meadow. The man was above him. The woman was somewhere else.

He turned and started down.

Roberta crouched in a thicket of manzanita, staring at the church. She clutched her stomach, sick with anxiety. In her mind she had seen the killer shaking her sister, had felt the hard wooden riser beneath her head.

Several moments later she saw Eckker appear out of the ground from a trapdoor. He hesitated, then moved out of sight behind one of the building's remaining walls. He reappeared on the slope, heading up toward Jake. She lost track of him a dozen yards farther up.

She watched. Waited. If she was going in there, she'd have to do it now. She hurried out of the thicket and ran the fifty feet to the ruins. She was well inside the shell when she stopped to listen.

Silence.

The silence was broken by a voice from above. The words carried downhill with crystal-clear clarity. "Hey, you big, stupid sonofabitch! You! Eckker! You're not king of the mountain anymore!"

Jake!

Robbi's heart leapt into her throat. He was trying to warn her. She saw Eckker then, about two hundred yards away, coming back down the slope.

She could hide. The three of them could play this game all night. But still her sister was his prisoner somewhere in those ruins. It would all be for nothing if he managed to escape and take Tobie with him.

Something below caught her eye. Lights, down the

mountain. Streamers of headlights, turning off the highway, moved up the road toward her parents' house. Police?

She hesitated. If she went down and the killer followed her, she'd lead him away from Jake and Tobie . . . and into the hands of the law.

Without trying to be quiet, she ran through the shell of the church. From the corner of her eye she saw him moving in her direction.

Turning, she started to run downhill.

FIFTY-FIVE

Jake cautiously worked his way down the steep incline. When he reached the ruins of the church, he skirted the building, staying in the cover of the trees and boulders. Gripping the shotgun, he moved in slowly.

A basement. Roberta had mentioned a basement. Jake advanced, entered the shell of the church, and began to look for some type of cellar entrance.

The rain began in earnest again. Jake swiped at the dripping hair on his forehead as he stepped behind the pulpit. With the barrel of the gun he tapped at the debris on the ground. A hollow sound. Jake dropped to his knees, used his knuckles to rap on the plank. He dug his fingers around the floor until he located the seam, then pulled up the trapdoor.

He cautiously stepped down into the dark basement. He wished he had a flashlight, a lighter, or even a match. But he soon realized he wouldn't need a light; less than three risers down, he heard a girl moan. When he touched her she made a noise deep in her throat and flailed out, fighting.

"Tobie, it's me, Jake," he said, trying to catch her hands.

She became perfectly still.

"Tobie, it's okay."

He heard her suck in her breath. Then she sobbed once.

Jake lifted her and carried her out into the pouring rain. "Are you all right. Are you hurt?"

"I'm okay."

"We've got to go after Robbi."

"There's a logging road." She held the back of her head with one hand and pointed southeast with the other.

"Can you walk?"

"Yes," she whispered. She came to her feet. Her knees buckled.

Jake handed her the shotgun, bent down, and said, "Climb aboard, you go piggyback to the road."

Tobie climbed on.

Roberta glanced behind her. He was back there, she heard him, caught a glimpse of him now and then through the trees. Her nightmare was playing itself out exactly as she'd dreamt it. Adrenaline pumped through her veins, her throat felt raw, her chest tight. She raced surefootedly through the trees, thankful for the cool rain, thankful for the stream of headlights weaving their way up a winding dirt road, but above all, she was thankful that her sister was out of his clutches. For now.

Through the quaking aspens in front of her, she saw

a streak of lightning snake to the ground. The meadow. She was about to enter the meadow. Thunder crashed like cymbals inside her head.

The procession of lights jounced along to the east of the open field. If she could just cut across diagonally, she'd reach the road and the safety within those lights. Behind her, like a charging grizzly, his breathing as tortured as hers, he closed the distance.

Robbi lunged forward into that immense open space. With the rain hammering her face and body, weighty footfalls pounding close behind her, she ran for her life.

Jake saw the headlights, bouncing, coming toward them on the deep rutted road. He held Tobie's hand as they ran. She was concentrating on the ground in front of her.

"Look," he said.

She raised her head. Wonder and relief sprang into her eyes at the sight of the cars.

A spotlight from one of the vehicles cut through the pouring rain and swept across the open field. Jake followed it with his eyes. More funnels of light crisscrossed the first. The span of trees on the far side of the meadow glowed with a dozen beams of lesser intensity. Flashlights. Lanterns. Men on foot, their beacons sweeping back and forth, were combing the land.

Through the driving rain and thunder the pinpoints of light seemed to sing. Help had arrived. They'd be okay. All they had to do was find Roberta.

His gaze followed the spotlight as it panned across the meadow. Just breaking through the trees he made out a running figure. And close behind, a mere twenty feet away and gaining, was a second, larger figure.

Panic rocked Jake. The way Eckker was bearing down on her, it was obvious he had little or no regard for the score of armed men surrounding him. If he caught her, he could snap her neck in an instant and no one could stop him.

Jake gave Tobie a slight nudge in the direction of the sheriff and his men, clutched the small .20-gauge shotgun, and, oblivious of the shouts behind him, took off across the meadow.

Roberta's breath was ragged in her throat. She thought her chest would burst, her heart explode. Every muscle in her body screamed. The toe of her shoe caught in a chuckhole. She tripped, staggered, *Oh, please, don't fall, don't fall.* If she fell, he would be on her instantly, tearing her to pieces. She smothered a sob.

Someone was running toward her. Someone was coming out to help her! She heard her name. It was Jake. He was shouting something, but the thunderous sounds of the storm tore his words away. He stopped abruptly, positioned the shotgun against his shoulder, and took a shooter's stance. His left hand slashed downward.

Drop, he wanted her to drop so he could fire. Obeying immediately, she threw herself to the side, falling, then tumbling over and over in the slick grass. Pain shot into her joints, cruelly twisted at her air-starved muscles. An explosion rang in her ears. Robbi turned to see the towering man, thrown back by the blast to his chest, stagger, then reel like a drunk before regaining his footing. The front of his shirt opened up; blood poured forth.

Eckker braced his feet, stood spread-eagle. He put his bandaged hand to his chest; blood instantly soaked into the porous fabric.

The wounded man opened his mouth and screamed, a savage, primal, beastly scream, then turned, glared at Roberta with eyes so wild, so enraged, so utterly mad that she thought her heart would stop, seize from the sheer malevolence of it.

Roberta scrabbled backward in the wet grass, trying desperately to get to her feet. He came for her, fell on her, his massive weight knocking the air out of her. His blood flowed over her, hot, sticky, the acrid smell mingling with the rank odor of his body and its particles of putrid, dying flesh.

The shotgun blast had failed to bring him down. He seemed to possess the power of ten men. *He must kill me before he can die,* Roberta thought in despair. *Nothing can stop him now.*

Beams of light danced over her. Through the storm's steady cadence she heard shouting, advancing forms, yet no one dared fire.

On his knees now, the man held her across her chest. His hands moved to her throat.

Jake charged. Hauling back, he swung the shotgun at the killer. The wooden stock grazed the back of the man's head.

Roberta screamed when Eckker wrenched the shotgun from Jake's hands and, with the barrel, clubbed him across the chest, sending him sprawling to the ground. He raised the weapon up, high above his head at arm's length, to club Jake again.

Suddenly, from nowhere, she heard pounding hooves rapidly approaching.

With the shotgun above his head, the killer gazed in confusion at the horse and rider bearing down on him. He released Roberta, fell backward.

The horse reared up as Hanley fired the powerful shotgun, pumping shell after shell into his grandson. The giant flew backward, a mass of bloody, ravaged flesh tumbling over and over to finally lie unmoving, facedown, in the marshy grass.

Hanley slid from the horse, the gun falling from his hands. "Joseph," he whispered, his hand stretching out toward his grandson.

Jake moved to Robbi.

Over Jake's shoulder Robbi saw a score of people running, advancing on them. Tobie led the pack.

Roberta buried her face in the soft, pulsing placc of Jake's neck and sobbed.

FIFTY-SIX

Three days after the storm the ground was once again hard, unyielding. The summer morning dawned calm. Easterly clouds blocked the sun.

Roberta and Jake stood on the springy grass of the cemetery grounds. She leaned against him, his arm circled her waist. Several feet away Lois and Tobie stood tall, proud, despite the presence of the man who scowled from his wheelchair on thc other side of the coffin.

The funeral service for Hanley Gates ended. An aide began to push the wheelchair toward the limousine. Lois and Tobie followed, holding hands. Tobie wiped tears from her eyes, turned to look at Robbi. She smiled weakly and raised her fingers in a gesture of parting.

Roberta waved back. Then, with the aid of the cane, she let Jake steer her off in the opposite direction. They walked in silence, the solemnness dropping away like falling leaves as they distanced themselves from Hanley's gravesite.

Crossing an arched latticework bridge, Jake said quietly, "Feel like getting away for a few days?"

She slowed, glanced at him. "I'd like nothing better. You must've read my mind."

"No, that's your department. I only work with minds, you read them."

"I hope not for a while. It's weird, isn't it . . . nothing for over twenty years, then in just a few weeks enough to last anyone a lifetime."

"You saved her, Robbi. You said you would and you did."

"I had help." She leaned over and kissed the corner of his mouth. "Now, back to the subject of a weekend getaway."

"It doesn't have to be just the weekend. We can make it a week, two weeks. What's a decent interval for a honeymoon?"

The sun broke through the clouds. A perfect omen.

Roberta felt a rush of happiness, then fear. She gazed into his keen blue eyes, now tender. "Jake, have you thought this through? What if it comes back? The nightmares, the visions, the telepathy . . ." The words faded.

"Then you'll have a doctor in residence. One who knows your case . . . *intimately.* You have no idea what a valuable asset you are. With you around, no more lost car keys, no more getting caught in the rain." He turned to her. "Honey, I love you and all that goes with you."

She smiled, looked away, her gaze following the path of the tiny stream beneath them. "I shall always remember this day. The day the man I love proposed to me in a cemetery."

He took her in his arms, held her tight. "Roberta," he said softly in her ear, "it could be you in that coffin back there. Belinda, Maggie, Carl, Avondale, Howe—Christ, it hurts just to think about what could have happened."

She felt stinging tears behind her lids. She thought of that day in the hospital when she had first met Jake. A blind woman, listening to the sweet mandolins of Harry Geller. She had refused to give in to the music that day. Yet she had promised herself a time, a very special time in the near future, to let it all out. She had much to be thankful for . . . much to reflect on.

Would there ever be a day more special than this one? A perfect day to treat herself to the Gypsy melodies, she thought, *and let the tears flow* . . . tears of happiness, tears of hope.

"Jake, that sounds so good . . ."

"I detect a but in there. What?"

"But—I hope you'll understand . . ." She squeezed his hand. "There's something I have to do today. And I have to do it alone."

He stared into her eyes, searching. Then he nodded. "And tomorrow?"

"Tomorrow I'm yours. Yours for as long as you'll have me."

On this day Hanley Gates was laid to rest.

And the women from the mountain, once lost souls, were free to go on with their journey.